'Invigorating and gripping . . . every word works quietly to establish the illusion that things are happening by themselves . . . A literary achievement' *Time*

'A brave, brilliant book.' *Sunday Herald*

'A tour de force . . . an unflinching novel of rare power.' Mordecai Richler

'Magnificent . . . prose as taut and cutting as cheese-wire.' *Guardian*

COLD SPRING HARBOR

'Yates writes with a sympathy so clear-hearted that it often feels like nostalgia for his own youth, and yet he is also thoroughly uncompromising in revealing their capacity for self-delusion, their bewilderment in the face of failure.' *New York Times*

'So consistently well-written, just, unsentimental and sympathetic.' *Washington Post*

COLLECTED STORIES

'An unforgettable and long-overdue compilation of work by one of the great, neglected American writers of the postwar era.' Stephen Amidon, *New Statesman* Books of the Year

'These stories show the devastating economy and intensity of a master of the form.' Lisa Allardice, *Daily Telegraph*

'The strength of Yates's sympathy and observation mark this out as a major literary event . . . A remarkable achievement.' *Independent*

'Yates is a realist par excellence . . . Read and weep.' *Guardian*

Also available from Methuen

Cold Spring Harbor
The Easter Parade
Revolutionary Road
The Collected Stories of Richard Yates

YOUNG HEARTS
CRYING

Richard Yates was born in Yonkers, New York, in 1926. After serving in the US Army during the Second World War, he worked as a publicity writer for the Remington Rand Corporation, and for a brief period in the sixties as a speech writer for Senator Robert Kennedy. His prize-winning stories first appeared in 1953, and his first novel, *Revolutionary Road*, was nominated for the National Book Award. He wrote six other novels, including *Easter Parade*, *A Special Providence* and *A Good School*, and two volumes of short stories, *Eleven Kinds of Loneliness* and *Liars in Love*. His collected short stories were published by Methuen in 2001. Richard Yates was twice divorced and the father of three daughters. He died in 1992.

YOUNG HEARTS CRYING

RICHARD YATES

Methuen

Published by Methuen 2005

3 5 7 9 10 8 6 4 2

First published in the USA by Delacorte Press/
Seymour Lawrence, 1984
First published in Great Britain by Methuen, 1986

Methuen Publishing Ltd
11–12 Buckingham Gate
London SW1E 6LB
www.methuen.co.uk

Grateful acknowledgement is made for permission to reprint excerpts from the
following copyrighted works:

'Watching the Needleboats at San Sabba' from *The Portable James Joyce*. Copyright 1946,
1947 by The Viking Press, Inc. Copyright © renewed The Viking Press, Inc., 1974,
1975. Copyright 1914, 1918 by Margaret Caroline Anderson. Copyright 1916, 1918 by
B. W. Huebsch. Copyright 1939 by James Joyce. Copyright © The Estate of James
Joyce, 1964, 1967. Copyright renewed 1942, 1944, 1946 by Nora Joseph Joyce.
Copyright renewed 1946 by Nora Joyce. Copyright © renewed George Joyce and Lucia
Joyce, 1967. Reprinted by permission of Viking Penguin, Inc.

Tennessee Williams, *A Streetcar Named Desire*, Copyright 1940 by Tennessee Williams.
Reprinted by permission of New Directions Publishing Corporation.

'I Want to Hold Your Hand' by JOHN LENNON and PAUL MCCARTNEY.
© Copyright 1963 by Northern Songs, Ltd., London, England. Sole Selling Agent
MUSIC CORPORATION OF AMERICA, INC., New York, N.Y. USED BY
PERMISSION. ALL RIGHTS RESERVED.

ISBN 0 413 15660 5

Methuen Publishing Limited Reg. No. 3543167

A CIP catalogue for this title
is available from the British Library.

Typeset by SX Composing DTP, Rayleigh, Essex
Printed and bound in Great Britain
by Bookmarque Ltd, Croydon, Surrey

To my three daughters

YOUNG HEARTS
CRYING

PART ONE

Chapter One

By the time he was twenty-three, Michael Davenport had learned to trust his own skepticism. He didn't have much patience with myths or legends of any kind, even those that took the form of general assumptions; what he wanted, always, was to get down to the real story.

He had come of age as a waist-gunner on a B-17, toward the end of the war in Europe, and one of the things he'd liked least about the Army Air Force was its public-relations program. Everybody thought the Air Force was the luckiest, happiest branch of the service – better fed and quartered and paid than any other, given more personal freedom, given good clothes to be worn in a "casual" style. Everybody understood, too, that the Air Force couldn't be bothered with the petty side of military discipline: Flying and daring and high comradeship were esteemed over any blind respect for rank; officers and enlisted men could pal around together, if they felt like it, and even the regulation Army salute became a curled-up, thrown-away little mockery of itself in their hands. Soldiers of the ground forces were said to refer to them, enviously, as fly-boys.

And all that stuff was probably harmless enough; it wasn't worth getting into any arguments about; but Michael Davenport would always know that his own Air Force years had been humbling and tedious and bleak, that his times in combat had come close to scaring the life out of him, and that he'd been enormously glad to get out of the whole lousy business when it was over.

Still, he did bring home a few good memories. One was that he had lasted through the semifinals as a middleweight in the boxing tournament at Blanchard Field, Texas – not many other lawyers' sons from Morristown, New Jersey, could claim a thing like that. Another, which came to take on philosophical proportions the more he thought about it, was a remark made one sweltering afternoon by some nameless Blanchard Field gunnery instructor in the course of an otherwise boring lecture.

"Try to remember this, men. The mark of a professional in any line of work – I mean *any* line of work – is that he can make difficult things look easy."

And even then, brought awake among the sleepy trainees by that piercing idea, Michael had known for some time what line of work it was that he wanted eventually to make his mark in as a professional: he wanted to write poems and plays.

As soon as the Army set him free he went to Harvard, mostly because that was where his father had urged him to apply, and at first he was determined not to be taken in by any of the myths or legends of Harvard, either: he didn't even care to acknowledge, let alone to admire, the physical beauty of the place. It was "school," a school like any other, and as grimly eager as any other to collect its share of his GI Bill of Rights money.

But after a year or two he began to relent a little. Most of the courses *were* stimulating; most of the books *were* the kind he had always wanted to read; the other students, some of them, anyway, were turning out to be the kind of men he had always craved as companions. He never wore any of his old Army clothes – the campus was crawling then with men who did, and who were largely dismissed as "professional veterans" – but he kept the modified handlebar mustache that had been his only affectation in the service, because it still served the purpose of making him look older than his years. And he had to admit, now and then, that he didn't really mind the light that came into people's eyes, or the quickening of their attention, when they learned he had been an aerial gunner – or that his playing it down seemed only to make it all the more impressive. He was prepared to believe that Harvard might, after all, provide a good-enough environment for learning how to make difficult things look easy.

Then one spring afternoon in his junior year – all bitterness gone, all cynicism drowned – he wholly succumbed to the myth and the legend of the lovely Radcliffe girl who could come along at any moment and change your life.

"You *know* so much," she told him, reaching across a restaurant table to grasp one of his hands with both of her own. "I don't know any other way to put it. You just – *know* so much."

The Radcliffe girl's name was Lucy Blaine. She had been chosen for the leading role in Michael's first halfway decent one-act play, which was then in rehearsal at a small campus theater, and this was the first time he had worked up the courage to ask her out.

"Every word," she was saying, "every sound and silence in this play is the work of a man with a profound understanding of the – you know – of the human heart. Oh, God, now I've embarrassed you."

That was true – he was too embarrassed to meet her eyes – and he could only hope it wouldn't make her want to change the subject. She wasn't the prettiest girl he had ever met, but she was the first pretty girl who had ever shown so much interest in him, and he knew he could get a lot of mileage out of a mixture like that.

When it seemed appropriate to offer a compliment or two of his own he told her how much he'd enjoyed her performance at the rehearsals.

"Oh, no," she said quickly, and for the first time he noticed she'd been tearing her paper napkin into careful, resolutely parallel strips on the table. "I mean, thanks, and of course that's nice to hear, but I know I'm not really an actress. If I were I'd have gone to *acting* school somewhere, and I'd be knocking myself out in summer stock and trying to get auditions and all that. No" – she gathered all the strips of napkin into her fist and gently thumped the table with it for emphasis – "no, it's just something I like to do, the way little girls play dress-up in their mothers' clothes. And the point is I could never've dreamed – could never've dreamed I'd be working in a play like this."

He had already discovered, in walking away from the theater with her, that she was exactly the right size for him – the top of her head floated just at the edge of his shoulder – and he knew she was the right age, too: she was twenty; he would soon be twenty-four. Now, as he took her back to the drab room on Ware Street where he lived alone in "approved student housing," he wondered if this persistent just-rightness, this pattern of near-perfection, could possibly hold. Wouldn't there have to be a hitch in it somewhere?

"Well, it's about like what I imagined," she said when he'd shown her into his place, while he made a quick furtive search of the room to be sure there were no dirty socks or underwear in sight. "Sort of stark and simple and a good place to work. Oh, and it's so – masculine."

The pattern of near-perfection held. When she turned away

6

from him to look out a window – "And I'll bet it's lovely and bright here in the mornings, isn't it? With these tall windows? And these trees?" – it seemed entirely natural to move up close behind her, put his arms around her, and take both of her breasts in his hands while he sank his mouth into the side of her neck.

In less than a minute they were naked and reveling under the Army blankets of his double bed, and Michael Davenport found he hadn't yet known such a fine and responsive girl, hadn't even guessed at what a boundless, extraordinary new world a girl could be.

"Oh, Jesus," he said when they were finally at peace, and he wanted to tell her something poetic but didn't know how. "Oh, Jesus, you're nice, Lucy."

"Well, I'm glad you think so," she said in a low, subtle voice, "because I think you're wonderful."

And it was springtime in Cambridge. Nothing else was of any consequence at all. Even the play had ceased to matter very much: when a Harvard *Crimson* reviewer called it "sketchy" and described Lucy's performance as "tentative" they were both able to take it in stride. There would be other plays soon enough; and besides, everybody knew what envious little snots the *Crimson* reviewers were.

"Can't remember if I've asked you this before," he said once when they were strolling in the Boston Common, "but what does your father do?"

"Oh, he sort of – manages things. Different kinds of business things. I've never quite known what he does, exactly."

And that was the first clue he had, apart from her elegantly simple clothes and manners, that Lucy's family might be very rich.

There were further clues a month or two later, when she took him home to meet her parents at their summer place on Martha's

Vineyard. He had never seen anything like it. First you drove to an obscure coastal village called Woods Hole, where you went aboard a surprisingly luxurious ferryboat that floated you out over miles of sea; then, once ashore again on the distant island of "the Vineyard," you followed a road between tall uncropped hedges until you came to an almost-hidden driveway that led around among lawns and trees and took you down near the edge of the gentle water, and there was the Blames' house – long and amply proportioned, made almost as much of glass as of wood, with its wooden sections finished in dark brown shingles that looked silver in the dappled sunlight.

"I was beginning to think we'd never get to meet you, Michael," Lucy's father said after shaking hands with him. "We've heard almost nothing but your name since – well, I suppose it's only been since April or so, but it seems much longer."

Mr. Blaine and his wife were tall and lean and graceful, with faces as intelligent as their daughter's. They both had the kind of taut, tan skin that comes with easy mastery of swimming and tennis, and their husky voices suggested a full appreciation of daily alcohol. Neither of them looked more than forty-five years old. Seated and smiling together on a long chintz-covered sofa, in their impeccable summer clothes, they might have been a photograph illustrating a magazine article with a title like "Is There an American Aristocracy?"

"Lucy?" Mrs. Blaine was saying. "Do you think you'll be able to stay through Sunday? Or would that mean keeping you away from any number of romantic imperatives back in Cambridge?"

A soft-treading Negro maid came in with a liquor tray, and the early tension of their gathering began to fade. Sitting back to savor the first sip or two of an ice-cold, bone-dry martini, Michael stole an unbelieving glance at the girl of his dreams and then let his gaze follow the lofty ceiling line of one bright wall until it met at right angles with another, far away, that opened onto other and still other rooms in the shadows of the afternoon. This was a place suggesting the timeless repose that only several generations' worth of success could provide. This was class.

"Well, but what do you mean, 'class'?" Lucy asked him, with an exasperated little puckering of her forehead, as they walked alone along the narrow beach the next day. "When you use a word like that it makes you sound sort of proletarian and dumb, or something, and you must know I know better than that."

"Well, compared to you I *am* proletarian."

"Oh, that's silly," she said. "That's the silliest thing I've ever heard you say."

"Okay, but listen: Do you think we might get out of here tonight? Instead of staying through Sunday?"

"Well, I suppose so, sure. But why?"

"Because." And he stopped to let her turn toward him so that his fingers could touch one of her nipples, very tenderly, through the fabric of her shirt. "Because there are any number of romantic imperatives back in Cambridge."

His own most important romantic imperative, all through the fall and winter of that year, was to find attractive ways of fending off her shy but persistent wish to be married.

"Well, of *course* I want to," he would say. "You know that. I want to as much as you do, or even more. I just don't think it'd be too smart a thing to do before I've even gotten started in any kind of work. Isn't that reasonable?"

And she would seem to agree, but he learned soon enough that words like "reasonable" didn't carry much weight with Lucy Blaine.

A wedding date was set for the week after his graduation. His family came up from Morristown to smile in courteous bewilderment through the ceremony, and Michael found himself a married man without being fully aware of how it had all come about. When their taxicab brought them from the church to the reception, in an old stone building at the base of Beacon Hill, he and Lucy emerged under the looming figure of a mounted policeman who raised one hand to the visor of his cap in a formal salute as his beautifully groomed horse stood straight and still as a statue at the curbside.

"Jesus," Michael said as they started up an elegant flight of stairs. "How much do you suppose it costs to hire a mounted cop for a wedding reception?"

"Oh, I don't know," she said impatiently. "Not much, I shouldn't think. Fifty?"

"Gotta be a lot more than fifty, honey," he told her, "if only because you'd have to buy oats for the horse." And she laughed and hugged his arm to show she knew he was only fooling.

A small orchestra played a medley of Cole Porter tunes in one of the three or four big, open rooms of the reception, and crouching bartenders raced under the pressure of their orders. Michael spotted his parents once in the sea of guests and was glad to find they had a sufficient number of strangers to talk to, and that their Morristown clothes looked all right, but then he lost sight of them again. A very old, wheezing man, wearing the silk rosette of some rare honor in the lapel of his custom-made suit, was trying to explain that he'd known Lucy since she was a baby – "in her *pram!* In her little woolly mittens and her *booties!*" – and another man, much younger, with a knuckle-crushing hand-shake, wanted to know how Michael felt about sinking-fund debentures. There were three girls who had known Lucy "at Farmington" and who rushed with squeals of happiness to embrace her, though she could scarcely wait until they were gone to tell Michael that she hated them all, and there were women of her mother's age who dabbed at invisible tears in saying they had never seen such a lovely bride. It was while pretending to listen to the drink-fuddled talk of a man who played squash with Lucy's father that Michael thought again of the mounted policeman at the curb. Surely it wouldn't be possible to "hire" a cop and his horse; they could have been stationed here only through the courtesy of the police department, or of the mayor, and that suggested an element of "influence" in Lucy's family as well as of money.

"Well, I think it all went pretty well, don't you?" Lucy said much later that night, when they were alone in a lavish suite at the Copley Plaza. "The ceremony was nice, and I guess the party did get a little messy toward the end, but then that always happens."

"No, I thought it was fine," he assured her. "Still, I'm glad it's over."

"Oh, Jesus, yes," she said. "So am I."

Not until about halfway through their week's stay in that splendid hotel, a week of paid-for luxury dispensed with casual rudeness under the stares of strangers – only then did Lucy make a shy announcement that would greatly complicate everything between them.

It happened after breakfast one morning, when the room-service waiter had trundled away their plates of melon rind and egg yolk and the heavy flakes of broken French croissants. Lucy was at the dressing table, using its mirror both to brush her hair and to watch her new husband pace the carpet behind her.

"Michael?" she said. "Do you think you could sit down for a minute, please? Because you're sort of making me nervous? And also," she added, putting her hairbrush down as carefully as if it might break, "also because there's something important I have to tell you."

As they took conversational positions, partly facing each other in two overstuffed Copley Plaza chairs, he thought at first she might be pregnant – that wouldn't be great news, though it wouldn't be bad news, either – or maybe that she'd been told she couldn't have children at all; then his racing mind touched on the frightful possibility that she might have a fatal illness.

"I've wanted you to know about this from the beginning," she said, "but I was afraid it might – change things, sort of."

It seemed to him now that he scarcely knew her, this leggy, pretty girl to whom the word "wife" might never be comfortably applied, and he sat with a chill of dread from his scrotum to his throat as he watched her lips and waited for the worst.

"So now I'll have to stop being afraid, that's all. I'll just tell you, and I can only hope it won't make you feel – well, anyway. The thing is, I have something between three and four million dollars. Of my own."

"Oh," he said.

Remembering it later, even after many years, it would always seem to Michael that they filled their remaining days and nights in that hotel with nothing but talk. Their voices only rarely took on the tension of an argument and never once broke into quarreling, but it was a steady, dead-earnest discussion that kept circling back over the same issues time and again, and there were decidedly two points of view.

Lucy's position was that the money had never meant anything to her; why, then, should it mean anything to him beyond an extraordinary opportunity for time and freedom in his work? They could live anywhere in the world. They could travel, if they felt like it, until they found the right setting for a full and productive life. Wasn't that the kind of thing most writers dreamed of?

12

And Michael would admit he was tempted – oh, Jesus, talk about tempted – but this was his position: He was a middle-class boy and he had always assumed he would make something of himself on his own. Could he really be expected to abandon that lifelong habit of thought overnight? Living off her fortune might only bleed away his ambition, and might even rob him of the very energy he needed to work at all; that would be an unthinkable price to pay.

He hoped she wouldn't misunderstand him: it was certainly fine to know she *had* all that money, if only because it meant their children would always have the security of trust funds and stuff like that. In the meantime, though, wouldn't it be better if she kept it all strictly between herself and her bankers, or her brokers, or whoever the hell it was that looked after it?

She assured him repeatedly that his attitude was "admirable," but he always turned away that compliment by saying it was nothing of the kind; it was only stubborn. All he wanted was to carry out the plans he had made for them long before the wedding.

They would go to New York, where he'd take the kind of job that other fledgling writers took, in some advertising agency or publishing house – hell, anybody could do that kind of work with his left hand – and they'd live on his salary like an ordinary young couple, preferably in some plain, decent apartment in the West Village. The only real difference, now that he knew of her millions of dollars, was that they would both have a secret to keep from the other ordinary young people they'd meet along the way.

"Isn't this really the most sensible thing," he asked her, "at least for the time being? Do you see what I'm getting at, Lucy?"

"Well," she said, "when you say 'for the time being' I guess I

— sure I do. Because we'll always have the money to fall back on."

"Okay," he conceded, "but who said anything about falling back? Have I ever struck you as a falling-back kind of man?"

And he was instantly glad he'd come up with that line. There had been times, in all this talk, when he'd caught himself almost at the point of blurting out that to accept her money would jeopardize his "very manhood," or even that it would "emasculate" him, but now all the queasy implications of such a weak and desperately final defense could be forgotten.

He was up and pacing again, fists in his pockets, and he went to stand for a while at the front windows, looking out over Copley Square at the sunny parade of weekday-morning pedestrians along Boylston Street and at the endlessly deep blue sky beyond the buildings. It was good flying weather.

"I just wish you'd take a little time to think it over, is all," Lucy was saying from somewhere in the room behind him. "Couldn't you at least keep an open mind?"

"No," he said at last, turning to face her. "No, I'm sorry, baby, but we're going to do this my way."

Chapter Two

The place they found in New York was almost exactly what Michael had specified: a plain, decent apartment in the West Village. They had three rooms on the ground floor, on Perry Street near the corner of Hudson, and he could shut himself into the smallest room and hunch over the manuscript of a book of poems he wanted to finish and sell before his twenty-sixth birthday.

Finding the right kind of work for his left hand, though, was a little more difficult. In the course of several interviews he began to suspect that a job in an advertising agency might drive him out of his mind; instead he settled for employment in the "permissions" department of a medium-sized publishing house. His duties there amounted to little more than idleness: he spent much of every office day at work on his poems, and nobody seemed to care or even to notice.

"Well, that certainly sounds like an ideal situation," Lucy said – and it might have been, except that the paychecks he brought home were barely enough to cover the groceries and the rent. Still, there was a reasonable hope that he'd be promoted – other people in that sluggish department were sometimes "taken upstairs" to receive real salaries – and so he decided to stick it out for a year. That was the year his twenty-sixth birthday came around and found his book still far from finished, because he had thrown out many of its earlier, weaker poems; it was also the year they discovered that Lucy was pregnant.

By the time their daughter Laura was born, in the spring of 1950, he had quit fooling around in the publishing house and found a better-paying job. He was a staff writer now for a slick, fast-growing trade magazine called *Chain Store Age*, hammering out copy all day about "bold, revolutionary new concepts" in the business of retail merchandising. It wasn't exactly the kind of work he could do with his left hand – these guys wanted a hell of a lot for their money – and there were times at his clattering typewriter when he would wonder what a man married to a millionairess could possibly be doing in a place like this.

He was always tired when he got home, badly in need of a couple of drinks, and there wasn't even any hope of seclusion with his manuscript after dinner, because the room he'd once used for writing was now the nursery.

He knew, though, even if he did keep having to remind himself of it, that only a God damn fool would complain about the way things were going. Lucy had become the picture of a serene young mother – he loved the look that came over her face when she breast-fed the baby – and the baby herself, with her petal-soft skin and her round, deep blue eyes, was a constant source of wonder. Oh, Laura, he wanted to say when he slowly walked her to sleep, oh, little girl, just trust me. Trust me, and you'll never be afraid.

It didn't take him very long to get the hang of the work at *Chain Store Age*. When he was singled out for praise on several of his "stories" he began to relax – maybe it wasn't really necessary to knock yourself out over this shit after all – and soon he made friends with another staff writer, an affable, talkative young man named Bill Brock whose disdain for the job seemed even greater than his own. Brock was an Amherst graduate who had spent a couple of years as a labor-union organizer for electrical workers – "the best, most rewarding time of my life" – and was now deep in the writing of what he called a working-class novel.

"Look, I'll give you Dreiser and Frank Norris and those guys," he would explain, "and I'll even give you the early Steinbeck, but for the most part there hasn't *been* a proletarian literature in America. We're scared shitless of facing the truth, that's what it amounts to." And then at other moments, as if sensing something faintly absurd in his own passion for social reform, he would laugh it off with a rueful little shake of the head and say he guessed he'd been born twenty years too late.

When Michael asked him over for dinner one night he said, "Sure; love to. Be okay if I bring my girl?"

"Well, of course."

Then when he saw Michael writing down the Perry Street address he said, "I'll be damned; we're practically neighbors. We're only a couple hundred yards from you, over on the other side of Abingdon Square. Good, then; we'll look forward to it."

And from the moment Bill Brock brought his girl into the Davenports' apartment – "This is Diana Maitland" – Michael began to be afraid he would find himself secretly, achingly in love with her forever. She was slender and black-haired, with a sad young face that suggested a fine mobility of expression, and she carried herself a little like a fashion model – or rather with the kind of heedless, lanky grace that any training as a fashion model might only have refined and destroyed. He couldn't take his eyes away from her, and he could only hope that Lucy wasn't paying attention.

When the four of them were settled over their first or second drinks, Diana Maitland cast a brief, twinkling look at him.

17

"Michael reminds me of my brother," she said to Brock. "Don't you think? Not so much in the face, I mean, but in the general build and manner; sort of the whole personality."

Bill Brock frowned and didn't seem to agree, but he said, "That's a great compliment anyway, though, Mike: she's always been crazy about her brother. Very nice guy, too; I think you'd like him. Little moody and morose at times, but essentially a very –" And he held up one hand to ward off any objection from Diana. "Well, now, come on, baby, I'm not being unfair. You *know* he can be tiresome as hell when he goes in for all this brooding, heavy-drinking, Great Tragic Artist horseshit." And as if confident of having silenced her, he turned back to the Davenports and explained that Paul Maitland was a painter – "Damn good one, too, from what I hear, and I mean at least you gotta give him credit: he works hard as hell at it and doesn't seem to care if he ever makes a nickel out of it or not. Lives way the hell downtown on Delancey Street or some awful place, in a studio as big as a barn that costs him about thirty bucks a month. Does rough carpentry to pay the rent and buy the booze – are you getting the picture? A real tough customer. Anybody ever came along and offered him a job like *we've* got – you know? As a commercial artist or something? – if that ever happened he'd punch 'em right in the mouth. He'd think he was being compromised. He'd say they were trying to make him sell out – and that's exactly the way he'd put it, too: 'sell out.' No, but I've always liked the hell out of Paul, and I admire him. I admire any man with the courage to go – you know – the courage to go his own way. Paul and I were at Amherst together, you see; if it hadn't been for that I'd never have met this creature here."

The phrase "this creature" echoed in Michael's head throughout their dinner and for a long time afterwards. Diana Maitland might be only a girl at the table, courteously praising Lucy's cooking; she might be only a girl in the conversational hour or two that followed, and still a girl when Bill Brock helped her on with her coat in the vestibule and they said goodnight and their footsteps rang and faded across Abingdon Square toward Brock's place, "their" place – but once they were home, with the door locked behind them and their clothes on the floor; once she lay thrashing and moaning in Brock's arms, in Brock's bed, she would be a creature.

There were other visits back and forth across Abingdon Square in the fall of that year. Each time Michael would steel himself to take the risk of glancing quickly from Diana to Lucy, hoping Lucy might turn out to be the more attractive of the two, and he was always disappointed. Diana kept winning the contest time and again – oh, Christ, what a girl – until, after a while, he decided to quit making those wretchedly secret comparisons. It was a dumb, dumb thing to do. It might well be something other married men did now and then, for little other purpose than to torture themselves, but you didn't have to be very smart to know how dumb it was. Besides, when he and Lucy were alone and he could look at her from different angles and in any kind of light, it was always easy to believe she was pretty enough to last him a lifetime.

One ice-cold December night, at Diana's urging, the four of them rode downtown in a cab to visit her brother.

Paul Maitland turned out to look nothing at all like Michael: he did have the same general kind of mustache, which he touched and stroked with shapely fingers in the momentary shyness of meeting strangers, but even that provided no real similarity because it was far more luxuriant – a fearless young iconoclast's mustache as opposed to that of an office worker. He was lean and limber, in a masculine version of his sister's style,

19

dressed in a Levi jacket and pants with a merchant seaman's sweater worn under the jacket, and he spoke very courteously in a light, almost whispering voice that made you bend a little toward him for fear of missing something.

As he led his guests across his studio, a big, plain loft once used for small-factory facilities, they found they couldn't see any of his paintings because everything lay in shadows cast by the glare of a streetlamp beyond the windowpanes. But in one far corner a great many yards of heavy burlap had been hung from ropes to form a kind of tent, and it was within this small enclosure that Paul Maitland made his winter home. He lifted a flap to usher them inside, and they discovered other people sitting around with red wine in the warmth of a kerosene stove.

Most of the names were lost in the perfunctory introductions, but by now Michael was less concerned with names than with clothes. Seated on an upended orange crate with a warm glass of wine in his hand, he was unable to think of anything but that he and Bill Brock must look hopelessly out of place here in their business suits, their button-down shirts and silk ties, a couple of smiling intruders from Madison Avenue. And he knew Lucy must be uncomfortable, too, though he didn't want to look at her face and find out.

Diana was plainly welcome in this gathering – there had been cries of "Diana!" and "Baby!" when she'd first come crouching in under the burlap – and now she sat prettily on the floor near her brother's feet, talking in an animated way with a partially bald young man whose clothes suggested he was a painter, too. If she ever got tired of Brock – and wouldn't any first-rate girl get tired of Brock soon enough? – she wouldn't have long to wonder where to look next.

There was another girl called Peggy who looked no more than nineteen or twenty, with a sweet grave face, a peasant blouse and a dirndl skirt, and she seemed determined to prove she belonged to Paul. She sat as close as possible to him on the low studio couch that was apparently their bed; she never took her eyes off him, and it was clear that she would like to have her hands on him, too. He seemed scarcely aware of her as he leaned forward and lifted his chin to exchange a few laconic remarks over the top of the stove with a man on the orange crate next to Michael's, but then when he sat back again he gave her a lazy smile, and after a while he put his arm around her.

Nobody in that dry, overheated little makeshift room looked more like an artist than the man on the crate next to Michael's – he wore white overalls daubed and streaked with many colors – but he was quick to explain that he was "only a dabbler; only a well-meaning amateur." He was a local businessman, a sub-contractor in the building trades: it was he who supplied Paul Maitland with the part-time carpentry work that kept him alive.

"And I consider it a privilege," he said, hunching closer to Michael and lowering his voice so that their host wouldn't overhear. "I consider it a privilege because this boy's good. This boy's the real thing."

"Well, that's – that's fine," Michael said.

"Had a rough time of it in the war, you know."

"Oh?" And this was one part of the Paul Maitland story that Michael hadn't yet heard – probably because Bill Brock, who'd been classified 4-F during the war and was still touchy about it, would not have been inclined to provide the information.

"Oh, God, yes. Too young to've seen the whole thing, of course, but he was up to his neck in it from the Bulge right on through to the end. Infantry. Rifleman. Never talks about it, but it shows. You can see it in his work."

Michael pulled his necktie loose and opened his collar, as if

21

that might give his brains a better chance to sort things out. He didn't know what to make of any of this.

The man in overalls knelt to pour himself more wine from a gallon jug on the floor; when he came back he took a drink, wiped his mouth on his sleeve, and began talking to Michael again in the same tone of confidential reverence. "Hell, New York's crawling with painters," he said. "The whole damn country is, for that matter. But you come across a boy like this maybe once in a generation. I'm confident of that. And it may take years; it may not even happen in his lifetime, God forbid" – here he reached down and rapped his knuckles on a slat of his crate – "but some day an awful lot of people are gonna walk into the Museum of Modern Art and it'll be Paul Maitland all the way. Room after room after room. I'm confident of that."

Well, okay, swell, Michael wanted to say, but do you think you could sort of shut up about it now? Instead he nodded in slow and respectful silence; then he peered across the kerosene stove at Paul Maitland's averted face, as if a close-enough scrutiny of it might reveal some gratifying flaw. He considered Maitland's having gone to Amherst – didn't everybody know Amherst was an expensive school for society boys and intellectual lightweights? – but no, all those stereotypes were said to have broken down since the war; besides, he might have chosen Amherst because it had a good art department, or because it allowed him more time to paint than he'd have had at other colleges. Still, he must have enjoyed at least a taste of aristocratic languor there, after all that infantry soldiering. He had probably joined in a general taking of pains over just the right cut of tweeds and flannels and just the right kind of light, witty talk, and in a general vying for perfection at knowing how best to spend each careless weekend ("Bill, I'd like you to meet my sister Diana . . ."). Didn't all that suggest something just a little ludicrous about this headlong descent into lower bohemia and odd-job carpentry? Well, maybe; maybe not.

There were still a few inches of wine in the glass jug, but Paul Maitland announced in his customary mutter that it was time for a real drink. He reached into some recess of the hanging burlap and brought out a bottle of the cheap blended whiskey called Four Roses – he sure as hell hadn't learned to drink *that* stuff at Amherst – and Michael wondered if they might now be permitted to see the side of him that Bill Brock had disparaged: the brooding, heavy-drinking, Great Tragic Artist horseshit.

But there was evidently neither time nor whiskey enough for that to occur tonight. Paul poured a generous round or two of real drinks for everyone, eliciting gasps and grimaces of appreciation, and Michael liked the jolt of it too, despite the taste. There was livelier and more spirited talk around the burlap enclosure for a while – several voices grew happily boisterous – but soon it was almost midnight, and people were getting up and putting on their coats to leave. Paul rose to wish his guests goodnight, but after the third or fourth handshake he crouched, froze, and gave all his attention to a small, smudged plastic radio that had been buzzing and crackling on the floor beside the bed all evening. The radio's static had cleared now, and it had begun to issue a sweet, fast melody full of clarinets that took everyone back to 1944.

"Glenn Miller," Paul said, and he squatted nimbly to turn up the volume. Then he switched on a bright overhead light beyond the burlap, took his girl by the hand, and led her out into the chill of the studio for dancing. But the muffled music wasn't loud enough for his liking out there, so he hurried back inside and brought the radio out with its wall plug ready in his free hand, looking along the baseboard for a socket and finding none. Then from a shadowed section of the floor he picked up the attachment end of an electrical-appliance cord, the kind of flat oblong device with twin holes meant to receive the prongs of an electric iron or an old-fashioned toaster, and he hesitated less than a second over whether or not it would work.

Michael wanted to say, No, wait; I wouldn't try that – it looked like something any child would know better than to try – but Paul Maitland jammed the radio plug into the other thing with all the aplomb of a man who knows what he's doing. A big blue-and-white spark went off in his hands but the circuit caught and held: the radio came up strong again, and he went back to the girl just as Glenn Miller's reeds gave way to the soaring, triumphant blare of his brass section.

Standing in his overcoat, feeling dumb, Michael had to acknowledge that it was a pleasure to watch them dance. Paul's heavy, high-cut work shoes were remarkably agile in performing their neat little movements on the floor, and the rest of him was all rhythm too: he would send Peggy spinning away as far as their joined hands would allow and then bring her spinning back, making her dirndl skirt whip and float around her pretty young knees. Neither in high school nor in the whole of his time in the Army nor at Harvard – and not for lack of trying – had Michael ever learned to dance like that.

And as long as he was feeling dumb anyway he supposed he might as well turn and inspect a big painting that now hung revealed in the single studio light. It was just as he'd feared: it looked incomprehensible to the point of chaos; it seemed to provide no sense of order, or any sense at all, except perhaps in the silence of the painter's own mind. It was what Michael had grudgingly learned to call Abstract Expressionism, the kind of picture that had once provoked him into a bad quarrel with Lucy, before they were married, as they stood in the murmurous hush of some Boston art gallery.

". . . What do you mean, you don't 'get' it?" she'd said irritably. "There's nothing to 'get,' don't you see? It isn't representational."

"So what is it, then?"

"Just what it looks like: an arrangement of shapes and colors, perhaps a celebration of the act of painting itself. It's the artist's personal statement, that's all."

"Yeah, yeah, sure, but I mean if it's his personal statement, what's he saying?"

"Oh, Michael, I don't believe this; I think you're teasing me. If he could have said it he wouldn't've had to *paint* it. Come on; let's get out of here before we—"

"No. Wait a second. Listen: I still don't get it. And there's no point in trying to make me feel dumb about this, baby, because that won't work."

"I think you're trying to make yourself feel dumb," she said. "I don't even know how to talk to you when you're like this."

"Yeah, well, you'd better try another line pretty soon, sweetheart, or it's only gonna get worse. Because you know what you are when you pull this snotty little Radcliffe condescension with me? You're a real pain in the ass. I mean that, Lucy. . . ."

But now, here in Paul Maitland's studio, when she came up as his neatly bundled, pleasantly tired wife and put her hand through his arm, he was glad enough to let her steer him away to the door. There would be other opportunities. Maybe, if he saw enough of Paul Maitland's work, he might begin to understand it.

As they followed Bill Brock and Diana in clumping down the cold, dirty stairs to Delancey Street, Bill turned back cheerfully and called, "Hope you folks are ready for a little walk – we sure as hell aren't gonna find a cab in *this* neighborhood." And in the

25

end, with freezing feet and streaming nostrils, they walked all the way home.

"They're both sort of – rare people, aren't they?" Lucy said later that night, when she and Michael were alone and getting ready for bed.

"Who?" he said. "Diana and Bill?"

"Oh, God, no, not Bill. He's just an ordinary loudmouthed, smart-assed – as a matter of fact I'm getting a little tired of Bill, aren't you? No, I meant Diana and Paul. There's something exceptional about the two of them, isn't there? Something sort of – unearthly. Something enchanted."

And he knew at once what she meant, though he might not have put it that way. "Well, yeah," he said. "I mean I know what you mean."

"And I have the funniest feeling about them both," she said. "Sitting there and watching them tonight I kept thinking, These are the kind of people I've wanted to know all my life. Oh, I suppose all I'm really trying to say is that I want them to like me. I do want that so much, and it makes me nervous and sad because I'm afraid they won't, or that if they do it won't last."

She looked forlorn, sitting on the edge of the bed in her nightgown like the very picture of a poor little rich girl, and her voice was perilously close to tears. If she allowed herself to cry over something like this he knew she would be ashamed, and that would only make it worse.

And so, in as low and comforting a voice as he could manage, he told her that he understood her fears. "I mean I don't necessarily agree with you – why *wouldn't* they like you? Why wouldn't they like both of us? – all I mean is, I know what you mean."

Chapter Three

The White Horse Tavern, on Hudson Street, became their most agreeable gathering place. They were usually a party of four – Bill and Diana and the Davenports – but there were a surprising number of other, happier evenings when Paul Maitland would bring Peggy uptown to join them around a big, damp brown table for drink and talk and laughter, and even for song. Michael had always liked to sing; he prided himself on having memorized all the lyrics of obscure songs and on usually having the sense to know when to stop, though there were some nights when Lucy had to frown or nudge him into silence.

This was at a time not long before the death of Dylan Thomas made the White Horse famous ("And we never even saw him in there," Michael would complain for years afterwards. "Isn't that the damndest thing? Sat around the Horse almost every night and never even saw the man – and how could anybody miss a face like that? Christ's sake, I didn't even know he was in America when he died.")

As a consequence of that death it seemed that everyone in New York wanted to come and drink at the White Horse every night – and so the place lost much of its appeal.

But by the spring of that year the city itself was no longer very appealing for the Davenports. Their daughter was four, and it

seemed only reasonable to look for a place in the suburbs –
assuming, of course, that they could remain within easy
commuting distance.

The town they chose was Larchmont, because it struck
Lucy as being more "civilized" than the others they visited, and
the house they found to rent there seemed to meet their
immediate needs. It was nice: a good place to work, a good
place to rest; and it had a good, grassy backyard for Laura to
play in.

"Suburbia!" Bill Brock cried as dramatically as a man
discovering the shore of a new continent, and he brandished the
bottle of bourbon he had brought as a housewarming gift. Close
beside him and clasping his arm with both hands, Diana Maitland
pressed her laughing face against his coat as if to suggest that this
kind of clowning was the very thing she had always loved best
about him.

And as they made their slow, mirth-encumbered way up the
short path from the Larchmont sidewalk into the Larchmont
house, Bill seemed reluctant to break the pattern of his own
hilarity. "My God," he said, "look at this! Look at the two of
you! You're like a couple of young marrieds in the movies – or
in *Good Housekeeping*!"

There was nothing for the Davenports to do but go along
with the laughs as best they could, even after drinks were poured
and they were settled in a conversational group around the living
room, though Michael had begun to hope the teasing would
soon be over. But Bill Brock wasn't quite finished: he extended
the index finger of the hand that held his glass, aimed it first at
Lucy and then at Michael, who were sitting together on the sofa,
and said "Blondie and Dagwood."

And Diana almost fell out of her chair. It was the first time
Michael had ever disliked her. Worse still, the second time came

later that same night, long after the talk had turned to other things and the tension had dissolved. Brock, as if in partial apology for his earlier comments, expressed a nonhumorous interest in seeing what the town was like, so the four of them took a long walk through the leaf-shadowed evening streets. And Michael was tentatively pleased because this was indeed the best time for a tour of Larchmont: all its glaring, oppressive tidiness was softened and made gentle in the dark. Its lighted windows, as seen through their dappling of green in house after house, suggested calm and order and well-earned peace. It was very quiet, and the air smelled wonderful.

". . . No, I can certainly understand the appeal of it," Bill Brock was saying. "Nothing's awry, nothing's screwed up, nothing's ever out of whack. That's certainly what you'd want, I guess, if you're – married and have a family and all that. Matter of fact there must be millions of people who'd give anything for a chance to live here – an awful lot of the guys I worked with in the union, for example. Still, for some temperaments it just wouldn't ever be right." And here he gave his girl a little squeeze. "Can you imagine Paul in a place like this?"

"God," Diana said quietly, and she gave an audible shudder that reverberated down Michael's spine. "He'd die. Paul would absolutely, literally die here."

". . . And I mean couldn't she see what a tactless fucking thing that was to say?" Michael demanded of his wife after their guests had gone. "What the hell does she take us for? And I didn't like her getting quite such a big fucking laugh out of that silly shit about Blondie and Dagwood, either."

"I know," Lucy assured him. "I know. Well, it was a very – awkward evening."

But he was glad he had been the one to explode. If he'd held it all in that night it might have been Lucy who broke first – and

29

her breaking, rather than in anger, would probably have been in tears.

He had established a working alcove in one corner of the attic of their Larchmont house – it wasn't much, but it was private – and he would look forward all day to the hours he could spend alone there. He had begun to feel that his book was almost in shape again, almost done, if only he could bring off the long, ambitious, final poem that was meant to justify and carry all the others. He had an adequate working title for it, "Coming Clean," but certain lines of it stubbornly refused to be brought alive; whole sections of it seemed ready to collapse or evaporate under his hand. On most nights he worked in the attic until he ached with fatigue, but there were other times when he couldn't get his brains together, when he would sit there stupefied in a paralysis of inattention, smoking cigarettes and despising himself, until he went back downstairs to bed. And even then there was seldom enough sleep to prepare him for the push and hustle of the Larchmont mornings.

From the moment he closed the front door behind him he was caught up and swept along in a heavy stream of commuters walking to the train station. They were men of his own age or ten or twenty years older, with a few in their sixties, and they seemed to take pride in their very conformity: the crisp dark business suits and conservative ties, the highly polished shoes brought down in almost military cadence on the sidewalk. Only rarely did a commuter walk alone; almost all of them had at least one conversational companion, and most of them moved in clusters. Michael's tendency was to look neither right nor left for fear of attracting a comradely smile – Who the hell needed these guys? – but he couldn't enjoy his solitude because it was too reminiscent of bad times in the Army: the sense of having to keep his own counsel among talking, laughing, better-adjusted men. And that discomfort was always at its most acute after they had filed and clumped inside the Larchmont station, because there was nothing to do in there but stand around and wait.

Then once he saw another stranger leaning alone against the wall, squinting down through steel-rimmed glasses at a lighted cigarette as if smoking required his full attention. The man was smaller and younger-looking than Michael, and he wasn't even dressed right: instead of a suit coat he wore an Army "tanker's jacket," the sturdy zippered wind-breaker once coveted by most ground-force troops in Europe because it was given only to the men who rode in tracked and armored assault vehicles.

Michael drifted over to within speaking range and said "You in an armored division?"

"Huh?"

"I said were you in an armored division during the war?"

The young man looked puzzled, blinking several times behind his glasses. "Oh, the jacket," he said at last. "Naw, I bought this off a guy, is all."

"Oh, I see." And Michael knew that if he said, Well, that was a good buy; they're nice to have, he would feel even more like a fool, so he kept his mouth shut and started to turn away.

But the stranger apparently didn't want to be left alone. "Naw, I wasn't in the war," he said in the same quick, automatically apologetic way that Bill Brock always said it. "Wasn't even in the service until forty-five, and then I never got overseas. Never even got out of Blanchard Field, Texas."

"Oh, yeah?" And this opened up further conversational possibilities. "Well, I spent a little time at Blanchard in forty-three," Michael said, "and I sure as hell wouldn't've wanted to stay. What'd they have you doing there?"

A small, witty spasm of revulsion worked in the young man's

31

face. "Band, man," he said. "Fucking marching band. I'd made the mistake of telling some personnel interviewer I played drums, you see, so the minute I finished basic they hung this fucking snare drum on me. Parade drum. Rattly-tat, rattly-tat. Retreat parades, full-dress parades, award ceremonies and all that Mickey Mouse. Jesus, I thought I'd never get outa there alive."

"Are you a musician, then? In civilian life?"

"Oh, not really. Haven't got my union card yet, but I've always liked to fool around with it. So what'd you do at Blanchard? Take basic there?"

"No, I took gunnery."

"Yeah?" And the young man's eyes were as wide and keen as a boy's. "You an aerial gunner?"

It was turning out to be as pleasant as any similar talk at Harvard, or in the offices of *Chain Store Age*: all Michael had to do was answer questions, as briefly as possible, and he could feel himself gaining stature in his listener's mind. Well, yeah, he had flown in combat – Eighth Air Force, out of England; no, he'd never been shot down or wounded, though he'd had the shit scared out of him a few times; oh, yes, it was certainly true that English girls were wonderful; yes, no; yes, no.

And as always before, he managed to change the subject before there could be any hint of a waning of interest. He asked the young man how long he'd been living in Larchmont – a year, was all – and if he was married.

"Oh, sure; who isn't? You know anybody here who isn't? That's what Larchmont's *for*, man." And he had four children, all boys, all about a year apart. "My wife's Catholic," he explained, "and she was stubborn as hell about all that for an awful long time. Think I got her pretty well talked out of it now, though – hope to hell I do, anyway. I mean, they're good; they're nice; but four's plenty." Then he asked where Michael lived, and said

"Wow, you got the whole house? That's nice. We've just got an upstairs apartment. Still, we're better off than we were in Yonkers. Spent three years in Yonkers; wouldn't want to go through that again."

By the time the train came clattering in they had shaken hands and exchanged names – the stranger's name was Tom Nelson – and as they moved out across the platform Michael noticed for the first time that he carried what looked like a sparse roll of paper towels held together with a rubber band. But they were neither soft nor clean enough to be towels; they had a mottled, handled look that suggested they were laboriously drawn-up "specification sheets" for spare parts or tools required today by Tom Nelson's employer (A garage owner? A construction boss?) and which Nelson would spend hours tracking down in the warehouses of some dismal place like Long Island City.

And if nothing else, riding into town with Tom Nelson might provide a few sad and funny things to tell Lucy about tonight: this hapless, Church-ridden, too-young father of four, this wry, rueful, rattly-tat parade drummer from the dust of Blanchard Field who hadn't even earned his tanker's jacket, let alone his union card.

For the first few minutes of the ride they sat together in silence, as if each were trying to think of a new topic; then Michael said "They still have the boxing tournament at Blanchard when you were there?"

"Oh, yeah, that was always a fixture. Big morale factor, or something. You like to watch that?"

"Well," Michael said, "as a matter of fact I went out for it. Middleweight class. Lasted through the semifinals; then some supply sergeant took me apart with left jabs – never met a man with a left jab like that, and he knew how to use his right hand, too. Technical knockout in the eighth round."

"Damn," Nelson said. "Course, I could never've done anything like that because of my eyes; still, even with good eyes I probably wouldn't've tried it. Right up to the finals; that's impressive. So what kinda work you doing now?"

"Well, I'm a writer, or at least that's what I'm trying to do: poetry and plays. Got a book of poems almost done; had a couple of plays produced in a very small way, up in the Boston area. Just for the present, though, I've got a dumb little commercial-writing job in the city – *you* know, to keep the groceries coming in."

"Yeah." And Tom Nelson gave him a sidelong look that glinted with amiable teasing. "Jesus. A gunner, a fighter, a poet, and a playwright. Know something? You're coming on like a fucking Renaissance Man."

And amiable or not, the teasing hurt. Who *was* this little bastard? But the worst and most sickening part was that Michael had to admit he'd asked for it. Dignity and reserve were qualities he had always prized more highly than almost any others; why, then, did he always, always have to shoot his mouth off?

And even if it might not be strictly true that a man like Paul Maitland would "die" in Larchmont, it was clear that Paul Maitland would never open himself to the ridicule of some fool on a Larchmont commuters' train.

But Tom Nelson seemed unaware of having inflicted pain. "Well, poetry's always been very big with me," he was saying. "Can't write it to save my ass, but I've always liked to read it. You like Hopkins?"

"Very much."

"Yeah, he kinda gets into your bones, doesn't he? The way Keats does; the way some of the later Yeats does, too. And I like the hell out of Wilfred Owen. Even Sassoon, to some extent. Like some of the French, too, Valéry and those people, but I don't think you can understand their stuff unless you know the language. I used to like to illustrate poems – got on a big illustration kick for a couple of years and I'll probably get back to it, but now I'm doing more just regular pictures."

"You're an artist, then."

"Oh, yeah, yeah; thought I'd told you that."

"No, you didn't. And you work in New York?"

"No; work at home. Take my stuff into the city once in a while, is all. Couple times a month."

"So you're able to—" and Michael was about to say "able to earn your living at it?" but he checked himself; the question of how any artist earned his living was apt to be a delicate one. Instead he said "—able to work full time at it, then?"

"Oh, yeah. Well, I had to teach back in Yonkers – taught high school there – but then things began to pick up a little."

And Michael ventured a careful inquiry about technique: Did Nelson work in oils?

"Naw, I can't seem to get much going when I try that. I do water-colors – pen-and-ink drawing with a color wash – that's all. I'm very limited that way."

Perhaps, then, he was limited to the art departments of advertising agencies, or perhaps, since "watercolors" did suggest pleasant little scenes of boats moored in their harbors or of flocks of birds on the wing, he might be limited to the kind of stifling gift shops where pictures like that were displayed for sale along with expensive ashtrays, with pink shepherd-and-shepherdess figurines, and with dinner plates bearing the portraits of President and Mrs. Eisenhower.

Another question or two might have been enough to establish all that, or to clear it up, but Michael didn't want to press his luck. He remained silent until the train had brought them into the echoing swarm of Grand Central.

"Which way you headed?" Nelson asked when they emerged blinking in the city sunshine. "Up or down?"

"Up to Fifty-ninth."

"Good; I'll walk you to Fifty-third. Gotta check in at the Modern there."

And it took a little while for that to sink in, as they walked, but by the time they'd turned uptown on Fifth Avenue Michael was no longer in any doubt that to "check in at the Modern" meant a business appointment with the Museum of Modern Art. He wished there were some way he could accompany Nelson on that visit – he wanted to see exactly what the hell went on in there – and in the end, as they came to the corner of Fifty-third, it was Nelson who made the suggestion. "Want to come along?" he said. "This'll only take a couple minutes; then we can head on up in your direction."

There seemed to be a touch of deference in the face of the uniformed man who opened a thick plate-glass door for them, and again in the bearing of the elevator operator, though Michael couldn't be sure he hadn't imagined it. But nothing was left to his imagination in the strikingly pretty girl whose reception desk stood at the far end of a big, hushed room upstairs, and who whipped off her horn-rimmed glasses so that her lovely eyes could shine with admiration and welcome.

"Oh, Thomas Nelson," she said. "Now I know it's going to be a good day."

An ordinary girl would probably have remained seated to pick up a phone and press a button or two, but there was nothing ordinary about this one. She got up and came swiftly around her desk to take Nelson's hand and to reveal how slender and well-dressed she was. She blinked and mumbled on being introduced to Michael, as if noticing his presence for the first time; then she turned quickly back to Nelson for a few moments of bright talk and laughter that Michael couldn't follow. "Oh, but I know he'll be waiting," she said at last. "Why don't you just go on in?"

And the bald, tan, middle-aged man who stood alone in the inner office, pressing the knuckles of both hands onto an empty table, did indeed appear to have been waiting for just this moment.

"Thomas!" he cried.

He was a little more polite than the girl in meeting Nelson's guest – he offered Michael a chair, which Michael declined – then he went back to the table and said "Now, Thomas. Let's see what wonderful things you've brought us this time."

The rubber band came off, the mottled roll of papers was unfurled and then gently rolled the opposite way to help them lie flat, and six bright watercolor pictures were laid out for the man's inspection – almost, it seemed, for the delectation of the world of art itself.

"My God," Lucy said that night, when Michael had gotten just that far in telling the story. "So what are the pictures like? Can you tell me?"

He was a little annoyed with the "Can you tell me?" part of it, but he let it pass. "Well, they're certainly not *ab*stract," he said. "I mean they're representational – there are people and animals and things in them – but they're not realistic. They're very sort of – I don't know"; and here he was grateful for the only technical information Nelson had given on the train. "He does a kind of scratchy, blurry pen-and-ink drawing with a water-color wash."

And she favored him with a slow, intelligent-looking nod, as if commending a child on a surprisingly mature insight.

"So anyway," he went on, "the museum guy started moving very slowly around the table, and he said 'Well, Thomas, I can tell you right away that if I let this one go I'd never forgive myself.' Then he walked around some more and said 'This one's rapidly growing on me too. Can you let me have them both?'

"And Nelson said 'Sure, Eric; help yourself.' He's just standing there calm as hell in his damn zipped-up tanker's jacket, looking like he couldn't care less."

"So are they acquiring these pictures for some – seasonal exhibit, then, or what?" Lucy said.

"That's the first thing I asked him when we were out on the street again, and he said 'Naw, these are for the permanent collection.' Can you imagine that? The permanent collection?" And Michael went to the kitchen counter to put more ice and bourbon into his drink. "Oh, and another thing," he said to his wife. "You know what he paints his pictures *on*? Shelf-paper."

"What–paper?"

"You know. Like what people cover shelves with, for storing canned goods and stuff like that. Said he started using it years ago because it's cheap, then he decided he 'likes the way it takes the paint.' And he does it all on his fucking kitchen floor. Says he keeps a big flat square of galvanized tin there, to make the right kind of surface; then he lays a soaking-wet piece of shelf-paper on it, gets down on his haunches and goes to work."

Lucy had been doing her best to prepare their dinner ever since Michael came home, but she'd been too frequently distracted. The pork chops were dried out and she'd forgotten to chill the applesauce; the green beans were limp and the potatoes weren't baked through. But Michael noticed none of it, or didn't care. He ate with one elbow on the table and his hand spanning his brow, and with a third or fourth glass of whiskey in readiness beside his plate.

"So I asked him," he said around his chewing, "I asked him

38

how long it takes him to make a picture. He said 'Oh, maybe twenty minutes if I'm lucky; usually more like a couple hours, sometimes a day or so. Then about twice a month I go through 'em and throw a lot of 'em out – maybe a quarter or a third – and whatever's left are the ones I bring into town. The Modern always wants first pick, and sometimes the Whitney wants a look at 'em, too; then I take the rest of 'em up to my dealer – you know, to my gallery.'"

"What's his gallery?" she asked, and when he repeated the name she said "My God" again, because it was a place made well-known by the art pages of *The New York Times*.

"And he told me – and he wasn't bragging; Christ's sake, nothing this little bastard ever says is bragging – he told me they give him a one-man show there at least once a year. Last year they gave him two."

"Well, it's all a little – hard to take in, isn't it?" Lucy said.

Michael shoved his plate aside – he hadn't even opened his baked potato – and picked up his whiskey as if it were the main course. "It's incredible," he said. "Twenty-seven years old. And I mean, Jesus, when you think of – Jesus, honey." And he shook his head in wonderment. "I mean, talk about making difficult things look *easy*." Then, after a while, he said "Oh, and he said he'd like us to come over for dinner some night soon. Said he'd check with his wife and give us a call."

"Really?" Lucy looked as pleased as a child on her birthday. "Did he really?"

"Well, yeah, but you know how those things are. It may slip his mind. I mean it's nothing to count on, or anything."

"Couldn't we call them?" she asked.

And he was silently exasperated. For a girl raised in the upper reaches of the upper class, she could be surprisingly dense about good manners. But then, perhaps good manners had never been especially characteristic of millionaires in the first place; how could ordinary people ever know about that?

"Well, no, baby," he said, "I don't think that'd be too good an idea. I'll probably run into him again on the train, though; we'll work something out." Then he said "No, but listen, let me give you the postscript to all this. When I finally got to the office my brains were kind of reeling. I knew I couldn't face the job, so I went in to waste a little time with Brock, and I told him about Tom Nelson. When he'd heard it all he said 'Well; that's interesting. I wonder who *his* father is.'"

"Oh, that's just *like* him, isn't it?" Lucy said. "Bill Brock is always going on and on about how he hates cynicism in any form, but he's really about the most cynical person I've ever known."

"Wait, though; it gets worse. I said 'Well, Bill, for one thing his father's a pharmacist in Cincinnati, and for another I don't see what the hell difference it makes.'

"And he said 'Oh. Well, okay, then, I wonder whose cock he's sucking.'"

Lucy was seized by a spasm of revulsion so acute that it forced her up from the table. The syllable "Ugh!" came from her distorted lips and she stood hugging herself with both arms as if chilled to the bone. "Oh, that's vile," she said, shuddering. "That's the vilest thing I've ever heard."

"Yeah, well, you know Brock. And anyway he's been in a lousy mood for weeks. I think he's having a few troubles with Diana."

"Well, I'm not surprised," she said as she began to clear the plates away. "I don't know why Diana didn't dump him long ago. I've never understood how she could've taken *up* with him."

★

40

One Saturday morning Bill Brock called up, in unaccustomed shyness, to ask if he could come out to Larchmont alone that afternoon.

"Are you sure he said 'alone'?" Lucy inquired.

"Well, he kind of slurred it, or elided over it, but I'm pretty sure that's what he said. And he certainly didn't say 'we.'"

"Well, then, it's over," she said. "Good. Only, now we're in for it: he'll want us to sit around for hours while he pours out his broken heart."

But it wasn't that way – not, at least, in the first part of Brock's visit.

"I mean, I'm all right in short-term relationships," he explained to them, hunching forward on the sofa in readiness for a serious discussion of himself. "I know I am, because I always have been in the past. What I can't seem to do is sustain a hell of a lot of interest over the – you know – over the long haul. I get *tired* of a girl, is what it amounts to. I get bored and then I get restless; simple as that. Frankly, I've never understood the concept of marriage. I mean, if it works for you people, fine – but then, that's your business, right?"

For the past several months, he reported, Diana had been "making marriage noises. Oh, just a hint here and a hint there at first – those were easy enough to handle – but then it started getting worse. Finally I had to tell her, I said 'Look, honey: let's face a few facts, okay?' So she agreed to move out of my place – she got an apartment with another girl – and we started seeing each other on a different basis, maybe twice a week at the most. That's the way things were when we came out here that last time. And she enrolled in an acting class – you know how they have these little 'Method' classes all over town now, mostly run by broken-down actors trying to put a few dollars together? Well, that sounded like a nice idea; I thought it might be good for her. But son of a bitch, it wasn't more than a couple of weeks before she started going out with a guy she'd met in the class – some actor-boy, actor-twerp, actor-asshole; rich father out in Kansas City who pays him to stay away from home. Then three nights ago – and I swear to you, this was the worst night of my life – I took her out to dinner and she told me in this very cool, distant way – she told me she'd moved in with this guy. She 'loves' him, and all that shit.

"Well, Jesus, I went home feeling crippled, feeling like I'd been run over by a truck. I threw myself down on the bed" – here he lay back in the sofa and flung one forearm over his eyes to suggest a total abandonment to grief – "and I cried like a child. I couldn't stop. I cried for hours, and I kept saying, 'I've lost her. I've lost her.' "

"Well," Lucy said, "it doesn't sound so much as though you'd lost her, Bill; it sounds more as though you'd thrown her away."

"Well, of *course*," he said, his arm still covering his eyes. "Of *course*. And isn't that the worst kind of loss? When you don't even realize the value of something until you've thrown it away?"

Bill Brock spent the night in their spare room – "I knew it," Lucy said later; "I knew he'd end up sleeping here" – and he didn't leave until after lunch the next day. "Have you ever noticed," she asked when they were alone again, "how your sympathy for someone's story – anyone's story – tends to evaporate when they get to the part about how long and hard they cried?"

"Yeah."

"Well, at least he's gone for now," she said. "But he'll be back, soon and often; you can count on that. And do you know what the worst part is? The worst part is we'll probably never see Diana again."

Michael felt his heart contract. He hadn't even thought of that, but from the moment Lucy said it he knew it was true.

"You're *always* expected to take one side or the other when a couple breaks up," she went on, "and isn't it funny how that can seem to work out almost entirely by accident? Because I mean if it had been Diana who called us – and it might just as easily have been – then *she'd* be our friend, and it wouldn't've been much trouble to sort of drop Bill Brock out of our lives."

"Well, I wouldn't worry about it, dear," Michael said. "Maybe she'll call us anyway. She might call anytime."

"No. I think I know her well enough not to expect that."

"Well, hell, we'll call her, then."

"How? We don't even know where she is. Oh, I suppose we could find out, but even so I don't think she'd be very happy to hear from us. We're all stuck with the way things are."

After a while, when she'd finished with the lunch dishes, she stood sadly drying her hands in the kitchen doorway. "Oh, and I did have such high hopes of being friends with her," she said, "and with Paul Maitland, too. Didn't you? They've both always seemed to be such good – such good people to know."

"Mike Davenport?" said a shy, light-textured voice on the phone a few nights later. "Tom Nelson. Listen, my wife and I were wondering if you folks might come over Friday night. Can you come for supper?"

And so it came to seem, for both the Davenports, that they hadn't lost out forever in their need for good people to know.

Chapter Four

"Place isn't much, as you'll see," Tom Nelson warned them after he'd come hurrying down from his upstairs apartment to let them in at the glass-paned front door. "Hard to keep things nice when you've got four kids." And at the top of the stairs his wife stood smiling in welcome, the girl whose once-stubborn Catholicism might almost have jeopardized her husband's career.

Her name was Pat. There were remnants in her face of a devout and fearful child of Cincinnati as she bent in the steam to pierce the boiling vegetables, or as she crouched and squinted at the oven door to withdraw and baste the roast, but when she sat laughing with her guests in the small living room, with a drink in her hand, it was clear that the Museum of Modern Art had had its way with her. She held herself very straight but without tension, wearing a fashionably simple dress, and her large, attractive eyes and mouth were able, as if by nature, to look merry and responsible at the same time.

The three younger boys had been put to bed, but the oldest, a pudgy six-year-old named Philip whose round face looked nothing like either of his parents, had been allowed to stay up and peer suspiciously at the visitors. At his mother's urging he passed around a plate of salted crackers spread with liver paste;

then, after depositing the plate on the coffee table, he went back to stand beside his mother's knee.

"We'd begun to think there wasn't anybody in Larchmont," Pat Nelson was saying, "who wasn't just – you know – who wasn't just sort of all Larchmont, inside and out."

And Lucy Davenport assured her, eagerly, that she and Michael had begun to think the same thing.

They didn't talk of painting or of poetry, as the Davenports had thought they might, but it didn't take the Davenports long to see how foolish that expectation had been: professionalism could be taken for granted in company like this. Instead they talked almost entirely of trivial things.

They all abhorred the movies, though all admitted to having seen a great many of them, and so they entertained one another with movie jokes. What if June Allyson had been cast as Scarlett O'Hara? What if Dan Dailey had been given the Humphrey Bogart role in *Casablanca?* Would Bing Crosby or Pat O'Brien be the better choice to star in a movie biography of Albert Schweitzer? Then Michael asked, rhetorically, if anyone would ever know how many hundreds of movies of all kinds – comedy, love, war, crime, or cowboy – had contained the line "Look: I can explain everything." And that, to his own shy surprise, struck the others as the funniest thing that had yet been said.

Philip was sent to join his brothers in what must have been a crowded, double-decked bedroom, and soon after that the party moved to the kitchen table. It was big enough to serve as a dinner table for four, but just barely, and the kitchen was still too warm from the cooking. On one corner of the floor, beyond the table and away from the stove, Michael saw the flat piece of galvanized tin beside a cardboard box, advertising Kellogg's Rice Krispies, from which several fresh rolls of shelf-paper protruded.

45

He supposed that the paints, the ink, and the pens and brushes must be kept in the same box.

"Oh, please take off your coat and tie, Michael," Pat Nelson said, "or you'll *die* in here." Then, a little later in the meal, she gazed at one of the steamed-up windows as if it might open onto bright vistas of the future. "Well, at least we'll only be here a few more months," she said. "Has Tom told you we're moving to the country this summer? For good?"

"But that's *terrible*," Lucy said, with more heartfelt emphasis than seemed warranted. "I mean it's wonderful for you, but terrible for us. We'll have hardly gotten to know you before you go away."

And Pat assured her, kindly, that it wouldn't be far away: they were only going up into Putnam County. That was the next county north of Westchester, she explained, and it was mostly rural – there was scarcely any suburban element at all. She and Tom had made several trips up there to look around, until they'd found what struck them as the right house on the right piece of land, near the village of Kingsley. The house itself needed work, but the work was being done now; they'd been promised it would be finished and ready in June. "And it's only a short drive from here – what is it, Tom, a little over an hour or something? – so you see it'll be easy to keep in touch with all our friends."

Lucy cut into another slice of cooling roast beef, and Michael could tell from her face that she was hurt by the phrase "all our friends." Hadn't the Nelsons made clear that they *had* no other friends in Larchmont? But then, chewing, she seemed to understand that Pat had meant all their friends in New York – the Museum of Modern Art crowd and the Whitney crowd, all the well-heeled, admiring people who'd taken to buying as many Thomas Nelson pictures as they could afford, as well as the jolly, witty, insiders' crowd of other young painters who were rapidly becoming successful too.

"Well, it sounds great," Michael said heartily. Since removing his coat and tie he had unfastened the top two buttons of his shirt and rolled up the sleeves; now, hunched over his wine and speaking in a voice that he knew might strike Lucy as being just a little loud, he was determined to suggest that he too might soon be a man unburdened of mundane necessity. "Once I can manage to get the damn job off my back," he said, "we'll be ready to make a move like that ourselves." And he winked conspicuously at his wife. "Maybe after the book's out, babe."

When dinner was over and they moved back to the living room, Michael discovered a bureau bearing six or eight precise miniatures of British soldiers in the full-dress uniforms of historic regiments – the kind of collector's items that might have cost a hundred dollars apiece. "Hey, Jesus, Tom," he said. "Where'd you get these?"

"Oh, I made 'em," Nelson said. "It's easy. You start with an ordinary tin soldier, melt it down a little to change the look of it, build it up here and there with model-airplane glue, and all the rest of it is in the painting."

"Well, I'll be damned." One of the soldiers held a tall staff with a partially unfurled Union Jack, and Michael said "How'd you make the flag?"

"Toothpaste tube," Nelson told him. "Piece of toothpaste tube'll give you a pretty good flag, if you can get it to wrinkle the right way."

Michael felt like saying You know what you are, Nelson? You're too fucking much. Instead, after taking a drink from the heavy glass of bourbon in his hand, he said only that the soldiers were beautiful.

"Well, it's just something I do for kicks," Nelson explained, "and besides, the boys like to watch. But I guess I always have been hooked on soldiers. Here, look——" and he pulled open a deep drawer of the cabinet. "These are the combat troops."

The drawer was packed with hundreds of jumbled tin soldiers from the dime store – riflemen in all firing positions, or hauling off to throw grenades, machine-gunners seated or prone, other men crouched at the tubes of mortars – and it brought an unexpected pang of longing to Michael's throat. He had once thought he must be the only boy in Morristown, New Jersey, if not in the world, who went on loving tin soldiers after the age of ten, when all other boys gave them up in favor of athletics. He had kept his own hoard of them in a box in the shadows of his closet and would often take them out and play with them during the hours before his parents woke up in the morning, until his father caught him at it once and told him to throw the God damn things away.

"You can have real battles with 'em, too," Tom Nelson was saying.

"Real battles?"

"Oh, well, you can't do the *small*-arms fire, of course, but you can do the artillery." And from another drawer came two plastic toy pistols of the kind made to shoot four-inch sticks tipped with rubber suction cups. "Friend of mine back in Yonkers and I used to have battles that'd last all afternoon," Nelson said. "First we'd get the right terrain – no grass; just dirt with a few little ridges and hills; or if it was supposed to be the First World War we'd dig ourselves a series of trenches on both sides. Then we'd divide up the troops and we'd spend a long time deploying them, trying to figure the best – you know – the best tactical advantages. Oh, and we had a strict rule about the artillery: you couldn't just blast away at random, or it would've been a shambles. You had to get back six feet behind the rear of your own infantry, and you had to keep the heel of your hand on the ground at all times" – and he demonstrated this by dropping to his haunches and setting the butt of one toy pistol firmly onto the carpet.

Across the small room, where the girls were sitting, Pat Nelson rolled her eyes in fond exasperation and said "Oh, God, they've started in on the soldiers. Well, never mind; pay no attention."

"You could control your elevation and your range," Nelson said, "and you could even change positions – we used to allow each other three changes of position during a battle – but you always had to fire from a fixed point on the ground, like real field artillery."

Michael was entranced by all this, and by the unashamedly boyish, dead-serious way Nelson was telling it.

"Then afterwards," Nelson went on, "I mean if it was a good battle, we'd lay down cigarette smoke very low over the whole scene and take photographs. It didn't always work, but some of those photographs really did look like the real thing. You'd think they were pictures of Verdun, or something."

"I'll be damned," Michael said. "And can you do this indoors, too?"

"Oh, we'd do that sometimes on rainy days, but it's nowhere near as good; you can't have hills or trenches or anything."

"Well, look, Nelson," Michael said in mock belligerence, and took another drink. "I fully intend to engage you in military combat at our earliest convenience – my backyard, your backyard, or wherever else we can find the best terrain" – he felt he was getting drunk but couldn't tell if it was on whiskey or friendship, and it pleased him to see that Tom Nelson was smiling agreeably – "but I'll be at a severe disadvantage unless I can get some experience on maneuvers first: I won't even know how to use my field artillery piece. So whaddya say we set up a few companies right here. Now. In this room."

"Naw, the carpet's no good, Mike," Nelson said. "You need a wood floor to get 'em to stand right."

"Well, hell, can't we roll the carpet back? Just until I get a little artillery practice?"

He was dimly aware of Nelson saying "Naw, look, it's—" but he had already lunged off to where the carpet bordered the kitchen doorway. He backed beyond it, crouched, and got a grip on the edge of it with both hands – noticing for the first time that it was green, cheap, and badly worn – and he'd just heaved it up from the floor when he heard Nelson call "Naw, I mean wait – it's tacked down."

Too late. A hundred carpet tacks flew and danced in shuddering clouds of house dust along three borders of the torn-up rug – all the way across the room to where it remained feebly secure, within a few inches of the coffee table and the girls – and Pat Nelson was instantly on her feet. "What're you *doing*?" she cried, and Michael would never forget her face at that moment. She wasn't angry, at least not yet: she was only shocked beyond belief.

"Well, I—" Michael said, still wretchedly holding his end of the rug at his chin, "I didn't realize it was fastened, is the thing. I'm terribly sorry if I—"

And Tom Nelson quickly tried to help him out: "We were gonna set up some of the soldiers, dear," he explained. "It's okay; we'll put it all back."

Pat set both small fists on her hips and she was angry as hell now, red in the face, but she addressed her husband instead of their guest, as if that were more in keeping with the rules of sociability. "It took me *four days* to drive all those tacks into the floor. Four days."

"Ma'am," Michael began, because he had found in the past that calling a girl "ma'am" could sometimes help to ease him out of difficult situations, "I think if you'll let me borrow a small hammer and some new carpet tacks, I can have this whole disaster repaired in practically no time."

"Oh, that's *dumb*," she said, and this time she wasn't speaking to Tom. "If it took me four days, it'd probably take you five. What you *can* do, though – both of you – is get down and start picking up the damn tacks. Every one of them. I won't have the boys coming out here in the morning and cutting their feet."

Only then did Michael risk a look at his own wife – he couldn't have borne it until now – and her face was partly turned away, but he was fairly sure he had never seen her so embarrassed.

For what seemed more than an hour, on their hands and knees, the two men slowly patrolled all sectors of the floor and the wrinkled rug in search of rusty or bent or broken tacks. They were able to exchange small, shy jokes as they worked, and once or twice the girls joined hesitantly in the laughter, until Michael began to entertain a wistful hope that the evening might still be saved. And with the pouring of what Pat Nelson called "one last drink," after the job was done, it seemed that her graciousness was mostly restored – though he knew that if it were wholly restored she wouldn't have said "one last drink." Mercifully, then, all their talk was of other things until the time came for the Davenports to say goodnight.

"Ma'am?" Michael inquired at the door. "If you can ever forgive me for the rug, do you think we can still be friends?"

"Oh, don't be silly," Pat said, and she touched his arm with what felt like kindness. "I'm sorry I got mad."

But walking home alone with Lucy was another matter.

"Well, of *course* she 'forgave' you," Lucy said. "What are you, some little boy who feels all goody-good again because his mother's 'forgiven' him? Oh, couldn't you see how poor they are from the moment we walked into that place? Or at least how poor they've always been until the past year or so? And now that he's begun to earn real money they're putting every dollar of it into the country place they've bought. They'll be making a whole new life for themselves on the strength of his work, and you can be sure it'll be a splendid life, too, because they're just about the most admirable people I've ever met. In the meantime they're stuck here for a little while longer, so they made the awful mistake of having us over tonight. And when I saw you rip up that carpet – I really mean this, Michael – when I saw you rip up that carpet it was like watching a total stranger do some insane, destructive thing. All I could think was: I don't know this man. I've never seen this person before."

She stopped talking then, as though talking could never lead to anything but exhaustion, and Michael had nothing to say. He felt more weak than resentful and he knew that no reply would be adequate, so he clenched his jaws to keep from making any reply at all. Once in a while, along the intervals of sidewalk between trees, he looked up at the winking stars in the black sky as if to ask if ever – oh, ever – there might come a time when he would learn to do something right.

Things got better before the end of that spring.

Michael did manage to get the job off his back – or almost. He persuaded *Chain Store Age* to let him become one of its several "contributing writers," rather than an employee. He would work on a freelance basis now, visiting the office only twice a month to deliver his copy and to pick up new assignments; he would lose the security of a salary and all the "fringe benefits," but he was confident he could earn at least as

52

much money this way. And the best part, he explained to his wife, was that he could set his own schedule: he could pack all the *Chain Store* stuff into the first half of each month, or maybe even less than that, and have the rest of the time to himself.

"Well," she said. "That's very – encouraging, isn't it?"

"Sure as hell is."

But far more encouraging, for both of them, was that he finished his book of poems – and that it was accepted almost at once by a young man named Arnold Kaplan, who'd been an acquaintance of his at Harvard and was now an editor at one of the more modest New York publishing houses.

"Well, sure it's a small house, Mike," Arnold Kaplan explained, "but it beats the shit out of some university *press* imprint." And Michael was ready enough to agree with that, though he had to acknowledge that some of the younger poets he most admired – people with steadily growing reputations – were published by university presses.

He was given an advance of five hundred dollars – a fraction, probably, of what Tom Nelson earned for a single twenty-minute watercolor – and because the amount was so meager the Davenports decided to spend it all in one place: they bought what turned out to be a surprisingly good used car.

Then came the galley proofs. Michael winced or cursed or cried out in pain as he pounced on each typographical error, but this was mostly to conceal from Lucy, if not from himself, the vast pride he felt on seeing his words in print.

Another heartening aspect of that spring was that Tom and Pat Nelson continued to give every sign of friendliness. They came to the Davenports' for dinner twice and entertained them once again at their own little place, where the incident of the rug was never mentioned. Tom read the corrected galleys of Michael's book and pronounced it "nice," which was a little

RICHARD YATES

disappointing – it would take Michael a few more years to learn that "nice" was about as far as Nelson ever went in praising anything – but then he made it better by asking if he could copy out two or three of the poems, because he said he'd like to illustrate them. When the Nelsons left town for their new home – and by then the very name of Putnam County seemed almost to have taken on the sound of happiness itself – there were easy promises that they would all be seeing one another soon.

A photographer from *Chain Store Age* offered to take Michael's jacket photograph free of charge, in order to have a credit line on the book, but Michael didn't like any of the man's contact prints; he wanted to throw them all away and hire "a real photographer" instead.

"Oh, that's silly," Lucy said. "I think one or two of these are very striking – this one especially. Besides, what're you trying to do? Get a screen test at Metro-Goldwyn-Mayer?"

But their only serious discord came over the "biographical statement" that would be printed beneath the picture. Michael secluded himself to try and get it right, knowing he was taking too long over it but knowing too how closely he had always read such statements by other new poets, knowing how subtly and infernally important these things could be. And this was the finished copy he brought out for Lucy's approval:

Michael Davenport was born in Morristown, New Jersey, in 1924. He served in the Army Air Force during the war, attended Harvard, lost early in the Golden Gloves, and now lives in Larchmont, New York, with his wife and their daughter.

"I don't get the part about the Golden Gloves," she said.

54

"Oh, honey, there's nothing to 'get.' You know I did that. I did it in Boston, the year before I met you; I've told you about it a hundred times. And I did lose early. Shit, I never even got beyond the third—"

"I don't like it."

"Look," he said. "It's *good* if you can work a light, self-deprecating touch into something like this. Otherwise it's—"

"But this isn't light and it isn't self-deprecating," she told him. "It's painfully self-conscious, that's all it is. It's as though you're afraid 'Harvard' may sound sort of prissy, so you want to counteract it right away with this two-fisted nonsense about prizefighting. Listen: You know these writers who've spent their whole lives in college? With their advanced degrees and their teaching appointments and their steady rise to full professorship? Well, a lot of them are scared to put *that* stuff on their book jackets, so they get themselves photographed in work shirts and they fall back on all the dumb little summer jobs they had when they were kids: 'William So-and-so has been a cowhand, a truck driver, a wheat harvester, and a merchant seaman.' Don't you see how ludicrous that is?"

Michael walked away from her across the living room, keeping his back straight, and didn't speak until he had turned and settled himself in an armchair that left at least fifteen feet of floor between them.

"It's grown increasingly clear lately," he said then, not quite looking at her, "that you've come to think of me as a fool."

There was a silence, and when he looked up into her eyes he found them bright with tears. "Oh," she said. "Oh, Michael, is that really the way I've been? Oh, how hateful. Oh, Michael, I never, never meant – oh, Michael."

And from the slow, almost theatrical way she came across that fifteen-foot space, he knew even before he got up to take her in

55

his arms that there would be no more fault-finding, no more condescension, and no more trouble in his house.

Larchmont would never be Cambridge, but the smell of this girl's hair and the taste of her mouth, the sounds of her voice and her impassioned breathing, hadn't changed at all from times under the Army blankets on Ware Street, years ago.

In the end, though, he decided she was probably right about the jacket copy. The world, or rather whatever infinitesimal fraction of the American reading public might bother to pick up and glance over his book, would never know that Michael Davenport had once lost early in the Golden Gloves.

Chapter Five

In Putnam County, in the fall, you can see pheasant break from cover and take off over long tan and yellow fields, and sometimes there are hesitant deer to be found among the slender trunks and shadows of oak and white birch. Serious hunters don't much care for the region, though, because it isn't "open" enough: there are many well-traveled asphalt roads, some with an occasional clustering of houses and stores and public schools, and there is the high, relentlessly solid intrusion of the New York State Thruway.

Near the southern edge of the county lies a lake called Tonapac, once a popular summer resort for middle-class vacationers from the city; the lake itself has long been out of fashion, but the small commercial settlement spawned at one end of it remains intact.

And it was into this drab village that the Davenports found their way one September afternoon: Michael at the wheel of the car and watching for the necessary left turn, Lucy frowning over a road map that lay unfolded on her thighs.

"Here we go," he told her. "This is the one."

They passed through a flat section of tidy, close-set little homes, several of whose front lawns displayed plaster Virgin Marys and lofty poles with American flags that hung limp in the windless day, and Lucy said "Well, it's beginning to look a little tacky, isn't it." But then they came to a long, curving stretch of road where there were nothing but low, old stone walls and dense masses of trees on either side, and at last they found what they were looking for: a brown shingled mailbox with the name "Donarann."

They were here to follow up a real-estate ad that had promised a "charming 4½-room guest house for rent on private estate; beautiful grounds; ideal for children."

"Driveway isn't exactly in top condition," Michael said as their tires rumbled uphill in the ruts and the billowing dust of it, but they were both intrigued by what a long and unenlightening driveway it was.

"Oh, good, you're the Davenports," the landlady said, emerging from her own house with a thick bunch of keys in her hand. "Did you have any trouble finding us? I'm Ann Blake." She was short and quick, with an aging, small-chinned face made almost comical by long false eyelashes; she reminded Michael of the old-time cartoon character Betty Boop.

"I think the best thing would be to show you the little guest house first," she explained, "in case you might find it unsuitable in some way – I love it, but I know it's not to everyone's taste – and then if you do think you'd like it well enough, I'll take you around to see the grounds. Because really, it's the grounds that are the main attraction here."

She was right about the guest house: it wasn't to everyone's taste. It was stubby and ill-proportioned, made of stucco in a pale shade of pinkish-gray, with the wooden trim and shutters at its windows painted lavender. Upstairs, at one end of it, French doors led out onto an abbreviated balcony that was overgrown with leafy vines, and from the balcony a frivolous, vine-entangled spiral staircase descended to a flagstone terrace at what proved to be the front door. If you stepped back on the grass to take it all in with a single searching glance, the house had a lopsided, crudely fanciful look, like something drawn by a child with an uncertain sense of the way a house ought to be.

"I designed it myself," Ann Blake told them as she sorted out her keys. "Actually, I designed all the buildings on this property many years ago, when my husband and I first bought the land."

But they were surprised to find that the brown-and-gray interior of the house was much more promising: it had, as Lucy pointed out, a lot of nooks and crannies. There was a nice fireplace, there were fake but attractive beams across the living-room ceiling, there were built-in cabinets and bookshelves; and the larger of the two upstairs bedrooms – the one that opened onto the balcony and the spiral staircase, the one both Davenports assumed would be their own – was bright and spacious enough for Lucy to describe it as "sort of elegant in a way, don't you think?"

Oh, it might be a funny little house, but who cared? It was basically okay; it wouldn't cost them much; it would be good enough, at least, to live in for the next year or two.

"So," Ann Blake said. "Are you ready for the grand tour?"

And they followed her out across the grass past a giant weeping-willow tree – "Isn't that a spectacular tree?" she asked them – and on to a place where broad stone steps began to take them up a hill.

"I wish you could've seen these terraces a month or two ago," she said as they climbed. "Each terrace was ablaze with the most brilliant, heavenly colors: asters, peonies, marigolds, and I don't know what else; and then here on the other side, all over this latticework, there were masses and masses of rambling roses. Of course we've been extremely fortunate in our gardener." And she looked briefly at both their faces to make sure they'd be impressed by the name she was about to pronounce. "Our gardener is Mr. Ben Duane."

Beyond the top of the steps and well back from the highest of the flower-garden terraces, Michael discovered a wooden shed that was more than tall enough to stand in and probably measured five by eight feet square. It struck him at once as a good place for working, and he lifted the rusty hasp of its door to peer inside. There were two windows; there was room enough for a table and chair and a kerosene stove, and he could sense the sweet labor of writing here in total solitude all day, through all seasons, bringing a pencil across the page time and again until the words and lines began to come out right as if of their own accord.

"Oh, that's just the little pump shed," Ann Blake said. "You won't have any need to bother with it; there's a very reliable man in the village who keeps the pump in good repair. If you'll step over this way, though, I'll show you the dormitory."

Years ago, she told them, and she was getting a little winded from walking and talking at the same time; years ago, she and her husband had founded the Tonapac Playhouse. "Did you happen to notice the sign for it as you were driving up? Just across the road from here?" In its time it had been one of the most celebrated summer-stock theaters in the state, though of course no reputation was easy to sustain nowadays. For the past five or six summers she had rented out the Playhouse to one sort of scruffy little free-lance production company after another, and it *was* a relief to be rid of the responsibility; still, she did miss the way things used to be.

"Now you'll see the dormitory," she said as a very long wood-and-stucco building emerged through the trees. "We built it to house and feed the theater people every summer, you see. We hired a wonderful chef from New York, and a good housemaid, or housekeeper as she preferred to be called, and we – Ben!"

A tall old man with a wheelbarrow full of bricks came slowly around the side of the building. He stopped, set the heels of the wheelbarrow down, and shaded his eyes from the sun with one forearm. He was stripped to the waist, wearing only a pair of brief khaki shorts, sturdy work shoes with no socks, and a blue bandana tied low and tight around his brow. When he saw he would be introduced to strangers his eyes and mouth took on a look of pleased expectancy.

"This is Ben Duane," Ann Blake announced, and after a moment's futile fumbling for the Davenports' name she said "These nice people came to look at the guesthouse, Ben, so I've been showing them around."

"Oh, the little guest house, yes," he said. "Very nice. Still, I think you'll find the real advantage here is the place itself – the acreage, the grass and the trees, the privacy."

"That's just what I've tried to tell them," she said, and looked at the Davenports for confirmation. "Isn't it?"

"We're well away from the world here, you see," Ben Duane went on, absently scratching one armpit. "The world can go about its brutal business every day and we're shielded from it. We're safe."

"What're the bricks for, Ben?" she asked him.

"Oh, one or two of the terraces could use a little shoring up," he said. "Thought I'd better get it done before the frost sets in. Well. So nice to've met you both. Hope it works out."

And as Ann Blake led them away she seemed scarcely able to wait until the old man was out of earshot before talking about him: "You *are* aware of Ben's work, of course, aren't you?"

"Oh, yes, certainly," Lucy said, allowing Michael to nod and keep his mouth shut. He had never heard the name.

"Well, it'd be really surprising if you weren't," she told them. "He's one of the real – he's an ornament of the American stage. His readings from Walt Whitman alone were enough to make him famous – he toured every major city in the United States with that production – and then of course he created the role of Abraham Lincoln in *Mr. Lincoln's Difficulties* on Broadway. And he's marvelously versatile: he even took an important singing part with the original Broadway cast of *Stake Your Claim!* – oh, what a lighthearted, fun show that was. Now he's been blacklisted, as I expect you know – one more vile, unspeakable act of Senator McCarthy, you see – and we're deeply honored that he's chosen to spend his time of exile here. He's one of the finest – one of the finest human beings I know."

They were walking on a gravel road or driveway now, but Mrs. Blake was out of breath again and had to stop for a few seconds, with a hand under one breast, before she could resume her monologue.

"So. Now if you'll look down through the trees, down into that clearing, you'll see our picnic area. See the lovely big outdoor fireplace? And the long tables? My husband built all those tables himself. We'd have wonderful parties there sometimes, with Japanese lanterns strung up all around. My husband used to say the only thing we lacked was a swimming pool, but I never minded that because I'm not a swimmer anyway.

"And now coming up here, straight ahead, is the annex of the dorm. There were times when we'd have so many theater people, you see, that we needed an extra building. Most of it's been closed off and boarded-up for years, but one section of it makes a really nice apartment, so we've been renting the apartment to a pleasant young family named Smith. They have four small children, and they love it here. They're the salt of the earth."

A girl of about seven sat carefully changing her doll's clothes on the fringe of grass that bordered the gravel road. Beside her was a baby's playpen in which a boy of four or five stood sucking his thumb, holding onto the railing with his free hand.

"Hello, Elaine," Mrs. Blake called brightly to the girl. "Or wait – are you Elaine or Anita?"

"No, I'm Anita."

"Well, you're all growing up so fast it's really hard for a person to keep track. And you," she said to the boy. "What's a big guy like you doing in a thing like that?"

"He has to stay in there," Anita explained. "He's got cerebral palsy."

"Oh."

And as they walked on, Ann Blake seemed to feel that some explanation was required. "Well, when I described the Smiths as 'salt of the earth,'" she said, "I suppose I really meant to imply that they're very, very simple people. Harold Smith is a clerk of some sort in the city – he wears half a dozen ballpoint pens clipped into his shirt pocket, and that kind of thing. He works for the New York Central, and you see one of the ways that dreadful old railroad manages to keep its employees is by offering them free commutation fares from any point along the tracks. So Harold took advantage of that and moved his family out here from Queens. His wife's rather a sweet, pretty girl, but I scarcely know her because whenever I've seen her she's at the ironing board – ironing and watching television at the same time, morning, noon, and night.

"No, but here's a curious thing: Harold once told me very shyly that he'd done some acting in high school and wondered if he could try out for a part. So to make a long story short he played the policeman in *The Gramercy Ghost*, and he was wonderfully good. You'd never guess it, but he has a natural gift for comedy. I said 'Harold, have you ever considered doing this professionally?' He said 'Whaddya – crazy? With a wife and four kids?' So that was that. Still, I'm afraid I really didn't – didn't know about the cerebral palsy. Or the playpen."

Then she fell silent at last and walked well ahead of the Davenports, giving them time to stroll and think it all over. The gravel road had brought them back around to where they could see the guest house again, far away on its shallow rise of grass in the fading afternoon, a house that might have been drawn by a child, and Michael squeezed his wife's hand.

"Want to take it?" he asked. "Or think about it some more?"

"Oh, no, let's take it," she said. "We aren't going to find anything better, at a rent like this."

And when they'd told her of their decision, Ann Blake said "Wonderful. I love to see that: I love to see people who know themselves well enough to make up their minds. Will you come into my house for just a minute or two, then, so we can get the paperwork taken care of?" And she led them in through the door of her cluttered kitchen, turning back to say "I'll have to ask you to excuse all the debris."

"I am not debris," said a young man who sat on a tall stool at the kitchen counter, hunched over a plate of poached eggs on toast.

"Oh, yes, you are," she told him, sidling past him and pausing to tousle his hair, "because you're always, always in the way when I have business to attend to." Then she turned back again to her smiling visitors and said "This is my friend the handsome young dancer, Greg Atwood. These are the Davenports, Greg. They're going to be our neighbors in the guest house – *if* I can find the papers, that is."

"Oh, nice," he said, wiping his mouth, and he got languorously down off the stool. He was barefoot, wearing skin-tight

64

"wheat" jeans and a dark-blue shirt that he'd left unbuttoned to the waist in the style newly popularized by Harry Belafonte.

"Do you – dance professionally?" Lucy asked him.

"Well, I've done some of that, in a small way," he said, "and I've taught, too, but now I work mostly for my own pleasure, trying new things."

"It's like practicing a musical instrument," Ann Blake explained as she closed a drawer, opened another, and went on rummaging. "Some artists practice for years between performances. And personally, I don't care what he does as long as he stays right here where I can keep an eye on him. Ah, *here* we are." And she laid two copies of the lease on the counter in readiness for signing.

On their way out to the Davenports' car she walked with one hand conspicuously locked and swinging in Greg Atwood's, until he detached his hand and put his arm around her.

"What does the name of the place mean?" Michael asked her.

" 'Donarann?' Oh, that was my husband's idea. His name was Donald, you see – *is* Donald, I mean – and mine's Ann, so that was his silly way of putting them together. I must always remember to say his name *is* Donald, because he's very much alive and well. He lives four and a half miles north of here on a place about twice this size that he bought for the twitchy little airline stewardess he made off with, seven years ago. Nothing ever stays the same, you see. Well. It's been so nice. See you again soon."

"I don't think we made a mistake," Michael said as they began the long drive back to Larchmont. "It's not perfect, but then nothing ever is, right? And I think Laura's going to like the hell out of it, don't you?"

"Oh, I hope so," Lucy said. "I do hope so."

After a while he said "Know something, though? It's a good thing you knew who the old wheelbarrow guy is, because I would've flubbed it."

"Well, actually," she said, "what I'd mainly heard about him is that he's sort of the queen of the road. There was a girl at college who came from Westport, and she said Ben Duane bought a house there during the run of his Abraham Lincoln play. Only she said he didn't stay there very long because the Westport police gave him a choice: either to get out of town or to stand trial for showing dirty movies to little boys."

"Oh," Michael said. "Well; too bad. And I guess young Greg the dancer is a little on the queer side, too."

"I'd say that's a fairly safe assumption, yes."

"Well, but if he and old Ann are shacked up together, how do you suppose they work it out?"

"It's called being ambidextrous, I think," she said. "It's called being able to swing from both sides of the plate."

Five or six more miles went by before Lucy began, in a gentler voice, to elaborate on her hope that their daughter would like the new place. "That's really all I was doing this afternoon," she said, "trying to see everything through Laura's eyes, wondering what she'd make of it. I felt pretty sure she'd like the house – she might even think it's sort of 'cozy' – and when we started up the hill I kept looking around at all that open countryside and thinking Oh, here's the part she's *really* going to like.

"Then when we saw the brain-damaged boy in the playpen I thought No, wait: this isn't right; this won't do. But then I thought Well, why not? Isn't something like this a little closer to the real world than anything she's likely to see in Larchmont – or anything I saw when *I* was growing up?"

He was nettled by her saying "the real world" – only the rich and their children ever talked that way, and it always implied a lifelong wish to go slumming – but he didn't call her on it: he understood what she meant, and he agreed with her.

"I think you have to sort of balance everything out on the scales," she said, "when you're trying to decide what's best for a child."

"Exactly," he told her.

Laura was six and a half and tall for her age – a shy, nervous girl with slightly protruding upper teeth and remarkably big blue eyes. Her father had recently taught her to snap her fingers, and now she would often snap the fingers of both hands in unison, without being aware she was doing it, as if to punctuate her thoughts.

She hadn't liked the first grade and was afraid of facing the second – afraid even to contemplate the all-but-endless train of other long, aching grades that would have to be endured until, like her mother, she would someday be grown up. But she loved the house in Larchmont: her bedroom there was the only truly private, secret place in the world, and her backyard offered daily excursions into hazardous adventure – or rather into adventure as hazardous as she might ever care to have it be.

There had lately been a great deal of talk in the house about "Putnam County," and she'd come to dread whatever that might turn out to mean, though both her parents assured her she would like it. Then one morning a huge red moving van backed carefully up to the kitchen door and men came tromping inside and began to take everything away – first the storage cartons that she'd anxiously watched her parents packing and sealing for the past few days, then the very furniture itself, and the lamps and the rugs – everything.

"Let's get started, Michael, okay?" her mother said. "I don't think she wants to watch this."

So instead of being allowed to stay and watch it she rode alone in the back seat of the car for a very long time, holding an old and grubby Easter bunny that her mother had said she could bring along if she wanted to, trying to overhear and understand as much as possible of what her parents were saying to each other up in the front.

And the funny part was that after a while she wasn't frightened anymore: she had begun to feel a reckless exhilaration. What if the men did take the whole Larchmont house apart until it fell into rubble and dust? What if the moving van did get lost on the road and never arrive at wherever it was they were supposed to be going? What, for that matter, if her father didn't know where they were supposed to be going either? Who cared?

Oh, who cared? Laura Davenport and her father and mother would always be safe in the shelter of their own car, traveling easily through space and time; and this very car might come to serve, if necessary, as a small but adequate new home for the three of them (or even for four of them, if her wish for a baby sister ever did come true).

"How're you doing, sweetheart?" her father called back to her.

"Fine," she told him.

"Good," he said. "Won't be much longer now; we're almost there."

That meant he did know where they were going. It meant everything was still essentially all right and life would probably soon come back to normal, or to something as close to normal as her parents were able to arrange. And Laura was relieved, but at the same time she was oddly disappointed: she couldn't help feeling she might have liked things better the other way.

*

A day or two after they'd moved into the new house, with their belongings intact but still in disorder, Laura went out to fool around on the terrace at the front door where her father stood working with an unwieldy pair of hedge-clipping shears. He was trying to cut some of the thicker vines away from the base of the spiral staircase, and she watched him until it got boring; then she was startled to see a girl of about her own age walking steadily toward her across the wide expanse of grass.

"Hi," the girl said. "My name's Anita; what's yours?"

And Laura acted like a baby, sidling around to hide behind her father's legs.

"Oh, come on, honey," he said impatiently, and he set the shears down in order to reach back and bring her out in front of him again. "Anita asked you what your name is," he told her.

So there was nothing to do but take a brave step forward. "My name's Laura," she announced, and snapped the fingers of both hands.

"Hey, that's neat," Anita said. "Where'd you learn how to do that?"

"My father taught me."

"You have any brothers and sisters?"

"No."

"I have two sisters and one brother. I'm seven. Our last name's Smith and that's very easy to remember because it's one of the most common names in the whole world. What's your last name?"

"Davenport."

"Wow, that's a big long one. Want to come over to my house for a little while?"

"Okay."

And Michael called his wife out onto the terrace to watch the two little girls walk away together. "Looks like her social life is beginning to pick up already," he said.

"Oh, that's nice," Lucy said, "isn't it."

They had previously agreed that it would only be a day or two more, as soon as they managed to make the house "presentable," before they could begin to do something about their own social life.

". . . Well, hey, this is great," Tom Nelson said on the phone. "You find a decent place? Good. How about coming over some afternoon? How about tomorrow?"

The town of Kingsley, where the Nelsons lived, would never have to be explained in terms of an almost-abandoned lakeside resort, a resultant blue-collar community, and a moribund summer-stock theater. It required no explanations, and it offered none.

There wasn't really any "town" to it at all, beyond a snug little lineup of post office, gas station, grocery and liquor store; all the rest of it was country. The residents of Kingsley were here because they had earned the right to be – had earned enough money in New York to put squalor and vulgarity behind them forever – and they valued their privacy. The few houses that could be glimpsed from the road were set well back among trees and shrubs, so that what may have been the most agreeable parts of them would never be known to strangers. Michael was reminded, in passing, of Lucy's parents' summer place on Martha's Vineyard.

The Nelsons' big, white, well-remodeled farmhouse was an exception: you could see the whole of it, at the top of a long, broad hill of grass, as soon as the hill itself came into view around the curve of a slender subsidiary road. Even so, the very look of it let you know at once that it was invulnerable to intrusion and impervious to compromise. There would be no old homosexuals wheeling bricks along the crest of this hill, or any young homosexuals dawdling over poached eggs at the base of it. This place belonged entirely to Thomas Nelson and his family. They owned it.

"Well, hey," Tom said in greeting at the top of the driveway, as his wife came smiling from the door behind him.

Then there began a happy inspection of the house, with Lucy saying "marvelous" at each discovery. The sun-bright living room was too big to comprehend all at once, and its most remarkable feature, for Michael, was that one long wall of it was packed floor to ceiling with open shelves of books. There were at least two thousand books here, and probably more like twice that many.

"Well, they've been accumulating for years," Tom explained. "Been buying books all my life. Didn't have room for 'em in Yonkers or Larchmont, so we had to keep 'em in storage. Nice to have 'em out again. Want to see the studio?"

And the studio too was long and wide and flooded with light. The old piece of galvanized tin lay on the floor in one corner, looking very small now, and several new pictures were carelessly displayed on a thumbtack board just above it, leading Michael to suspect that this might be the only corner actually used for working.

"First studio I ever had," Tom said. "Feel a little lost in here sometimes."

But to ease the times when he felt a little lost there was a full set of trap drums at the far end of the room, along with an arrangement of stereo components and a great many shelved record albums. Tom Nelson's collection of jazz recordings was almost as substantial as his library.

On their way out to the kitchen, where the girls were talking, Michael noticed that a new place had been found for the soldiers: the parade figures stood apart from one another with their swords and wrinkled toothpaste-tube flags, and there was enough deep drawer-space beneath them to accommodate the combat troops.

"Oh, I'm so happy for you both," Lucy said when the four of them were settled in the living room. "You've found the perfect place to live, and to raise your children. You'll *never* have to think about moving again."

But then the Nelsons wanted to know what kind of place the Davenports had found, and both Davenports nervously interrupted each other before they could get the information out.

"Oh, well, we're just renting, of course," Michael began, "so it's only a temporary deal, but it's—"

"It's a funny-looking little house on an old private estate," Lucy said, brushing flecks of cigarette ash off her lap, "so there's quite a lot of land with it, but the people are kind of—"

"It's kind of a fruit farm," Michael said.

"A fruit farm?"

And Michael did his halting best to explain what he meant by that.

"Ben Duane," Tom Nelson said. "Isn't he the one who did the Whitman readings? And didn't he get shafted by the McCarthy committee a couple years back?"

"Right," Lucy said. "And of course I'm sure he's perfectly – you know – perfectly harmless and everything, though I suppose I'd be uneasy if we were bringing a *boy* into the place. And I imagine we can sort of keep our distance from the landlady, too, *and* her boyfriend. Still, we'll never really have a sense of being alone there, the way you are here."

"Well," Pat Nelson said, drawing her mouth a little to one side, "I don't know what's supposed to be so wonderful about the sense of being alone. I think Tom and I'd go utterly stir-crazy if we didn't see a lot of our friends. We've started having parties every month or so now, and some of them have really been fun;

but my God, when we first moved here it was gruesome. We were *i*solated. Once we went to some little party up the road – I can't even remember the people's name – and this one man got me cornered and started grilling me. He said 'What does your husband do?'

"I said 'He's a painter.'

"He said 'Yeah, yeah, okay, but I mean what does he *do*?'

"I said 'That's what he does; he paints.'

"And the guy said 'Whaddya mean, he's a commercial artist?'

"I said 'No, no, he's not a commercial artist; he's just – you know – he's a *painter*.'

"He said 'You mean a *fine*-arts painter?'

"And I'd never heard that term before, have you? A 'fine-arts' painter?

"Well, we kept going around and around like that, missing each other's points, until he finally went away; but just before he went away he gave me this very narrow, unpleasant look, and he said 'So whadda you kids got, a trust fund?' "

And the Davenports slowly shook their chuckling heads in appreciation of the story.

"No, but you're going to find a lot of that up here," Pat told them, as if in fair warning. "Some of these Putnam County types assume that everybody does one kind of work for a living and another kind for – I don't know – for 'love' or something. And you can't get through to them; they don't believe you; they'll think you're putting them on, or else they'll think you've got some *trust* fund."

There was nothing for Michael to do now but look down into his nearly empty whiskey glass, wishing it were full, and be silent. He couldn't explode in this house because it would be humiliating, but he knew he would almost certainly explode later, when he and Lucy were alone, either in the car or after they got home. "Christ's *sake*," he would say. "What the fuck does she think *I* do for a living? Does she think I make my fucking living out of *poems?*"

But then a sobering, cautionary line of thought reminded him that he couldn't afford to explode alone with Lucy, either. To explode with Lucy over a thing like this would only open up the long, subtle, tantalizing argument that went all the way back to their honeymoon at the Copley Plaza.

When, she might ask, would he ever come to his senses? Didn't he know there had never been a need for *Chain Store Age*, or for Larchmont, or for this dopey little house in the decadence of Tonapac? Why, then, wouldn't he let her pick up the phone and call her bankers, or her brokers, or whoever it was who could instantly set them free?

No; no. He would have to control his temper one more time. He would have to be silent tonight and tomorrow and the next day. He would have to sweat it out.

Chapter Six

One day in the village of Tonapac, where he'd come to buy snow tires, Michael saw a familiar figure on the sidewalk ahead of him: a tall young man in a Levi jacket and pants, walking in a way that suggested a cowboy actor in the movies. "Paul Maitland?" he called, and Maitland turned around in surprise.

"Mike!" he said. "I'll be damned. What're *you* doing here?" And there was a heartening vigor in his handshake. "Got time for a drink?" he asked then, and he steered Michael into a dark, grubby little workingman's bar where he seemed to have been headed in the first place.

Several slouching customers along the bar said "Hi, Paul" and "Hey, Paul," as Maitland moved toward a table in the back, and Michael was impressed that an artist could be on easy terms with these roughhewn men.

When their whiskey arrived, Paul Maitland held his glass just short of his lips as if to savor this small postponement of pleasure, and his eyes twinkled in reminiscence of old times at the Horse.

"I'll never forget the night you astonished that crusty old merchant seaman from Yorkshire," he said, "by singing all the verses of 'On Ilkley Moor 'Thout Hat' – and with a perfect accent, too. Damn good performance."

"Yeah, well, I was stationed in England in the service, you

see, and I knew a Yorkshire girl who taught me the words."

This was fine. Drinking whiskey in the middle of the day with a man believed to be a genius, a man who'd only rarely shown any particular sign of liking him before, and who was now at pains to remind him that he'd once done something memorable in the White Horse Tavern.

". . . You remember Peggy," Paul Maitland was saying. "Well, we're married now, and her stepfather has a nice place a few miles from here, over in Harmon Falls. We rented a little house on his property and at first it was sort of touch-and-go, but then I began to find fairly steady carpentry work here in Tonapac and a couple of other towns as well, so we're doing all right."

"And you have enough time for your painting?"

"Oh, sure; paint every day. Paint like a fool; paint like a madman. Nothing ever stops that. So where are you and Lucy living?"

In telling him, Michael found himself about to say "It's really kind of a fruit farm," but held it back. He had begun to learn that explaining certain things could be more trouble than it was worth. Then he said "How's your – how's your lovely sister?"

"Oh, Diana's fine. I think she'll probably be getting married soon – fellow named Ralph Morin. Seems like a nice-enough guy."

"Is he the actor?"

"Well, he's been an actor; now I think he's more of a director, or trying to be." And Paul looked thoughtfully into his drink. "I suppose I always hoped she'd wind up marrying old Bill Brock, because they did seem good together, but what the hell. Nobody ever has any influence in matters like that."

"Right."

And over the second drink Michael opened what he hoped might be a happy new topic. "Listen, Paul: there's another painter out here that I think you'd really like – or maybe you know him already. Tom Nelson?"

"Well, I know *of* him, of course."

"Good. Anyway, he's one of the nicest, most unassuming guys in the world, and I think the two of you might really hit it off. Maybe we can all get together sometime."

"Well, thanks, Mike," Paul said, "but I don't think I'd care for that."

"Oh? Why not? You don't like his work?"

The fingers of Paul's right hand were busy with half of his mustache, and he seemed to choose his words very carefully. "I think he's a good illustrator."

"Well, but his illustrations are only part of it," Michael said. "His paintings are the main thing, and they're—"

"Yeah, yeah, I know; very big with the museums and all that. But what those people're buying as paintings, you see, as pictures, are really illustrations."

Michael's lungs felt shallow, as if he were about to get into an argument beyond his understanding: no terms would be defined and nothing would be clear. "Because they're – representational, you mean?" he asked.

"No," Paul Maitland said impatiently. "No, of course not. Matter of fact I wish people'd stop using that asinine word. Wish they'd stop saying 'abstract-expressionist,' too. We're all just trying to make pictures, after all. But if a picture's any good it's self-sufficient; it needs no text. Otherwise, all you're getting is something clever, something ephemeral, something of the moment."

"So you're suggesting Nelson's work won't last?"

"Oh, that's not for me to say," Paul Maitland said, looking comfortable with having made his point. "It's for others to decide in the course of time."

"Well," Michael said, because it seemed necessary to find some amiable conclusion to this tense little talk, "I suppose I see what you mean." And then he felt weak inside, as though he'd been bullied into betraying a friend.

"Mind you, I have nothing against the man personally," Paul was saying; "I'm sure he's very pleasant and all that; it's just that I can't imagine how we'd find anything to talk about. We're at opposite ends of the spectrum, you see." And after they'd sat drinking in silence for what seemed a long time, he said "You still see much of Bill?"

"Some. In fact he may be coming out this weekend; I think he wants to show off his new girl."

"Oh, well, good," Paul said, "and listen, if he does come out, will you give us a call?" But then he struck his forehead with the heel of his hand. "Or no, wait – that won't work: Diana and what's-his-name are coming out this weekend, too. Damn nuisance, isn't it? How we all have to keep taking *sides*?"

"Yeah."

Paul knocked back his whiskey and signaled for another round. Three drinks with no lunch before an afternoon of rough carpentry might be a little reckless; but then, Maitland had always seemed to know what he was doing.

"I've always liked old Bill," he said. "Loud and arrogant and full of himself, I know, and of course all that Marxist bullshit can be tiresome as hell. What little of his stuff I've read could easily have passed for a *parody* of the Party line, if it hadn't been so dead serious. I remember one story that began something like: 'Joe Starve threw down his wrench on the assembly line. "Fuck this," he said.' Still, he can be jolly and funny and a good companion; I've always liked having him around."

And there was a slight easing in Michael's conscience. If Maitland could disparage a man and still value him, then maybe his own knuckling-under in the question of Tom Nelson hadn't been wholly dishonorable.

When they emerged blinking into the bright street to shake hands again, Michael knew it would be all he could do now to get the damn snow tires home before he'd hit the sack and sleep the afternoon away, while Paul Maitland climbed scaffoldings in the sun and fitted heavy boards together and drove sixteenpenny nails, or whatever the hell it was he did for a living.

". . . And this is Karen," Bill Brock said as he courteously helped her out of the car. She was small and slim and dark, and she was very shy at meeting Bill's friends in the country.

"Know what this is like?" Bill said, coming to a stop on the grass. "It's kind of like an F. Scott Fitzgerald place. Little on the shabby side, but that only makes it all the more so. You can almost see him coming to the window up there in his bathrobe, with half a bottle of gin, to find out if it's morning yet. He's spent the night finishing another story, so his daughter'll be able to finish another year at Vassar; now maybe this afternoon, when he's got his brains back together, he'll start writing 'The Crack-up.'

"Well, anyway," Bill concluded, with an expansive gesture that seemed to take in the whole estate, "it sure beats the hell out of Larchmont."

And as the four of them sat around the living room ("We sort of like all the nooks and crannies in here," Michael explained), Bill remained in charge of the talk.

"All this'll probably be a bore for Karen," he began, "because she's heard nothing else for weeks, but there've been a couple of big moves in my life. For one thing, I've given up on the Left. As a writer, I mean. Took my two proletarian novels and all the stories, put 'em in a cardboard box and tied a string around it and shoved it into the back of my closet, and I can't tell you what a relief that was. 'Write what you know' – Jesus, I've been hearing that advice all my life and I always thought it was too simple-minded, or I was too smart for it or something, but it's the only real advice there is, right? Oh, I might be able to salvage some of the material from the electrical-workers' book eventually, but the whole concept'll have to be different. It'll have to focus on the problem of why a prep-school-and-Atnherst kid would ever want to work as a union organizer in the first place – you see what I'm getting at?"

They all saw what he was getting at, though only Karen seemed enthralled by it. And the second of his two big moves, announced with unaccustomed shyness, was that he had gone into psychotherapy.

It hadn't been an easy decision, he explained: it had probably required more courage than anything he'd ever done, and the worst part was that it might take years – years! – before the help he was getting now could have any profitable effect in his life. Still, he had come to a point where no other choice was possible. He honestly felt that if he hadn't taken this step he might have gone out of his mind.

"How exactly does it work, Bill?" Lucy asked him. "I mean do you lie on a couch and sort of – free-associate? Is that it?" And Michael was surprised that she'd been interested enough to inquire.

"No; no couch – this guy doesn't believe in the couch – and no real free-association technique either, at least not in the Freudian sense. We sit on two chairs in his office, facing each other, and we talk. All very down-to-earth, for the most part. And that's another thing: I feel I was extremely fortunate in finding this particular man. I can respect his intelligence; I think I'd have liked him as a person if I'd met him socially rather than professionally, though of course that's speculation. And we even seem to have a lot in common: he's something of an old Marxist too. Well, look, it's almost impossible to explain a thing like this to outsiders; it can't be – you know – can't be summarized or anything."

Then, as if aware that he might have held the floor a little too long, he subsided with his drink to let Michael take over. And Michael did have a few things to say: he began by telling them that he'd been working hard as a bastard. "So I think I'll be able to finish this new play by the end of the year," he said, "and it's beginning to feel like it really does have commercial possibilities. . . ."

Listening to the tone and rhythm of his own voice as it warmed to its subject, as it enlarged on its theme of high hopes and modest expectations, and as it came to a graceful conclusion on a note of wry self-effacement, he realized what he was doing: he was trying to impress the shy, attentive young stranger at Bill Brock's side. She wasn't even an especially pretty girl, but she was here, brand new, and Michael had never been able to resist showing off for a new girl.

"Let's have another drink," he said, "and then we'll take a stroll around the rest of the place before the sun goes down."

Soon they were all drifting past the giant willow tree, which Karen said was "magnificent"; then, following Ann Blake's original route, they climbed the stone steps beside the flower-bed terraces. "This funny little shed here on top is where I work," Michael told them. "Doesn't look like much, but I like the privacy of it.

". . . And talk about nooks and crannies," he continued as they came around the corner of the big dormitory building, "there's a nook or a cranny along in here somewhere that serves as a refuge for one of America's most celebrated faggot actors –

I mean this old guy's so queer the cops once threw him out of Westport for showing dirty movies to little *boys*."

"Good evening," Ben Duane said from the shadows of a doorway. He was dressed in a rumpled suit and a clean shirt, adjusting the turquoise clasp of a string necktie as if in readiness to descend the hill for dinner at Ann Blake's house. There was no way of telling whether he'd heard Michael or not, but the chance of it was enough to prevent either of the Davenports from stopping to introduce their guests.

"Hello, Mr. Duane," Michael said quickly, and they all moved away faster than they'd come.

"Jesus!" Michael said, smiting his forehead with his hand. "That was the dumbest, the all-around dumbest thing I've done since we moved here."

"Well, I don't think he heard you," his wife said, "but it wasn't one of your better moments."

And he was still weak with chagrin when they'd completed their circuit of the grounds and come back to the living room, where he sank into a chair to nurse his feelings.

Then Lucy briskly got their supper on the table – early, she explained, because they were all going to a party at the Nelsons'.

"Nelson?" Brock inquired. "Oh, yeah, the hotshot water-color guy. Well, fine, that oughta be nice; a party's a party."

When Tom Nelson greeted them at his bright front door he was wearing the field jacket of an airborne infantryman.

"Where'd you get the paratrooper's jacket?" Michael asked him as soon as the introductions were over.

"Bought it off a guy, is all. Nice, huh? I like it because of the pockets."

And Michael was nettled: the tanker's jacket of Larchmont had been "bought off a guy," too. What the hell was Nelson trying to do – be a different kind of war veteran every time he moved to a new town?

The Nelsons' big living room was swarming with people, and so was the studio beyond it. There were a few lovely girls among the women, almost as if a movie director had organized the scene, and the men ranged from youth to hearty middle age, some of them with beards. There were three or four Negroes who looked like jazz musicians, and the crisp recorded sounds of Lester Young seemed to lace all the disparate talk and laughter of the room into wave on wave of pleasurable discourse. At first sight, and even on closer inspection, there was nobody there who didn't seem to be having a good time.

This was Arnold Spencer, a professor of art history at Princeton.

This was Joel Kaplan, a jazz critic for *Newsweek* and *The Nation*.

This was Jack Bernstein, a sculptor whose new show had just opened at the Downtown Gallery.

And this was Marjorie Grant, a poet, who said at once that she'd been "dying" to meet Michael because she'd "loved" his book.

"Well, that's very nice," he told her. "Thank you."

"I'm crazy about your lines," Marjorie Grant said. "One or two of the poems themselves didn't strike me as wholly successful, but I love your lines." And she recited one of them, to prove she had memorized it. She was about Michael's age and pretty in an old-fashioned way: she wore a heavy shawl drawn close around her upper arms and torso, and her blond hair was fixed in a thick, tight braid that circled her head like a crown. If you could get the shawl off her and take the hair apart, she might be great. But a tall, strong-looking man named Rex hovered close beside her, smiling patiently while she had her little exchange with Michael, and it was clear that Rex was the only man in the world, for the present, who knew what she was like without the shawl and the braid.

"Well," Michael said, "I'm afraid I'm not familiar with your work, but that's only because I don't keep up nearly as much as I—"

"Oh, no," Marjorie Grant answered him. "I've only had one book and it's just a little Wesleyan University Press sort of thing."

"Well, but Wesleyan's one of the finest—"

"Yes, I know people say that, but in my case it doesn't really apply. One reviewer called it 'kittenish,' and after I stopped crying I began to see what he meant. I'm working on some much better stuff now, though, so I hope you'll—"

"Oh, I certainly will," Michael told her. "And I'll get the first book, too, whether you like it or not."

"Marjorie?" Rex inquired. "Want to move on into the studio and look at some of Tom's new things?"

When they'd gone Michael felt a happy glow from her praise – the line she'd quoted had never seemed especially good before – though he wished he could have found a way to ask which of the poems hadn't struck her as wholly successful.

And after another drink or two, watching Tom Nelson move courteously among his guests, he decided he didn't really mind the paratrooper's jacket. Most of these people must surely know that Nelson hadn't been an airborne soldier; and what if they didn't? The war had been over for eleven or twelve years; wasn't it about time for people to wear whatever they felt like? Wasn't it essentially dumb and "square" to think otherwise? And maybe, in all innocence, Nelson did like it because of the pockets. What would be the matter with that?

"Know something?" Lucy asked, drifting up to his side an

hour or so later. Her eyes were unnaturally bright. "I don't think I've ever seen so many intelligent-looking people in one place in my whole life."

"Yeah, you're right."

"Well," she amended, "with the exception of those two over there near the wall. They're awful – I can't imagine where the Nelsons ever dug them up, or why, but I'm glad Bill Brock is stuck with them now: they deserve each other." One was a sturdy young man whose dark hair kept falling almost into his eyes as he talked; the other was a plain girl in a cheap dress that looked uncomfortable and moist at the armpits. Both their faces were so earnest and humorless, so charged with the effort of making their conversational points clear at all cost, that they didn't seem to belong in this gathering. "Their name's Damon," Lucy said. "He's a linotype operator in Pleasantville and says he's writing 'a work of social history'; she writes what she calls potboilers to help support their family. They're some kind of communists, I think, and I mean I guess they're nice enough, but they're *awful*." And she turned away from the sight of them. "You want to go into the studio?"

"Not just yet," Michael told her. "I'll be along in a minute."

". . . in a cardboard *box*," Bill Brock's loud voice was explaining to the Damons, while Karen clung to his arm as if for protection, "with a *string* around it. And that represents six and a half years' work. So you see I can agree with everything you say, Al, and with everything you're *likely* to say – but in political terms only. That kind of material simply doesn't lend itself to the novel form. Probably never has, probably never will."

"Ah," said Al Damon, raking his hair back from his brow with nervous fingers. "Well, I'm not going to charge you with 'selling out,' my friend, but I'll suggest that you're chasing after false gods. I'll suggest that you're still hooked on the 'lost generation' crowd of thirty years ago, and the trouble is we no longer have anything in common with those people. We're the *second* lost generation."

And because Michael Davenport thought he had never heard anything quite as foolish as a full-grown man saying "We're the second lost generation," he moved over close beside Bill in order to meet the Damons.

". . . and I understand you run a linotype machine, right, Al?" he inquired. "In Pleasantville?"

"Well, that's what I do for a living, yes," Al Damon said.

"Makes sense," Michael assured him. "Learn the trade, get the union wages and the fringe benefits; probably makes a lot better sense than what Bill and I do."

And Bill Brock agreed that it probably did.

"And you look to be in pretty good shape, too, Al," Michael said. "What do you do for exercise?"

"Well, I ride a bike to work," Damon said, "and I lift a few weights."

"Good; those are both good things to do."

Mrs. Damon, whose name was Shirley, was beginning to look a little anxious.

"Tell you what, Al," Michael said. "Let's try something, just for laughs." And he pointed to the upper part of his own abdomen. "Hit me as hard as you can. Right here."

"You kidding?"

"No, I mean it. Hard as you can." And Michael tightened and locked the muscles of his midsection, a trick that even amateur fighters are taught to do.

Damon's foolish, uncomprehending smile gave way to an angry narrowing of the eyes as he gathered and set himself for the punch, and he drove his right fist powerfully into the appointed place.

It didn't quite take Michael's breath away and it sent him only two steps back, but it hurt more than he'd thought it would. He hadn't played this game since college. "Pretty good one, Al," he said. "Now it's my turn. You ready?" And he placed his feet properly.

Michael's fist traveled only a short distance but it was fast, it connected in just the right way, and Al Damon lay unconscious on the rug.

Shirley Damon fell beside him with a scream, and Lucy, appearing from nowhere, rushed up to grasp and shake Michael's arm as if she'd just caught him killing a man with a pistol. "Why did you *do* that?" she demanded.

There was a light but general shriek of women around the room now, and a muttering of "Drunk . . . drunk" among the men. At first Michael thought they must mean Damon was drunk for having fallen down; then, as Lucy continued to shake and berate him, he knew the charge of drunkenness was meant for himself.

The high, wavering voice of Marjorie Grant could be heard across the room saying "Oh, I can't bear violence; I can't bear violence in any form."

"Look, it's a game," Michael was explaining to Lucy and to anyone else who would listen. "It's called trading punches. It's perfectly fair; he hit me first. Jesus, I never meant to—"

Tom Nelson was smiling in the entrance of his studio, blinking through his glasses and saying "What's the deal?"

Al Damon regained his senses after a few seconds; he rolled to one side, hugged his belly, and drew up his knees.

"Give him air," someone commanded, but he had air enough to get unsteadily to his feet, with his wife's help, at what would have been about the count of seven. Shirley Damon lingered just long enough to give Michael a look of withering hatred; then she carefully steered her husband toward the front door, while someone else brought their coats, but they didn't quite make it before Al Damon had to stop, crouch, and vomit on the floor.

". . . And if he'd vomited while he was still unconscious it could have gone into his lungs and killed him," Lucy said. "Then what? *Then* how could you have laughed it off?" She had taken the wheel, as she always did when she wanted to prove that Michael was too drunk to drive, and it always made him feel humiliated – even emasculated – to ride on the passenger's side.

"Ah, you're making too much of it," he said. "I traded punches with the guy, that's all; there wasn't any tragedy or any slaughtering of innocents. And most of the people *were* able to laugh it off. Tom *Nelson* certainly was – he said he wants me to teach him how to do it. And Pat said it was okay, too. She gave me a little kiss at the door and said I mustn't worry about it. You *heard* her say that."

"Personally," said Bill Brock, riding in the back seat with his arm around Karen, "I was delighted to see it happen. The guy's an asshole. His wife's an asshole, too."

"Oh, exactly," Karen said in a sleepy voice. "Neither of them have any – you know – any charm or anything at all."

"Well, she's a drab little thing," Lucy said on Sunday evening, after Bill and Karen had gone back to the city, "but she's pleasant. And she's certainly a lot more appropriate for Bill than Diana *Maitland* ever was."

"Sure is," Michael said, and he was heartened because this was the first civil thing his wife had said to him since the Friday night of the Nelsons' party. With luck, they would now be on good terms again.

But they would never know what became of Karen, because

88

a very few weeks later Bill showed up with another girl. This one's name was Jennifer, and she was blond, broad-shouldered and given to blushing smiles.

They were only passing through, Bill said. They were on their way up to Pittsfield to visit Jennifer's parents, who wanted to look him over.

"Bill and I've only been seeing each other for about three weeks, you see," the girl told them, "and I made the awful mistake of letting my parents know. What actually happened was, I happened to be taking a shower one morning when the phone rang, so I asked Bill to answer it and it was my mother. And the point is she and my father've both been worried about me since I moved to New York – oh, I know this sounds ridiculous because I'm almost twenty-three, but they're very old-fashioned. They're from another time."

"Hell, I'm not worried," Bill said, jingling his car keys. "I'll charm their socks off."

And he may well have done so, though it turned out that they'd never know what became of Jennifer, either, or of Joan or Victoria or any of the other girls he would bring for their inspection over the next few years; they could only assume that Bill, as he'd once explained to them, was all right in short-term relationships.

One Friday afternoon, a month after the Al Damon incident, there was nothing for the Davenports to do but sit reading magazines in different parts of their living room. Neither of them mentioned it, but they were eaten with anxiety that there might be another party at the Nelsons' tonight and that they might have been dropped from the invitation list.

And then, that same day, Paul Maitland called up to say that Diana was out for the weekend again, with her boyfriend, and that she'd love to see them both. Could they come over to Harmon Falls at about five?

During the short ride Michael steeled himself for this new meeting with Diana. Maybe she had become a silly girl, now that she'd spent all this time with her actor-boy, actor-twerp, actor-asshole – girls did change – but then, maybe not. And from the moment he saw her standing in the driveway with her brother and his wife and her tall young man, smiling in welcome as the car pulled up, he knew she hadn't changed at all. She might as well have been the only person there: graceful and awkward at the same time, a girl so unique and complete that you'd have to be a fool to want any other girl in the world.

There were kissings and handshakes – Ralph Morin seemed determined to prove he could crush all of Michael's knuckles if he felt like it – and then the party moved into a big fieldstone house that had been built for Walter Folsom, the retired engineer who was Peggy's stepfather. In the main room of it, where Mr. Folsom and his wife rose to greet the young people, there was a great window overlooking a leafy ravine that fell away to a bright, rapid stream a hundred yards below. "All my life," Mr. Folsom told his guests, "I've wanted a house equipped with a spigot in the wall that pours whiskey; so now you see I have my wish at last."

Ralph Morin, sinking into one of the sofas that bordered the big window, was explaining to Mrs. Folsom that he always felt "this really great sense of peace out here." And he flung one arm along the sofa back to illustrate his point. "If I ever lived in a house like this I'd spend all my time right here, beside this window, reading. I'd read all the books I've always meant to read, and then some more."

"Yes," his hostess said, looking as if she wished she had someone else to talk to. "Well, it's a pleasant spot for reading."

If you didn't know Ralph Morin had been trained as an actor, Michael decided, you could guess it from his movements and gestures: the way he held his head to its best advantage in the available light, the falsely casual draping of his arm along the sofa, even the poised clasp of his other hand around his drink and the careful placement of his shapely, well-buffed shoes on the floor. He did everything as if he were having his picture taken.

Walter Folsom had taken up painting in his retirement, as had his wife, and they were both plainly delighted with young Peggy's choice of a husband. For the rest of the afternoon, whenever Paul wasn't listening, they seemed eager to let the Davenports know how highly they thought of his work, and once Mr. Folsom spoke the same line as the subcontractor on Delancey Street, long ago: "This boy's the real thing." Paul Maitland seemed unable to go anywhere without attracting admirers.

But Michael spent most of that time contriving ways to find Diana alone, in some corner or part of the room away from the mainstream of talkers. He didn't know what he wanted to say to her; he just wanted to have her at close range, all to himself, so that he could make interesting replies to whatever she might feel like saying to him.

And it happened only once, when they were all leaving the Folsoms' house to go over to the Maitlands' for supper: Diana fell into step with him and said "That was an awfully nice book of poems, Michael."

"Yeah? You mean you read it? And liked it?"

"Well, of course I read it and liked it. Why else would I've told you?" Then, after a perilous moment, she said "I especially liked the last one, the long one, 'Coming Clean.' That's a lovely thing."

"Well," he said, "thank you" – but he was too shy to speak her name.

Paul and Peggy lived in a small, rude clapboard cottage that had been here for years before Walter Folsom bought the property, and there were signs of honest young poverty all around the front room. A mud-caked pair of Paul's work shoes stood near the front door, beside his carpenter's toolbox; there were several cardboard cartons of unpacked books, and not far away was an ironing board where it was easy to picture Peggy pressing her husband's denim clothes. As the party sat huddled over bowls of the beef stew she had served, they might as well have been inside the burlap hangings of the old Delancey Street place.

"Oh, this is wonderful, Peg," Diana said of the stew.

And Mrs. Folsom, whose handsome face seemed incapable of hiding her feelings, looked pleased that her daughter's cooking had been praised. Then she said "Paul? A little later, can we have a look at what you've been doing in the other room?"

"Oh, I'd rather not show anything now, Helen, if you don't mind," Paul told her. "I've just been roughing-out a few things; it's all very tentative work. I don't think I'll have anything to show until after we're back from the Cape. But thanks anyway."

Michael would always remember that "tentative" was the word a Harvard *Crimson* reviewer had used to dismiss Lucy's performance in his first play; now he wondered if he would have been able to tell the difference between Paul's "tentative" paintings and his finished ones, and he was glad to be spared the task of trying.

A little later he heard Lucy saying "Well, but *why*, Paul?" and saw Paul Maitland shake his chewing head at her in kindly but firm refusal, as if to explain that any question of "why" was irrelevant. And he knew at once that she hadn't asked to see the paintings; this was something else.

"Okay, but I don't get it," she persisted. "The Nelsons are wonderful people and they're good friends of ours; I know you'd like them. Just because you and Tom may not see eye to eye professionally, does that really suggest you couldn't enjoy them in a *social* way?"

Then Ralph Morin leaned over to squeeze Lucy's forearm and said "I wouldn't press him on it, dear; there are times when an artist has to use his own judgment."

And Michael wanted to strangle him for calling Lucy "dear," as well as for his fatuous little remark.

". . . Oh, but the Cape's lovely in the off season," Peggy Maitland was saying. "The landscape's all bleak and windswept, and there are these wonderfully subtle colors. And there's this carnival that spends the winters near where we stayed last year. They're delightful people. They're gypsies, and they're very friendly but very proud. . . ."

Michael had never heard her talk at such length: all she usually did was answer questions in monosyllables or cast silent, adoring glances at her husband. Now she was coming to the point of her anecdote:

". . . So I asked one of the men what his act was – his act in the carnival? – and he said 'I'm a sword swallower.' I said 'Doesn't that hurt?' And he said 'Think I'd tell *you?*'"

"Oh, that's *mar*velous," Ralph Morin exclaimed, laughing. "That's the very heart and spirit of the entertainer."

On their way back to Tonapac that night, Lucy said "What did you think of what's-his-name? Morin?"

"Didn't much go for him," Michael said. "Pretentious, self-conscious, boring – I think he's probably a fool."

"Well, you'd say that anyway."

"Why?"

"Why do you think? Because you've always had such a terrible crush on Diana. It was all over your face today. Nothing's changed."

And because he didn't feel up to denying it – didn't especially want to deny it anyway – they rode in silence the rest of the way home.

Except for Harold Smith and several other clerks whose fares were paid by the railroad that employed them, there were very few daily train commuters from Tonapac to New York: the ride took an hour and fifty minutes. When Michael was obliged to take his twice-monthly trips to the city he would always exchange brief neighborly greetings with Harold on the station platform; then, aboard the train, he would read the paper alone while Harold joined the other railroad men across the aisle, in two facing seats, for a card game that lasted all the way to town. But one morning, looking pleasantly shy, Harold came over and sat beside Michael instead.

"My wife and I were saying just last night," he began, "that we're really glad to have you folks living in the guest house. I mean Ann Blake's very nice, but we were afraid she might rent it out to a couple of queers or something. Makes it a lot nicer to have a regular family in there, is all I meant. And our Anita really thinks the world of your little girl."

Michael told him quickly that Laura was very fond of Anita, too – and he added that this was especially nice because Laura was an only child.

"Well, good," Harold Smith said. "So they'll always have each other for playmates, right? And our other girls are only nine and ten, so they can really all be playmates together. Our boy is six. He's – handicapped." Then after a while he said "So what do you do with your free time, Mike? You like to bowl? You play cards?"

"Well, mostly what I do is work, Harold. I'm trying to finish a play, you see, and I've got some poems going, too."

"Yeah, well, I know about that; Ann told us that. And you've fixed up the old pump shed to work in, right? No, but I mean how about when you feel like taking a break?"

"Well, my wife and I do a lot of reading," Michael said, "or sometimes we visit friends of ours over in Harmon Falls, or up in Kingsley" — and only too late, after hearing himself say "friends of ours" and "up in Kingsley," did he realize how rude he had been.

Harold Smith bent well forward in the train seat to scratch one ankle above the top of its very short sock, his suit coat gaping open to prove that he really did wear five or six ballpoint pens clipped into his shirt pocket, and Michael was afraid that when he settled back he might open his newspaper and spend the rest of the long ride in injured silence.

Something would have to be said. Well, I'm afraid I don't care much for bowling, Harold, he might begin, and I never really learned to play poker; but I like to watch the fights — do you? Oh, the girls probably wouldn't go for it, but maybe you and I could get together in whatever bar you like, some night when there's a good fight card coming up, and we could —

Wrong; wrong. Harold Smith might say Nah, I don't follow the fights, or Nah, I don't go to bars; or worse, he might say Yeah? I wouldn't of figured you for a fight fan — and that would only lead to one more treacherous stroll down the dust of Memory Lane, to Blanchard Field or even to the unmentionable Golden Gloves.

At last, and in what seemed the nick of time, Michael let his voice start to work without any thought or plan of what he was saying.

"Harold?" he inquired. "Why don't you and Nancy come

95

over to the house for supper some night soon? Or if you can't make it for supper, come a little later and we'll just have a drink and get acquainted. Because I mean as long as we're neighbors, the least we can do is be friends, right?"

"Well, that'd be very nice, Mike. Thanks." And for just a second Harold Smith's plain, pleased-looking face, blushing very slightly, seemed to hint at what Ann Blake had called his natural gift for comedy.

As easy as that! When both of their newspapers had rattled open, suggesting an agreeable separateness for the rest of the ride, Michael couldn't get over his discovery that sometimes – and maybe only once in a while – social life wasn't infernally difficult after all.

On the appointed evening the Smiths used a strong flashlight to find their way across the grass to the guest house.

Harold had changed into his country clothes, a heavy red-and-black-checked hunting shirt with the collar up and the tails out; Nancy looked very trim in a blue sweater and well-faded blue jeans. And the Davenports had made the mistake of dressing up for them – Michael in a suit and tie, Lucy in what might easily have been called a cocktail dress. But Michael was fairly sure that if there could now be talk enough, and drink enough, the question of clothes would no longer matter.

Well, sure, working for the railroad was a pain in the ass, Harold Smith confided, settling back in an easy chair with a gin and tonic in his hand. He hadn't much liked it when he was hired there as an office boy, years ago, and he couldn't honestly claim he liked it much better now. "My father said 'Better get a job, kid,' so I got a job, and there you have the story of my career." And he took a drink to allow time for a ripple of laughter around the room.

"Still," he went on, "there were certain unexpected

advantages right from the start. My first summer on the job I went stumbling into the personnel department one morning and I spotted old skinny here." He winked at his wife. "She was sitting at her typewriter like all the other girls, but she wasn't typing: she had both arms up over her head and she was yawning – she looked like this was the last place in the whole world she wanted to be – and I remember thinking *There's* a girl I might be able to talk to. But I was very shy then, you see. Oh, a smart-ass and a wise guy, and I'd been in the Navy and all that, but still very shy with girls."

"So you had an office romance," Lucy Davenport said. "Oh, this is a charming story." And Michael was instantly afraid that "charming" might have a patronizing sound.

"Well, it sure as hell didn't happen right away," Harold said. "I took to walking into personnel three and four times a day, whether I had any business there or not – sometimes all I'd do would be bring in a handful of paper clips – and it must've been three weeks before I worked up the nerve to say anything to her."

"It was more like six," Nancy Smith said, winning another small laugh. "And all that time I kept wondering Why does this attractive boy keep coming in here, and why doesn't he ever speak to me?"

"Now, hold it right there, funny-face," Harold commanded, aiming a stiff index finger at her. "Who's telling this charming story – you or me?"

And when he was confident of having the floor again, he resumed his own version. "Now, back in those years, you see, they only gave us half an hour for lunch. You were supposed to run around the corner to the Automat, plug in your nickels, eat your sandwich and your lousy little piece a pie, and then come running back to the office like a rat. In other words, I knew there

97

wouldn't be a hell of a lot of percentage in asking her out to lunch, you follow me? So I got a better idea. I said 'Look, it's a beautiful day. Feel like going for a walk?' And we walked up Park Avenue all the way from Forty-sixth to Fifty-ninth, taking our time, talking and talking. Couple of times she said 'Harold, we'll be *fired*,' and I'd say 'Wanna bet?' And she'd just laugh. Because, you see, in the kind of kids' jobs we had then we both knew it'd cost the company more to fire us than to keep us on – and besides, all we'd done was disappear for the afternoon: maybe nobody even noticed it. So anyway, we finally did have lunch about four o'clock that day in the Central Park cafeteria, the one by the zoo, but I don't think either of us ate much: we were too busy holding hands and smooching and saying all kinds of dopey things to each other – stuff we'd both learned from the movies, I guess."

"Oh, I think that's beautiful," Lucy said.

"Well, okay, but we ran into quite a lot of trouble later on," Harold said. "My family's Catholic, you see, and Nancy's is Lutheran, and those two don't mix at all. And then her parents thought she ought to marry some better-established guy – that was another shitty little problem. Took us more than a year to talk everybody into it, but they finally came around."

For a tense moment Michael was afraid the Smiths might now ask to hear the story of the Davenports' courtship, which would involve an awkward slurring-over or throwing-away of words like "college," let alone of names like "Harvard" and "Radcliffe," but Harold seemed to feel that any such inquiry could wait. He was well into his second drink, he had grown accustomed to dominating the talk, and now he brought it back to what he had apparently wanted to tell about from the start, which was his ambition.

Even in a rinky-dink old company like the Central, he said,

you had to give credit where credit was due. This deal of the free commutation fares, for instance: wasn't that a pretty fair example of enlightened management at work? How else could he and Nancy ever have been able to raise their kids in a place like this, while they were all still young enough to get the good out of it? And hell, he had to admit he liked the guys he worked with in Data Processing. They'd been together a long time; they understood each other. And there was a men's handball club that met on Friday afternoons; he'd found he really enjoyed that. Kept him in shape, too.

But the best thing, he said, sitting back with a fresh drink, the most promising thing, was that the Central had now made an executive training program available to its higher-level data processing people. He himself might not be eligible for another two years, but it certainly gave him something to look forward to. Part of the course work was done "within the corporate structure," he explained, but the biggest share of it was undertaken by "business-administration professors at several of the leading universities in the metropolitan area. . . ."

All three of Harold's listeners, whose eyes had been quick and bright when he'd told of taking Nancy out for a walk, had subsided now into attitudes of stoic patience. Nancy looked as though she wasn't listening because she'd heard it all before; Lucy managed to award the speaker a dumb-faced little nod at each pause in his voice, to show she was following the points he made; Michael stared down into his glass as if alcohol, taken in reasonable quantities, might turn out to be an effective precaution against dying of boredom.

But at last Harold came forward in his chair in a way that suggested he was almost finished. "So you see," he said, "in the transportation industry of the future it won't matter whether a man's come up through the rails *or* the airlines. He'll be a member of responsible, decision-making management in the – you know – in the transportation industry itself."

"Well, that's certainly very – interesting," Lucy said.

"You're right," he told her. "It's interesting. And I'm very interested in your field, too, Mike."

"My field?"

"*Chain Store Age*. Because I mean Jesus, talk about *changes*. Only a few years ago you had your little neighborhood grocery and your little drugstore and your little guy around the corner selling fish. And now there's a revolution in the entire concept of retail merchandising, am I right? So you take a magazine like yours, right up at the forefront of all those changes; I'd think you must find yourself in a world of opportunity every time you walk into the office."

"Well, no, Harold," Michael said. "I don't think of it as anything but a way of paying the bills, you see, so I can get my own stuff done."

"Well, sure, I understand that, but you still *work* for the magazine, right? What was the last thing you wrote for them? I'd really like to know."

Michael set his bite and felt a prickling in his scalp. All this would be over soon. "Well, let's see," he said. "I wrote a series of articles about some guy in Delaware named Klapp. He's an architect who's built a shopping-mall kind of thing in some town down there and he thinks it's really swell and he wants to do the same thing in other towns, but he says he keeps being stymied by 'politics.' "

"Did you meet the guy?"

"Talked to him on the phone a couple of times. He sounds like an asshole. The only reason my editor wanted these pieces at all is because the magazine's planning a special issue on Urban Renewal, or some horseshit like that."

"Well, okay," Harold Smith said. "Now. Supposing your articles really do make this guy look good. Then supposing *Life* magazine picks up the story for a big picture spread, and the guy makes a fortune building his stuff in a whole lot of other towns. And supposing he's so grateful to you he says 'Mike, I'd like you to come and be my public-relations man.' Well, sure, he'd still be an asshole; agreed. But look" – and Harold's face crinkled, winking, in the way it must have done when he first worked up the nerve to speak to Nancy in the personnel department – "Wouldn't it be a little nicer to write your poems and your plays on fifty thousand a year?"

When the Smiths had followed the efficient beam of their flashlight home at last, Lucy said "Well, now that we've made the gesture I don't imagine we'll have to do it again, at least for a while." Then she said "It's funny, you know? You can see how he *would* be good in a stage comedy: he can make you laugh. But my God, when he doesn't feel like making you laugh he can really put you to sleep."

"Yeah, well, that's what years of grubbing along in white-collar work can do. It's not too bad until they start believing in Management, but then they're lost. The magazine is crawling with people like that too. Sort of frightening."

She had collected the empty glasses and was carrying them to the kitchen. "Why 'frightening'?" she asked.

And he was just tired enough, with just enough drink in him, to express and even exaggerate his fears. "Well, because what if this play doesn't turn out to *be* my big-assed breakthrough? Or the next play either?"

She was standing at the sink, washing out the glasses and the plate that had held crackers and cheese. "In the first place," she said, "that's unlikely, as you know. In the second place you'll have two or even three good collections of poems soon, and you'll be sought-after by universities."

"Yeah, well, swell. Only, you know something? The college English departments of America are loaded with guys an awful lot like Harold Smith. They may not believe in Management, but the things they do believe in are enough to make your eyeballs dry out and wrinkle up like prunes. If I ever turn into a college English teacher I can guarantee you'll be bored shitless with me inside of two years."

She made no reply to that, and the silence in the kitchen began to feel almost like shame. He knew what she had left unsaid: In the third place, there would always be her money. And he was appalled now that the fretful aftermath of this one dull evening could have brought him so close to making her say it again.

He moved up beside her and ran one hand down the straight, firm length of her spine. "Well, okay, dear," he said. "Let's just go on upstairs now."

He didn't finish his play by the end of the year. All through the late winter months he worked day and night in the pump shed, where the kerosene stove left a fine coating of soot on his hands and face and clothes. By March or April, when he could stop using the stove and open the windows, he thought he had made enough good changes in the second and third acts to bring them alive, but the first act still lay inert on its pages. It was all labored exposition, the kind of writing he could have sworn he'd outgrown years ago, and it stubbornly resisted improvement. If the mark of a professional was to make difficult things look easy, this playwright seemed to be straining in the opposite direction: every new device he tried in that wretched first act had the effect of making easy things look difficult.

Then it was the middle of July, and his only encouragement came from knowing he could literally lose himself in concentration for many hours at a time. He didn't feel the heat or the strict confinement; he wasn't aware of the pencil in his hand or the dribbling sweat that constantly had to be wiped from his eyes; sometimes he would emerge from the shed at dusk when he'd expected it to be noon.

He was so hard at work one sweltering afternoon that he scarcely noticed a heavy thump shuddering the door of the shed from the outside, as if a man had fallen against the base of it. And half an hour must have passed before he began to realize that the shed itself was filling with a foul, intolerable smell. What the hell was this? He had to struggle to push the door open because of what proved to be a damp hundred-pound burlap sack, and when the sack fell over and came open it spilled many soft, trowel-shaped objects that couldn't be identified at first because each of them was swarming with blue-bottle flies. Then he saw they were the rotting heads of fish.

"Oh!" Ben Duane called from fifty yards away, and he came hurrying toward the shed in his scanty khaki shorts. He was a little bow-legged but very agile for an old man, and he smiled engagingly. "Didn't know anyone was in there," he said, "or I would've put that somewhere else."

"Yeah, well, I work here, you see, Mr. Duane," Michael said. "I've been working here for several years now. Every day."

"Is that a fact? Funny I hadn't noticed. Here, I'll get all this out of your way." Squatting low, he used both hands to gather up the spilled fish heads, flies and all, and put them back in the sack. "These are mackerel heads," he explained. "Don't smell very nice at this stage, but they make good fertilizer." Then he stood erect again, still smiling, heaved and slung the sack over one naked shoulder, and said "Well. Sorry about the

103

inconvenience, my friend." And he walked off toward the flower beds.

There was no hope of getting any more work done that day. The mackerel heads were gone but their smell hung as heavy as if it had seeped into the very walls of the shed, and whenever Michael let his eyelids close he saw crawling clots of blue-bottle flies.

"And you know something?" he demanded of Lucy later. "I'll bet the old son of a bitch did it to me on purpose."

"Oh?" she said. "Well, but why would he do that?"

"Ah, I don't know; fuck it. I don't know anything anymore."

Chapter Seven

Michael's parents drove up from Morristown about once a year, and they were model visitors: they never stayed too long or too short a time for comfort; they didn't seem to find anything strange about the Tonapac place as compared with the house in Larchmont, and they didn't ask embarrassing questions. It was always clear that their main purpose in making the trip was to see their grandchild, and Laura seemed to love them both whole-heartedly.

But Lucy's parents were far less reliable. Two or three years could pass without a word from them, except for scribbled-up Christmas cards and perhaps some small remembrance at the time of Laura's birthday; then, and never with adequate notice, they would suddenly appear in the flesh – two handsome, talkative rich people whose every glance and gesture seemed a calculated unkindness.

"So *this* is where you've been hiding," Charlotte Blaine called as she stepped from a very long, clean automobile. Then, pausing on the lawn to look the place over, she said "Well, it's – different, isn't it." And just before they went into the house she said "I love your little spiral staircase, dear, but I don't quite see what it's *for*."

"It's a conversation piece," Lucy told her.

Michael thought his father-in-law looked a lot older than the last time he'd seen him. Stewart ("Whizzer") Blaine might still play a fast game of squash in town and a fast game of tennis in the country; he might still dive from the high board and accomplish any number of vigorous laps in the pool; but his face had taken on the bewildered look of a man who can't imagine where the years have gone.

He was reported to have told Lucy, once, that he thought Michael's refusal of her fortune was "commendable"; now, though, as he sat blinking over the rim of his bourbon and water, he was almost visibly changing his mind.

"Well, Michael," he said after a long silence. "How're things down at the retail whaddyacallit – the trade journal?"

And it was Lucy who answered him, with a casual little smile that warmed Michael's heart.

"Oh, we've almost forgotten all about that," she said. And she explained about Michael's free-lance arrangement, making it sound as though he scarcely needed to bother with *Chain Store Age* from one month to the next. Then she wound it up, after a significant pause, by saying "And he has another book of poems almost finished."

"Well, that's fine," Mr. Blaine said. "And how about the plays?"

This time Michael spoke for himself. "Well, I haven't had very much luck with those yet," he said, and the truth was that he'd had no luck at all. Several of his early plays might still be on the desks or in the files of a few off-Broadway producers, but the big one, the three-act tragedy that had cost him so much, had earned only a cursory letter of acceptance from his agent and was now "making the rounds" – an endless avenue of little hope. At times during the summer he had even thought of offering the script to the Tonapac Playhouse, but he'd always held back. The director of that year's itinerant company was a nervous, hurrying, indecisive man who didn't inspire much confidence; the actors were either undisciplined kids, dying for their Equity credentials, or incompetent veterans forever too old for their roles. Besides, it would have been almost too much to bear if they had considered the play and turned it down. "The theater's a very – a very difficult business," he concluded.

"Oh, I know it is," Mr. Blaine said. "I mean, I can imagine it must be."

Laura came home from school then, and Michael knew this meant the visit would soon be over. Stewart and Charlotte Blaine had never had more than a little of themselves or each other to spare for being parents, so it was only reasonable not to expect them to show much interest in the child of another generation. After their first false cries of delight they seemed unable even to pay attention to the shy, big-eyed, grass-stained little girl who came up to stand too close to their knees, whose presence obliged them to hold their whiskey glasses aloft and well out of harm's way as they craned their faces comically from one side of her to the other in an effort to keep the grown-ups' talk alive.

As soon as the Blaines had gone, Michael clasped his wife in a hug and thanked her for the way she had answered her father's question. "You really came through for me," he said. "That was great. It's always so great when you – when you come through for me that way."

"Well," she said, "I did it as much for myself as for you." And she seemed to stiffen in his arms, or maybe it was his arms that stiffened; it might have been that he stepped on her shoe, or that they broke apart too quickly; in any case, it felt like the clumsiest embrace of their lives together.

★

One autumn day there was a knock on the pump shed door and Michael found Tom Nelson smiling there in his old GI tanker's jacket.

"Want to go out for pheasant?" Nelson inquired.

"I don't have a shotgun," Michael told him. "Or a hunting license, either."

"Hell, they're not hard to come by. You can get a fairly decent gun for twenty-five bucks or so, and the license is easy. I've been going out alone the past couple mornings, and I thought I'd like some company. Thought an old aerial gunner'd make a pretty good wing shot."

It was a nice idea – and flattering, too, that Tom Nelson had come all the way from Kingsley to suggest it; Michael took him down to the house so that Lucy could have a share in the pleasure. They had been to many parties at the Nelsons' house, and the Nelsons had often sat talking and laughing in theirs; even so, Lucy still seemed glad of any reassurance that the Nelsons were their friends.

"Shooting *birds*?" she said. "Is that really such a good idea?"

"Ancient spirit of the hunt, ma'am," Tom Nelson said. "Besides, it gets you outdoors. It's exercise."

And very early one morning, when Michael self-consciously carried his cheap new shotgun through yellow fields toward what Nelson had described as "a natural spot," he felt a quickening of interest. Except for boxing, which he knew he'd taken up for complicated reasons, he had never pursued or enjoyed a sport in his life.

But when they sat down on a lichened rock, it soon appeared that Tom was less concerned with pheasant than companionship: he wanted to talk about girls.

Had Michael noticed the little black-haired number at that last party? With the sweet mouth and the kind of tits you could die for? She was shacked-up with that bullshit art historian from Yale – wasn't that a heartbreaker? – and the worst part was she seemed to like the old clown.

Oh, and Jesus, talk about heartbreakers: A couple of weeks ago Tom had been hanging around the Modern trying to talk to this lovely young thing, looked to be fresh out of Sarah Lawrence or someplace, real doe eyes and sweet, sweet legs, and he'd just gotten to the point where he managed to tell her he was a painter.

"She said 'You mean you're Thomas *Nel*son?' But son of a bitch if some flaming faggot curator didn't pick that very moment to call out to me from the other side of the room in this fluty voice: 'Oh, *Thomas, do* come and meet Blake So-and-so of the National Gallery.' And man, I mean I *shrank* across that floor. I was absolutely positive she had me figured for a fag."

"Couldn't you've gone back to her later?"

"Lunch, man. Had to eat *lunch* with that National Gallery asshole. Spent half an hour looking around for her afterwards, but she'd taken off. They always take off." He sighed heavily. "My trouble is I got married too young. Oh, I'm not knocking it: it's home, it's family, it's stability and all that." And he stubbed out his cigarette on the rock between his boots. "But some of these girls are – some of these girls are too much. Want to try flushing out a bird or two?"

And they did, conscientiously, but they found none.

Deer season came later. The only legal way to hunt deer in Putnam County was with shotgun slugs, rather than rifles – and the blunt snouts of those slugs, protruding from their tight paper shell casings, looked so brutal that many hunters must have been only halfhearted in stalking their prey. Michael and Tom weren't even halfhearted: their mornings in the woods were mostly given over to conversational strolls or to taking long rests, seated with their guns across their laps.

"Ever have a girl write you a fan letter about your poems?"

"Nope. That hasn't happened."

"Be pretty nice, though, wouldn't it? Some neat girl fall in love with you and write you a breathless little letter; you write back and set up a meeting someplace? Take a lot of careful planning, but it might really be nice."

"Yeah."

"I almost had something like that once. I mean *al*most. Girl went to one of my gallery shows and wrote me this letter: 'I feel you have something to say to me, and perhaps we have something to say to each other.' Like that. So I played it cool, and it's a good thing I did. Wrote back and asked her for her photograph, and there went the ballgame. She'd had the picture taken with these shadows of leaves partly covering her face, to make herself look more arty, I guess, but there was no hiding it: tiny little eyes, pursed-up mouth, frizzy hair – I mean not exactly a dog, but a semi-dog. Talk about disappointment, man. And I mean it wouldn't've been so bad if I hadn't had this altogether *other* girl built up in my mind. Christ, what imagination can do to you."

Another time Nelson complained that he never really got away from home these days except when *Fortune* magazine gave him an illustration assignment. "And I usually enjoy those jobs; the work's easy, and I like to travel. Last year they sent me down to south Texas to do some sketches of the oil rigs there. That part was all right. Trouble was there were these two guys in charge of showing me around down there in a jeep, you see, and I couldn't figure out why they didn't like me: they kept calling me 'the artiste.' One of 'em would say 'Hey Charlie, wanna run the artiste over to Number Five?' or 'Think the artiste has had enough for the day?' Like that. Then once the three of us were eating lunch in this truck-stop kind of place and they got to talking about their families, and I happened to mention I had four sons.

"Wow! You shoulda seen their jaws drop! Made all the difference in the world, just hearing me say 'four sons.' Point is, you see, a lot of those characters think 'artist' equals 'fag,' and I guess you can't blame them; anyway, from then on they couldn't do enough for me. Buying me drinks at night, calling me 'Tom,' asking me all about New York, laughing at my jokes. And I think they were about ready to fix me up with a girl, but there wasn't time. Had to catch the damn plane."

As they made their way home for breakfast on the last day of deer season, trudging as slowly as tired infantrymen with their weapons balanced on their shoulders, Tom Nelson said "Ah, I'll never know what the hell was the matter with me when I was a kid. I was a very slow developer. Reading books, playing the drums, fooling with tin soldiers – *that's* what I was doing when I should've been out getting laid."

Lucy took longer than usual over washing the dishes one evening, and when she came out into the living room she wiped back a fallen lock of her hair in a way that suggested she had a difficult announcement to make.

"Michael," she began, "I've decided I ought to see a psychiatrist."

His lungs seemed to shrink, as if breathing might now be severely curtailed. "Oh?" he said. "Why?"

"There isn't any why in the sense of something that can be explained," she told him. "If there were, I could explain it."

And he was reminded of her impatience with him over the abstract-expressionist painting in that dimly remembered Boston art gallery: "If he could have said it, he wouldn't have had to paint it."

"Well, but I mean is it mainly what you'd consider a marriage problem?" he asked, "or other kinds of problems?"

"It's – all kinds. Current things, and things going all the way back to my childhood. I've come to feel I need help, that's all. And there's a man in Kingsley named Fine who's supposed to be quite good; I've already made an appointment with him for Tuesday, and I think I'll be going twice a week. I just wanted you to know about it because I think I'd feel funny if you didn't. Oh, and of course there's no need to worry about the expense of it or anything; I'll be using my own – you know – my own money."

And so he had to stand at a window on Tuesday afternoon and watch her drive away. There was a chance that she might soon come back, disgruntled by the psychiatrist's questions or his manner, but the far more likely thing was that from now on she would disappear every Tuesday and Friday into a world of secrets that couldn't be confided; she would grow ever-more distant; she would evaporate and be lost to him.

"Daddy?" Laura asked him once when they were alone together. "What does 'dilemma' mean?"

"Oh, it means when you can't quite decide what to do. Like maybe you want to go out and play with Anita Smith, but there's a good show on television and you sort of feel like staying home and watching that instead. Then you're in a 'dilemma.' See?"

"Oh," she said. "Yes. That's a good word, isn't it."

"It sure is. You can use it in a lot of ways."

When the heaviest snowfalls hit Putnam County it always took four or five days before Ann Blake could arrange to get her driveway plowed. On those mornings, holding hands and shuddering or laughing, Michael and Laura would plod all the way down through the drifts to the place where the school bus stopped, and they always had Harold Smith and his children for company. Harold would carry Keith, his brain-damaged boy, and he'd say "You're not getting any lighter, buddy," as his daughters trailed behind. When the children had been deposited at the bus stop, all looking forlorn in their ice-flecked mufflers, their stiff mittens and their rubber boots, it was time for Harold to wave goodbye and strike off up the road for the mile-and-a-half walk to the train station – and if it happened to be a *Chain Store Age* day, Michael would go along with him. They'd walk fast, pausing now and then to crouch and blow the congestion of their nostrils into the snow, and they'd talk like hardbitten comrades.

"Well, marriage is funny, Mike," Harold said once with the wind whipping the vapor of his voice over his shoulder. "You can go along for years without ever knowing who you're married to. It's a riddle."

"You're right," Michael said. "It is."

"Course, most of the time it doesn't seem to matter: you get by; you get through; the kids get born and start growing up, and pretty soon it's all you can do to stay awake until it's time to go to sleep."

"Yeah."

"Then maybe once in a while you take a look at this girl, this woman, and you think: What's the deal? How come? Why her? Why me?"

"Yeah, I know what you mean, Harold."

By the spring of 1959 Michael had come to feel he was discovering poetry all over again. The publication of his second book had been disappointing – not very many reviews, most of them tepid – but now he was putting together a new one that gave every promise of excellence.

Some of the new poems were short but none were slight, none were loose, and it pleased him to read the better ones aloud in the solitude of the pump shed. Sometimes, almost wholly without shame, he would cry over them. There was still a lot of work to be done on the long, rich, ambitious poem that would conclude the book – something comparable to the one called "Coming Clean" that Diana Maitland had said she liked so much – but he had some strong opening lines for it and a generally sound idea of how it would develop: he felt confident he could bring it off by September, if the summer went well. It would begin slowly and accelerate as it gathered complexity; its controlling images would be of time and change and decay, and at the end, very subtly, it would turn out to be about the falling-apart of a marriage.

Words and phrases rode in his head as he walked home from the shed every evening, and later as he sat with his whiskey in the living room while Lucy moved around in the steam and savory smells of the kitchen.

Only very slowly, absentmindedly, was his attention drawn to a bright purple-and-white book on the coffee table that might have been lying there for days. It was called *How to Love*, by Derek Fahr, and the photograph on the back showed a bald man whose keen eyes had been caught looking straight into the camera.

"What's this?" he inquired when she came in to set the dinner table. "Some kind of sex manual?"

"Not at all," she told him. "It's a work of psychology. Derek Fahr is a philosopher, and he's also a practicing psychiatrist. I think you might find it extremely informative."

"Yeah? Why me?"

"Well, I don't know. Why *me*?"

The following Sunday, when all sounds and activity in the living room were swamped under the Sunday newspapers, he looked up from *The New York Times Book Review* to say "Lucy? Did you know this guy Derek Fahr's been up at the top of the best-seller list for twenty-three weeks?"

"Yes, sure, I knew that," she said as she paged through fashion advertisements across the room, and then she looked at him. "You think everything on the best-seller list is trash, don't you? You always have."

"Well, not everything, no; I've never said that. It's certainly true that *most* of the stuff is trash, though, isn't it?"

"I don't think that's true at all. If a man can write something that appeals to a great many people; if his ideas and his way of expressing them turn out to be what a great many people want, or need – isn't that a substantial achievement?"

"Oh, come on, Lucy, you know better than that. It's never been a question of what people 'want' or 'need' – it's a question of what they're willing to put *up* with. It's the same rotten little commercial principle that determines what we get in the movies and on television. It's the manipulation of public taste by virtue of the lowest common denominator. Oh, Jesus, I *know* you know what I mean." And he rattled his paper back into reading position, to make clear that the subject was closed.

There was a silence of ten or fifteen seconds before she said "Yes. I know what you mean, but I don't agree with you. I've always known what you meant about everything; that's never been the trouble. The trouble is I've never agreed with you – ever – and the appalling thing is I've never even come to realize it until the past few months." And she stood up, looking defiant and oddly fearful at the same time.

The book section slid to the floor as Michael got to his feet.

"Now, wait just a God damn minute," he said. "Is this something you and Dr. Fine have worked out in those cozy little intimate sessions of yours?"

"I might have known you'd jump to a cheap conclusion like that," she said. "As it happens, you're entirely wrong – I'm not even sure if I'll go on seeing Dr. Fine – but I suppose you can believe whatever you wish. Could you just stop talking now?"

She went swiftly into the kitchen then, but he was right behind her. "I'll stop talking," he told her, "when I'm fucking ready to stop. Not before."

She turned on him and looked him up and down. "Oh, this is strange," she said. "This is really interesting. I mean it's been surprising enough to find I've always hated all your precious, elitist little *Kenyon Review* ideas – and my God, if I never hear you say 'poem' or 'play' again it'll be too soon – but what I know now is that it's your voice itself I hate. Do you understand me? I simply can't bear the sound of your voice anymore. *Or* the sight of your face." And she wrenched open both taps of the sink at full blast, preparing to wash the dishes.

Michael went back and wandered trembling among the strewn Sunday papers. This was worse than bad; this was the worst. In other fights he had sometimes managed to give her time enough alone, in silence, to recover and be sorry, but now the old rules no longer applied. And besides, he had a few more things to say.

She was hunched over the steaming suds when he came up to stand behind her, keeping his distance. "Where do you get 'precious'?" he demanded. "Where do you get 'elitist'? Where do you get '*Kenyon Review*'?"

"I think we'd better stop this at once," she told him. "Laura can hear us, and she's probably crying up there."

He left the house, slamming the kitchen door, and made his

way up past the extravagance of Ben Duane's flower beds. But once he was at his desk he couldn't lift a pencil or even see straight. He could only sit with half his fist in his mouth, breathing hard through his nose, trying to comprehend that the bottom had dropped out of everything. It was over.

He was thirty-five, and he was as frightened as a child at the thought of having to live alone.

Lucy wasn't breathing very easily either as she finished her job at the sink. She hung the damp dish-towel firmly on its rack and the rack fell away from the wall, leaving four funny-looking little wounds in the cheap plaster. Nothing had ever worked in this makeshift kitchen; nothing had ever been right in the whole of this makeshift house or in the secondhand, second-rate piece of real estate around it.

"And I'll tell you something else," she whispered fiercely at the wall. "A poet is someone like Dylan Thomas. And a playwright – oh, God! – a playwright is someone like Tennessee Williams."

For as long as she could remember, Laura Davenport had wanted a younger sister. Sometimes she felt she would have settled for a younger brother, if the choice were between that and nothing, but it was a sister that she wished for, and dreamed of. She had chosen a name for her long ago – Melissa – and she would often spend hours in whispered conversation with the phantom child.

"You ready for breakfast, Melissa?"

"Not yet. I can't get this dumb comb through my hair."

"Well, here, then; let me help. I'm good at snarls. This'll only take a second. There. Is that better?"

"Oh, yes, it's fine now. Thanks, Laura."

"You're welcome. Hey, Melissa? After breakfast, want to go

over to the Smiths'? Or would you rather just fool around here with the dolls and stuff?"

"I don't know; I can't decide. I'll tell you later, okay?"

"Okay. Or you know what else we could do, if you feel like it?"

"What?"

"We could go up to the picnic place and see if we can climb that big tree."

"You mean the really big tree? Oh, no. I'd be scared, Laura."

"How come? You know I'd be right there to hold you if you started to slip or anything. Why do you keep getting scared all the time, anyway, Melissa?"

"Because I'm not as *old* as you, that's why."

"You're even scared of the kids at school."

"I am not."

"You are too – and second grade is just baby stuff; everybody knows that. If you're scared in the second grade, I hate to think how you'll be in *fourth* grade."

"So? I bet *you're* scared of the kids in fourth grade."

"That's the most ridiculous thing I ever heard. I'm a little shy sometimes, but I'm not scared. There's a big difference between shy and scared, Melissa. Bear that in mind."

"Hey, Laura?"

"What?"

"Let's not fight anymore."

"Well, all right. But you still haven't said what you feel like doing today."

"Oh, it doesn't matter. You decide, Laura."

Then there were times, for no clear reason and for days and weeks on end, when Melissa would fade to nothingness. Laura might think of interesting new things to talk over with her, new things to plan or do; she might even whisper appropriate questions and replies to represent Melissa's half of the conversation, but in those times she couldn't help knowing, with more than a touch of shame, that she was talking to herself. And once Melissa was gone, it always seemed she would never come back.

That was how things were for Laura on a warm September afternoon when she was nine. It was after school. She was alone in her room, carefully combing out the long brown nylon hair of a miniature doll, when her mother came to the foot of the stairs and called "Laura? Will you come down here, please?"

Bringing the doll and the comb, she went out to the landing and said "Why?"

Her mother looked strangely embarrassed. "Because Daddy and I have something important to tell you, dear, and to discuss with you; that's why."

"Oh." And as she started down to the living room, taking her time, Laura began to know beyond all hope that it was going to be something awful.

PART TWO

Chapter One

For a long time after the separation, and then after the quick divorce, Lucy didn't know where to go or what to do. It often seemed that this was because her range of choices was too wide – she knew she could go almost anywhere and do almost anything in the world – but there were times when she wondered, secretly and in fear, if it might be a matter of simple inertia.

"Well, but why stay *here,* dear?" her mother asked during a brief and impatient visit.

"Oh, I think it's only sensible, at least for the time being," she explained. "It wouldn't be fair to Laura to make some big impulsive move just for the sake of moving. I don't want to uproot her, take her out of school and everything, until I'm really sure of what I'm looking for and where I want to be. And meanwhile this is probably as good a place as any for – well, for taking stock; for sorting out my ideas; for trying to make plans. Besides, I have friends here."

Later, though, after her mother had gone, she wasn't altogether sure if she knew what she'd meant by "friends."

People were consistently welcoming and attentive; everyone seemed eager to let her know that they liked and valued her as much now as when she'd been Michael's wife – or even more, since they'd come to know her better. And she was touched and pleased by that; she was grateful – but there was the trouble. She didn't especially like being grateful; she didn't like the way her face felt in its almost continual smile of thanks.

"I really admire your mother and stepfather," she told Peggy Maitland one evening as they walked away from the big house in Harmon Falls, and Peggy looked baffled by that remark. It had been a gracious and enjoyable afternoon: whiskey had poured freely from the celebrated spigot in the wall; Mr. and Mrs. Folsom had both been charmingly at ease as they chatted and laughed beside the enormous window overlooking the ravine.

"How do you mean 'admire'?" Peggy asked her.

"Well, because they're so – settled," Lucy said. "It's as if they'd both figured out a lot of things and considered a lot of alternatives and then decided to be just the way they are. I mean there doesn't seem to be any strain in their lives."

"Oh," Peggy said. "Well, that's just because they're old." And she slipped one graceful hand and wrist through Paul's arm. "Personally, I'd rather be young. Wouldn't you? Wouldn't everybody?"

Back in the Maitlands' cottage, while Peggy got the supper started, Paul sat in a creaking armchair and offered their guest an engaging look of old affection. "Diana always asks after you, Lucy," he told her.

"Oh? Well, that's nice," Lucy said, and she almost said "That's very kind," but caught herself in time. "How does she – how does she like Philadelphia?"

"Oh, I don't imagine either of them cares much for Philadelphia," he said, "but they both seem very interested in the work they're doing."

Ralph Morin had been appointed "artistic director" of a new enterprise called the Philadelphia Group Theater; he and Diana had been married for a year or more.

"Well, be sure to give her my very best, Paul," Lucy said. "Both of them, I mean."

Then Peggy came out of the kitchen with a little cellophane bag that held an inch or two of what looked like tobacco. "You smoke, Lucy?" she inquired.

Michael Davenport had always said he hated marijuana, the few times he'd tried it, because it made him feel he was losing his mind, and Lucy hadn't liked it much either; but now, perhaps because Peggy's proud talk of being "young" had seemed a little challenging, she said "Sure. Love to."

And so they scrupulously rolled their joints and sat around getting high together, while the meat and vegetables shriveled on the stove.

"This is better-than-average stuff," Peggy confided as she tucked her pretty legs up into the sofa. "We get it from a friend of ours on the Cape. Costs a little more, but it's worth it. Because I mean most of what you can find around here is strictly childrensville. High-school City."

Lucy had been mildly irritated in the past by Peggy's "hip" vocabulary, her reliance on all this "-ville" and "city" jargon self-consciously borrowed from Negroes, but tonight it no longer seemed an affectation. There wasn't anything the matter with Peggy. All of her fresh young life was honest and whole. She had been born to marry Paul Maitland, and to serve and inspire him; she was a girl to be envied.

"Curious thing, you know?" Paul said. "Can't paint when I'm drunk; I found that out years ago. But I can paint when I'm stoned." And so, after three or four mouthfuls of what little supper they'd been able to salvage, he excused himself and went into the other room, with a switching-on of great overhead lights, to be secluded with his work.

Lucy found she had to drive very slowly on the way home that night. She kept thinking she would have a great many things on her mind in the morning – new insights, good new ideas about herself and her future – but when she woke up there was nothing much to think about at all, other than the task of getting Laura ready for the school bus.

Sometimes Lucy and the Nelsons would go to the movies together – laughing among themselves at what a silly idea it was but enjoying it anyway, the three of them sitting like hushed children in the darkness and wholly absorbed in the screen, dividing their popcorn three ways. And the best part of those entertainments was demolishing them afterwards, back at the Nelsons' house or at Lucy's, staying up a little too late as they agreed on all the flaws and vulgarities of whatever movie had enthralled them, having a drink or two until it was time to say goodnight.

And then there were the Nelsons' parties. Lucy was shy at first about attending them alone, but she almost always had a good time. She had come to know most of the party crowd over the years – there were rarely more than a few newcomers at each gathering – and she could count at least three other recently divorced women in those happily seething, sophisticated rooms.

One night she glanced up to find a burly fellow smiling at her from across the studio in a way that suggested he'd been watching her for some time. He was one of the regulars, a college teacher with whom she'd sometimes had small, amiable talks, and he'd never shown any particular interest in her before. Then suddenly he spoke to her – or rather called out to her, in a jovial voice so loud that it silenced most other voices within its range:

"Well, Lucy Davenport. Got yourself a new man yet?"

She could have walked over and slapped his smiling face. She couldn't remember ever having been so mortified, and there now seemed nothing to do but find a place to put her drink down, get her coat, and get out of here.

"Oh, I'm sure he didn't mean to be rude," Pat Nelson said in the doorway, trying to persuade her to stay. "He's nice; he'd *die* if he knew it'd made you angry. Look: he may have had a little too much to drink and he – *you* know. That's just the kind of thing that happens when people – I mean that's parties, right?"

And Lucy did agree to stay a little longer, though she was very quiet and kept mostly to herself. She felt damaged.

It seemed very important these days to have everything nice in the kitchen when Laura came home from school. A freshly made peanut-butter-and-jelly sandwich had to be set out on the flawlessly clean kitchen counter, with a glass of cold milk beside the plate, and Lucy had to be waiting there too, nicely dressed and groomed, as if the whole of her life were at Laura's disposal.

". . . And the really neat part was, they made a contest out of it," Laura said around the chewing of her sandwich.

"A contest out of what, dear?"

"I *told* you, Mom. Building statues of Abraham Lincoln out of snow. You know how he is in the Lincoln Memorial, where he's sitting down? Well, we made him that way. And you see each of the three fourth grades built their own statue, and then when they were done they held this contest, and our class won because ours was the best."

"Well," Lucy said. "That sounds like it must have been fun. What part of the statue did you make?"

"I helped make his legs and his feet."

"And who made his face?"

127

"Well, there're two boys in our class who're good at faces, so they made his face. It looked really neat."

"And was there a prize of some kind for winning the contest?"

"Well, not a prize, exactly, but the principal came into our room later and hung this banner kind of thing over the blackboard, and it said 'Congratulations.'" Laura finished her milk and wiped her mouth. "Hey, Mom? Okay if I go over to Anita's?"

"Sure. You'll have to get bundled up again, though."

"I know. Only, Mom?"

"What?"

"Will you come too?"

"Well, I don't – why?"

And Laura looked shy. "Just because. Anita said her mother said you never pay attention to her anymore."

They found Nancy Smith where it seemed she could always be found, standing at the ironing board between toppling piles of children's clothes and underwear.

"*Lucy*," she said, looking up from the rhythm of her work. "What a nice surprise. Been a long time. Come and sit down, if you can find a place. Here, wait a second, I'll turn off the TV."

And when the little girls had gone off to another room, their mothers sat on either side of a wide table.

"I don't think I've seen you more than once or twice since you and Mike broke up," Nancy Smith said. "What's that been now – six months?"

"Five, I think."

Nancy looked as though she knew her next question might be indelicate but felt like asking it anyway. "You miss him?"

"Oh, no more than I'd expected to. It seemed like the right

decision at the time, and since then I haven't had any – you know – any regrets."

"So is he still living alone in the city?"

"Well, I don't suppose he spends too much time alone; I imagine there've been a few girls in and out of that apartment. But he's very good with Laura when she goes in for weekends. He's taken her to a couple of Broadway shows – she really liked *The Music Man* – and they do a lot of other things; she always seems to have fun with him."

"Well, that's nice."

There was a silence then, and Lucy began to sense that the talk would now develop in either of two ways: Nancy might allude to the peace and happiness of her own marriage; or she might, hesitantly and with averted eyes, express a wish that she too could work up the courage to seek a divorce.

But Nancy's thoughts were far away from matters like that. "Tomorrow's my brother's birthday," she said. "My brother Eugene. He always got a kick out of having been born on Abraham Lincoln's birthday, and he sort of took it to heart. By the time he was eleven or twelve I think he knew more about Lincoln's career than any of the history teachers did, and he could recite the Gettysburg Address from memory. They asked him to do that in front of the whole school once, at assembly, and I remember being scared the kids would make fun of him, but my God, you could've heard a pin drop in that auditorium.

"And talk about proud! Wow, I was proud of him. I was a year older, you see; I spent practically my whole life hoping nobody'd pick on him or push him around, even though it always turned out I had nothing to worry about. Nobody ever did give Eugene any trouble; people couldn't help knowing he was an exceptional boy. And I mean there *are* kids like that, you know? Kids so bright and so – out of the ordinary – that everybody understands they need to be left alone?

"Well, he was drafted right after high school, in 'forty-four, and once during basic training he told me he couldn't seem to qualify with the rifle. That's what they called it, 'qualifying.' You had to be a qualified rifleman, you see, and Eugene couldn't get a high enough score on the target range. He said he'd keep wincing and blinking when he pulled the trigger; that was the problem. He came home for a three-day pass just before he went overseas, and I remember how funny his uniform looked: the sleeves were way too short and the neck of it stuck way out in back, as if it belonged to somebody else. I said 'Well, so did you qualify?' And he said 'No, but it didn't matter; in the end they faked up the scores and qualified everybody.'

"I guess the Bulge was almost over by the time Eugene's bunch of replacements got to Belgium, so they were kept in reserve for a few days until the rifle companies came back off the line and picked them up, and then they all had to go down into eastern France because of something called the Colmar Pocket. I've never met anyone who ever heard of the Colmar Pocket, but it was there. A whole lot of Germans were defending this city of Colmar, you see, and somebody had to go in and clean them out.

"So Eugene's company started walking across this big plowed field, and I've always been able to picture that part of it – all these kids plodding along with their rifles in their hands, trying to look as if they weren't scared and doing their best to keep ten yards apart from each other because that was the rule, you had to keep ten yards apart – and Eugene stepped on a land mine and there was hardly anything left of him. In another week he would've been nineteen. The boy who wrote to my parents about it said we could be grateful that he hadn't suffered any pain, but I must've read that letter twenty times and I still didn't get it. 'Grateful' didn't seem like the right word.

"Oh, listen, don't get me wrong, Lucy, I don't really think about this much anymore; I mean I don't let it prey on my mind or anything; it's just that Abraham Lincoln's birthday always – Abraham Lincoln's birthday always kills me. Every year."

Nancy's head was bowed low over the table and she appeared to be crying, but when she looked up again her eyes were narrow and dry. "And I'll tell you something else, Lucy," she said. "A lot of people feel sorry for Harold and me because our boy is handicapped, you know? Well, but do you know the first thing I thought when we found out about his handicap? I thought Oh, thank God. Thank God. Now they can never take him into the Army."

Ann Blake sat hunched on one of the tall stools in her kitchen, hugging herself and seeming to shiver slightly as she stared into a cup of coffee. She got up promptly to open the door, but she could barely achieve a little smile when Lucy came in to deliver her check for the month's rent.

"Well," she said. "And how are you faring, Lucy?"

"How am I what?"

"Holding up. Managing to survive."

"Oh, we're doing pretty well, thanks," Lucy said.

"Ah, yes, 'we.' You'll always be able to say 'we,' won't you, because you have your daughter. Some of us are less fortunate. Well, I don't mean to sound – here; come and sit down, if you have a minute."

And it didn't take long, then, for Ann to confide that Greg Atwood had left her. He had signed up for a six-week tour with a dance troupe, and when the tour was over he'd telephoned her to say he wouldn't be coming home. He'd decided to join a new

131

troupe being formed from the nucleus of the old one, with plans for a much more extended tour that might keep him on the road for what he called an indefinite period of time. "He's flown away, you see," Ann explained.

"Flown away?"

"Well, of course. With all the other fairies. Listen. Promise me something, Lucy. Never fall in love with a man who's essentially – essentially homosexual."

"Well," Lucy said, "that's not very likely."

Ann gave her a slow, frowning, appraising look. "No, I don't suppose it is. You're still young, and you're pretty – I love the way you've been fixing your hair lately – and there'll be any number of men in your life. It'll be years before your luck starts to change, if it ever does." Then she got off her stool and stepped back two or three paces, straightening her clothes. "How old do you think I am?" she asked.

Lucy couldn't guess. Forty-five? Forty-eight? But Ann didn't wait long for an answer.

"I'm fifty-six," she said, and came back to sit at the counter again. "It's been more than thirty years since my husband and I built this place. Oh, and you can't imagine what high hopes we had. I wish you could have known my husband, Lucy. He was a foolish man in many ways – *is* a foolish man – but he loved the theater. We wanted a summer-stock company that might be the envy of the whole Northeast, and we almost had it. A few of our people really did go straight from here to Broadway, though I don't think I'll tell you their names because you'd only say you never heard of them. Oh, but I can tell you this place was alive with wonderful young people in those years – wonderful boys and girls destined for things they never quite achieved. Well. I won't keep you. And I'm sorry I spilled my troubles all over you, Lucy. It's just that you're the first person I've seen since Greg –

132

since that ugly little phone call, and I—" Her lips began to tremble out of control.

"No, really, Ann, that's okay," Lucy said quickly. "You're not keeping me from anything. Let me stay with you for a while, if you'd like, until you feel better."

Lucy had never been invited beyond the kitchen of this house, and she felt oddly privileged as Ann made her welcome in the living room. It was surprisingly small – the whole house was on a smaller scale than it appeared to be from the outside – and the staircase probably led up to a single luxurious bedroom for two. It was the kind of house that certain songwriters of the nineteen twenties must have had in mind with the phrase "a love nest."

"Well, you see the fireplace is bigger than necessary," Ann was saying. "That was my husband's idea. I think he liked to picture the two of us cuddled up here on the sofa, watching the flames and getting all toasty-warm before bedtime. He was a terrible sentimentalist. I've never seen the house he built for the little airline girl, of course, but I'd be willing to bet it has a fireplace at least as big as this." She fell silent for a while; then she said "Greg always liked it, too. He'd sit here staring into the fire for hours, mesmerized by it, and sometimes I'd go upstairs alone and lie there thinking Well, but what about me? What about me?" And she looked desolate again. "So the hell with it. I suppose I'll live here for years without ever building a fire."

"Why don't we build one now?"

"Oh, no, dear. That's very sweet, but I'm sure you must have better things to—"

Out in the late February wind again Lucy knocked the snow off three or four logs that lay in a pile beside the kitchen door and gathered up enough kindling to get them started, and when she carried her load back into the living room she found that Ann had broken out a bottle of scotch.

"It's much too early in the day," Ann said, "but I don't think anybody's going to care. Do you?"

Soon, when the first steady flames were beginning to climb around the hissing logs, there was a sense of well-earned peace in the room: Ann Blake had curled herself girlishly into the sofa and her guest was settled in an easy chair. Lucy had never liked scotch, but she was discovering now that once you got past the taste it wasn't really much worse than bourbon. It did the job. It took the harshness out of the day.

"You're sort of – rich, aren't you, Lucy?"

"Well, I'm – yes; but how did you know?"

"Oh, it's just a thing I can smell on people. Michael never gave off that particular smell, but you do; you always have. Well, 'smell' is probably the wrong word; I hope I'm not offending you."

"No."

"And besides, I've caught a glimpse or two of your parents. They've got money written all over them. Old money."

"Yes, I suppose they do. There's always been quite a lot of – quite a lot of money in my family."

"Then I don't understand why you go on living here. Why don't you take your daughter away someplace where you can be with your own kind?"

"Well," Lucy said, "I suppose it's because I don't really know what kind my own kind is."

And that didn't sound like much of an answer at first, but the more she thought it over the better it became. It was certainly closer to the truth than saying "I have friends here"; it was closer even than saying "It wouldn't be fair to Laura to make some big impulsive move." Oh, she was getting closer to the truth all the time – or maybe she needn't even try to get closer; maybe all she had to do now was give in to what she'd known in her heart all along. The truth – and what if it did take Ann Blake's whiskey in her veins to make it come clear? – was that she didn't want to leave Dr. Fine.

Twice now she had severed relations with the man, driving home from his office on each of those afternoons with her head held high in defiance and pride – and both times, after a few weeks, she had gone humbly back. Did other people feel this bondage to their psychiatrists? Did other people find themselves savoring the events of each day in order to have something to say, something to tell about at their next damned psychiatric session?

Well, on Wednesday I got drunk with my landlady, she began to rehearse in her mind, knowing it would come out almost exactly this way in Dr. Fine's consulting room. She's fifty-six and she's just been abandoned by a much younger man, and I guess she's about the most pitiable person I know. I think I hoped that being there and drinking with her might help take me out of myself a little, do you see? Sort of in the same way that Nancy Smith's telling about her brother helped take me out of myself that other time? Because I mean nobody can live, Doctor, nobody can breathe and be nourished on self, self, self. . . .

"Well, I can't imagine having a great deal of money," Ann Blake was saying as the flames crackled. "I've never even given it much thought, because all I ever wanted was a great deal of talent – and I'd gladly have settled for even a modest amount of that. Still, I suppose the two things are sort of alike. Having either one sets you apart. Being born with either one can bring you more than most people allow themselves to dream of, but they both require an unfailing sense of responsibility. If you ignore them, or neglect them, all the good of them slides away into idleness and waste. And the terrible thing, Lucy, is how easily idleness and waste can become a way of life."

. . . Then all at once she startled me, Doctor. She said 'The terrible thing, Lucy, is how easily idleness and waste can become a way of life' – and it was like a prophecy. Because that's what my life here is becoming, don't you see? This neurotic preoccupation with myself that you constantly encourage – oh, yes, you do encourage it, Doctor; don't deny that – and this helpless sense of inertia. It's all idleness. It's all waste. . . .

"Lucy?" Ann said. "Would you awfully much mind closing the curtains, dear, so I won't have to know what time it is? Oh, thank you." And when the room was dimmed she said "That's better. I want to have it be night. I want to have it be night and I don't want the morning ever to come."

The whiskey bottle was still almost a quarter full – Lucy could tell by holding it up to the firelight – and she poured herself another deep, authoritative drink to make sure she would remember all the things she planned to say to Dr. Fine.

"I think I'll just sort of stretch out here for a while, Lucy, if you don't mind," Ann said. "I haven't been – haven't been sleeping at all well."

"Sure," Lucy told her. "That's okay, Ann." And the silence in the room seemed wholly appropriate to her own need for solitude and contemplation.

On her way to the door she collided softly with a wall and had to stand leaning against it for a few seconds to regain her balance; she was lucky, though, in finding that her winter coat was still where she'd left it.

The expanse of snow and ice between Ann Blake's kitchen door and Lucy's house couldn't have been more than fifty yards, but it seemed to go on forever; then even after making the distance she stood for a long time, with the wind cutting her face, in order to stare with revulsion at the ice-encrusted spiral staircase. It was no damned conversation piece and never would be, unless you wanted to have the dumbest and most pointless conversation in the world.

When she'd flung her coat over a living room chair she went swiftly into the kitchen because it was time for the sandwich and the milk. She got out the peanut-butter jar and fumbled around for the jelly jar, but that was as far as she could go because she had to lean heavily on the counter with both hands, hanging her head.

It was all right, though; Laura was old enough to make her own sandwich. Everything would be all right now if she could only get up to the bedroom. She did it slowly, using the wall of the staircase for guidance; then she turned back the covers and got into bed with her clothes on. For just a moment she wanted Michael there to take her in his arms ("Oh, Christ, you're a lovely girl") but that passed quickly in the peace that came from knowing she was alone.

In another breath or two she would be too sound asleep to hear Laura coming home and calling "Mom? Mom?" – and there might be an edge of fright in the child's voice when she called again and got no answer – but that was all right, too. If Laura wanted to know where her mother was, she could come upstairs and find out.

"This fear of 'bondage,' " Dr. Fine said, "is by no means unusual. A patient will often come to feel dependent on a therapist, and the sense of dependency may then seem constricting. But it's an illusion, Mrs. Davenport. You're not 'bound' to me, or to the work we've done here, in any way at all."

"Well, you've got an answer for everything, haven't you?" Lucy said. "You guys run a pretty slick racket, don't you?"

And he looked as if he thought she was kidding. "Oh?" he said.

"Well, certainly. Your whole profession is a slippery, irresponsible business. You suck people in when they don't know where else to turn; then you seduce them into telling you all their secrets until they're utterly naked – yes, and so utterly absorbed in their own nakedness that nothing else in the world seems real. And if anybody ever does say 'Wait – stop – let me *out* of this,' then you shrug it all off and say it's an illusion."

She was almost ready to get up and walk out of the office again. There might not be a very pure sense of defiance and pride in it this time – she might even feel a little foolish, having done the same thing twice before – but there would almost certainly be a slow gathering of strength, all the way home, in her knowledge that this time was the last.

It was embarrassment, more than anything else, that kept her in her chair. She didn't like the shrill and reckless way her voice had risen just now, and those high, broken notes of near-crying still hung in the silent consulting room. If she couldn't leave with some measure of dignity, it might be better to stay.

"Suppose we go back a little, Mrs. Davenport," Dr. Fine said, looking at her steadily over his softly clasped hands. It had often struck her that there was something wormlike about this small, bald, pale and quiet man, and now that impression made her outburst seem all the more unworthy. How could anybody be in bondage to a worm?

"Sometimes it can be helpful just to summarize and clarify," he said. "The central problem we've discussed here, since the end of your marriage, is how best to take full advantage of your wealth and of the personal freedom it provides."

"Yes."

"There have been two persistent uncertainties – where to go

and what to do – and while we've discussed both questions at length we've recognized from the start that the two are inter-dependent: finding a satisfactory answer to one would resolve the other."

"Right."

And so much for summary; so much for clarification. Now it was time for Dr. Fine to get down to business. Lately, he said, Lucy seemed no longer to be "dealing" with the central problem. She was apparently allowing her attention to drift, letting herself be distracted by various inadequacies or elements of dissatisfaction in her present circumstances. And while these matters might indeed be distasteful, they were only transitory; only temporary. Wouldn't it be more profitable to look ahead?

"Well, of course," she told him. "And I do, or at least I try to. I know this is just a transitional period; I know it's only a time for taking stock; for sorting out my ideas; for trying to make plans . . ." and she remembered that these were the same three tidy activities she had reported to her mother, last fall.

"Good," Dr. Fine said. "Now perhaps we're moving in the right direction again."

But he had begun to look tired and even a little bored, as though he might be allowing his own attention to drift, and Lucy couldn't blame him for that. Even a small-town psychiatrist would have more interesting things on his mind than assessing the emotional balance of a rich, rich girl who didn't know where to go and didn't know what to do.

Nothing worth remembering took place in what little was left of the winter, or in March or April or early May. Then, one bright and fragrant day, she answered a knock on the kitchen door and found a strikingly handsome young man standing there with both thumbs hooked into the pockets of his jeans.

"Mrs. Davenport?" he inquired. "Be okay if I use your phone for a minute?"

He said his name was Jack Halloran, and that he was the director of a new theater group that would soon begin rehearsals at the Playhouse. Then he called the telephone company, in a tone of crisp, businesslike impatience, and arranged for phones to be installed "at once" in the theater, the dormitory, and the annex.

"Can I – get you a cup of coffee?" she asked when he was finished. "Or a beer or something?"

"Well, if you've got enough beer," he said, "I'd love one. Thanks." And when he was settled across from her in the living room he said "It's hard to believe, but whoever's been running this theater's been trying to do it without phones. Can you imagine that? Doesn't that sound like amateur night in Dixie?"

She had never heard that expression before, and wondered if he'd made it up. "Well," she said, "I think things *have* been a little on the sleazy side here for quite a few summers now. But the place did have a very good reputation once, years ago."

"Be pretty nice then, wouldn't it, if somebody could bring it back?" He took a deep swig of beer, making his prominent Adam's apple rise and fall. "And it might even happen this summer," he said when he'd wiped his mouth. "Can't promise anything, but I've spent more than a year getting this company together, and we're not just fooling around. We've got some fine young talent and we'll be putting on some good shows."

"Good," Lucy said. "That certainly sounds – certainly sounds good."

Jack Halloran had pale-blue eyes and black hair, and the kind of tough, sensitive face she had admired in the movies ever since she was a child. She already knew she wanted him; the only question now was how best and most gracefully it could be

140

brought about. And the first thing to do was keep him talking.

He told her he was from Chicago, and that he'd been raised there by "well-meaning strangers" – first in a Catholic orphanage and later in a succession of foster homes – until he was old enough to join the Marine Corps. And it was on a three-day pass in San Francisco, shortly before his discharge from the service, that he'd walked into a theater for the first time in his life and seen a touring Shakespeare company's production of *Hamlet*.

"I don't think I understood more than about half of it," he said, "but I knew I'd never be the same again. I started reading all the playwrights I could get my hands on, Shakespeare and all the others, and seeing plays – any kind of plays – and one way or another I've managed to keep hanging around the theater ever since. Hell, it may turn out that I'll never make it, either as an actor *or* a director, but that doesn't mean I'll ever quit. This is the only world I understand."

Over his second or third beer he let something slip that he probably wasn't used to confiding on such short acquaintance: he had made up his name. "My real name's Lithuanian," he explained, "and it's got more syllables in it than most people can work their mouths around. So I settled on 'Jack Halloran' when I was sixteen because it seemed to me the Irish kids were getting all the breaks; that's the way I signed up in the Marines. Then later it came to feel more natural, once I started working in show business, because a lot of show people have stage names."

"Sure," Lucy said, but it was a disappointing piece of information. She had never known anyone who lived under an assumed name; she wouldn't even have thought people did that kind of thing unless they were criminals, or unless – well, unless perhaps they were actors.

"Well, I think we'll have a good summer," he said, getting up in readiness to leave. "I like it here. Tell you a funny thing, though: I never would've expected to find an actor of Ben *Duane's* stature in a place like this. I asked him if he might consider working with us, but he's a stubborn old bastard: if he can't work on Broadway, all he wants to do is grow flowers."

"Yes. Well, he's quite a – quite a character."

"It was Mr. Duane who gave me your name," Jack Halloran said. "He told me you're divorced, too – I hope it's okay to mention that."

"Certainly."

"Well, good. And look: as long as we're going to be neighbors, Lucy, maybe I can see you again, okay?"

"Sure," she said. "I'd like that, Jack."

After closing the kitchen door behind him she began to dance around on tiptoe. She executed six or eight neat, whirling steps all the way back into the living room, where she made a little curtsy.

. . . And from the moment I met him, Doctor, I began to feel this strange, warm, wonderful sense of –

But she didn't even finish that sentence in her mind, because it was something Dr. Fine might never have to hear. All she could do, as her heart slowed down, was stand looking out an open window into the colors of spring.

Chapter Two

For a day or two, waiting for him to come back, she entertained a sobering, cautionary thought: Could you really make love with a man when you didn't even know his name? But in almost no time at all, after he did come back, she learned the answer to that question.

Yes. You could. You could rapturously kiss and clasp and writhe and heave with a man all day in what had once been your husband's bed; you could crave a man so badly it was almost like dying; you could open your legs wide for him if that was the way he liked it, or bring them close around him if he seemed to like that better; you could even cry "Oh, Jack! Oh, Jack!" while knowing all the time that "Jack" was part of an alias conceived because the Irish kids were getting all the breaks.

She meant to ask him about the name right away – she knew the longer she waited the more awkward it might be – but she could never quite find the words because there was too much of Jack Halloran in her life now, filling all her senses and her very bloodstream, filling her dreams.

And there never seemed to be enough time. Every afternoon, at first, they had to be up and dressed and downstairs, seated at a conversational distance, when Laura got home from school. And the ending of the school year imposed a subtler, more hazardous kind of secrecy: Laura might be far away for hours with the Smith girls, up in the woods or out across acres of grass, but there was no telling when she might come slamming back into the house. Then the actors and the stage technicians began to arrive on the estate, five or six or more of them each day, and this required Jack to be gone a lot of the time on business.

On the last day before rehearsals began he stole most of the afternoon to be alone with her, and their knowing it was stolen time made it all the more exquisite. When they'd fallen apart at last they lay weak with laughter at some small funny thing he had said; they were still laughing in helpless, subsiding spasms as they went lazily about the business of putting on their clothes and making their way downstairs. In the kitchen, fully recovered, he stood holding her close in a long romantic embrace.

Then very shyly, with her face against his shirt, she said "Jack? Do you think you might tell me your real name now?"

He drew away and gave her a short, speculative look. "Nah, let's hold off a while on that, honey, okay? I'm sorry I even told you about it."

"Well, but I thought it was charming that you did," she said, afraid he could tell she was lying. "It was one of the first things I liked about you."

"Yeah, well, okay, but that was before we got to know each other."

"Well, exactly. And the point is I can't go on saying 'Jack Halloran' indefinitely, don't you see? It's like taking something counterfeit and pretending not to care. Oh, listen: I can work my mouth around any number of syllables, and I'd love to. Do you think I'm a snob or something?"

He seemed to be turning that question over in his mind. Then he said "No; it's more that I'm the snob. You'll find your average Lithuanian slum child can be snobby as hell around high-class New England girls – didn't anybody ever warn you about that? My kind of people always feel superior to your kind, you see, because we've got the brains and the guts and all you've got is the money. Oh, maybe we can take you one at a time, once in a while, but even then there's bound to be an element of condescension in the deal. So I really think we're both better off this way, Lucy, don't you? As long as I'm Jack Halloran we can have a lot more laughs, and that's a promise."

Then suddenly he was gone, out in the sunshine where he'd come from, heading for the hill to the dormitory. And at least half the dormitory, by now, would be filled with girls.

But he was back that very evening, soon after dark, barely visible through the screen door except for the burning end of his cigarette. When she let him into the kitchen he seemed to feel that no apologies were necessary, unless she chose to find an implicit apology in the way he winked and murmured "Lucy" just before he kissed her. Then he said "Listen, baby. I'll be working every day now, and of course I can't spend any time here at night without upsetting Laura, so how's this: I've got a nice room up in the dorm – it's all my own and it's big enough for two. Think you could manage to come up there once in a while?"

"Well, is it – does it have a private entrance?"

"How do you mean?"

"Well, would I have to walk through a whole dormitory full of people every time I—"

"Ah, that won't matter; they won't notice, or if they do they won't care. They're all nice kids."

Lucy had never been inside the dormitory building before. It smelled of dust and old lumber, and the shadowed ground floor of it, where the theater people took their meals, was still warm

145

with the redolence of recent cooking: there had been liver and bacon for supper tonight.

Upstairs she discovered that almost all the living quarters were arranged in an open space, with narrow beds placed at intervals along the walls in the style of an infantry barracks. Here and there some shy person had made an attempt at privacy by hanging sheets or blankets around a bed like curtains, but those few ineffectual hiding places only called attention to themselves: most members of the company were apparently contented to live in the open. And a good many of them were gathered now in talking, laughing clusters around the big, bright room. Except for an occasional middle-aged face they looked very young, and Lucy was careful to pick one of the boys, rather than one of the girls, for making her inquiry.

"Excuse me; do you know where I can find Mr. Halloran?"

"Mr. who?"

"Jack Halloran."

"Oh, *Jack*. Sure; there."

And when she turned to where the boy pointed she knew she could easily have found it herself because it was the only door in sight.

"Hi, baby," Jack said. "Sit down. Be with you in just a second, okay?" He was standing with his shirt off at a small sink and mirror, shaving with an electric razor. There was nowhere to sit except on his bed, which was a cot of the same size and kind as the ones outside, but Lucy wasn't ready to sit down anyway. She moved around like a housing inspector, peering closely at everything. There was a bathroom, or rather a closet containing a toilet bowl; there was a window that might by day command a view of Ben Duane's flowers, and there were two big, cheap suitcases sagging against the wall, ugly with age and grime and heavy use. If you saw such dismal bags in a bus station, would you have any way of guessing they might belong to a bright, ambitious young actor-director on the road? Well, probably not; more likely your glance would dismiss them at once as pitiful emblems of strain and failure – the kind of luggage carried by worn-out Negroes, say, on a journey from one state's welfare program to another.

When she did sit down on the bed she saw that the door of the room had a keyhole of the big old-fashioned kind used for peeping, with no big old-fashioned key thrust into it, and at about the same time she found that the small unvarying sound of the electric razor was making her teeth ache.

"Is there a key?" she asked him.

"Huh?"

"I said is there a key for the door?"

"Oh, sure," he said. "Got it in my pocket."

Then at last he switched off the razor and put it away. He locked the door with what seemed some difficulty – he had to try the knob several times to make sure the job was done – and came to sit close beside her, slipping one arm around her ribs. "I was careful to reserve this room before the kids came up," he said, "because I knew I'd want privacy, but I didn't know I'd have somebody so nice to share it with. Oh, and I got us some beer, too." He reached under the cot and pulled out a six-pack of Rheingold Extra Dry. "Probably isn't very cold anymore, but what the hell. Beer's beer, right?"

Right. Beer was beer; bed was bed; sex was sex; and everybody knew there were no social classes in America.

When she'd taken off her clothes she said "Jack? How am I going to get out of here?"

"Same way you got in, I guess. How do you mean?"

"Well, I can't stay very long, you see, because Laura isn't used to being left alone, and the point is I really don't know if I—"

147

"Didn't you give her the phone number up here? Case she needs you for anything?"

"No. I didn't. And the point is I really don't know if I can go out and face all those people again."

"Ah, I think you're being a little silly about this, Lucy, don't you?" he said. "Now come on, settle back. If we haven't got much time we might as well make the most of it."

And they certainly did. Getting laid on a cot was even better, in a way, than getting laid in a double bed: it meant you were never apart; it made you feel that both of you were only halves of a single aching animal in urgent and overwhelming need. And in the final throes of it, when Lucy was afraid her helpless sounds could be heard throughout the dormitory, a phrase from Shakespeare floated into her mind for the first time in years: "Making the beast with two backs."

"Oh, God," she said when she'd recovered her breath. "Oh, my God, Jack, that was – that was really—"

"I know, baby," he told her. "I know. It really was."

The New Tonapac Playhouse would begin its season with a light comedy – "Just to get our muscles in shape," Jack Halloran explained – and Lucy attended the last few rehearsals of it, sitting alone in the big old barnlike theater across the road.

The show was far enough along now so that most of it moved and developed without requiring much help from Jack, but it was a pleasure just to watch him standing tense with concentration on one shadowed side of the stage and to know he was wholly in charge. He held the open script in one hand, and he slowly wagged the loose forefinger of the other at the thigh of his jeans as if it were a metronome subtly attuned to the rhythm of the play. Sometimes he would call out to one of the actors: "No, to the left, Phil; to the left" or "Jane, you're still not getting the right inflection in that line; let's try it again."

Once, when a contagious series of fumbled lines threatened to wreck a whole scene, he called everything to a stop and walked out into the lights.

"Now, look," he began. "An awful lot of time and talent has gone into this show, and we're going to get it right. We're going to get it right if we have to double up and rehearse around the clock, is that clear?"

He paused there as if to allow for questions or complaints, but nobody said anything. Most of the actors were looking at the floor like embarrassed children.

Then he said "I just don't understand how we can still have mistakes like this. Some of you people seem to think this is amateur night in Dixie or something."

There was another silence, and when he spoke again it was in a lower, less exasperated voice. "Okay. We'll go all the way back to Martha's line about happiness and take it from there. Only, this time, pay attention."

The opening-night audience filled only a little more than two thirds of the theater, but the encouraging thing was that they didn't all look like local people. It seemed evident that some kind of New York crowd really might be expected to come all the way out here this summer – even for this first and relatively minor offering.

And the performance went well. There were no visible mistakes; the laughter came up full and spontaneous in all the right places, and the applause at the end was long and loud enough to warrant three curtain calls. Then, just before the curtain came down for the last time, one of the actors brought Jack Halloran out from the wings to take a shy, courteous bow, and Lucy was so proud she could have cried.

★

Jack owned a noisy, bad-smelling, eleven-year-old Ford, seldom repaired and never washed; he always apologized for it, but there were quite a few nights that summer when he found it useful for taking Lucy out on long drives to "get away from the whole damn place for a while."

Once the car was on the road it seemed as good as any other car, and they would ride for miles over Putnam County while he told her about the daily rehearsals and the nightly performances, about certain people in the company who weren't shaping up very well and others who were a pleasure to work with.

They would stop to drink at bars featuring pinball machines and tall jars of pickled pigs' feet, the kind of quaint "townie" bars she hadn't visited since college, but they never stayed very long in those places because Jack would begin to worry about the many things he had to do the next day. And that was all right with Lucy: after an hour or two of traveling she was always eager to get back to his little room.

By late summer, with a new show every week, the company had presented plays by Chekhov, Ibsen, Shaw, and Eugene O'Neill, as well as an overly ambitious production of *King Lear* that Jack had come to consider their only failure so far ("Ah, we all tried too hard on that one, and it showed").

There was never enough sleep or even enough rest for the performers, and there were tearful outbursts among the girls at more than a few rehearsals. Even one of the boys broke down and cried once, clearly ashamed of himself as he turned on Jack and called him a fucking slave-driving prick.

But the people from New York kept coming out, in ever-increasing numbers, and most of the evenings began to seem triumphant. A man from the William Morris Agency went backstage to tell Jack he would like to "handle" him, but later, when Lucy said "Wonderful!" Jack said it was no big deal.

"These Morris people are a dime a dozen," he explained; "besides, I already have an agent. No, the only one of us who got a real break tonight is Julie. God damn, isn't that fine? I'm very – I'm really very proud for her."

"Well, so am I," Lucy said. "And she certainly deserves it."

Julia Pierce was a thin girl of twenty-four with straight dark hair and big, luminous eyes. She had played the leading roles in *The Sea Gull*, in *A Doll's House*, and again in *Major Barbara* – and her "real break" was that she had now been asked to audition for a part in a new comedy by a well-known Broadway playwright.

She was very quiet and shy offstage, and often seemed acutely nervous – Lucy had noticed that her fingernails were bitten down to the flesh – but the nervousness always vanished when she went to work. Three or four other girls in the company were prettier than Julia Pierce, and they knew it, but they could only envy and admire what they called her "terrific authority" as an actress. Her clear and resonant voice, filling the theater even when she murmured, was a marvelously subtle instrument for bringing make-believe situations to life.

And one sweltering night, after a little knock on the door of Jack Halloran's room, it was Julia Pierce's unmistakable voice that called, quietly, "Mrs. Davenport? Your daughter's on the phone."

Lucy had been drifting off to sleep with Jack's arm close around her and his hand cupping one of her breasts, but she struggled free and got dressed in such haste that she left her stockings and underwear on the floor.

Out at the telephone, which was attached to a wall near the stairs, she said "Laura?"

"Mom, can you come home now? Because Daddy just called and he sounded all funny."

"Well, dear, sometimes your father does have too much to drink, and then he——"

151

"No, this wasn't drunk; this was different. I mean he wasn't even making any sense."

She couldn't hurry past the heavily fragrant flower-bed terraces because she was afraid of missing each downward step in the darkness, but once she was on level ground she broke into a run for the lighted house. In the living room she gave Laura a quick, reassuring hug and said "Tell you what we'll do. I'll call Daddy now and find out if he's sick or anything; then if he is, we'll do everything we can to help him get better."

She settled herself at the phone and began to dial Michael's number in New York, and even before she'd finished dialing she was afraid he wouldn't be there: he might have called Laura from any of a million phone booths, anywhere.

But he answered on the first ring. "Oh, Lucy," he said. "Oh, I knew you'd call back. I knew you wouldn't let me down. Listen, can you stay on the phone a minute? I mean can you just sort of stay on the phone a minute?"

"Michael?" she said. "Can you tell me what the trouble is?"

"What the trouble is," he repeated, as if the question had helped to clear his head. "Well, I haven't had any sleep for about five – no, about seven – shit, I don't know how many days. I keep watching the sun come up over Seventh Avenue and then I turn around half an hour later and it's the middle of the night again. And I don't think I've been out of this place for a week – or maybe it's more like two or three weeks now. There are paper bags full of trash standing all around this room, and a couple of 'em have fallen over and spilled. Are you getting the picture, Lucy? I'm scared. I'm scared shitless, you see. I'm scared to walk out the door and up the street, because every time I do I see all kinds of people and things that aren't even fucking *there*."

"Well, wait, Michael, listen. Do you have a friend I could

call? Someone who might come over and sort of look after you?"

"A 'friend,'" he said. "You mean a girl. No, there isn't anybody like that. Oh, but don't get me wrong, sweetheart: I've had a whole lot more than my share of girls since you threw me out of the house. Jesus God, I've been having pussy for breakfast, pussy for lunch, pussy for—"

"Come on, Michael," she said impatiently. "Listen: let me call Bill, okay?"

"—pussy for dinner," he was saying, "oh, and plenty of pussy for leftovers at midnight, too. Bill who?"

"Bill Brock. He might be able to come over and—"

"No. That's out. I won't have Brock walking into this place. He's been wallowing in psychoanalysis for years. He'll sit here trying to psychoanalyze me, and the point is I may be crazy but I'm not *that* crazy. Oh, Jesus, Lucy, try to understand. All I need is sleep."

"Well," she said, "perhaps Bill can get you some sleeping pills."

"Ah, yes, 'perhaps.' Tell me something, Lucy: How come you always say 'perhaps' instead of 'maybe' when you're in this Miss-Purse-the-Nurse frame of mind? You've always had about six artificial, affected ways of speaking, you know that? Your whole personality changes to suit the occasion. I noticed it way the hell back in Cambridge, but I thought it was something you'd outgrow. Only you never have, so now I guess you're stuck with it for life. And I guess it comes from being a millionaire girl among ordinary people, because I mean you feel you've gotta be up there on stage all the time, right? Playing one fucking role after another? Gracious Lady Bountiful dispensing favor? Well, that's exactly the kind of horseshit I came to find very, very tiresome over the years, Lucy. And do you want to know something else? For most of the time we were married I was in love with Diana Maitland. Never had her, never came within a mile of her, but, oh, Christ, I could've died for that girl. Ah, I used to wonder if you knew what I was going through, but then I'd figure it didn't matter anyway because you were probably in love with Paul – or if not with Paul then with Tom Nelson, or else with some romantic abstraction of a man who'd turn out to be about twenty-nine times stronger and better than me. Know what we did, Lucy? You and me? We spent our whole lives *yearning*. Isn't that the God damndest thing?"

She told him they had better get off the phone now, so she could call Bill Brock; then after hanging up she took a minute to comfort Laura, whose eyes were still round with fear.

"Listen, this is going to be all right, baby," she said. "You'll see. Promise not to worry now, okay?"

"Was he making any sense this time?"

"Well, it was a little confused at first, but after we got to talking he was – yes. He was making very good sense."

Bill Brock sounded as though the phone had awakened him, and she pictured some sleepy girl in the bedclothes beside him – she had never been able to imagine Bill without a girl.

"Well, sure, Lucy," he said when she'd explained the trouble. "I'll get over there right now. I can bring him a couple of my own sleeping pills – they're very mild, but they might do the job – and I'll stay there with him until it's time to call my shrink in the morning. And I mean this shrink of mine is a good, solid man – you'd like him, and you'd trust him, and I'm pretty sure he'll have a few ideas. Then I'll call you back when I can. So listen: Don't worry, okay? This is no big deal. These things happen to practically everybody."

"Well, Bill, I can't thank you enough," she said, and then she chewed her lip because he was someone she'd disliked for years.

"Ah, honey, don't be silly," he told her. "This is what friends are for."

She had barely put the phone back in its cradle before it rang. It was Michael, and she thought he was convulsed with laughter until she realized he was in tears.

". . . Oh, Lucy, listen, I didn't mean any of that," he was saying as he struggled to control his voice. "I didn't mean the stuff about Diana Maitland or any of the rest of it, do you understand me?"

"It's okay, Michael," she said. "Bill's on his way over now. He's bringing some medication, and he's going to stay with you."

"Well, but listen. I may never have another chance to tell you this, so please for God's sake don't hang up on me."

"I won't hang up."

"Okay. This is something I want you to remember, Lucy, and I think it's probably the last chance I'll ever have to say it. There's only been one girl in my whole life. There's only been one shining, splendid—"

"Yes, well, that's nice," she said dryly, "but I think I liked the first version better."

He seemed not to have heard her. ". . . Oh, baby, do you remember back on Ware Street? Remember when we were both so young we thought anything in the world was possible – when we thought the world itself stopped turning every time we got laid?"

"Well, Michael, I think that's about enough, don't you?" she said. "Just be quiet now, and stay there, and wait for Bill."

There was a long silence before he spoke again, and then it was hard to believe he'd been crying only a minute before: his voice was as terse and flat as that of a soldier acknowledging orders. "Right. Gotcha. Got the message." And he broke the connection.

She went upstairs with Laura and tucked her into bed with as much care as if she were four or five instead of ten and a half.

And it wasn't until she was alone in her own room, taking off her dress, that she remembered the underwear and stockings strewn on Jack Halloran's floor.

As soon as she'd left him, Jack might easily have gotten up and pulled on his pants and opened the door again and said "Julie? Can I offer you a beer?"

And that shy, talented girl might easily have come in to sit on the cot beside him while they talked about her brilliant future. She would have told him, breathlessly, that she knew she could never have "found" herself this summer without his help, and he would have insisted that her achievements were all her own.

Oh, he probably hadn't made a lunge for her right away – Jack had an impeccable sense of timing – but while listening to her talk he would almost certainly have taken the key from his pocket, gone to the door one final time, and locked it for the night.

Bill Brock called back in the morning, well after Laura had left for school, and his voice betrayed a striving for command.

"Listen, it's gonna be okay, Lucy," he told her. "Michael's safe, and he's in good hands, and he's getting treatment."

"Oh," she said. "Well, good. Was your – doctor able to help, then?"

"No, that part of it didn't work out. Look, I'll tell you exactly what happened, okay?"

"Okay."

"Well, when I got over there last night he was pacing around and talking steadily – talking compulsively. Sometimes he'd be coherent for five minutes or so, and then he'd get all unfocused again. All irrational. Diana Maitland's name kept coming into it:

156

he kept trying to tell me a whole lot of disjointed stuff about Diana Maitland, and I figured that was just because he still associates her in his mind with me. You know."

"Sure," Lucy said.

"Oh, and the place was a wreck, Lucy: I don't think he'd taken out the trash for a month, and I've never seen so many cigarette butts in my life. So I straightened up the bed for him and I got him to take the pills I'd brought. But they didn't work – I told you they're a very mild prescription – and after a while he started saying he wanted to go out for a walk. Well, at first I tried to talk him out of it, but then I began to think it might not be a bad idea: I thought the physical exercise might help him sleep. So we started walking up Seventh Avenue, and all the way up to about Fourteenth Street he was fine: very quiet, very docile, not even talking much. Then all of a sudden he got manic."

"Got 'manic'?"

"Well, he kept getting these terrific bursts of energy, and he kept getting away from me, and there wasn't any way I could control him. He'd go running out in the street, right into the traffic and everything, as if he was trying to kill himself, and I knew I couldn't deal with the situation alone. So I got this cop to help me – and I know you may not like that part of it, Lucy, but there are times when you really need a cop – and the cop called a police ambulance and we got him safely over to Bellevue."

"Oh."

"Well, look, Lucy: we've all heard stories about Bellevue, and I suppose it's true that he won't be getting much rest there for the first few days, but you have to remember it's a thoroughly up-to-date facility. Some of the finest psychiatrists in New York are consultants there, and those guys know their business. I had a long talk with the admitting physician – this very nice, very bright young guy out of Yale Med School – and I really wish you could've talked to him too because he was very reassuring. He said Mike'll probably only be in there a week, or two weeks at the most, and he said he'll be given the best available medications, stuff that'd cost him a fortune if he were getting it under private care. And then I called my own shrink first thing this morning, because I wanted to check all this out with him, and he said it sounded to him as if I'd done the right thing."

"Sure," Lucy said. "I mean I'm sure that's what he would – I'm sure that's probably true."

"So I'll keep you posted, Lucy, okay? I'll be going over there again as soon as they have visiting hours on Mike's ward, and I'll find out how he's doing and everything, and I'll let you know."

Lucy said that would be fine, and she thanked him again. She even said "Thanks so much for your help, Bill," and "Thanks for everything."

But she could hardly wait to be rid of his voice.

And she had indeed heard stories about Bellevue. Crowds of men, barefoot and in wretched pajamas, were made to walk the filthy floors of locked and airless wards in there all day – made to walk to a wall and turn, walk to the opposite wall and turn again, because that was the easiest way for the hulking Negro orderlies to keep an eye on all of them. Some of the men would shout or scream and others would fight, and the punishment for each disturbance was the same: the man would be forcibly injected with a heavy sedative and locked alone in a padded cell.

She could picture Michael trudging along with his head down in that dreadful parade, or sprawled in humiliation on the stained canvas mats of a cell, and she knew he would find it all impossible to believe. None of this could really be happening to him, because he was – well, because he was Michael Davenport, and because all he had needed was sleep.

When Jack Halloran arrived at the house to take her down across the road for rehearsals, he said "What was the trouble last night? When Laura called?"

"Oh, nothing much. She got a little upset about something – mostly just about being alone, I think – so I thought I'd better stay with her. She was fine this morning." Lucy hardly ever told lies because they always made her feel she might be turning into somebody else, but this time there was clearly no point in telling the truth.

The day would be as hot and windless as yesterday and the day before. They were walking down Ann Blake's driveway now, and Lucy was careful to wait until they were almost at the foot of it, until there were no other members of the company in sight, before she turned on Jack with a bright artificial smile.

"So," she said. "Did you and Julie have a good time last night?"

His face looked so blank, and then so honestly puzzled, that she felt a tentative sense of relief.

"I think you're out of your mind, Lucy," he told her.

"Maybe I am. Maybe picturing the two of you on that damned little cot is enough to *drive* me out of my mind."

They had come to a stop, facing each other, and he took hold of her shoulders with both hands. "Lucy, will you cut this out?" he said. "My God, what kind of a slob do you take me for? You really think I'd bring some other girl into my room the minute you've left it? That'd be like something out of a French farce, for Christ's sake, or like something out of a dirty joke."

So she allowed him to lead her out across the warm asphalt road and along the far side of it toward the theater.

159

"And besides," he said as they walked, and he put his arm around her. A short lock of his black hair was lifting and falling attractively on his forehead with every step. "Besides, I don't even *want* Julie Pierce. Why the hell would I want Julie Pierce? She's way too skinny and she hasn't got any tits at all. And she may be talented as hell but I think there's something a little cracked upstairs. So can I just please get started on the day's work now, sweetheart, without taking any more of this crazy shit from you?"

"I'm sorry," she told him. "Oh, I'm sorry, Jack."

"Hey, baby?" he asked softly, a few nights later. "You awake?"

"Yes."

"Be okay if we sit up for a minute, and talk?"

"Sure." She knew he'd had something on his mind for hours, even for days, and she was glad of the chance to find out what it was.

"Want a beer?"

"Oh, I don't care. Sure, I guess so."

And then he came out with it. "You used to do some acting, right? Up around Harvard? In a couple of your husband's plays and things like that?"

"Oh, well," she said, "sure, but that was just – you know – that was just college-girl stuff. I never had much training or anything."

"Well, the thing is I'd really like to work with you," he told her. "I'd like to see what you can do, and I've got a feeling you'd do very well."

And she was about to protest, or to laugh it off, but she kept still because a slow sense of pleasurable expectancy had begun to rise in her chest.

Jack wanted something big to close the season with, he

explained. He wanted a final show so powerful that nobody sitting out there in the New Tonapac Playhouse would ever forget it. He had given this a lot of thought all summer and he knew the play he wanted, but now he wasn't sure if he could cast it. Had Lucy ever seen *A Streetcar Named Desire?*

"Oh, my God," she said.

Michael Davenport had taken her to the original Broadway production, on a weekend trip to New York soon after they'd met, and she would always remember the stunned, enraptured look on his face as they left the theater. "Know something, sweetheart?" he'd said. "That's the greatest fucking American play ever written. This guy Williams makes O'Neill look empty." She had hugged his arm and told him she'd loved it too – loved it; loved it – and a month later they'd come all the way back from Boston just to see it again.

". . . And the trouble is I've worked the hell out of Julie all summer," Jack Halloran was saying. "I'm getting a little concerned about her nerves. Besides, she's not old enough for Blanche Dubois. I suppose she could play Stella, but then that's a very demanding part too; might be better to use one of the other girls. Still, the main problem is finding somebody who's right for Blanche, and that's why I thought of you. Now, wait; listen" – and he quickly held up one hand to ward off her refusal – "before you say no to this, dear, let me tell you something. There's plenty of time; you won't have to worry about that. We've got two whole weeks."

And he explained that the play wouldn't be going into rehearsal until a week from tomorrow; that would give them seven days for what he called preliminary coaching. The two of them would meet alone on the stage every afternoon, when the regular working day was over and all the kids were gone, and he'd take her through her part line by line until she was

161

"comfortable" with it; until she'd "gained enough confidence" to begin rehearsing with the other members of the cast. Did that sound fair enough?

"Well, Jack," she said, "this is certainly a – certainly an honor" – here she had to glance at his face to make sure he wouldn't think "honor" was a silly word – "and I'd love to try. But you'll have to promise me one thing. If it turns out that you don't think I'm good enough, promise to tell me right away, okay? Before it's too late?"

"Well, sure; of course I'll promise that. And listen, it's great that you're willing to do this, Lucy. It's really a load off my mind."

From under his bed, where the beer was kept, he pulled out a cardboard box packed with copies of the play. She could take one home and read it, and make notes in it; then she'd be ready for the first of their working sessions.

"Who do you have in mind for the man?" she asked him. "For what's-his-name? Stanley Kowalski?"

"Well, that's the other thing," he said. "I know there are two or three kids in the group who could probably handle it, but I've really come to miss performing – the hell, this'll be the last show, right? So I thought I'd do it myself."

Chapter Three

". . . Hello, Stanley," Lucy recited. "Here I am, all freshly bathed and scented, and feeling like a brand new human being!"

But instead of delivering the next line in his Stanley Kowalski voice and his menacing Stanley Kowalski slouch, Jack Halloran broke out of character and became her coach again. "No, look, dear," he said. "Let me try to explain something. We know the audience has to suspect from the start that Blanche is gonna go crazy; otherwise they'll never believe the final curtain. But I'm getting a little afraid you're gonna make her go crazy too soon. When you let hysteria come up into your face and your voice that way, you're robbing us of a lot of tension and suspense. You're kind of giving the whole show away, if you see what I mean."

"Well, of course I see, Jack," she said. "It's just that I wasn't aware of any – hysteria, that's all."

"Well, I may not have put it very well, but that's the idea. And another thing. We know Blanche hates Stanley; she's revolted by everything about him, and you've got that part of it right. But beneath the surface – unconsciously, or against her will – she's attracted to him. It's only an undercurrent, but it's gotta be in there if it's gonna pay off later. And I know you're aware of all this, baby, but the point is I don't think you've quite established it yet. Now, these next few lines are important, where she asks him to button up the back of her dress. And I don't want to see just a mockery of flirtation, the way you read it last time; I want to see at least a subtle element of real – you know – of real flirtation in there, too."

And all Lucy could do was tell him she would try. It was the third or fourth afternoon of their coaching sessions and she seemed to be losing confidence with each day, rather than gaining it. She had come to dread the very smell of the stage.

". . . Would you think it possible," she asked, a few lines later in the same scene, "that I was once considered to be – attractive?"

"Your looks are okay."

"I was fishing for a compliment, Stanley."

"I don't go in for that stuff."

"What stuff?"

"Compliments to women about their looks." Jack knew every nuance of the Stanley Kowalski role; he had played it in summer stock before. "I never met a woman that didn't know if she was good-looking or not without being told, and some of them give themselves credit for more than they've got. I once went out with a doll who said to me 'I am the glamorous type, I am the glamorous type.' I said 'So what?' "

"And what did she say then?"

"She didn't say nothing. That shut her up like a clam."

"Did it end the romance?"

"It ended the conversation – that was all. . . ."

"Jack, I don't think this is going to work," she told him as they climbed the driveway in the brilliant orange sunset of their last afternoon. "I don't see how I can possibly—"

"Look, I made a promise, didn't I?" And he slung one arm around her waist. Whenever he did that it made her feel safe and important. "I promised you that if I didn't think you could handle the part I'd tell you so. Well, listen, it's gonna be all right. Maybe there're still a couple of rough spots, but just wait. Tomorrow we'll have Julie and all the others working with us, and you'll begin to see what a difference real rehearsals can make. The play'll carry us along in its own momentum – make us all better than we thought we could be – and by opening night we'll have it licked."

"Is – Julie going to play Stella Kowalski, then?"

"Well, I kind of halfway tried to talk her out of it, because I know how tired she is, but she kept saying she'd rather work than rest. So I pretended to be very reluctant – and I mean it's true that I've been concerned about her nerves and everything – but in the end I said okay. And of course I'm delighted to have her. Julie's the kind of performer who can hold a whole show together with her bare hands."

That was the evening that Michael called up again, just before dinnertime. Laura answered the phone – "Hi, Daddy!" – and talked to him in a happy, chattering way for a few minutes before she covered the mouthpiece and handed the phone to Lucy. "He wants to talk to you, Mom. He sounds all better."

"Well, that's fine," Lucy told her. "Now, why don't you run along upstairs, dear, in case there are things Daddy and I need to discuss in private."

"What kind of things?"

"Well, I don't know; you know; grown-up things. Just go on upstairs, okay?"

Then she took up the phone and said "Hello, Michael. I'm – really glad you're out of that place."

"Good," he said. "Thanks. Still, I wonder if you have any idea what that particular place is like."

"Oh, I think I sort of do. I think anyone who's lived in New York has heard about Bellevue."

"Yeah, well, okay, except that Bellevue's about twenty-nine times worse than anyone who's lived in New York can possibly imagine. Never mind, though; I'm out. I'm all scrubbed down with antilice soap, delousing soap, and I'm on what they call an outpatient basis now – it's kind of like being on parole. I've gotta go back there once a week to get 'therapy' from some pompous little Guatemalan asshole in a purple suit. Oh, and I've got pills, too. I've got more different kinds of pills than you ever saw. And they're wonderful things, these pills: they keep your brains working even after your mind is dead."

She knew it was a mistake to let him go on this way – he was talking as if she were still his wife – but she didn't know what to say that would make him stop.

"No, but the worst part of all this," he said, "is what it's done to my record."

"Your 'record'? What record is that?" And she was instantly sorry she'd asked.

"Oh, Jesus, Lucy, don't be dense. Everybody in America's got a record – the FBI files are only one small part of it – and there's no hiding from it. There's no escaping it, ever. Oh, I imagine my record'll start *out* nicely enough, with stuff about Morristown and the Air Force and Harvard; then there'll be stuff about you and Laura, and about *Chain Store Age* and all the published poems – and I mean even the divorce'll look okay in there, because nobody cares about that kind of thing. But then all of a sudden: Whammo. It'll say 'Psychotic Episode, August, nineteen sixty.' There'll be some New York City policeman's signature, or his badge number, because it was the cops that brought me in, and there'll be some Bellevue flunky's signature too; and then, dear God, there'll be the signature of William fucking Brock –

166

concerned citizen, guardian of the public health and morals – because he's the son of a bitch who committed me. Oh, Lucy, don't you see what I'm saying? I'm a certified lunatic. I'll be a certified lunatic for the rest of my life."

"I think you're still very tired," she said, "and I don't think you really believe any of the crazy things you're saying."

"Wanna bet?" he asked her. "Wanna bet?"

"I want to get off the phone now," she told him, "before Laura starts worrying again. This hasn't been an easy time for her. But first I want to tell you something. I'm only going to say this once, so listen carefully. From now on, when you call Laura, don't ask to speak to me. Because if you do I'll refuse, and then we'll both be hurting Laura in a wholly unnecessary way. Is that clear?"

"But there are things that happen between a man and a woman in the dark," said Julie Pierce in the role of Stella, "that sort of make everything else seem – unimportant."

"What you are talking about," said Lucy Davenport in the role of Blanche, "is brutal desire – just – Desire! – the name of that rattle-trap streetcar that bangs through the Quarter, up one old narrow street and down another."

"Haven't *you* ever ridden on that streetcar?"

"It brought me here," Lucy said. "– Where I'm not wanted and where I'm ashamed to be."

"Then don't you think your superior attitude is a bit out of place?"

"I am not being or feeling at all superior, Stella. Believe me I'm not. It's just this. This is how I look at it. A man like that is someone to go out with – once – twice – three times, when the devil is in you. But live with? Have a child by?"

"I have told you I love him."

"Then I *tremble* for you. I just – *tremble* for you. . . . He acts like an animal, has an animal's habits! Eats like one, moves like one, talks like one! There's even something – subhuman . . . Yes, something apelike about him. . . . Thousands and thousands of years have passed him right by, and there he is – Stanley Kowalski – survivor of the Stone Age! Bearing the raw meat home from the kill in the jungle! And you – *you* here – waiting for him . . ."

"Okay," Jack Halloran called. "I think we can knock off now. Tomorrow we'll pick it up from Scene Five. Hey, Julie?"

"Yes, Jack?"

"You're really doing fine in there."

But he said nothing at all to Lucy, even when they were alone and plodding up the lumpy driveway together, slow with fatigue. He didn't put his arm around her, either.

"Well, so did you qualify?" Nancy Smith had asked her brother. And he'd said "No, but it didn't matter. In the end they faked-up the scores and qualified everybody."

Late that night they sat fully clothed on the edge of Jack's bed for what seemed a long time, as if each were waiting for the other to make the first move toward getting undressed.

"Know something, dear?" he said. "You might be able to learn a lot just from watching Julie work."

"Oh? Well, I – how do you mean?"

"Well, it's her whole – her whole performance. Notice her timing. She's never off by so much as half a beat. And notice how she understands the stage. She never looks lost on the stage except when the play calls for her to look lost; then she knows how to look lost as hell. I mean she's the kind of actress you find once in a – I don't know; once in a long while. She's the real thing."

And I'm not, Lucy wanted to say. And I'll never be, and you

168

know it, and all you're doing is using me in this play. You're using me and using me, and I hate you. I hate you. But all she said was "Well, I'll try to pay closer attention to her, then, in what little – what little time we have left."

They seemed to have hardly any time left at all – and with each rapidly vanishing day, right up into the dress rehearsal, Jack kept after her about what he called the hysteria in her face and voice.

"No, dear," he would say, coming quickly out of his Stanley Kowalski role. "You're still a little shrill in there – a little unbalanced. You'll have to try for more control in this speech, Lucy. You'll have to try for control as hard as Blanche *Dubois* is trying, okay? Okay. Let's take it again."

But a couple of hours before curtain time, on opening night, he walked into her house and kissed her in a way that suggested an impending triumph.

"Know what we're gonna do?" he said. "You and me?" And he ceremoniously pulled a bottle of bourbon out of a paper bag. "We're gonna have a drink. I think we've both earned this, don't you?"

And it might have been the whiskey, or it might have been that what Jack had promised about the momentum of the play came true for her at last, but Lucy made her way through that opening night with an authority she could never have foreseen. She was almost sure her face and voice didn't once betray hysteria too soon; she knew she established just the right blend of mock and real flirtation in the subtle early scene with Stanley; and she couldn't help noticing, if only with part of her mind, how tame and modest Julie Pierce's performance came to seem beside her own. Julie's role was secondary, after all: if anyone was going to hold this show together with her bare hands, it would have to be Lucy Davenport herself.

At certain quiet moments – times, for instance, when the play called for her to look lost on the stage – she would catch herself wondering if the Nelsons or the Maitlands, or all of them, might be in the audience. And she'd try to rid herself quickly of such thoughts – no real actress would let her attention drift like that – but she'd go on wondering anyway. She could almost feel their presence out there, two couples seated in separate parts of the darkness because they were strangers to each other – her "friends"; the people whose lives had changed her own. And if they had pitied her for years, as an unhappy wife and a poor little rich girl, then let them all sit back and take a look at her now.

She had a high, clear sense of doing everything right, and nobody could say she wasn't doing it alone. It was Lucy Davenport alone who brought Blanche Dubois from neuras-thenia and self-delusion into terror; and at last, with the final scene of the play, it was Lucy Davenport alone who set her adrift in madness of a kind no audience in the world could fail to believe, or fail to care about, or ever forget.

The thunderclap of applause became a long ovation that went on and on as the supporting actors gathered at the footlights to take their curtain calls. Lucy was crying, but she managed to stop at once – managed to arrange her face into a look of shyness and courtesy – when the moment came for her to walk out with Jack and stand there alone with him under the rising curtain. He clasped and held her hand as if to suggest to the crowd that they were really in love, and there was a renewal and swelling of applause that continued long after the curtain had fallen for the last time – people seemed to be calling for one more look at the two of them holding hands.

But Jack was already hurrying her through the dimly lighted bustle and disorder backstage.

"You were good, Lucy," he said as he steered her carefully

around a tall stepladder, heading for an outside door. "You did well." And that was all he said until they were out across the road and walking up the driveway, guided by the weak and wavering beam of his flashlight.

"There were – a couple of problems," he began. "Well, really only one problem."

"Jack," she said, "if you start talking about 'hysteria' again, I honestly don't think I'll be able to—"

"No, that part was okay. You had good control on that tonight. This is nothing specific; it's more of a general thing. And it's more important."

His arm was around her, but it didn't bring much comfort. "What I'm getting at," he said, "is that your whole performance tonight was – stagey. You were acting almost as if none of the rest of us were there. You kept kind of upstaging everybody else, all the way through, and the point is that's never a good idea because it shows. The audience can see it."

"Oh." And it may not have been the first time in her life that she'd felt shame all over her skin and deep inside her, too, crawling in her bowels – there must surely have been other such times in childhood, or in college, or even in the years since then – but it seemed now that never before had she fully understood the meaning of the word. This was shame. "Oh," she said again, and then in a small voice she said "So I made a fool of myself."

"Ah, Lucy, come on, I didn't mean anything like that," he told her. "Listen, it's no big deal. This happens all the time with beginners. Having a real audience out there is sort of intoxicating, and it makes a lot of people want to be 'stars,' you see, before they've learned to work with other actors. All you have to remember, dear, is that the theater is a communal enterprise. Hey, listen: whaddya say we go to your place and get some more of that good whiskey. That'll pick you up."

And they sat drinking in the living room for half an hour, but it didn't make the shame go away.

Lucy wasn't sure if her voice would work, but she tried it. "And I suppose Julie Pierce was the one who minded all my 'upstaging' the most?" she inquired.

"Nah, nah, Julie's a pro," he said. "She'll always understand this kind of thing. Besides, I don't think anybody 'minded' anything, dear. We all like you, and we're proud of you. You came in out of nowhere and learned an extremely difficult part, and you brought it off. I think you'll find ordinary people are nicer than you give them credit for being, Lucy – probably nicer than you've ever let yourself believe."

But her mind was far away, thinking of people who weren't so ordinary.

"Well, sure she hammed it up," Tom Nelson might well be saying to his wife as they went about their preparations for bed, "and sure she was embarrassing. Still, isn't it good that she's finally got something to do? And isn't it nice that she's fixed up with what's-his-name? The guy that runs the show?"

And in another, very different house, Paul Maitland might be fingering his mustache with a small, devilish smile as he said "What'd you think of Lucy?"

Then Peggy would say, "Yuck," and "Squaresville, man," and "Emotional City," and whatever other cool little disparagements she'd managed to pick up, along with her dirndl skirts and her gypsy friends, in her time as a child of bohemia.

"Would it be helpful," Jack said, "if I try to give you a few pointers about tomorrow night?"

"No. Please. I don't think I can bear any more pointers."

"Well, hell, I probably exaggerated the whole thing. I'd never've said anything if I'd known it'd make you feel so bad. Listen, though, Lucy. Can I tell you just one more thing?"

He came over to her chair and took her chin in his hand, tilting it up to make her look into his remarkably good-looking face. "None of this matters," he told her, and he winked. "Do you understand? None of it matters at all. It's only a dumb little summer-stock theater that nobody ever heard of. Okay?"

He let go of her face then and said "Feel like coming on up to the – up to the dorm with me?" And the hesitation in his voice told her at once that he wouldn't care if she said no.

"I don't think so, Jack; not tonight."

"Okay, then," he said. "Sleep well."

She was scrupulously careful to avoid any suggestion of wanting to be a 'star' as the second night's performance got under way. She took pains to be considerate of all the minor actors, and she almost wanted to evaporate in her scenes alone with Julie Pierce, so that Julie could get the most out of whatever it was that Julie wanted to do. All this, she kept telling herself, all this would soon be over.

But when she walked into the wings at the end of Scene Three, Jack Halloran intercepted her with an imploring look, incongruously dressed in Stanley Kowalski's bowling shirt.

"Listen, dear," he said. "Don't get mad at me, but listen. You're going off in the opposite direction this time. You're too subdued out there; you're too remote. And we may get away with it in these early scenes, but the point is you've gotta start pulling out the stops pretty soon, Lucy, or we're not gonna have any show at all tonight. You follow me?"

And she followed him. He was the director; he'd never been wrong before; and she'd spent most of this day regretting that she hadn't gone up to the dorm with him last night.

It was all a matter of balance – of going far but not too far – and Lucy was almost sure she achieved the right balance in the rest of that second performance.

But then she had to find ways of getting through the third night, and the fourth and the fifth – and sometimes the final curtain would fall before there was time for her to tell whether she'd achieved the right balance or not. Certain nights were better than others – she knew that – but by the end of the week she could no longer sort them out; couldn't remember which were which.

Her most vivid memory, when it was all over, was of going out for the curtain call with Jack after the final performance, and of holding hands for the people one last time. She wouldn't forget knowing she had better be happy to take this applause – stand here and take it however it came – because it was something that would never happen again.

Jack didn't have much to say to her backstage that night except that she'd done very well. Then he said "Oh, and listen, the kids're throwing a little party up in the dorm later on. Can you make that? Say about an hour from now?"

"Sure."

"Good. Well, look, I've gotta stay here and help 'em get started tearing down some of this stuff. You want to take the flashlight?"

"No, that's okay." And she assured him, meaning it as a wry little joke, that she was used to walking home alone in the dark.

The party, as she could have predicted, was less a celebration than a nice try. Jack seemed glad to see her there and so did Julie Pierce; so, too, did most others among the oddly assorted people she had come to think of as "the kids" – and several of them, carefully holding cans of beer or paper cups of wine, wanted to tell her what a pleasure it had been to know her this summer. From the sound of her own voice in repaying those compliments, Lucy knew she was doing pretty well; she was holding up nicely.

But she ached with tiredness. She wanted to go home and sleep – this whole damned summer had robbed her of privacy and silence – still, she knew it might look rude if she left early.

For what seemed half an hour she stood in a shadowed section of the room and watched Jack and Julie talking quietly together. It was only reasonable that they'd have things to discuss: Julie's New York audition would be coming up soon, and Jack would be in the city too, looking first for an apartment and then for whatever work he could find. ("I always try to spend as much time as I can in New York," he'd explained once, "because that's where the – you know – that's where the theater is.")

But when Lucy found she was trying *not* to watch them talk – when she'd begun willing herself to look into all other parts of the big room before allowing her eyes to go back to them, briefly and almost furtively – she knew it was time to get out of here.

She went around to all the people who'd been nice to her and wished them goodnight and good luck, and three or four of them kissed her cheek. Then she went up to Jack, who said "I'll give you a call tomorrow, dear, okay?" and to Julie Pierce, who told her she'd been "wonderful."

The next morning she drove into White Plains – it was the only town for miles around that had decent department stores – and there she bought two handsome, identical, dark-tan suitcases that cost a hundred and fifty dollars apiece.

When she'd brought them home she hid them away in her bedroom closet, so that Laura wouldn't find them and ask questions; then she settled herself in the living room and began to wait for Jack to call.

When the phone rang she sprang for it, but it was Pat Nelson.

"Lucy? I've been trying to call you all week but you're never home. Listen, we really enjoyed the play. You were *very* impressive."

175

"Oh, well, thanks, Pat, that's – very kind."

"Oh, and listen, Lucy." Pat lowered her voice to a husky murmur of girlish confidence. "This Jack Halloran of yours is really something. He's adorable. Will you bring him over to the house sometime?"

There was no call from the Maitlands, and Lucy supposed it had been foolish to imagine they would squander a nonunion carpenter's pay on theater tickets – let alone on tickets for some dumb little summer-stock theater that nobody ever heard of.

That afternoon she stood at the window to watch a straggling procession of New Tonapac Playhouse people setting out on the long walk to the train station. And from this distance they all did look like kids – boys and girls from far and wide with their cheap hand luggage and their Army duffel bags, brave entertainers who might travel for years before it occurred to them, or to most of them, that they weren't going anywhere.

Julie Pierce was not among them – but then, nobody would have expected her to be. Julie had undoubtedly chosen to stay here a day or two more, to get some rest for her celebrated nerves and begin to regain the strength she would need in meeting the challenges of a real career.

Then at dusk the phone rang again.

"Lucy? This is Harold Smith?" Some people always spoke their names in the form of a question, as if you might not think them worthy of a statement. "I don't know how to tell you this," he began, "because I haven't quite recovered yet, but Nancy and I thought you were absolutely marvelous. We were over-whelmed."

"Well, that's – awfully nice of you, Harold."

"Isn't it the damndest thing," he said, "how you can live across the yard from somebody for years, be on friendly terms and all that, and never even know who they are? Oh, listen, I'm

176

saying this all wrong and I knew I would; all I'm trying to do is convey our – our very great admiration, Lucy, and our thanks. For what you gave us."

She said that was the nicest thing she'd heard in a long time; then, shyly, she asked him which performance they had seen.

"We saw it twice – the first night, and then again the night before last. And I couldn't begin to make comparisons because they were both tremendous; both great."

"Well, actually," she said, "I was told I sort of overdid everything on that first night. I was sort of told I'd embarrassed people by trying to be a 'star' or something."

"Ah, that's crazy," he said impatiently. "That's just crazy talk. Whoever told you that is outa their mind. Because listen. Oh, listen, baby, you were in *command* of that stage. You went straight for everybody's throat and you never let go. You *were* a star. And I want to tell you something: I'm not very big in the crying department, but when that curtain came down you had me crying out there like a little bastard. Nancy too. And I mean for Christ's sake, Lucy, isn't that what the theater's for?"

She managed to fix an adequate supper for Laura and herself, though she could only hope Laura didn't notice that she ate almost nothing.

It was after eight o'clock when Jack called her at last. "Dear, I can't ask you up to the dorm tonight because I've gotta be an accountant," he said, "and it'll probably keep me up till morning. There're all these accounts to be settled, you see, for the whole company, and I've been neglecting most of 'em all summer. This is one aspect of show business I was never cut out for."

And maybe he was a good actor, even a born actor, but any child could have told from the texture of his voice that he was lying.

For almost the whole of the following day she walked around

the house with her knuckles pressed to her lips – the very mannerism specified, in the stage directions of the play she knew by heart, as being characteristic of Blanche Dubois.

"Still up to my neck in paperwork, I'm afraid," Jack told her on the phone that evening, and she wanted to say Oh, well, look: let's forget it. Why don't you just forget everything and go back to wherever you came from and leave me alone?

But then he said "Be okay if I come down to your place for a drink tomorrow? Say about four?"

"Well," she said, "sure, that'd be nice. And I've got something for you."

"Got something for me? What's that?"

"Well, I think I'd rather have it be a surprise."

Some kind of private, giggling business with the Smith girls kept Laura far away from the house all afternoon, and Lucy was grateful for that; still, at the moment when she shyly brought the suitcases into the living room and up to Jack Halloran's chair, she almost wished Laura could have been there with her to see his eyes growing as round in wonder as those of a little boy on Christmas morning.

"Son of a bitch," he said in a hushed voice. "Son of a bitch, Lucy, those are the two prettiest things I ever saw." And she knew Laura would have liked that.

"Well, I thought they might be useful," she said, "because you travel a lot."

"'Useful,'" he repeated. "Know something? I've wanted stuff like this as long as I can remember." Putting down his glass, he reached forward and unfastened the clasps of one of the bags to open it and inspect its interior. "Built-in coat hangers and everything," he announced. "And my God, look at all these separate compartments. Lucy, I don't know how to – don't know how to thank you."

One of the small misfortunes of being a rich girl, and she'd known it all her life, was that people would often exaggerate their pleasure when you gave expensive gifts. It came from embarrassment, because they couldn't offer anything comparable in return, and it nearly always made her feel foolish, but it hadn't ever stopped her from making the same mistake the next time.

When she'd brought in fresh drinks and settled herself across from him again, it became increasingly clear that they didn't have much to say to each other. They couldn't even seem to meet each other's eyes, except at long intervals, as if each were afraid of the other's pleasant, precarious smile.

Then she said "So when are you planning to leave, Jack?"

"Oh, sometime tomorrow, I guess."

"Think the car'll make it to the city?"

"Oh, sure. Got me up here, it'll get me back. No, all I'm dreading now is the business of finding a place to live. Have to go through that every year, if I want to stay in New York. Still, it always works out; I always manage to hole up for the winter."

"And this year it'll be especially nice, won't it," she said, "because you'll be holing up for the winter with Julie Pierce."

The look on his face gave everything away. He seemed to know at once that there would be no further point in trying to keep his secret.

"Well, and so what?" he said. "Why shouldn't I?"

"If memory serves," Lucy began, "she's way too skinny and she hasn't got any tits at all. She may be talented as hell but there's something a little cracked upstairs."

"That's in very poor taste, Lucy," he said when she was finished. "I'd think a girl of your class would have much better taste than that. I thought it was something you people were born with."

"Ah. And what are *you* people born with? An endless capacity for lust and betrayal, I imagine, and a crafty little talent for inflicting senseless pain. Right?"

"Wrong. We're born with an instinct for survival, and it doesn't take most of us long to learn that nothing else matters in the world." Then he said "Ah, Jesus, Lucy, this is dumb. We're talking like a couple of actors. Listen: is there really any reason why you and I can't be friends?"

"It's often occurred to me," she said, "that 'friend' is about the most treacherous word in the language. I think you'd better get out of here now, Jack, okay?"

And the worst part – for both of them, it seemed – was that he had to make his exit with the two new suitcases hanging from his hands on either side.

She was cleaning up the kitchen the next morning, trying and trying to put him out of her mind, when he came to stand outside the screen door in exactly the way he had appeared the first time, a strikingly handsome young man with his thumbs in his jeans.

When she let him into the kitchen he said "Casimir Micklaszevics."

"What?"

"Casimir Micklaszevics. That's my name. Would you like me to write it down?"

"No," she said. "That won't be necessary. I'll always remember you as – Stanley Kowalski."

And he awarded her a wink. "Not bad, Lucy," he said. "Pretty nice little curtain-line you came up with there. Guess I could never top a line like that. Well, anyway, listen: Have a good life, okay?" And he was gone as abruptly as he'd come.

Later, from a living-room window, she saw the snout of his old car coming around the trees at the far side of the dormitory building. A gleam of sunlight eclipsed its windshield, and she turned quickly away and crouched and covered her eyes with both hands: she didn't want to see Julie Pierce riding beside him.

Later still, when she lay on her bed and gave in at last to the kind of crying Tennessee Williams described as "luxurious," she wished she had allowed him to write down his name. Casimir what? Casimir who? And she knew now that her nice little curtain-line about Stanley Kowalski had been worse than cheap and spiteful – oh, worse; worse. It had been a lie, because she would always and always remember him as Jack Halloran.

Chapter Four

When Lucy finally did decide where to go, it wasn't very far away. She found a solid, comfortable house at the northern edge of Tonapac, almost on the Kingsley town line, and arranged to buy it at once. She had been saying "rent" for so many years, aloud and in her mind, that the very act of walking into a bank to buy a house gave her a sense of brave beginnings.

She liked everything about this new house. It was high and wide without being too big; it was "civilized." No neighbors were visible on any side because of tall shrubs and trees, and she liked that, too; but what she liked best was that there would now be only a short stretch of gently curving blacktop road between her door and the Nelsons'. She could walk over there any time she happened to feel like it, or the Nelsons could walk over here. On summer afternoons whole groups of the Nelsons' guests might come strolling along in the dappled sunshine of this road, laughing and carrying their drinks, calling "We want Lucy! Let's get Lucy!" and so the possibilities of romance were almost infinite.

The Maitlands would be more remote now; but then, she had come to think of them as being more remote in the other sense as well. If they wanted to persist in their willful poverty – if Paul was stubbornly determined to go on shunning the Nelsons and all the bright opportunities implicit in the world of the Nelsons' parties – then it might be only sensible to leave them behind.

She knew Laura would miss the Smith girls, and possibly the ragged expanse of the old estate itself, but she promised to take her back there for visits as often as she wanted to go. And the great practical advantage of staying within the limits of Tonapac, as Lucy explained several times to her mother and others on the phone, was that Laura wouldn't have to change schools.

Within a very few days she bought a whole houseful of good new furniture, along with a few antiques of the kind called "priceless," and she bought a new car. There was no reason why any of the things in her life should not be the best she could find.

All she knew about the New School for Social Research, in New York, was that it was an adult-education university. There had been rumors, some years ago, that it was a haven for old-line communists, but she'd never minded that because she had often considered that she herself, if born a decade earlier, could easily have been an old-line communist too. Some of her comrades might have despised her for her money, though her modest way of living would always have been beyond reproach, but others might have esteemed her all the more for it. Even in her own time she had never been impatient with communist talk except when it came from someone like Bill Brock, and that was because she'd always suspected that Bill Brock would be among the first to fold up under any kind of political pressure.

But now the surprisingly thick spring catalogue of the New School lay open before her on the new coffee table in the new living room of her new house, and she was taking her time over it, beginning to plan a new life.

The departmental section called "Creative Writing" offered five or six courses, each with a paragraph or two of descriptive material, and it didn't take her long to figure out that each instructor must have written his own course description in a painstaking effort to compete with the others.

One or two of the teachers were writers she'd heard of but hadn't read; the rest were unknown to her. In the end she settled on one of the strangers, someone named Carl Traynor, and marked him heavily in the margin with her pencil. His credentials weren't very striking ("Stories in numerous magazines and several anthologies") but she'd found herself coming back time and again to his course description until she had to acknowledge it as her favorite.

This is a course in writing short stories. There will be assigned reading of stories by established authors, but the main part of each weekly class will be devoted to critical evaluation of students' manuscripts. It is expected that students will attain a working knowledge of the craft, and the ultimate aim of the course is to help each new writer find his own literary voice.

For days, waiting for the spring semester to begin, Lucy was almost at peace with the idea of herself as a writer. She pored over the two stories she had managed to finish during the past year or so, making small changes until it began to seem that any further revision might spoil them. The stories were there; they were adequate, and they were hers.

When you wrote it didn't matter if hysteria sometimes came up in your face and voice (unless, of course, you let it find its way into your "literary voice") because writing was done in merciful privacy and silence. Even if you were partly out of your mind it might turn out to be all right: you could try for control even harder than Blanche Dubois was said to have tried, and with luck you could still bring off a sense of order and sanity on the page for the reader. Reading, after all, was a thing done in privacy and silence too.

The morning was unusually mild and clear for February, and it felt grand to be walking down lower Fifth Avenue. This calm and stately neighborhood was where Michael Davenport had always said he wanted to live, "as soon as one of the plays pays off"; one day long ago she had made the mistake of reminding him that they could move here anytime – right away, if they felt like it – and that had brought on one of his fiercely frowning silences as they walked all the way home to Perry Street, letting her know that she'd broken the rules of their old agreement once again.

She had remembered the New School as a dark, Soviet-Union kind of place, and that part of it was still there, but now it was dominated by a new adjacent building, bigger and taller and all made of steel and glass, as bright and greedy-looking as the United States itself.

A silent elevator took her up to the appointed floor and she walked shyly into her classroom: a long conference table with chairs placed around it. Some students were already seated, looking uncertain about whether to smile at one another, and others were gathering. Most of them were women – this was disappointing because Lucy had dimly hoped for a roomful of attractive men – and except for one or two young girls they were all in middle age. She had a quick general impression, possibly mistaken, of housewives whose children were grown and gone, freeing them at last to pursue the ambition of their lives. Of the few men, the most conspicuous was a blunt-faced, truck-driverly fellow wearing a green work shirt with some company's insignia on its left breast pocket – probably the kind of writer who would want to employ the word "fuck" as often as possible in his

185

clumsy stories – and he had struck up a tentative conversation with the smaller man beside him, who was so pale and bland in his business suit and his pink rimless glasses that Lucy imagined he must be an accountant or a dentist. Farther down the table sat a much older man, with white hair bristling from his scalp and tufting in his nostrils; he had probably come out of retirement to try his hand at this game, and his humorous lips were already moving very slightly as if in rehearsal for his self-appointed role as class comedian.

The last to come in, and to take his place self-consciously at the head of the table, was the teacher. He was tall and thin and looked at first like a boy, though Lucy could tell he was well over thirty by his slump, by the slight tremor of his hands and the heavy shadows under his eyes. "Melancholy" was the first word that occurred to her, and she decided that might not be a bad quality to have in a writing teacher, assuming there'd be livelier qualities too.

"Good morning," he said. "My name's Carl Traynor, and I expect it'll take me a little time to find out who all of you are. Maybe the best way to begin is to call this roll they've given me; then if possible – and I don't want anyone feeling obliged to do this, if you'd rather not – but if possible you might say a few words about yourself and your background when your name is called." His voice was pleasantly deep and steady, and Lucy could feel herself beginning to trust him.

When he called her name she said "Yes; here. I'm thirty-four. I'm divorced" – and she wondered at once why she'd felt it necessary to say that – "and I live in Putnam County with my daughter. I've had very little writing experience except in college, many years ago."

But at least half of the other students declined to provide personal information, and Lucy knew that if her name had come later in the alphabetical order she would have made that choice too – she should have made it anyway. Reticence was important in a room where any amount of emotional nakedness might soon be on display. She could only wonder now if the odd little blunder of saying "I'm divorced" would make her uncomfortable as long as she stayed in this group.

With the roll call out of the way, Carl Traynor settled down to deliver his opening remarks. "Well," he began, "I think I could probably tell you everything I know about fiction writing in half an hour – and I'd be happy to give that a try, because there's nothing I like better than showing off." Here he waited for a laugh that didn't come, and his hands began to tremble more noticeably on the table. "But this isn't a lecture course. The only way any of us can learn this craft is by saturating ourselves in examples of it, in and out of print, and then trying to put the best of what we've found into our own work."

He went on at some length to explain what he considered the value of a "workshop" like this: each manuscript would attain a kind of publication, in that it would be evaluated by fifteen people. Then he talked about the kind of criticism he would expect from this group. Constructive criticism was always to be desired, he said, except when it amounted to a hedging of bets or a pulling of punches; still, "honesty" was a word he had come to distrust because it was too often used as a license for harshness. He hoped they would be able to achieve dispassion without discourtesy.

"We're all strangers here today," he said, "but over the next sixteen weeks we'll come to know each other pretty well. And there's something volatile in the very nature of a writing class; we'll have raised voices here sometimes, and hurt feelings, too. So how's this for a guiding principle: The work is more important than the personalities. Let's be friends if we can, but let's not be sweethearts."

RICHARD YATES

And once again there was silence where he'd expected laughter. He had put both hands out of sight now, dropping one of them to his leg under the table and sinking the other into his coat pocket. Lucy thought she had never seen a teacher so ill at ease. If talking made him nervous, why did he talk so much?

And he was still talking, though she might have stopped listening if he hadn't brought his talk around to what he called "the procedure."

"Now, unfortunately," he said, "the New School doesn't make mimeograph facilities available to any of these writing courses, so it won't be possible for me to give out copies of each story to be read for the following week's class. That would be much the best way, of course, but we're stuck with things as they are. All we can do here is have the stories read aloud, either by their authors or by me, and base our discussion on what we've heard."

This was bad. Lucy had assumed her manuscripts would be read, like real stories, and that copies of them would then come back to her with written comments by the readers. Having them only listened to would be inadequate and hazardous – a whole sentence might fall out of the listener's mind before the next sentence began – and besides, it would be too much like working on the stage.

"Several of you sent in stories ahead of time," Carl Traynor was saying, "so I've been able to choose one for this morning's class. Mrs. Garfield?" and he peered uncertainly down the table. "Would you prefer to read this piece for us yourself, or—"

"No, I'd rather have you read it," said one of the matronly women. "I like your voice."

And it wasn't easy for Carl Traynor to hide his pleasure; this might have been the first nice thing anybody had said to him in months. "Okay, then," he said. "This is a fifteen-page manuscript, and the title is 'Renewal.' " Then in a voice that seemed overly measured and sonorous, as if to prove itself worthy of Mrs. Garfield's liking, he began to read.

Spring was late that year. Scarcely a crocus had yet emerged from the few patches of earth amid the long, gray spaces of slowly melting snow, and all the trees were bare.

At dawn a stray dog loped down the homely main street of the town, sniffing for signs of life, and from a distance, across the plains, came the lonely, mournful wail of a train whistle.

After what seemed about two pages the author introduced a boarding house in the poorer section of town, meticulously describing both the house and its neighborhood; then she brought the reader inside to discover a twenty-three-year-old man named Arnold in the slow and difficult process of waking up. Arnold was said to have had a bad night of drinking and of "loss." But the reader, or listener, had to follow him through every step of his morning ritual – fumbling to make coffee on an old hot-plate, sipping it, taking a shower in a rusty tub and putting on the kind of clothes suggesting the lower middle class – before learning what it was that he'd lost. His young wife had left him a month ago, because of his "wild ways," and gone back to stay with her parents in another town. Now Arnold climbed into his "battered" pickup truck and drove to that town, where he found that both parents were conveniently away from home for the day.

" 'Think we could have a talk, Cindy?' " he asked the girl, and they had one. It didn't last long, but it was a "good" talk, because each of them said what the other most wanted to hear, and Mrs. Garfield's story came to an end with their heartfelt embrace.

"So that's it," Carl Traynor said, looking tired. "Any comments?"

"I think it's a beautiful story," one of the women said. "The theme of renewal is announced in the title, it's developed in the nature descriptions – the renewal of the earth with the coming of spring – and it finds its resolution in the renewal of the young people's marriage. I was deeply moved."

"Oh, I agree," another woman said. "And I want to congratulate the author. I have only one question: if she can write as well as this, why does she consider herself a student?"

Then it was the turn of the truck-driverly man, whose name was Mr. Kelly. "I had a lot of trouble with the opening," he said. "I think it's much too slow. We gotta get the weather and the town and the dog and the train whistle and God only knows what else before we even get the boarding house, and then even after the boarding house we gotta wait too long before we get the kid. I don't know why we couldn't've gotten the kid right away and all the other stuff later.

"But my main problem," he went on, "is with the dialogue at the end. I don't think hardly anybody ever says exactly what they mean the way these kids do, with one person feeding the next line to the other. In the movies you might get away with lines like that because there'd be all this sweet music coming up on the soundtrack to let people know it's the end of the show. But this isn't the movies. All we've got here is ink and paper, so the writer's gonna have to work an awful lot harder to get the dialogue right.

"And even then – even then I'm not sure if talk alone is gonna do the job. I'm not sure if anybody's life ever got turned around by talk alone. Seems to me we need some kind of a thing in there too. I don't suppose a crocus'd work because it'd be a little heavily on the symbolic side, and I guess we don't want the girl telling the boy she's pregnant because that'd take the whole story away in another direction; but something. An incident; an event; something unexpected that rings true. Well, hell, I guess I'm shooting my mouth off."

"No you're not," said the white-haired man. "You're making sense." And he turned to the teacher. "I'm with Mr. Kelly all the way down the line on this one. He's said everything I wanted to say."

When most of the other students had been heard from – there were several who abstained from comment – it was time for Mr. Traynor's summing up. He talked for what seemed twenty minutes in an alternately smooth and hesitant voice, repeatedly glancing at his wristwatch, and all he did was try to appease every difference of opinion in the room. At first it seemed clear that he sided with Mr. Kelly – he reviewed each of Mr. Kelly's points and suggested that Mrs. Garfield might do well to take note of them – but then he began making concessions to the women who'd been deeply moved. He, too, he said, found it strange that Mrs. Garfield considered herself a student, but he was glad she did because otherwise they might not have the pleasure and the benefit of her presence here.

"Well, okay," he said when he was finished – or rather when his watch told him he had fulfilled his day's obligation to the New School – "I guess that's all for this week."

It wasn't much. It seemed scarcely worth the effort of having come all the way in from Tonapac. But Lucy was willing to believe it might get better; and besides, she had nothing else to do.

The second or third week's story was by one of the young girls – a slim, pretty girl who frowned and blushed and stared at her clasped hands on the table throughout Mr. Traynor's reading.

191

It was a ginger-aley day. As Jennifer wandered among the old campus buildings she had grown to love during the past three years – almost four now, she reminded herself – she couldn't help feeling it was the kind of day when something wonderful might happen at any moment.

And it did. In the student cafeteria she met a wonderful-looking boy she'd never seen before: he had recently transferred here as a senior from another college. They "had coffee" and spent the afternoon walking and talking, getting along wonderfully well. The boy owned a blue MG that he drove with "admirable" skill, and he took her to a wonderful restaurant in a neighboring town. In the candlelight, over dishes with names that were given in correctly accented French (though Mr. Traynor had trouble pronouncing them anyway), Jennifer found herself thinking "This could be a real relationship." Back at school they strolled together into the deep shadows behind her residence hall, and there on the grass, for a long time, they made out.

Lucy could remember "making out" as a wartime expression for getting laid; she didn't know until now, in the context of this story, that for a later generation of girls it had come to mean necking or petting – maybe unfastening your "bra" for a boy and maybe letting his hand stray into your pants, but nothing more.

Jennifer invited the boy up to her room "to have some tea," and that was where everything went terribly wrong. He was crude. He wanted to go to bed with her right away, without even being nice to her first, and when she declined he "became another person, more maniac than man." He shouted at her. He called her names too horrible to be recorded, even in memory, and as his violence mounted she cowered in fear, but luckily there was a heavy pair of scissors on her dresser: she snatched it up and held it tight in both hands, aiming the point of it at his face. When he'd left the room at last, slamming the door, she found that all she could do was curl up under the covers and weep. She understood now that this boy was a mentally ill person, seriously disturbed, badly in need of professional help – and that might also explain the strangeness of his having changed colleges in senior year. Sometime toward morning she remembered her father's wise and gentle voice: "We must always be considerate of those less fortunate than ourselves." And her last thought, just before sleep, was that a real relationship would have to wait.

Several women around the table offered guarded praise for the economy and swiftness of the writing, and one said she'd enjoyed the restaurant scene, though she added quickly that she couldn't say why.

Then Mr. Kelly was called on, but he only folded his big arms across his company shirt and said he'd rather not say anything today.

It was left to Mr. Kaplan, the dentist – or accountant-looking man, to do the main part of the job. "It struck me as a very immature piece of work," he said. "There's more unintentional silliness revealed all through it – and I mean on the author's part, not the character's – than I would have thought possible in anything written by an adult. When something as serious as that is wrong in a story, it seems to me that no amount of technical competence is going to help."

"I'll go along with all that," the old man said, "and I'll tell you something else: I wouldn't mind hearing the *boy's* version of the story. I'd like to know how he felt when she pulled the scissors on him."

"Well, but she was terrified," one of the women said. "He was wholly out of control. For all she knew she could have been raped."

"Ah, raped my ass," the old man said. "I'm sorry, lady, but this is a story about prick-teasing and that's *all* it is. Oh, and another thing: I never saw a ginger-aley day and neither did you."

Lucy was almost afraid to look at the girl who'd written the thing, but she risked a glance. No longer blushing, the girl's face was set in a calm shape of disdain now; she had even managed a wan little smile suggesting tolerance and pity for all the fools in this room and in the world.

The girl was okay; she would survive the morning; and Mr. Traynor seemed to know it. He didn't even chide the old man for unnecessary roughness, though that would have been in keeping with his opening-day stricture against "discourtesy" in criticism; instead, he made a chuckling observation that some kinds of material would always be more controversial than other kinds. Then he told the girl her story probably did need work. "If you can find ways to soften the tone of self-righteousness here," he said, "or of ap*par*ent self-righteousness, you may have a more satisfying — a more satisfying statement."

The first and lesser of Lucy's two stories, "Miss Goddard and the World of Art," was presented the following week. She sat stiff with fear as Traynor read it aloud, though she had to admit he read it well enough; the trouble was that many small mistakes in it, all unrecognized before, were now made clear in the sound of his voice. When it was over she felt weak; she wanted to hide; she could only hope Mr. Kelly wouldn't choose to remain silent again today.

And he didn't: he was the first to speak. "Well, this time we've got some dignity here for a change," he said, and it struck her at once that "dignity" was an uncommonly lovely word. "This lady understands sentences — that's rare enough — and she knows how to make them work together, which is even more unusual. You get a lot of strength in writing like this, and a lot of grace, and a lot of – well, I already said dignity, but that's in there too.

"As for the substance of the story, though, I'm not so sure. I mean what do we have? We have this little rich girl who doesn't like boarding school because the other girls make fun of her all the time, and she doesn't like going home on vacations either because she's an only child and her parents are all wrapped up in each other. Then she's befriended by this unconventional young art-teacher girl who tells her she's got a natural talent for drawing, and for a minute or two there I thought we might have some kind of lesbian story on our hands, but that was a wrong guess. The teacher helps the girl find self-esteem through art, so in the end the girl comes to realize she can face her life after all.

"And that may be part of the trouble right there: basically it's what used to be called a come-to-realize story, and that was a commercial formula that went out of business when the big slick fiction magazines folded up after television came in.

"No, but never mind that," he amended quickly. "That's secondary, and it may be a cheap line of criticism anyway. I think all I'm trying to say" – and he frowned hard in the effort of choosing the words – "all I'm trying to say is that I'm afraid I got a kind of who-cares feeling out of this. Very strong writing, fine writing; still, the material kept making me think Yeah, yeah, I get it, but who cares?"

And others, up and down the table, seemed to agree with both parts of Mr. Kelly's opinion. That made it an easy day for Carl Traynor: there was nothing to challenge the timidity of his leadership. There were no conflicts for him to mollify or retreat from, and his summing-up required nothing as brave as an original idea.

But Lucy kept coming back to the New School every week because there was a chance that her second and more ambitious story might be read aloud. She needed to know what George Kelly and Jerome Kaplan and one or two others would have to say about it. And she was obliged to wait through a good many other people's stories, with their bland or tumultuous critical discussions, but eventually it happened.

"We have another piece by Mrs. Davenport this morning," Traynor announced. "It's twenty-one pages, and the title is 'Summer Stock.'"

This time she could hear no mistakes in the pages being read. She was confident that her sentences would again be acclaimed, and that the new material would leave nobody able to ask who cared. Toward the end she even found herself moved by it – there was a faint swelling in her throat – as if it had been written by someone else.

"Well, okay," George Kelly said when it was over. "Once again I can't fault the language – this lady controls her language like a pro – and this time the story's a lot more interesting, too. We have this young divorced woman falling in love with this summer-theater director, and all that part is plausible and well-developed. The sexual episodes are as tastefully done as anything I've read along that line, and they're very strong and convincing too. So the man talks her into taking the most difficult part in an important play, and she knows she's not ready for it but does it anyway and exhausts herself; then, even before she's recovered from that, she finds out she's lost the man to a younger girl – and that's plausible too because it's been in the cards from the beginning – so everything's over. I think it's very good stuff.

"My only problem" – and here he settled back for the second part of his critique, while Lucy set her bite – "my only problem is that I didn't know what I was doing in the last three or four pages, or however many it is – the part that comes after the man takes off with the girl. I couldn't see what there was to find in those pages except more and more words about the woman's state of mind. There's this little philosophical essay about betrayal and loneliness, and you can't work abstract material like that into fiction, or at least I've never thought you could. Then we're supposed to believe she's afraid she'll go crazy, like her ex-husband, and that's boring because we know she won't; and we even have to follow her into fooling around with ideas of suicide, which is even more of a waste of time because she's never going to do a thing like that. Oh, there are a few nice moments in this section, like the little girl coming home from school for the peanut-butter sandwich, but there's no reason why those things couldn't have been worked in earlier, back in the body of the story. Mostly, all we have in this last part is the woman being sorry for herself in a whole lot of different ways. There's a word for this kind of thing, and if I had a better vocabulary I'd know it. Wait – 'maudlin.' Okay?

"And I hate to bring this up again, Mrs. Davenport, because I didn't even like having to mention it the last time, but this time I felt you were trying to bend all your good work out of shape just to bring it around into the formula of one more come-to-realize story. You want to tell us the woman finds she's been 'strengthened' by what's happened to her, and nobody's going to believe that because it's nonsense. What's the deal? Has anybody with any brains ever said unhappiness is beneficial? And I wouldn't want you to claim she's been 'weakened,' either, because neither one of those terms has any bearing. Neither one is appropriate. Matter of fact, the distinction between strong people and weak people always falls apart under scrutiny anyway, and everybody knows it, and that's why it's always been too sentimental an idea for a good writer to trust.

"So, look. What happens to your woman is that she's let down. We can assume she feels lousy about it, and I guess that's all we can assume, but that's plenty. That's the story. All you have to do, Mrs. Davenport, is cut away practically everything you wrote after the man takes off with the girl, and I think you'll be in business."

Mr. Kaplan cleared his throat and said "I liked the suitcases. I thought the suitcases were an excellent touch." And one of the older women said she'd liked the suitcases too.

"Mr. Kelly?" Lucy said after class that day, cornering him near the drinking fountain in the corridor. "I want to thank you for being so helpful with my stories. Both of them."

"Well, it's been a pleasure," he said. "I'm glad you're not mad at me. Excuse me." And he turned away to take a long, gulping drink of water, as if all that classroom talk had left him badly parched.

As he wiped his wet mouth on his sleeve she asked him, in the shy and respectful manner she had learned at the Nelsons' parties, what he "did." And it turned out that he didn't drive a truck; he was an elevator repairman, working mostly in tall buildings.

"That must be very dangerous."

"Nah, nah. They give us about twenty-seven times as many safety devices as we ever need in those shafts; we might as well be typewriter mechanics, except we're better paid. Thing is, though, all my life I've wanted to work with my brains."

"Well, it seems to me," she said, "that you work with your brains very well."

"Yeah, okay, but I meant for a living, you see. Work with my brains for a living. That's a little harder to arrange, if you see what I mean."

She saw what he meant. Then she said "When are we going to have something of yours in the class?"

"Well, that's not easy to say. Maybe not at all this year. I'm working on this very long novel – too long, I think; it may be out of control – and Carl told me I could take a few excerpts out of it for the class; find episodes or sections in it that might work as stories. Sounded good when he said it, but the trouble is I keep going over it and over it, and I can't find anything that works like that. It's all one big – you know – one big story."

"Well, it may not have been very good advice in the first place," Lucy said. "I'm afraid I don't have much confidence in Mr. Traynor."

"*Oh*, no." And George Kelly looked troubled. "No, you don't want to underestimate Carl Traynor. I've read four of his stories in magazines, and he's good. He's damn good. I mean, this boy's the real thing."

Julie Pierce, Paul Maitland, Tom Nelson, and all the more notable guests at the Nelsons' parties – how had she come to know so many real-thing people in her life? And what in God's name did you have to "do" to earn an accolade like that?

George Kelly was taking leave of her now with what seemed an exaggerated proletarian courtesy: he might as well have been holding a cloth cap at his chest with both hands. "Well," he said, backing away. "Listen. Been very nice talking to you, Mrs. Davenport."

She spent an hour or two walking around the Village that afternoon, surprised at every turn to discover how much things had changed. And it wasn't an aimless walk: she was looking for what she had come to think of as "material."

Far to the west on Perry Street she found the house where she and Michael Davenport had lived long ago, but it was almost a different house now – surely it couldn't have been as shabby as this in the old days. All the mailbox locks were smashed, and the sparse, carelessly lettered, hastily Scotch-taped names of tenants suggested it had become a place for transients.

Even so, as she lingered in the dirty vestibule, there was enough of the old house left to provide a flood of memories. Bill Brock's loud voice still echoed here, and she could still see Michael looking so dense he didn't even seem to know she knew that he was aching for Diana Maitland with every breath. There had always been kissing in this vestibule late at night, because Diana liked to kiss. She would kiss men and girls alike in the same swift, sweet little way that meant nothing beyond goodwill. There, she seemed to say. You're nice. I like you.

Then Bill Brock would put his arm around her and take her home to his place, "their" place, over across Abingdon Square, and Lucy always knew what a torture it must be for Michael to think of them there together.

Well, yes; there might be a story in those old times – the four young people in their separateness, with their secrets. Bill Brock could be the least important character, if she found him distasteful to write about, or she could change him into someone else – no; better keep him as he was, because much of the irony would arise from the riddle of Diana Maitland's being in love with such a man. The focus of the story would be on Diana, on how she could flirt around and draw attention to herself for hours in ways that nobody ever minded, because everybody knew what an exceptional girl she was. The protagonist would be the young wife (first-person? third-person?), and the sad young husband, possibly giving intimations even then of emotional wreckage, could serve as a kind of – well, never mind; she could work it all out when she got home.

But the idea had begun to seem thin even before she was back in Tonapac that night, and she sat in her expensive house feeling untalented. Except for George Kelly's qualified praise, and for an occasional grace-note of approval from Mr. Kaplan, nobody had yet given her any encouragement. Even the "dignity" of her sentences might be only a consequence of her having gone to private schools, and so there was still no reason to suppose she could be a writer at all. She might now spend a month or two at work on this Perry Street story only to find it falling apart on every page, in every paragraph, until she came to realize it amounted to nothing – and how would that be, Mr. Kelly, for the come-to-realize story of the year?

Fretfully, she couldn't even decide whether or not to go on with the New School course. Now that her two stories had been read and discussed there was no real reason to stay: Traynor could scarcely do much to help her find her "literary voice" in the few remaining sessions. Still, if she dropped out it might be interpreted by the others as a selfish and even a snobbish thing to do.

And so it was the fear of seeming to be a snob that drove her into New York for the following week's class – and it wasn't the first time in her life that the fear of seeming to be a snob impelled her, perversely, to become one.

She sat blowing thin, disdainful jets of cigarette smoke all through the reading of that week's manuscript, and she felt she ought to be congratulated for heroic patience as the critical discussion limped and fumbled its way around the table. She wasn't sure she'd be able to endure the teacher's summing-up but it was mercifully brief that day, and the moment his voice stopped she knew it was time for action. Everyone else in the room was still seated, almost as if they were waiting for it – asking for it – when Lucy Davenport shoved back her chair and stood up.

"This class," she announced, "this class is amateur night in Dixie. I'm sorry, Mr. Traynor, because I know you're a decent

201

man, but we've sat around here accommodating each others' mediocrity all these weeks; that's all we've done. And I suppose there may be a certain therapeutic benefit in activity like that, for those who need it, but it has nothing to do with writing and it never will. Can anybody really believe a fiction editor would spend three minutes on any of the stories we've had here? *Any* of them?"

She was dizzy, and her mouth was dry. George Kelly looked as embarrassed as if she had broken an important, implicit rule of conduct – as if she had fallen down drunk in his home, in front of his wife and family.

"Well, okay, I'm sorry," she said, meaning it mostly for George Kelly, though she couldn't quite raise her eyes from the table to face him. "I'm sorry." And then she hurried out of the room.

If she'd timed her outburst a few minutes earlier she might have made her escape alone, but now she had to ride down in the elevator with a dead-silent cluster of other women from the class.

Out on the street and free of them all – rid of them; rid of them – she started walking fast. She was almost a block away when she heard "Hey, Mrs. *Dav*enport! Hey, *Lucy!*"

And there he came, running down the sidewalk with his raincoat flapping around his skinny legs: Carl Traynor.

"Listen," he said when he'd caught up with her, and as soon as he'd recovered his breath he said "I think I owe you a drink. Don't you?"

When he'd steered her into a bar – and he looked tentatively pleased at having done even that, as though the first part of a difficult job had now been accomplished – he settled her at a small table near a window that faced Sixth Avenue.

"I'm sorry you were so disappointed in my course," he said,

"but I can understand it completely. That's the first thing I want you to know, and there's a couple of other things too. Could we just sort of talk a minute?"

"Sure."

"Let me make this as clear as I can," he began, and he was settling down to the serious business of a straight bourbon with a short glass of ice water on the side. She hoped it wouldn't be the first of many drinks, far into the afternoon, because he looked too thin to absorb much alcohol. "Every time I walk into that classroom I feel lost and scared and I know the people can sense it – *you've* sensed it – so it's only reasonable to explain why I even try to do it at all. God knows it's not for the money: this job pays less than a quarter of what I need for my family and myself – I mean I'm divorced, but I have two kids so there're still quite a few obligations back there. No, the whole point of this is that I need the credentials. The New School is the only university in America that would ever have hired me, you see, because I don't have a college education. I barely made it through twelfth grade. I still have no idea what a college teacher is supposed to do; I don't even know what a college teacher is supposed to *sound* like. There are times when I sit up there and hear myself talking away, droning and droning, and I think Who *is* this asshole? And all I want to do is go home and blow my brains out. Is this beginning to make any sense?"

"Well," Lucy said, "I certainly wouldn't have guessed you hadn't gone to college." And his slightly offended look told her at once it had been the wrong thing to say, almost as if she'd told a Negro that he seemed as intelligent as a white man. She tried to make up for it by saying "How did that happen? That you missed college, I mean."

"Well, it'd take too long to tell," he said, "and it's a story that doesn't reflect very favorably on me. I don't think I've ever really

203

been ashamed of it, but I've never been proud of it either. The thing is, though, there are universities all over the country now with graduate-school programs in writing – it's kind of an academic fad, I guess, but it looks like it's going to last awhile – and they're paying real salaries. That's what I'm after, do you see? I want to qualify for something like that."

And she was reminded briefly, once again, of Nancy Smith's brother: in the end they had faked-up the scores and qualified everybody.

"Oh, I don't suppose it'd be great," Carl Traynor was saying, "but it'd give me as much security as most other people have, whether I ever learn to do it well or not. And it'd sure beat the hell out of all the garbage I've done for a living – still *am* doing."

"What kind of garbage is that?"

"Free-lance commercial hackwork," he told her. "Grubby little writing for hire; picking up a hundred bucks here and fifty bucks there; years and years of it, going all the way back to when I should've been in college – and all of it for no other purpose than to buy time. Just to buy time. It's been very – tiring."

"Yes, I can imagine," Lucy said. And he did look tired – that, as well as sadness, was the main thing she'd seen in his face as long as she'd known him. After a moment she said "Mr. Kelly told me you've published some excellent stories."

"Well, that was very kind of Mr. Kelly," he said, and he finished off his second drink, or possibly his third. "But I'll tell you something Mr. Kelly doesn't know. I've got a whopper of a book coming out in October."

"Oh? Well, that's – fine. What's it called?"

And he recited the title but it went out of her head right away, like the name of some smiling stranger introduced at a party.

"What's it about?" she asked.

"Oh, I'm not sure I'd be able to say what it's 'about,'" he said, "but I can tell you what it is. It's everything I've managed to learn about the world at the age of thirty-five."

"Is it" – and here she asked the one question novelists were said to find tiresome, if not infuriating – "is it autobiographical?"

"Well, maybe," he said as if he were thinking it over. "But only to about the same extent that *Madame Bovary* is autobiographical."

And that struck her as an intriguing reply. He was rapidly becoming a new Carl Traynor – no tremor, no slump, no diffidence. He might still be tired and sad but he looked pleasingly cocky now, too, and for the first time she was able to imagine him having his way with a girl – perhaps even with any number of girls.

"Took me five years," he was saying of his book, "and it cost me a hell of a lot more than I'll ever want to remember, but I think it's good. Fact is, I think it's a whole lot better than good. It may not set the world on fire or anything swell like that, but people are gonna pay attention."

"Well, I'll – certainly be looking forward to it, Carl." And she knew it was the first time she'd used his first name, but she felt he had earned it.

It wasn't long then, as the day and the alcohol wore on, before he said he had thought her terrifically attractive ever since the first day of school. He had always wished he could get to know her better; wouldn't it be only fair, now, for Lucy to tell him something of herself and her life?

"Well—" she began, and in the same breath she found she was more than a little drunk. She had lost all count of how many gin-and-tonics had been set before her and disposed of, each empty glass promptly replaced by a full one. She must have had at least as much to drink as Carl Traynor, who was now signaling for another round.

"Well," she said again, and she launched into a monologue that she could never afterwards remember. She knew she told him a lot but not too much; she knew everything she said was true, but it was all the kind of carefully selective, drink-inspired truth that amounts to the stuff of flirtation.

It was no surprise when his hand came across the table and closed firmly around her own.

"Hey, Lucy?" he said huskily. "Will you come home with me?"

There was too much drink in her blood to let her make a quick decision, but she knew it would be awful to keep him waiting; she answered him as soon as she could.

"Well, no, I don't think so, Carl. I'm not very good at these casual things."

"Wouldn't necessarily be all that casual," he said. "We might find we can get something pretty nice going. Might even find we were made for each other, like people in the movies."

But she only said no again, trying to soften it this time by covering his hand with hers. She knew saying no could easily be something she'd regret; still, more damaging regrets might arise in the consequences of saying yes.

Out on the street corner he gave her a quick kiss and a long hug, and she responded fully to the hug because it seemed an agreeable and tender way of saying goodbye.

"Lucy?" he said into her hair. "Why did you stop and wait when I ran after you?"

"Because I was sorry I'd made such a scene upstairs, I guess. Why did you run after me?"

"Oh, hell, you know; because I've wanted you all this time and I couldn't let you take off that way. But listen, Lucy." He was still holding her, and she felt no impatience to be free: she was holding him, too, and his raincoat felt nice. "Listen," he said again. "There was another reason too. Will you try to understand this, if I tell you?"

"Of course."

"It was because – oh, baby, because you called me a decent man."

Chapter Five

Lucy worked on her Perry Street story for two or three months, but the material turned out to be subtle and slippery: it kept getting away from her. When she thought she'd brought most of it under control she devised a final episode that had, at least, the virtue of nobody's coming to realize anything: Late one night the young wife flew into a jealous rage at her husband, after the girl had kissed them both and gone. The husband could make only feeble attempts to deny his "yearning" for the girl, which drove the wife into further anger and reproach; then a heavy, costly dinner plate was smashed in the sink, symbolic of the marriage soon to be broken, and that was the end.

She guessed this might be all right; it might "work," except that – well, except that it hadn't really happened, and so it seemed to cast an unhealthy glow of fraudulence over the whole story. How could you ever learn to trust the things you made up?

On days when she felt she couldn't face that manuscript she would try to revise one or the other of her earlier stories, often hearing George Kelly's voice in quiet counsel and sensing his presence as keenly as if he were standing at her chair and peering over her shoulder.

She knew he'd been right. The boarding-school story did require a more dramatic resolution, and there was indeed an embarrassing glut of words after what should have been the final section of "Summer Stock."

One proud morning she found the right way to end "Summer Stock" – three sentences, terse but eloquent in their resonance – and it made her feel like a professional to tear up the old superfluous pages and drop them into her wastebasket.

But once that was done she began to find bad places back in the main part of the story: scenes that went on too long and others that didn't go on long enough, paragraphs that weren't pulling their narrative weight, sentences that had somehow eluded George Kelly's standards of dignity, and far too many easy, poorly chosen words. The only truly professional approach now, it seemed, would be to write the whole damned thing over again.

And the manuscript of "Miss Goddard and the World of Art" just lay there for weeks, stubbornly refusing to come alive. The weakness of its ending had come to seem only part of the trouble: the main trouble, she decided after a long time, was that she didn't like it. She wouldn't have liked it if somebody else had written it. She even thought up a disparaging little summary of it that George Kelly might have approved of: it was an oh-what-a-sensitive-child-I-was story.

Still, rather than destroy it, she put it away in a bureau drawer. There might be parts of it she would want to salvage and improve some day, like the girl's first meeting with Miss Goddard ("For a minute or two there I thought we might have some kind of lesbian story on our hands, but that was a wrong guess. . . .")

By August she had begun to spend less and less time at her writing table. On bright days she would put on an old bathing suit – a blue cotton bikini that Michael Davenport used to tell her was enough to drive him crazy – take out a blanket, and lie sunbathing for hours in her big backyard, with supplies of gin and tonic and an insulated bucket of ice cubes close at hand. Twice or three times, in the late afternoons, she went back into the house to change into a fresh summer dress and set off up the road on the way to the Nelsons', but each time she turned back after half the distance and came home again because she didn't know what she would have said to either of the Nelsons when she got there.

At first she described all this to herself as being "blocked" – all writers were blocked sometimes – but then, while trying to sleep one night, she began to suspect she was finished with it.

Acting might bring on emotional exhaustion, but writing tired your brains out. Writing led to depression and insomnia and walking around all day with a haggard look, and Lucy didn't feel old enough for any of that. Even the pleasures of privacy and silence could sink into nothing but loneliness when your brains got tired. You might drink too much or punish yourself by staying away from it, only to find that either alternative robbed you of writing itself. If your brains got tired enough, for long enough, some dizzying series of blunders might get you hauled away and locked into Bellevue, to be frightened and diminished for life. And there was still another hazard, one she couldn't have discerned without working so hard on these first three stories: if all you did was write about yourself, total strangers might come to know you too well.

Once years ago, back in Larchmont, she had shyly criticized one of Michael's poems by saying it seemed "too reticent."

And he'd paced the floor for a while without speaking, hanging his head. Then he'd said "Yeah, that's probably true. And it isn't a good idea to be too reticent; I understand that. Still, you don't ever want to drop your pants in Macy's window, either, right?"

Right. And Lucy could see now, on the evidence of these apprentice stories, that dropping her pants in Macy's window might be all she would accomplish, time and again, no matter what better things she might ever hope and try to do.

At one of the Nelsons' parties, in the fall of that year, she met a man who almost literally swept her off her feet. She cared nothing at all about what he "did" – he was a stockbroker and a faithful collector of Thomas Nelson watercolors – but she liked his face and his big chest and his flat belly, and within five minutes she found that the resonance of his deep, courteous voice could send out subtle vibrations along both wings of her collarbone. She was helpless.

"I have a terrible confession," she said when he drove her over toward Connecticut that night, on the way to his place in Ridgefield. "I've forgotten your name. Is it Chris something?"

"Well, that's close," he told her. "It's Christopher Hartley, but I've always been called Chip."

It occurred to her during that same drive that Chip Hartley was exactly the kind of man she might have married if she hadn't met Michael Davenport first – the kind of man her parents would always have been comfortable with. Another thing she learned in his car that night, after a series of bantering but relentless questions, was that he too had been born rich: he had inherited almost as much money as she had.

"Why do you work, then?"

"Because I enjoy it, I guess. I don't even think of it as 'work'; I've always seen the stock market as a kind of game. You learn the rules, you accept the challenges and take the risks, and the whole point is trying to come out ahead. If I ever find I'm beginning to let my clients down I'll get out of it, but in the meantime it's stimulating; it's fun."

211

"Well, but isn't a lot of it just boring? Just sort of daily routine?"

"Sure it is, but I like that part, too. I like the train ride into town every morning. I think *The Wall Street Journal* is the best daily newspaper in America. I like having lunch with my friends in restaurants where all the waiters know our names. And I even like the kind of afternoons when there's nothing much to do but fool around the office until the clock says it's time to quit. I often find myself thinking Well, okay, this may not amount to much, but it's my life."

Except for the handsomely framed Thomas Nelson pictures on every wall, there was nothing about his place to suggest excessive wealth. It was what real-estate agents call a carriage house – modest, stylish quarters appropriate for a childless man in the third or fourth year of his divorce – and from the confident way he steered her upstairs to the bedroom she could tell he rarely spent much time here alone.

Girls must always have spoiled this big, straightforward, plain-spoken man; each girl's impulse toward reserve or coyness would probably have been checked by her knowledge that plenty of other girls were waiting. And he was a good lover, in ways perhaps similar to those that made him a reliable handler of other people's money: he was thorough, attentive to detail, careful and adventurous at the same time, seemingly free of anxiety in every move.

He took her twice in the first night, then fell asleep with one hand still roaming her flesh until it came to a stop cupping one breast. When she awoke late in the morning, feeling good, she could hear the sounds of his puttering around in the kitchen downstairs. She could even smell the faint, drifting scent of coffee as she allowed herself a languorous stretch and then snuggled back under the bedclothes. This was nice.

And the best part was that it soon turned out there were no other girls in his life just now: he wanted to spend all his leisure time with her, either in Ridgefield or Tonapac or New York. A good many weeks flew by without any apparent need to count their passing.

But he was the first man she'd known who didn't have artistic ambitions of any kind, and that made him seem oddly incomplete. Well, but look, Chip, she wanted to say time and again, usually when their talk had flagged in some good restaurant, is this really all there is for you? Make money and get laid; get laid and make money? And she never asked that question for fear it would only make him look up blinking from his iced plate of oysters, or his hot platter of prime rib, and say Well, sure; why not?

"Is Nelson the only painter you collect?" she asked him one Sunday afternoon in Ridgefield.

"Yup."

"Why's that?"

"Oh, I think it's because I like the no-bullshit quality of his work. You get a sense of honest goods. Most of the other stuff being done these days is either over my head or beneath my notice, and most of the time I can't tell which, so I don't want to mess with it either for pleasure *or* investment."

"I've heard it argued," she said, "that he's more an illustrator than an artist."

"Could be," he conceded. "Still, I like the way it looks on my walls. And I like knowing that an awful lot of other people do too. They must, or he wouldn't be so successful."

And that seemed to settle it. Sundays, in Chip Hartley's well-organized life, were given over entirely to rest, to measured amounts of alcohol, and to the reading of world news – just as Saturdays were given over to sports and entertainment; just as all

213

five weekdays, except for their shrunken evenings, were given over to work.

Carl Traynor's first novel didn't exactly set the world on fire, but Lucy paid close attention to its several excellent reviews, and she bought it at once. The first thing she did was remove its ugly dust jacket – a cheap illustration on the front and a photograph on the back that might have been the picture of an unhappy college boy – then she settled down to read.

She was pleased with the "dignity" of the sentences and the clarity of the scenes, and along in the third or fourth chapter she could dimly begin to see what he'd meant about *Madame Bovary*. Parts of it were very funny, for a man who could never get a laugh at the New School, but there was a pervasive tone of sadness all through the story and a well-earned sense of impending tragedy toward the end.

It kept her sitting up in bed all night and it made her cry a little, turning away from the page to hide her loose mouth in her free hand; then, after trying and failing to sleep for most of the morning, she found his name in the Manhattan phone book and called him up.

"Lucy *Dav*enport," he said. "Well. Good to hear from you."

And in a shy voice, fumbling for the words, she tried to tell him how she felt about his book.

"Well, thanks, Lucy, that's fine," he said. "I'm very glad you liked it."

"Oh, 'liked' isn't the right word, Carl; I loved it. I can't remember when a novel has moved me so deeply. And I'd love to discuss it with you, but a phone call isn't really – do you think we could meet somewhere in town for a drink? Soon?"

"Well, actually, I've got company here now," he said, "and I'll probably be – you know – tied up for some time; so maybe

I'd better take a rain check on the drink, okay?"

And for hours after they'd hung up she was still bothered by the clumsiness of his message. Wasn't "I've got company here now" a funny way of telling her he had a girl? And she hadn't heard anybody say "take a rain check" for years, so that was funny, too – especially from a man with a writer's abhorrence of clichés.

But she couldn't deny that her own part of the talk had been all wrong – too open, too direct, too aggressive. If she'd had any sleep last night she would almost certainly have found a subtler approach.

And the worst thing, however she might dwell on the bungled little phone call, the worst thing now was that she was terribly, terribly disappointed. All night, and especially toward morning, she had repeatedly let her mind float away from Carl Traynor's powerful story into romantic little reveries of the man himself. Her having misjudged and belittled him all those weeks seemed only to lend piquancy to their long afternoon together in that Sixth Avenue bar. She deeply regretted having said no to him that day – if she'd said yes, she might now be alone with him in rejoicing over this very book – and she knew she would never forget how good he had felt to her clasping hands in that lingering embrace on the street.

At the dead-silent hour of five this morning, when she'd put the book aside before starting to read the last chapter because she knew the last chapter was going to break her heart, she could remember whispering audibly against her pillow: "Oh, Carl. Oh, Carl . . ."

And now, though it wasn't yet noon – wasn't even time to allow herself a drink – there was nothing left to dream of. Everything was gone. Everything was desolation and wreckage, because Carl Traynor had said he'd better take a rain check.

215

She had found in the past that a voluptuously long, hot shower could be made to seem almost as health-giving as a night's sleep; she had learned too that taking exquisite pains over the selection and putting-on of clothes could sometimes be as good a way as any of helping the hours to pass.

And luck was with her on this particular day: by the time she was ready to settle herself at the telephone table, with her first drink gleaming as deep and substantial as the love of a generous friend, it was after four. The New York Stock Exchange had been closed for more than an hour, and this might easily be the kind of afternoon when even a conscientious broker would have nothing much to do but fool around the office until the clock said it was time to quit.

"Chip?" she said into the phone. "Are you terribly busy, or can you talk for a minute? . . . Oh, good. I just wondered if you're – you know – if you're free tonight, because I'd really love to see you. . . . Oh, that's wonderful. . . . No, *you* say when; *you* say where. I want to place myself entirely at your disposal."

"Mom? Mom?" Laura called urgently from the living room one evening, when Lucy was finishing up in the kitchen. "Mom, come and look, quick. There's this neat new series on TV, and guess who's *in* it."

For a moment Lucy thought it might be Jack Halloran, but it wasn't. It was Ben Duane.

"It's all about this farm family, I think in Nebraska," Laura explained when Lucy came to sit beside her at the mottled, droning screen, "and I think it's really gonna be neat. It's supposed to be back in Depression times, you see, and they're very poor and all they've got is this little plot of—"

"Sh-sh," Lucy told her, because the girl's words were

216

tumbling out too fast to follow. "Let's just watch. I think I'll be able to pick it up."

Most of these television "series" entertainments were dreadful, but once in a while they stumbled onto a lucky formula, and this one did look fairly promising. The father was proud and taciturn, still a young man but prematurely aged by hardship, and the handsome mother was serene and patient to the point of nobility. There was a puzzled-looking boy just emerging from adolescence, and a girl a year or two younger – still a little coltish, perhaps, but large-eyed and brimming with incipient beauty.

Ben Duane played the spry old grandfather, and from the moment he came jauntily downstairs for breakfast you could tell he was going to be lovable all the way through. The scriptwriters hadn't given him many lines in this opening or "pilot" episode – he would look up briefly now and then to deliver pungent wisdom over his bowl of oatmeal – but he got most of the laughs, or rather most of the spasms of "canned" laughter on the soundtrack.

"I bet the girl turns out to be the star, don't you?" Laura said when the show was over.

"Well, or it could be the boy," Lucy said, "or either of the parents. And with so many more episodes to work with, I wouldn't be at all surprised if they make Ben the featured player sometimes. He was a very distinguished actor, you know, for many years."

"Yeah, I know. Anita and I used to think he was kind of a creepy old guy, though."

"Oh? Why?"

"I don't know. He never seemed to have enough clothes on."

Then Laura got up, switched off the set, and wandered out of the room. She seemed to wander everywhere she went

217

nowadays, rather than to walk. In a few more weeks she would be thirteen.

Peggy Maitland had studied drawing and painting at the Art Students League of New York for six months or so, before dropping out to devote her life to Paul, and she often said she had "loved" it there. The League had no entrance requirements and no formal program of study: beginners and advanced students were "all mixed up together," and the teachers gave individual attention to each student according to his needs.

So Lucy decided to give it a try. She didn't feel she needed drawing lessons – her drawing had been extravagantly praised by that much-admired teacher in boarding school, more than half a lifetime ago – but the challenge of oil painting on canvas would be something entirely new. And what did she have to lose?

The first thing she learned about oil painting, on her first day in one of the big, clean, light-flooded studios of the League, was that it smelled wonderful. It smelled like the very stuff of art itself. Then, slowly and with many mistakes, she began to learn more. Everything was light and line and form and color: you had a limited space, and your obligation was to fill it in a satisfying way.

"Now you're getting something," her instructor said quietly when he came to stand at her shoulder one afternoon – and God only knew how many weeks it had been since her enrollment. "I think you're getting something, Mrs. Davenport. If you stay with this one, you're going to have a picture."

He was a short, tan, bald man named Santos, a Spaniard who spoke English with almost no trace of an accent, and Lucy had known from the beginning that he was a real teacher. There was neither fear nor carelessness in his method; he never flattered the dullards or the fools; he expected everyone's standards to be as

218

high as his own – and his highest praise, so rarely given as to make it exquisitely valuable, was to say "You're going to have a picture."

"And I *love* it," she exclaimed in Chip Hartley's house one Saturday night, whirling to face his chair in a way that made her skirt swing and float attractively around her legs. "I *love* the feeling that I'm doing something well – something I can do without any sense of strain or fear of failure; something I may even have been born to do."

"Well, that's great," he told her. "Finding a thing like that does make all the difference, doesn't it." But he could look up at her only briefly because he was dismantling an expensive new German camera on the lap of his Bermuda shorts. Something had gone wrong with the thing this afternoon, spoiling the long day of picture-taking he had planned, and now his need to finger and scrutinize loose parts of it obliged him to sit with his thighs pressed together and his shoes pigeon-toed on the rug.

"I remember your saying about Tom Nelson's work once," she said, "that he gave you a sense of honest goods. Well, I'm beginning to think I might be able to do that, too – oh, not in his way, of course, but in a way of my own. Does that sound terribly immodest?"

"Sounds fine to me," he said, holding up a small piece of the camera for inspection in the lamplight. "Speaking of honest goods, though, I'm afraid the Germans may have put something over on us this time."

"Wouldn't it be better to take it back to the store?" she inquired. "Instead of trying to fix it yourself?"

"As a matter of fact, dear," he said, "I came to that same conclusion half an hour ago. All I'm trying to do now is get it put together well enough to *take* it back to the store."

This wasn't the first time Chip Hartley had struck her as less

219

than an ideal companion, and it wouldn't be the last. He would probably sit here fretting over his broken toy until bedtime; then soon it would be Sunday, always the most tedious of their days together, and once the new week began the only spice of uncertainty in her life would be wondering which of them would call the other first.

Well, being Chip Hartley's girl might not amount to much – it might even turn out to be little more than a way of waiting for something better to come along – but it would always permit some small things to be accomplished. Later tonight, for example, she could probably find a way to tell him that she'd never liked Bermuda shorts.

Whether she made her daily trips to New York by car or by train, it was necessary first to drive through the village of Tonapac and out along the winding asphalt road that took her past the weathered old sign for the New Tonapac Playhouse on one side and the base of Ann Blake's steep driveway, with its "Donarann" mailbox, on the other – and one of the reasons Lucy had come to believe the League was better than the New School was that she could now acknowledge those poignant landmarks without a second glance. Sometimes, in fact, she would get all the way through to the parkway entrance, or to the train station, without having noticed them at all.

But one morning she came upon Ann Blake standing alone at the roadside, all dressed up in a nice fall suit, with bright earrings, so she brought the car to a stop and leaned smiling from the driver's window.

"Can I give you a lift somewhere, Ann?"

"Oh, no, thanks, Lucy, I'm just waiting for the town taxi. They always hate to come up the driveway here, and I've never known why. I mean I suppose it's bad, but it's not that bad."

"Taking a trip?"

"Well, I'm going to New York for an – indefinite period of time," Ann said, though the small suitcase at her feet was the kind meant for carrying a single change of clothes. "Actually, I'm very—" And she lowered her false eyelashes in embarrassment. "Well, I might as well tell you this, Lucy; why not? I'll be checking into Sloan-Kettering."

And Lucy may have known at once what "Bellevue" meant, but it took her two or three seconds to realize that Sloan-Kettering was a hospital for cancer patients. She got out of the car – this wasn't the kind of talk you could have through a car window – and went quickly to Ann Blake's side without any idea of what she was going to say.

"Well, Ann, I'm terribly sorry," she began. "This is a rotten break. This really is a lousy, rotten break."

"Thanks, dear; I knew you'd be kind. And I suppose the world hasn't dealt me a very good hand this time, but then I never wanted to be an old woman anyway, so who cares? As my husband always used to say, who cares?"

"A lot of people care, Ann."

"Well, that's a nice thought, but try counting them up on your fingers. Name me four. Name me three."

"Listen, come along with me," Lucy said. "Let me take you up to the station, and we'll have a cup of—"

"No." And Ann looked as though she couldn't be budged. "I'm not leaving here any sooner than I have to. Walking down this driveway was the last concession I'm going to make, and I regretted every step of that. All I want to do now is stand here and wait until they come and – until they come and get me. Do you understand?" Her eyes were suddenly filled with tears. "This is my *place*, you see."

When the cab drew up and stopped for her, she got into it so slowly and carefully that Lucy could tell she was in pain. She might well have lived in pain for weeks or even months, alone in her love-nest house, before allowing herself to call a doctor. And she sat facing straight ahead as if determined not to look back, as the cab pulled away, but Lucy stood waving anyway until it was out of sight.

From old habit it occurred to her then that there could easily be a story in Ann Blake. It could be a long story, essentially very sad but with funny moments all through it, and this taxicab scene could serve as its perfect conclusion. There needn't even be anything to make up.

And she was halfway to the city that day before she fully understood that stories were no longer her business. She was a painter now. If she couldn't be a painter – well, if she couldn't be a painter she had better give up trying to be anything at all.

"Lucy Davenport?" said a strong and vigorous voice on the phone one evening. "Carl Traynor."

It was well over a year now since the strain and awkwardness of their last phone call, and she could tell at once that he didn't have company anymore.

". . . Well, I'd love to, Carl," she heard herself saying, as if her voice were an instrument suddenly freed from her mind's control, and "Actually, I'm in town every weekday now, so that should make it easy for us to – you know – to get together."

Chapter Six

The address he'd given her, as she might have expected, turned out to be the same little Sixth Avenue bar where they'd spent those hours the last time. And he was waiting for her at the same table, getting to his feet in a mote-filled shaft of afternoon sunlight as she came in the door.

"Well, Lucy," he said. "I hope you don't mind this place. I thought it might be sort of like taking up where we left off."

He looked less skinny, though it might have been a gaining of self-confidence more than weight, and he was much better dressed. His hands were steady, too, even before the first drink, and she noticed for the first time that they were nice-looking hands.

He had spent six months in Hollywood, he told her, employed to write a screen adaptation of a contemporary novel that he'd always liked, but the movie project had fallen apart in the casting because "they couldn't get Natalie Wood for the lead." Now he was home and almost broke again, almost back where he'd started – except, of course, that his own first book was long behind him.

"It's a beautiful book, Carl," she said. "Did it sell well at all?"

"Nah, nah, not well, but the paperback sale was fairly nice. And I still get enough mail to let me know that a few people out there are reading the son of a bitch; I guess that's all I should ever really have hoped for. What's bugging me now, though, is that I'm about a third of the way into another one and I can't seem to get it off the ground. I'm beginning to see what writers mean about second-novel panic."

"You don't seem panicky to me," she said. "Everything about you now suggests a man who knows exactly what he's doing."

He knew what he was doing, all right. In less than twenty minutes he had her out of that bar and up in the dim seclusion of his apartment, a block or two away.

"Oh, baby," he murmured as he helped her out of her clothes. "Oh, my lovely. Oh, my lovely girl."

The only trouble at first was that one small, cold-sober part of her mind floated free of the rest of her; it was able to observe how solemn a man could be at times like this, how earnest in his hairy nakedness, and how predictable. You had only to offer up your breasts and there was his hungering mouth on one and then the other of them, drawing the nipples out hard; you had only to open your legs and there was his hand at work on you, tirelessly burrowing. Then you got his mouth again, and then you got the whole of him, boyishly proud of his first penetration, lunging and thrusting and ready to love you forever, if only to prove that he could.

But she liked it – oh, she liked it all, and that traitorous little part of her mind winked out to nothingness long before it was over. Then, as soon as her breathing and her voice came back to normal, she told Carl Traynor he was "marvelous."

"You always know how to say just the right thing," he said. "I wish I could do that."

"Well, but you can; you do."

"Sometimes, maybe; other times not. I can think of one or

two girls who might want to give you an argument on that point, Lucy."

His place wasn't very clean – she had an impulse to fall heavily to work with a scrub brush and a bucketful of hot water and ammonia – and the bathroom appeared to be the grubbiest part of it. But when she stepped out of the shower she found two freshly laundered towels on the rack, hung there as if in readiness for her visit. That was nice, and it was nice too when he brought her a long flannel bathrobe to wear: it hung to her ankles and made her skin feel good all the way down.

She straightened up his bed, though he told her not to bother with it; then, walking barefoot on the naked floor, she explored the rest of his apartment. It was a lot bigger than it had seemed at first, high and well-proportioned and probably bright in the morning hours, though its windows were filled with the sadness of sunset colors now, but it was almost bare – sparsely furnished and without decoration. There weren't even very many books, and what few there were had been so carelessly shoved and jumbled on the shelves as to suggest impatience with the whole idea of being expected to own any books at all.

His writing table gave a first impression of jumble and impatience too, or even of chaos, until you saw the small, clean section of it where a portable typewriter had been shoved out of the way, where sharpened pencils were gathered in readiness, and where several pages of new manuscript lay face up, the top one showing almost as many words crossed out as words allowed to stand. It might not be Chip Hartley's idea of a desk; but then, the idea of it was a far cry from anything in Chip Hartley's understanding.

"Baby?" he asked from somewhere in the shadows behind her. "Can you stay awhile? I mean can you spend the night with me, or do you have to go back to wherever it is?"

And it took her no time at all to decide. "Well, if I can use your phone," she said, "I think I'll be able to stay."

Soon she was spending three or four nights a week with him, and as many afternoons as she could manage; that was how they worked things out for almost a year.

There were times when she'd find him so lost in his nervous pacing and chain-smoking, talking too fast and absently pulling at the crotch of his pants the way little boys do, that she couldn't believe he had written the book she admired so completely. But there were other times, more and more often, when he was calm and wise and funny and always knew how to please her.

"You're really a very shy man, aren't you?" she said one night when they were walking home from a small, awkward party that neither of them had enjoyed.

"Well, sure I am. How could you've sat through all those gruesome little New School sessions without knowing that?"

"Well, you always did seem ill at ease there," she said, "but you were never at a loss for words."

" 'At a loss for words,' " he repeated. "Jesus, I'll never understand why so many people think shyness means being tongue-tied and bashful and not having the nerve to kiss a girl. That doesn't even begin to cover the subject, don't you see? Because there's another kind of shyness that has you talking and talking as if you're never going to stop, has you kissing girls even when you don't feel like it because you think they may expect it of you. It's a terrible thing, this other kind of shyness. It can get you into nothing but trouble, and I've suffered from it all my life."

And Lucy settled her hand and wrist more snugly in his arm as they walked. She felt she was getting to know him better all the time.

Carl said once that he wanted to publish fifteen books before he died, and to have no more than three of them – "or four, tops" – be the kind of books that would have to be apologized for. She liked the bravery of that ambition and told him she was sure he'd fulfill it; then later, secretly, she began to seek out an important place for herself in his career.

The idea of devoting her life to a man had stirred in her only once before, in the early days with Michael; and if it had come to nothing then, was that any reason to disparage the possibilities this time?

Carl might well be "hung up" in his second novel, as he kept saying he was, but Lucy's presence could help him work it through. Then there'd be another book, and another and still others, with Lucy always faithfully at his side. And she knew there was no fear of Carl's being intimidated by her money. He'd told her more than once – jokingly, but saying it anyway – that he'd love to let her fortune pay his way through life.

The difference in attitude here, she guessed, was that Michael Davenport's stern independence arose from his never having known what poverty was. Carl Traynor had always known what it was, so he understood that it held no virtue – and he understood too that having an unearned income would imply no corruption.

There often seemed to be nothing Carl didn't understand, or couldn't understand after a moment's reflection; that may have been part of what made him a compelling writer, and in any case it made him effortlessly kind.

Lucy discovered she could tell him things about herself that she'd never told anyone else – not even Michael; not even Dr. Fine – and that alone was enough to make her feel she had a profound investment in him.

And she would never have to give up painting. Her pictures might get steadily better and more plentiful with the years until she became as thoroughly professional as he was, but there would never be any conflict – there'd be no basis for rivalry or even for comparison. The worlds of their work would be separate, and each might come to form a pleasurable complement to the other.

She could happily attend his publication parties or even go along on his book-promotion tours, if he asked her to, just as he could stand tall and proud and courteously smiling at the openings of her gallery exhibitions – lively, civilized gatherings where the presence of people like the Thomas Nelsons and the Paul Maitlands could always be taken for granted.

By the time they were both in their fifties, if not before, they might well command the admiration and envy of everyone they knew – and they might even be the kind of people that any number of strangers would give anything to meet.

But almost from the beginning there were harsh little troubles between them – quarrels that could sometimes seem bad enough to spoil everything.

Once in their early weeks together, at an old steak-and-potatoes restaurant that Carl said was his favorite place in the Village, she asked him about the girl who'd been his "company" at the time his book came out.

"Well," he said, "that's a story that doesn't reflect very favorably on me. I'll tell you the whole damn thing sometime, but suppose we let it ride for a while, okay?" And he stuffed his mouth with bread as if that might put a stop to any further questions.

She was willing enough to let it ride, if that was what he wanted, but instead he began to tell her the whole damn thing only a night or two later, in bed and within minutes after their lovemaking, which struck her as curiously inappropriate. And it took a long time to tell.

The girl was very young, he said, fresh out of college and filled with dreamy ideas about what she always called "the arts." And she was an extremely pretty girl, too: Carl Traynor had thought she was wonderful, and when she first moved in with him he remembered thinking If I can just help her grow up a little, she'll be perfect. But before long she turned out to be the only girl he'd ever known who drank more than he did.

"She'd fall down in bars," he said, "and she'd fall out of chairs at parties. She'd be smashed out of her mind every night, and that meant I always had to be the responsible one: every morning I'd have to get her out of bed and into her clothes and out on the street for a cab – it always had to be a cab because she said the subway was 'terrifying' – and off to whatever dumb little editorial job it was she had uptown.

"So when the screenwriting deal came through I sort of dumped her – told her I wanted to go to California alone – and that night she tried to open the arteries in both of her wrists with a razor blade. Well, Jesus, talk about scared. I wrapped her up as well as I could and then I carried her all the way up to St. Vincent's. Can you imagine that? Carrying her? There was some young Spanish doctor on duty in the emergency room that night, and he told me she hadn't touched an artery; all she'd done was slice into a couple of veins, and he said he could stop the bleeding with tight bandages. She knew more than I did, though – she knew that any attempted suicide in New York can get you an automatic six weeks in Bellevue – so as soon as the bandaging was done she was up and off that table quicker than a cat. She got out through an alley and went running down Seventh Avenue so fast not even the cops could have caught her. And when I finally got her cornered in the vestibule of her old apartment house, where she'd lived before moving to my place, all she said to me was 'Go away. Go away.'"

He sighed heavily. "So that was it. I think I did sort of love her – probably always will, in a way – but I don't even know where she is now, and I'm not in any hurry to find out."

There was a considerable silence before Lucy said "That isn't a very good story, Carl."

"Well, Jesus, I know it isn't a – how do you mean?"

"There's a little too much pleasure on the narrator's part," she said. "It's a self-aggrandizing story. It's a sexual braggart's story. I've never cared much for stories like that. Why, for example, was it necessary to stress your having carried her to the hospital?"

"Well, because the traffic runs down*town* on Seventh Avenue, that's why. A cab would've taken much too long, and for all I knew she was bleeding to death."

"Ah, yes. Bleeding to death for love of you. Listen, Carl: don't ever write that story, okay? At least not the way you've told it. Because if you ever do it'll only damage your reputation."

"Well, I'll be God damned," he said. "Here we are in my bed at one o'clock in the morning, and you're warning me about 'damage' to my 'reputation.' You've got some nerve, Lucy, you know that? Besides, I *told* you it was a story that didn't—"

"—reflect very favorably on you. I know. That's one of your favorite expressions, isn't it? It's a way of whetting people's interest, right? Put 'em off, make 'em wait; then, when it's least expected, let 'em have it."

"Are we having a fight now?" he inquired. "Is that the deal? Am I supposed to launch some counterattack so we can be up and shouting at each other all night? Because if that's what you have in mind, sweetheart, you're outa luck. All I want to do is sleep." And he turned away from her, but he wasn't quite finished. After a moment, in a carefully controlled voice, he said "In the future, dear, I think it might be helpful if you could refrain from advising me on what not to write or how

230

not to write it or any other horseshit along that line. Okay?"

"Okay." And she put her arm around his ribs to let him know she was sorry.

In the morning she was even sorrier, because she could see then that much of her anger had come from jealousy of the drunken girl, so she delivered a demure, well-worded apology that he didn't even let her finish because he was laughing and hugging her and telling her to forget it.

And it was always easy to put those clashes behind them, because so many weeks could pass in near-perfect harmony; still, there was never any telling when the next one might erupt.

"Have you kept in touch with Mr. Kelly at all?" she asked him one day.

"Mr. who?"

"You know; George Kelly, from the class."

"Oh, the elevator guy. No, I haven't. How do you mean, 'kept in touch?'"

"Well, I was hoping you might have, is all. He was very helpful to me, and he always struck me as a remarkably intelligent man."

"Yeah, well, sure, 'remarkably intelligent.' Look, baby, the world is crawling with these diamond-in-the-rough types, these salt-of-the-earth characters, and they're all remarkably intelligent. My God, I knew half-literate guys in the Army who could scare the shit out of you with their intelligence. So if you're running a writing course you're glad enough to have one or two of those people in the group – you may even let 'em do most of the work for you, the way I did with Kelly – but when school's out, it's out. They know it as well as you do, and it'd be crazy to expect anything else."

"Oh," she said.

"Well, for Christ's sake, Lucy, what the hell do you want to do? You want to get on the subway and ride for an hour out into Queens so we can have a nice little evening with George Kelly? There'd be Mrs. Kelly serving up the coffee and cake and talking a mile a minute, wearing seven different kinds of costume jewelry for the occasion, and there'd be four or five little Kellys standing around the carpet and staring at you, all working on their bubble gum in unison. Is that what you want?"

"It's curious," Lucy said, "that for a man with a twelfth-grade education you should have such a highly developed sense of social snobbery."

"Yeah, yeah, I knew you'd say that. Know something, Lucy? It's getting so I can predict everything you're going to say before you've said it. If I ever write a story about you, the dialogue'll be a cinch. It'll be child's play. I'll just sit back and let the typewriter do that part of it all by itself."

And she walked out of his place that time, after a parting statement about how "hateful" he was.

But she came back three hours later, bringing four well-chosen Impressionist reproductions for his walls, and he was so glad to see her that he seemed almost in tears as he clasped and held her in a long, staggering embrace.

"My God," he said later, after she'd carefully taped the pictures into place. "It's amazing what a difference they make. I don't know how I managed to live here all this time with nothing but bare walls."

"Well, these are only temporary," she explained, "because I have a plan. I'm full of plans where you're concerned, did you know that? The plan is, as soon as I have enough paintings of my own that I like, and enough that Mr. Santos likes too, I'm going to bring them down and hang them here, and then they'll be yours."

And Carl Traynor said that would be the nicest thing he could imagine. He said it would be an honor far beyond anything he could ever hope to deserve.

They were sitting on the edge of the bed now, holding hands as bashfully as children, and he told her he had never meant to be such a "pill" about George Kelly. He said he'd be perfectly willing to call George Kelly tonight, or this weekend, or whenever she liked.

"Well, that's awfully nice, Carl," she said, "but it's something we can easily put off until you feel more comfortable with it. Wouldn't that be better?"

"Okay. Good. Only there's one more thing, Lucy."

"What?"

"Please don't ever take off like that again. I mean, God knows I can't stop you from walking out of here – even walking out for good, if that's what you decide you want to do – but next time try to give me a little warning first, okay? Just enough so I can do everything in my power to make you stay."

"Oh, well," she said, "I don't think that's the kind of thing we'll ever have to worry about, do you?"

And the only way to spend the rest of that oddly exhilarating afternoon was to take off their clothes and get under the covers and be extravagantly in love.

He had never used his kitchen for anything but making instant coffee and for chilling beer and milk, but it wasn't long before she had it fully equipped with copper-bottomed pots and pans all hung in a row, with ample supplies of dishes and silverware, and even with a spice shelf. ("A spice shelf?" he asked her, and she said "Well, certainly, a spice shelf. Why *not* a spice shelf?")

She often cooked dinner for them that winter and he was always touchingly grateful, but she came to understand that he preferred restaurants because he "had" to get out of the place at night after working there all day.

His anxiety about his book seemed only to increase with the approach of spring. Sometimes it made him drink too much, which left him unable to work at all, but Lucy had at least a beginner's knowledge of troubles like that. She helped him establish the right amount of alcohol each day – beer all afternoon, as required, but no more than three bourbons before dinner, and nothing afterwards; still, she couldn't help him with the book itself. He wouldn't let her read the manuscript because "most of it's lousy, and anyway you could never read my handwriting – not to mention all the damn little marginal inserts I can hardly read myself."

Once he typed up a twenty-page section for her and went into the kitchen to hide while she read it. And when she called him out and told him it was "beautiful," his haggard face took on a look of tentative peace. He asked her a few questions to confirm that the parts he had hoped she would like were the very parts she'd liked best; then, after a minute or two, he began to look anxious again. She could almost see him thinking Well, okay, she's being nice, but what does *she* know?.

She knew by now it would be a novel about a woman, told from the woman's point of view – and that in itself was one of the big problems, he said, because he'd never tried a woman's point of view before and didn't know if he could sustain it in a convincing way.

"Well, it's certainly convincing in this part," she said.

"Yeah, well, okay; but twenty pages aren't exactly the same as three hundred."

She knew, too, from hints he'd dropped as well as from small indications in the excerpt itself, that the character, whose name was Miriam, would be substantially based on his former wife.

And she found nothing displeasing in that: he was much too good a writer to let the portrayal be distorted either by malice or nostalgia; besides, everybody knew it was a writer's privilege to find his material where he could.

"And even if I do get the point of view under control," he said, "there's still an awful lot to worry about. I'm afraid there may not be enough happening to this girl. I'm afraid there may not be enough *story* in this thing to make a novel."

"I can think of many fine novels that don't have much 'story' in them," Lucy said, "and so can you."

And he told her once again that she always knew how to say just the right thing.

One night they came back late to his place, hours after having broken the three-bourbon rule. They'd had plenty to drink – easily enough to make them fuddled and unsteady and ready for sleep – but the pleasant thing about this particular night was that they both seemed to have "held" it well: they were in a keyed-up, conversational mood, as if talk tonight might be brighter and more interesting than talk at any other time. They even made new drinks for themselves before settling down companionably in facing chairs.

There was one troubling aspect of the woman's-viewpoint problem, Carl said, that Lucy might be able to help him with. And he asked if she could tell him how it felt to be pregnant.

"Well, I've only been through it once, of course," she said, "and that was long ago, but I remember it as an essentially peaceful time. You get physically slowed down and you worry about being ungainly, or at least I did, but your nerves are quiet and you have a nice sense of being in good health: good appetite; good sleep."

"Good," he said. "All that's good." Then his face changed just enough to show that his next question would have nothing

235

to do with research. "Have you ever had a hysterical pregnancy?"

"A what?"

"Well, you know. There are some girls so eager to get married they can fake pregnancy. They don't just *say* they're pregnant; they develop all the symptoms of it in a very persuasive way. I knew a girl like that, three or four years ago, kind of a nice, cute little girl from Virginia. She'd bloat up every month and her tits would swell until it looked exactly like the real thing; then, wham, she'd have her period and it'd be all over."

"Carl, I think you're getting into another one," Lucy said.

"Another what?"

"Another bragging little anecdote to prove what a devil with the girls you've always been."

"No, wait," he said, "that's not fair. Whaddya mean, 'devil'? If you'd known how scared I was every month you wouldn't've seen anything 'devilish' about it. I'd be wringing my hands like some meek, timid little wretch. Then finally, maybe the seventh or eighth time she got that way, I took her to see this big-shot Park Avenue obstetrician. Cost me a hundred bucks. And you know what happened? That asshole came smiling out of his examining room and he said 'Good news, Mr. Traynor, and congratulations. Your wife has a healthy young pregnancy going.' Well, that was a jolt, as you can imagine, but two or three days later she got her period again. One more false alarm."

"And what did you do then?"

"I did what anybody else in his right mind would've done. I packed her up and sent her back to Virginia, where she belonged."

"Well, all right," Lucy said. "But tell me something else, Carl. Have you never been the loser where a girl is concerned? Haven't any girls ever broken up with you, or dropped you, or told you to get lost?"

"Oh, baby, don't talk nonsense. *Sure* they have. My God, I've had girls walk all over my face. I've had girls act as if I were shit on a stick. Christ Almighty, you oughta hear my *wife* on the subject of me."

In June or July Carl gave her a stack of a hundred and fifty typewritten pages – a little less than half the book, he said – and asked her to take it home to Tonapac for a couple of days.

"You're going to find it's nothing at all like my first book," he told her. "There isn't any thunder and lightning in it; there aren't any stunning confrontations or surprises or anything like that. I don't think the first book was necessarily more ambitious than this one, it was just ambitious in a more obvious way: it was a big, rich, 'tough' novel.

"This time I'm trying for an entirely different kind of thing. I want it to be a quiet, deceptively modest piece of work. I'm trying for a kind of serenity and balance in the writing. I'm trying more for esthetic values, you see, than for dramatic effects."

They were standing at his door, with Lucy holding the manuscript in its manila envelope, and she had begun to wish he'd stop talking. She would rather just have been given the thing, and been allowed to read it the way any stranger would, but he couldn't seem to let her go without all this explaining and instruction.

"I think the best thing," he was saying, "would be to go through it first at your normal reading speed, then go through it again more slowly to look for any places that you think might be improved – might be expanded or cut back or changed in some other way. Okay?"

"Okay," she said.

"Oh, and listen: you know the old analogy of the iceberg? How seven eighths of it are under the surface and only the tip is the part you can see? Well, that's sort of what I'm after here. I want the reader to sense that all these ordinary little events imply the presence of something huge and even tragic down beneath. Do you see how that works?"

And she told him she would keep it in mind.

In Tonapac that night, after a dinner with Laura and a talk with her that was long and careful enough to prove she was still a conscientious mother, Lucy went to bed early and settled herself to read.

She read it through without quite being able to acknowledge how disappointed she was; then, after a fitful sleep and a small breakfast eaten without appetite, she sat down to read it again.

She guessed she could appreciate the esthetic values, and she could certainly see what he'd meant by "modest," if not by "deceptively" modest.

It was tame, bland, boring stuff. Making her way through its technically perfect sentences, waiting and waiting for something to come alive on the page, she couldn't believe this was the same writer whose other book had enthralled her with its bite and power and swiftly gathering momentum, and the comparison made her feel betrayed.

There was a further sense of betrayal when she came upon the twenty pages that she'd once told him were "beautiful" – they seemed enervated now by being embedded in the larger dullness.

And she could no longer believe that Carl had based the character of Miriam on his former wife, because no woman of flesh and blood could ever have been as insipid as this. The trouble wasn't that he'd tried to make her excessively virtuous, it was that he'd allowed her always to be right. Her every perception was something Carl plainly agreed with and plainly expected his readers to agree with too; and hardly any of the dialogue rang true because she always said exactly what she meant.

Miriam was prone to philosophical ruminations – shapely little essays that would interrupt the narrative for whole pages at a time, and their very shapeliness betrayed a fiction writer's straining to meet the requirements of an alien form. Lucy couldn't help but wonder, in one essay after another, if Carl had gone to all that trouble because he thought it was the way a college-educated man would write.

There was probably enough "story" in the thing – he needn't have worried about that – but it was the kind of story any competent, mediocre novelist could have told. Miriam was shown in the early chapters as a neglected child; then she was a lonely girl, briefly in love with several boys who had little time for her, until she met the man you knew she would marry, a poor and unstable young commercial writer with high ambitions, and that was as far as the first half went.

But it seemed clear that almost anyone could guess at how the second half would go: you could already tell it wouldn't be a successful marriage; you knew there'd be disagreements in which Miriam would always speak with the voice of reason; you knew she would emerge from the divorce as a brave and self-sufficient woman, and that her orderly, philosophical habits of thought would sustain her through the final page.

If Carl Traynor ever did produce fifteen books, this one was almost certainly destined to be among those that would have to be apologized for. This particular iceberg would always be safe at any distance: there was nothing under the water.

Even so, Lucy didn't like the harshness of her own judgment. Walking alone in the shade of her big yard, on her last day before going back to the city, she tried to give the manuscript the benefit of every doubt. She was willing to admit now that she might have been unfair to it because – well, because she might be getting tired of Carl. And how could you ever tell when you

239

were getting tired of a man? Any intimacy had to accommodate certain amounts of impatience and boredom; didn't everybody know that?

It often seemed that she'd been tired of Michael Davenport for years before their separation; still, she knew that if it hadn't been for the acute discomfort of their final few months they might still be married. They might have found a renewal of interest in each other, and that might even have been a good thing, if only for Laura's sake.

The way to handle this business with Carl, she decided, was to offer encouragement. If she couldn't say she "loved" the thing, at least she could express praise for the sentences and a few of the scenes; the more she thought it over, the more she found there were any number of nice things she could tell him that wouldn't exactly be lies.

So that was how she handled it, once she was back in his apartment, and he took it well. He was clearly disappointed, but it was clear too that his own interest in the book would be enough to keep him working until it was done. The analogy of the iceberg didn't come up again, and she was glad enough to leave it alone: she was afraid that if she asked him what huge and tragic element was supposed to lie beneath the surface of Miriam's story he might give her a ponderous look and say "The human condition," or something like that.

There were hot summer afternoons in Carl's place when Lucy would torture herself by thinking of him as a failure. She would sit pretending to read a magazine but paying close attention to the subtly moving shape of his back as he hunched over his pencil, and for an hour or more she'd let her imagination do its worst.

There could never be fifteen books in this uncertain, mistake-making, self-pitying man. There might at best be two or three more, each worse than the last; then he would talk and drink his way through the rest of his life, having girls and telling them about his other girls, getting teaching jobs and being as ineffectual in all of them as he'd been at the New School. He might die early or late, but he would die knowing that except in a single novel he'd had nothing to say.

And she would despise herself for that pattern of thought. If she had so little belief in Carl Traynor, what was she doing here?

Sometimes she'd get up and go into the kitchen, because the kitchen could always remind her of domesticity with Carl at its best, and there her bitterness would usually subside. It wasn't "belief" in a man that mattered anyway – certainly not in terms of his professional future; if it were, there wouldn't be hundreds of millions of women devoted to men with no discernible future at all. And besides, this second novel was only half finished. There was still a chance that he could find ways of bringing it to life. There was even a chance that she might help.

"Carl?" she said one day, coming out of the kitchen in a determinedly casual stroll. "I think I have what may be a pretty good idea about Miriam."

"Oh?" he said without looking up. "What's that?"

"Well, this is nothing specific; it's more of a general thing." And she remembered at once that those were the words Jack Halloran had used, the night he said her whole performance had been stagey.

"I wonder," she said, "if you might be a little in danger of letting her develop into a strong person."

"I don't get it," he said, and he was looking steadily at her now. "Where's the danger? What's supposed to be the matter with a strong person?"

"Well, I was thinking of something George Kelly said once. He said the distinction between strong people and weak people

241

always falls apart under scrutiny, and that's why it's always been too sentimental an idea for a good writer to trust."

"Oh. Well, look, sweetheart, I think I have what may be a pretty good idea too. Suppose we let George Kelly repair the fucking elevators, okay? And suppose we let me write the fucking novels."

One September afternoon the big-windowed, handsome old façade of the Art Students League had been made to glisten nobly in a very light, drizzling rain. Lucy could take time to study the way the building looked, almost as if she were planning to paint a picture of it, because she was comfortably settled in a bright delicatessen across the street. For some weeks now it had been her habit to come here every day after school for a bagel and cream cheese, with a cup of tea; that was the small reward she allowed herself for having worked hard and well. But she'd known from the start that it had another purpose too: it was a way of stalling, of killing at least half an hour until she had to go down to Carl's place.

And on this particular afternoon, from the moment he opened the door for her, she knew there was going to be trouble.

"Jesus, talk about bad days," he said. "All I did today was fight with my agent – he thinks I ought to have this book *done* by now – and throw away twenty-seven pages that must've cost me six weeks' work." She could tell from his voice and his breath that he'd been drinking whiskey. "How do other people get through their lives?" he demanded, and he pulled hard at the crotch of his pants. "I mean lawyers and dentists and insurance men and guys like that? I guess they play tennis and golf and go fishing, but all that's out of the question for me because I've gotta *work* all the time. Oh, and I got a deadly little notice from the IRS this morning – they want a whole lotta money outa me. Everybody wants money outa me, even the phone company; even the landlord. I'm a month late with the rent and he's making it sound like the end of the world. Course, I can't expect you to understand this kind of thing: rich people don't even know what money means. Or I guess they know what it means, but they don't know what it costs."

They were seated across from each other in his dim living room now, and Lucy hadn't yet said a word.

"Well, I'm not wholly unfamiliar with what it costs," she began, "but that's something we needn't go into now. The main thing now is that you shouldn't be distracted by these financial problems. I can easily let you have whatever it'll take to settle your debts."

And his face made clear that he didn't know what to say. He had certainly wanted her to make the offer, but hadn't thought it would come so quickly. If he accepted it at once, all the drama would go out of his evening; still, if he made some show of pride and defiance, he might not get the money.

And so, for the present, he avoided both alternatives. "Well," he said. "This is going to take a little thinking over. Get you a drink?"

No other man she'd known had made drinking such a necessity – even made her feel incomplete without it – and for that reason it was extremely heartening tonight, as she took hesitant sips of a bourbon and water, to find that she didn't really want it. She didn't much care for the taste.

She didn't really want to be sitting in this big, awkwardly furnished room, either, and it was hard to believe that she'd spent so much time here for so long. If she had ever felt she belonged here, even at first, it wasn't an easy thing to remember.

Except for her house, where her daughter lived, there was only one place now where Lucy Davenport belonged.

She had worked for nine hours today on a painting that was almost finished and almost excellent. In another day or two she'd have it – she'd know that it didn't need another stroke or another touch – and Mr. Santos would know it too. That was where she belonged: in a bright, murmurous, fine-smelling studio where everything was light and line and form and color.

"Okay," Carl said. "I guess we might as well get down to business on this thing. The Federals want something close to five thousand dollars, and all the little bills'll probably bring it up to six. How does a loan of six thousand strike you?"

"I expected it to be more than that," she said, "from the way you were talking." And she got her checkbook out of her purse.

"We can establish the payment period at whatever number of months seems reasonable to you," he said. "And we'll make it include whatever the current rate of interest is; I can find that out tomorrow at the bank."

"Oh, I don't think any of that'll be necessary, Carl," she told him as she finished writing out the check. "I don't think we need to talk about payment periods and interest rates. It doesn't even have to be a loan, as far as I'm concerned."

He was up and walking, pulling at his pants again; then he turned on her, his eyes narrow and bright, and pointed to the check in her hand. "Okay," he said. "So it doesn't have to be a loan. Well, if it's not gonna be a loan, I'll tell you what you'd better do. You'd better take that check and turn it over; then on the other side, just above the place where I'm supposed to endorse it, you'd better write: 'For services rendered.'"

"Oh," Lucy said. "Oh, that's vile. Even if you're drunk, Carl, even if you think you're only kidding, that's vile."

"Well, there's a nice little new one for my ever-growing collection," he said, walking away from her again. "I've been called a lotta things by a lotta girls, sweetheart, but nobody ever said 'vile' before."

"Vile," she said. "Vile."

"So maybe this is the fight we've both been waiting for. Wouldn't that be a break? Take us both off the hook? Maybe now you'll never have to drag yourself all the way down here from art school when you don't want to see me. Maybe I'll never have to spend any more afternoons getting half smashed because I don't want to see you. Jesus, Lucy, has it really taken you this long to figure out we're bored half to death with each other?"

She was on her feet and going through his closet, looking for things of her own. There were three or four dresses, a good suede jacket, and two pairs of shoes. But there was nothing to carry the stuff in – not even a paper shopping bag – so she shut the closet door on all of it with a resolute little slam.

"I think I've been fully aware of this boredom," she said, "or at least of my own intense boredom with you, for a great deal longer than you might care to believe."

"Good," he said. "Swell. That means there won't be any crying, right? There won't be any recriminations or silly shit like that. We're clean. Well: Good luck to you, Lucy."

But she made no reply. All she did was get out of there as fast as she could.

On the long journey back to Tonapac that night she began to wish she had said "Good luck" to him, too. It might have lessened the clumsiness of her departure; and besides, he was a man who needed to be wished good luck. She couldn't remember now whether she'd torn the six-thousand-dollar check in half or whether she'd dropped it whole and negotiable on his floor; but that didn't matter. If the check was whole it would probably come back to her in the mail in a few days, along with a gracefully worded little note of apology and regret. And that would enable her to return it to him, with a very brief note of her own in which the phrase "Good luck" would be easy to achieve.

Chapter Seven

Laura gained forty pounds when she was fifteen, and there were other surprising changes in her too.

Words like "cool" and "groovy" came to replace "neat" in her vocabulary, but the more remarkable thing was that she now only rarely employed her vocabulary at all.

This child who'd been a chatterbox all her life, sometimes driving both her parents to exasperation by seeming never to know when to stop talking – this quick, nervous, skinny little girl had taken on the habits of silence and secrecy, along with all that excess flesh, and she wanted to be alone most of the time.

Her bedroom, once a place of teddy bears and scattered Barbie-doll clothing, was now a dim and private sanctuary for the sweet soprano wailings of Joan Baez.

After a while Lucy found she could tolerate Joan Baez – there was even a faintly soothing quality in that voice, if you listened with only part of your attention – but she couldn't bear Bob Dylan.

What had given this college kid the arrogance to appropriate a poet's name? Why couldn't he have learned to write before writing songs for himself, or learned to sing before singing them in public? Why hadn't this bogus folk troubadour taken a few lessons on his guitar – or even on his wretched harmonica

– before setting out to capture children's hearts by the tens of millions? There were afternoons when Lucy had to walk around the backyard for an hour or more, hugging her arms or clasping her hands tight at her waist, just to escape the sound of him.

When the Beatles broke out she thought they were agreeably spirited, disciplined performers, but in their first few recordings she wondered why they were trying to sound like American Negroes:

> Whin Ah-ah-ah
> Say thet suh'thin'
> Ah think you'll unduh-stan'
> Whin Ah-ah-ah
> Say thet suh'thin'
> Ah wunna hole yo' *han'*

She liked them better later, after they'd relaxed into their own English accents.

Most of the decorations in Laura's room were giant photographs of singers, boys and girls, but one day Lucy found her putting up a new poster that had nothing to do with music. It seemed, in fact, to have nothing to do with anything at all: it was a reproduction of an abstract painting that might have been the work of an insane person.

"What's that, dear?"

"Oh, it's just psychedelic art."

"*What* kind of art? Can you give me that word again?"

"You never heard of it?"

"No, I never have. What does it mean?"

"Well, it means – it means psyche*del*ic, Mom, that's all."

★

Laura wasn't there when Lucy got home from the city one night. That was strange enough – she had always been there before, secluded with her records or messing around in the kitchen with some other starving, overweight girl from school – and it became more and more strange as the hours passed. Lucy knew the names of two or three girls that Laura might be visiting, but she didn't know any of their last names, so there was no hope in the telephone book.

By ten o'clock the idea of calling the police had occurred to her, but she didn't do it because she wouldn't have known what to say. You could scarcely report a child "missing" at ten o'clock after a single day; even if you could, it would only lead into a labyrinth of dumb, dumb questions by some cop.

It was almost eleven when the girl came slouching into the house at last, looking vague, prepared with an apology as awkward and irritating as adolescence itself.

"Sorry I'm late," she said. "A bunch of us got to talking and we lost track of the time."

"Well, dear, I've been a little on the frantic side. Where *were* you?"

"Oh, over at Donarann, is all."

"Over where?"

"Donar*ann*, Mom. Where we *lived* for about a hundred years."

"Well, but that's miles from here. How did you get there?"

"Chuck drove me over, with a couple of his friends. We go there all the time."

"Chuck who?"

"His name's Chuck Grady. Look, he's a senior, okay? So he's had his license for two years, okay? And he even has a commercial license now because he drives a bread truck after school."

"And for another thing," Lucy said, "what possible reason can there be for your wanting to go there?"

"We go up to the dorm, is all, with a bunch of the other kids. It's a – good place to go."

"Up to the dorm?" Lucy felt there might be a little hysteria rising in her face and voice.

"You know," Laura told her. "Where the actors used to stay before they shut the theater down. It's a good place to go, is all."

"Dear," Lucy said, "I'd like you to tell me how long you and your friends have been making use of that abandoned building. And I'd like you to tell me what you do there."

"Whaddya mean, 'do' there? You think we go there to get laid?"

"You're fifteen years old, Laura, and I won't accept that kind of language from you."

"Shit," Laura said. "Fuck."

And it might have gotten even worse, as they stood staring at each other like enemies, if Lucy hadn't found a way to break the tension. "Well," she said. "Now. Suppose we both try to calm down. You sit over there, please, and I'll sit here, and I'll wait for you to answer my questions."

The girl looked ready to cry – was that a good sign or a bad one? – but she was able to provide the information. Two boys she knew had found a broken lock on the dormitory building last summer. They had gone inside and discovered the kitchen facilities and all the electrical wiring still intact; then, with the help of a few girls, they had cleaned the whole place up and made it into a kind of clubhouse. Odds and ends of furniture and dishware were brought in, as well as a stereo and a good collection of records. There were now ten or twelve regular members of the group, usually more girls than boys, and anybody could see they weren't doing any harm.

"And do you smoke marijuana there, Laura?"

"*Nah*-o," the girl said, but then she qualified her statement.

"Well, the kids bring it in and I guess some of 'em get stoned, or at least they say they do, but I tried it a few times and didn't like it. I don't like beer much, either."

"All right; tell me something else. When you're with these boys, these older boys like Chuck Grady, do you ever – have you ever – are you still a virgin?"

Laura looked as if the question were preposterous. "Mom, you've gotta be kidding," she said. "*Me*? I'm big as a house and funny-looking anyway. God, I'll probably be a virgin all my *life*."

And the tragic way her voice rose and broke on "all my life" was enough to bring her mother quickly over to the arm of her chair.

"Oh, baby, that's the silliest, silliest thing I ever heard," Lucy said. She gently clasped the side of Laura's head against her breast, ready to release it at the first subtle hint that Laura might rather be free. "And I don't know how you ever got the idea you're funny-looking, because it's never been true. You have a sweet, lovely face and you always will. If you're overweight now it's mostly because of the snacking problem we've discussed many times; and besides, it's perfectly normal. I was heavy too at your age. But will you let me tell you something, dear, with all my heart? Two or three years from now there'll be boys on the phone all the time. You'll have as many or as few boys in your life as you choose; and the choice – the choice, dear – will always be entirely your own."

Laura made no reply to any of this – it wasn't even clear that she'd been listening – so her mother had no alternative but to go back to the other chair, facing her again, and get down to the difficult part of the business.

"In the meantime, Laura," she said, "in the meantime you are not permitted to go to that dormitory again. Ever."

251

And there was an appropriately heavy silence in the room, while they looked at each other.

"So?" Laura said in a small voice. "How you gonna stop me?"

"I'll give up all my work at the League, if necessary, and stay in this house around the clock. I'll pick you up after school and bring you home. *That* might give you some idea of what a child you are." And Lucy took a deep breath so that her next words would sound empty of all emotion. "Or, come to think of it, there's a much simpler way: I'd have only to make a phone call. You kids are all trespassers on that property, as you know, and trespassing is against the law."

There was fright in the girl's face then, though it was the kind of cheap fright shown in crime movies: the eyes briefly wide and then suddenly narrowed.

"That's blackmail, Mom," she said. "Pure blackmail."

"I think you might do well to grow up a little, dear," Lucy told her, "before you use a word like that to me." She allowed another silence to develop, and to gather weight, before she tried a new and gentler line of argument. "Laura, there's no reason why you and I can't discuss this sensibly," she said. "I'm fully aware that young people like to have gathering places of their own; that's always been true. My objection to this particular arrangement is simply that it's not suitable for you. It's unwholesome."

"Where do you get 'unwholesome'?" Laura asked, and that was a habit of speech she had picked up from her father ("Where do you get 'precious'? Where do you get 'elitist'? Where do you get '*Kenyon Review*'?"). "Mom, would you like to know something? Would you like to know who hangs out in the dorm all the *time*, for God's sake? Phil and Ted Nelson, that's who, and you think the Nelsons are *wunn*derful people. That's just the way you've always said it, too, Mom, as long as I can remember: 'Oh, the Nelsons are *wunn*derful people.' "

252

"I don't appreciate the mimicry," Lucy said, "or the ridicule, either. And I'm surprised to hear the Nelson brothers are falling into habits like this, because they've been raised in a very cultivated home." She instantly regretted saying "a very cultivated home" because it was just the kind of phrase that would make Tom Nelson weak with laughter, but she couldn't take it back now. "Still, whatever the Nelson brothers may happen to feel like doing is beside the point. My concern is entirely for you."

"I don't get it," Laura said. "How come boys can do whatever they feel like and girls can't?"

"Because they're *boys*," Lucy cried, rising from her chair, and she knew at once she was out of control. "Boys have done whatever they've felt like since the beginning of *time*, don't you even know that? Haven't you even learned *that* yet, you poor, ignorant little – how smart do you have to *be* to know a thing like that? They're irresponsible and self-indulgent and careless and cruel, and they get away with it all their lives because they're *boys*."

Her voice stopped then, but she could tell it was too late. Laura was up and backing away across the room, looking at her with a mixture of apprehension and pity.

"Mom, you really oughta watch it, you know?" she said. "Maybe you could get your shrink to give you some stronger pills, or whatever it is those people do."

"I think we'd better let that be my business, dear, don't you? Now." And Lucy swept back her hair in a poor attempt at composure. "Can I – fix you something to eat before you go to bed?"

But Laura only said she wasn't hungry.

★

". . . And the point is I was wholly irrational," Lucy said in Dr. Fine's office a few days later. "I was raging at her like one of these madwomen whose only abiding passion is their hatred of men. It frightened me terribly and I've been frightened ever since, because I've never been that kind of person and I don't want to be that kind of person."

"Well, these adolescent years can be very trying for parents," Dr. Fine began, as carefully as if he were telling her something she didn't know, "and they're especially difficult in the case of a single parent. The more exasperating the child's behavior, the more severe the parent's response; this in turn provokes further flare-ups of rebellion in the child, and so a kind of vicious cycle is established."

"Yes," she said, straining for patience. "But I don't think I've made myself clear here, Doctor. As I've tried to explain, the matter of Laura and the dormitory is something I'm fairly sure I can deal with on my own. What I wanted to discuss with you today, you see, is this other thing – this sense of genuine alarm about myself; these increasing fears about myself."

"I understand," he said in the quick, automatic way that always suggested no understanding at all. "And you've expressed those fears, and I can only say I think they're exaggerated."

"Well, that's – swell," Lucy said. "So I've come here for nothing, once again."

If this had been a few years ago she might have sprung to her feet, gathered up her coat and purse, and headed for the door. But she felt she had used up all the dramatic possibilities of exits like that. She had walked out on Dr. Fine too many times for any new points to be made; and besides, there had never been any way of telling, in the next session, whether he'd minded her doing it at all.

"It's regrettable," he said, "that you sometimes feel you've come here for nothing, Mrs. Davenport, but perhaps that in itself is something we might do well to explore."

"Yeah, yeah, okay," Lucy said. "Okay."

"Mr. Santos?" she inquired in the League one afternoon. "May I speak with you for a minute, if you're free?"

And when she had his attention she said "I have two friends who are professional painters, and I'd like very much to show them something of what I've done. There are twelve canvases here that I've saved for myself, but I wondered if you could go through them and pick out perhaps four or five that you think are the better ones."

"Certainly," he said. "That would be a pleasure, Mrs. Davenport."

She expected him to linger over each painting lifted from her heavy stack, examining it, tilting his head this way and that as he did when confronting a picture that wasn't yet finished; instead he went through all of them so quickly, and with such apparent impatience to get the job done, that she began to wonder for the first time if there might be something a little – well, a little inauthentic about him.

He set six pictures aside, then looked doubtful and put two of them back. "These," he told her. "These four. These are your best."

And she almost said How can you tell? Instead, from long habit, she said "Thank you so much for your help."

"You're very welcome."

"Can I give you a hand with those, Lucy?" said an agreeable boy named Charlie Rich who worked in her studio, and together they got all twelve canvases out of the Art Students League and down the sidewalk and into the trunk of her car, with Mr. Santos's four selections placed carefully on top.

255

"You're not leaving us, are you, Lucy?" Charlie Rich asked her.

"Oh, I don't think so," she told him. "Not yet. I'll be back."

"Good. Glad to hear it. Because you're one of the very few people I look forward to seeing every day."

"Well, that's – very nice, Charlie," she said. "Thank you." He was a sturdy, attractive kid and a good painter; she guessed he was probably ten or twelve years younger than herself.

"I've often wanted to take you to lunch," he said, "but I never had the nerve to ask."

"Well, I think that'd be nice," she said. "I'd enjoy it. Let's do it soon."

Charlie's hair was blowing awry in the wind and he used one hand to try and keep it in place. He wore his hair a little longer and fuller than average – a little like the Beatles; a little like the Kennedy brothers – and that was something she'd noticed in any number of other young men lately. In a few more years there might no longer be an "average" haircut for men, any more than there were hats.

"Well," she said, with the car keys out and ready in her hand. "I ought to be getting started. I'm going to show my pictures to two very good professional painters tonight, and I'm a little scared. Maybe you'd better pray for me."

"Oh, I don't pray for anybody, Lucy," he said, "because I've never believed in that stuff. Tell you what I'll do, though." And he came up close and touched her arm. "I'll think about you all the time."

Harmon Falls would be her first stop. She had called Paul Maitland last night to arrange this visit, and he'd tried to shy away from it by saying he'd never been a very good judge of other people's painting, but she'd persisted. "Whoever said you're supposed to be a 'judge,' Paul? I only want you to look at these pictures and see if you like them, that's all, because if you do it'll mean a great, great deal to me."

And her imagination had taken it from there. She knew she'd be able to tell at once if he liked them. If he glanced back at her face with even a slight nod or a slight smile, after looking at each picture, it would mean he thought they were good. And if he impulsively slung his arm around her, or anything like that, it would mean he thought she was a painter.

Peggy Maitland might then come and join them in a long, three-way hug of comradeship — they'd all be laughing because they'd be off balance and stepping on each other's shoes — and on the high wave of that exhilaration it might be easy for Lucy to bring them along with her to the Nelsons' party tonight.

"Isn't it about time, Paul?" she would say. "Isn't it about time you got over this senseless prejudice? The Nelsons are wonderful people, and they'd love to meet you."

And there could then be a fine joining of three painters in Tom Nelson's studio. The two men might be a little reserved at first — they'd shake hands firmly enough, then step back to look each other up and down — but all the tension would dissolve when Lucy put her pictures out for display.

"My God, Lucy," Tom Nelson might say in a hushed voice. "How'd you ever learn to paint like that?"

Still, nobody had to tell her how treacherous the imagination could be. This was what Dr. Fine called "fantasizing," as wretchedly graceless a word as most of his others, and she resolved to put it all out of her mind.

Paul was still out on some carpentry job when Lucy got to the Maitlands' house; that was too bad, because she always knew she wouldn't get a very gracious welcome from Peggy.

". . . I never drink until Paul gets home," Peggy explained when they were seated uncomfortably together, "but I can offer you a cup of coffee. And I made some raisin cookies this morning; would you like one?"

Lucy didn't really want coffee, and the trouble with the raisin cookie was that it looked at least six inches wide. She didn't know how she was ever going to get through it. There were only a few topics she could discuss with Peggy Maitland, and she lingered over each of them as a way of warding off silence.

Yes, her mother and stepfather were "fine." Yes, Diana and Ralph Morin were also "fine", though still in Philadelphia; they had two little boys now and were expecting a third child soon. "And speaking of that," Peggy said, "I'm pregnant too. We just found out."

Lucy told her that was wonderful; she said she was delighted; she said she was sure it would make them both very happy, and she even said she hoped it would be only the first of a good many children because she'd always imagined Paul and Peggy as ideal parents of a big family.

But while listening to herself saying all those things, holding the giant cookie just short of her lips, she was fully aware that silence would fall in the room as soon as her voice stopped.

And it did. She managed to take a bite of the cookie and to say "Oh, this is good" around her chewing, but from then on the silence was complete. Peggy asked no questions of Lucy – not even about Laura; not even about the Art Students League – and because there were no more questions there was no more talk. All they were doing now, adrift in all this silence, was waiting for Paul to come home.

I've never liked you, Peggy, Lucy said in her mind. You're very pretty and I know everybody thinks you're a treasure, but you've always struck me as a spoiled, selfish, rude little girl. Why haven't you ever grown up enough to be kind, like most people?

Or even considerate? Or even courteous?

But at last there was a stamping outside the front door and Paul came into the house. "Hey," he said as he put down his heavy toolbox. "Good to see you, Lucy."

He looked tired – he was getting a little old for manual labor in the service of art – and he made straight for the liquor supply. That was a lucky thing for Lucy because it meant that as soon as both the Maitlands' backs were turned she was able to open her purse and stuff the damned cookie inside it.

Paul was well into his second drink before he seemed to remember why Lucy was here. "How about those pictures?" he asked her.

"They're out in the car."

"Want a hand with them?"

"No; sit still, Paul," she said. "I'll get them. There're only four."

She was already steeled for disappointment when she brought them in and arranged them on the floor against the living-room wall. She was ready to regret having come to this house in the first place.

"Well, these are nice, Lucy," Paul said after a while. "Very nice."

Mr. Santos had a way of saying "nice" that could fill you with pride and hope, but that wasn't how Paul Maitland used the word. And he didn't once look back from the pictures at Lucy's face.

"I've never been much of a judge, as I told you," he said, "but I can certainly see how the League's been good for you. You've learned a lot."

It took less time to gather up and stack the paintings than it had to set them out, and she carried the four of them easily under one arm as she went to the door.

Paul got up to wish her goodnight, and that was when he

looked into her eyes for the first time, with the sorrow of an old friend's apology for not having been able to say more.

"Come back and see us again soon, Lucy," he said, and Peggy didn't say anything at all.

Lucy went home just long enough to take a shower and change her clothes, because she had promised to be in Tom Nelson's studio well in advance of the party crowd. And while she was brushing her hair a small, nice thing occurred to her before she could quite remember what it was: Charlie Rich would be thinking about her all the time.

Tom was playing the drums along with a Lester Young recording, and his face looked lost in the music, but he stopped at once and got up and turned off the record player when he saw Lucy come in.

"Now, listen, Tom," she began. "I want you to promise me something. If you don't like these pictures I want you to tell me so. If you can say *why* you don't like them it might be helpful, because I might learn something, but the main thing is to let me have it straight from the shoulder. No fooling around."

"Oh, that goes without saying," he said. "I'll be merciless. I'll be brutal. Would it be okay if I tell you first, though, that you look terrific tonight?"

And she couldn't fake much shyness when she thanked him for that, because she knew she did look good. She was wearing a new dress of the kind said to do wonders for her; her hair was exactly right, and her need to know about the paintings might well have brought a certain radiance to her face and eyes.

She placed the four pictures along the studio wall, not far from the trap drums, and Tom dropped nimbly to his haunches to examine each one. He took so long over them that she began to suspect he was stalling, using the time to figure out what he would say.

"Yeah," he said at last, and one of his expressive hands followed a curving line in the painting she had decided she liked best. "Yeah, that's nice, the way you did that. This whole area over here's nice, too, and so's this here. Then here in this other one, you got a nice design going for you. Colors are pretty, too."

Then he stood up, and she knew that if she didn't ask a question or two there would be no more talk at all.

"Well, Tom," she said, "I didn't think they'd take you by storm, exactly, but can you tell me one sort of general thing about these paintings? Do you think they're a little on the amateur-night-in-Dixie side?"

"A little on the amateur what?"

"Well, that's just an expression. I mean do you think they're amateurish work?"

He backed away from her and sank both hands into the side pockets of his paratrooper's jacket, looking irritated and compassionate at the same time.

"Aw, Lucy, come on," he said. "What can I say? Sure they're amateurish, dear, but that's because you're an amateur. You can't expect to do professional work after a few months at the League, and nobody else can expect it of you, either."

"It hasn't been a few months, Tom," she told him. "It's been almost three years."

"Can I peek?" Pat Nelson called from the kitchen, and she came into the studio drying her hands on a dish towel. After she'd peeked, after she'd inspected the four paintings for a conscientious length of time, she told Lucy they were very impressive.

But the first party guests would be arriving soon, so Lucy took the pictures out to the driveway where her car was parked. She placed the four of them on top of the other eight, then slammed and locked the trunk on them all – and with the finality of that slam she knew she would never go back to the Art Students League.

For a long time she stood alone under the high, heavily whispering trees and pressed her knuckles to her lips like Blanche Dubois, but she didn't cry. Blanche had never cried either; it was Stella who did all the "luxurious" crying. Blanche had no need to cry because she was acquainted with despair, and Lucy felt she was coming to be acquainted with it too.

But despair would have to wait at least a few more hours, because this was a party night at the Nelsons'. Chip Hartley would probably be among the guests, but she'd learned long ago not to dread that: they had often met and talked pleasantly at these parties since the end of their time together. Once or twice – three times, actually – she had even gone back to Ridgefield and slept with him. They were "friends."

And as she walked around to the Nelsons' kitchen door she changed her mind about the League. She would go back there, but it would only be for the purpose of seeing Charlie Rich. He might turn out to be older than he looked; and besides, however treacherous the word "friend" might be, she knew she was going to need all the friends she could get.

In the humid brightness of the kitchen she stood with one hand on her hip like a fashion model and the other calmly smoothing her hair. She was thirty-nine and didn't know much about anything and probably never would, but she didn't need Tom Nelson or anyone else to tell her she had never looked prettier.

"Pat?" she said. "As long as everybody knows I'm practically an alcoholic anyway, do you suppose I could fix myself a drink?"

PART THREE

Chapter One

For Michael Davenport, looking back, the time after his divorce would always fall into two historical periods: pre-Bellevue and post-Bellevue. And although the first lasted only a little more than a year, it came to seem longer than that in memory because so many things happened to him then.

It was a year of melancholy and regret – he had only to look into the infinite sadness of his daughter's face to be reminded of that, even when she smiled, even when she laughed. Still, he soon found there could be an unexpected vigor in his days alone – a frequent quickening of the spirit, a brave and youthful readiness for anything; and it would always nourish his secret pride to know that within three weeks after leaving Tonapac he won a young and stunningly pretty girl.

"Well, sure it's a good-enough place," Bill Brock said, pacing around the cheap apartment Michael had found for himself on Leroy Street, in the West Village, "but you can't just hole up here alone all the time, Mike, or you're gonna go crazy. Look: there's this big-assed party uptown Friday night – some advertising guy I hardly even know. He comes on like an extra-smooth gangster or something, but what the hell: almost anything might turn up at a party like that." And Brock crouched over Michael's desk to write down a name and address.

The door there was opened by a hearty man who said "Any friend of Bill Brock's is a friend of mine," and Michael ventured into a loud roomful of talking, drinking strangers who might have been picked at random off the street: they seemed to have nothing in common but their various kinds of new and expensive clothes.

"Pretty big crowd," Bill Brock said when Michael had found him at last, "but I'm afraid there isn't much good stuff – much available stuff, anyway. There's an extraordinary little English girl in the other room, but you'll never get near her. She's surrounded."

She was surrounded, all right: five or six men were trying to claim and hold her attention. But she was so extraordinary – all eyes and lips and cheekbones as she stood chatting in an upper-class English accent, like the prettiest girl in an English movie – that any chance of getting near her seemed worth the effort.

". . . I like your eyes," she told him. "You have very sad eyes."

Within five minutes she'd agreed to meet him at the front door, "as soon as I can get away from all this"; that took five minutes more; then they spent half an hour having a drink in a bar around the corner, where she told him her name was Jane Pringle, that she was twenty, that she'd come to this country five years ago when her father was "appointed to direct the American part of an enormous international corporation," but that her parents were now divorced and she'd been "sort of at loose ends for a while." She wanted him to know, though, that she was wholly independent: she earned her living as a secretary in a theatrical press-agent's office, and she loved her job: "I love the people there, and they love me."

But Michael got her out of that bar and into a cab even before she stopped talking, and then in almost no time at all she was naked in his bed with her sweet legs locked around his own, writhing and gasping and having at last what she later declared, in tears, to be the first orgasm of her life.

Jane Pringle was almost too good to be true, and the best part was that she wanted to stay with him indefinitely – or, as she said, "until you get tired of me." Their first days and weeks together may not quite have been the happiest in Michael's memory – there were a few too many artificial smiles and sighs for that – but they let him know that all his senses had come alive again, in surprisingly fresh and vivid ways, and that was enough for the time being.

She was agreeably quick to remove all traces of her presence every other weekend, when Laura came into town to visit him; but on each of those Sunday nights, after seeing Laura safely aboard the train for Tonapac again, he knew he could ride the subway home and find his windows lighted on Leroy Street: Jane was always there and waiting for him.

Her nominal residence, where she kept most of her belongings, was the home of a "tiresome old aunt" near Gramercy Park. Didn't the aunt wonder about her new living arrangement? "No, no," Jane assured him. "She never asks questions. She wouldn't dare. She's fearfully bohemian herself. Oh, Michael, aren't you ever going to take off your clothes?"

She found so many ways of saying he was wonderful that he might have come to believe it, if he hadn't had to face the diminished self-esteem implicit in each day's work. Nothing had come right in any of the poems he'd taken up since moving back to New York. At first he thought having Jane might make a difference, but after she'd been with him a month or two he was still struggling with the words.

He couldn't complain of needing more time alone, because

Jane was away all day during the week; but that in itself was part of the trouble: he missed her when she was gone.

And she did seem to love her job. She called it "a fun job," no matter how often he told her "fun" wasn't an adjective; she never allowed herself to be late to work in the morning, or to be less than perfectly dressed and groomed, and he was always surprised in the evening to find how fresh and exhilarated she could be after those long secretarial hours. She would walk back into his life with her face smelling of the sharp fall weather, humming a song from a new musical comedy, sometimes bringing a bag of expensive groceries ("Aren't you getting a little bored with restaurants, Michael? Besides, I love to cook for you; I love to watch you eat the things I've made.")

Even at times when her job wasn't fun, it was always a romance.

"I cried at work today," she reported once, lowering her eyes. "I couldn't help it – but Jake held me in his arms until I felt better, and I thought that was awfully nice of him."

"Who's Jake?" And Michael was startled at how quickly she could make him jealous.

"Oh, he's one of the men; one of the partners. The other one's Meyer, and he's nice too, but sometimes he's gruff. He shouted at me today and he's never done that before; that was why I cried. I could tell he felt rotten about it later, though, and he apologized very sweetly before he went home."

"So how big an agency is it? Just those two guys, or what?"

"Oh, no, there's a staff of four. One of them's Eddie; he's twenty-six and we're really good friends. We have lunch together almost every day, and once we tangoed all the way down Forty-second Street, just to be crazy. Eddie's going to be a singer – is a singer, I mean – and I think he's terrifically good."

He decided not to ask any more questions about the office.

He didn't want to hear that stuff, and none of it would matter anyway as long as she came home eager to please him every night.

Bill Brock's word "extraordinary" kept recurring to him as he watched Jane move around the apartment, as he walked with her in the evening streets, or sat with her in the old White Horse. She *was* an extraordinary girl. He had come to feel he could never have enough of her flesh, and his missing her in working hours seemed to suggest a gentler attachment, too. He scarcely even noticed her artificial smiles and sighs anymore – they were part of her style – but he often wished there weren't such an abundance and variety of information in the story of her life.

She had been married at seventeen to a young teacher at the exclusive New Hampshire boarding school she'd attended, but the marriage was so "horrible" her parents had it annulled in less than a year.

"And that was the last time I had to depend on my parents in any way at all," she said. "I'd never dream of asking them for anything again. They're so busy hating each other now, and so busy being in love with their new people, that I've sort of come to despise them both. And the worst of it is they feel so *guilty* about me: God, that's infuriating. It's not so bad in my mother's case, way out in California, but my father's a real nuisance because he's right here in town. And then there's lovely Brenda – that's his wife, you see; my stepmother. The curious thing is I was quite fond of Brenda at first: she seemed sort of like an older sister and we were very close for a while, until I began to learn what a manipulative person she is. Brenda would absolutely dominate my life if she had her way."

But all this family bitterness could vanish in a breath. Jane sometimes used Michael's telephone to call her father, and she would talk for an hour with an almost flirtatious enthusiasm, calling him "Daddy" in every sentence and helplessly laughing at his jokes, then asking to speak to Brenda and spending half an hour more in the kind of soft, cryptic, gossipy conversation that most girls reserve for their best friends.

And perhaps because he had a daughter of his own, Michael was mostly pleased with the harmony of those talks: he would even smile to himself as her sweet English voice went on and on at the phone across the room, and it occurred to him more than once that he'd like to meet her father someday. ("I'm so glad," the man might say; "so glad Jane seems to have found a sense of stability and direction at last. . . .")

Her father hadn't always been a corporate executive, Jane explained after one of the phone calls; journalism was his first love, and during the war he'd been one of the top correspondents for a leading London newspaper. In an earlier version her father had spent the war in hazardous espionage work for the British government, but Michael didn't call that to her attention because for all he knew it might have been possible for a journalist to serve as a spy.

There were further discrepancies, though, in some of the other things she told him.

It was her "horrible" former husband who had taken her virginity, so clumsily that the thought of it could still make her shudder; but happier memories once brought her back to the year she was sixteen, when she'd given "everything, oh, everything" to a boy she'd met at a lakeside resort in Maine.

The summer before last she had undergone an extremely painful abortion, in New Jersey; she'd been obliged to find the abortionist herself and to pay him out of her own salary, and the consequences of his bungled work had left her weak and ill for months; yet the summer before last was also when she had hitchhiked all over Western Europe with a boy named Peter and

270

had a marvelous time until Peter's father insisted he come home and go back to Princeton in the fall.

Michael tried to clear up a few points in some of her stories, but there were so many others that he lapsed into a bewildered silence most of the time. And then it began to seem that she was willfully testing the limits of his credulity, as troubled children sometimes do.

On one side of her exquisite face there was a small patch of scar tissue, suggesting that a boil or a cyst had once been removed from that spot, and Michael told her one afternoon, in bed, that he thought it made her all the prettier.

"Oh, that," she said. "Well, I hate that scar, and I hate everything it stands for." Then, after a significant pause, she said "The Gestapo wasn't very well known for gentleness."

He took a long breath. "Baby, where do you get the Gestapo? Please don't give me the Gestapo, sweetheart, because I just sort of happen to know you were six years old when the war ended. Now, suppose we talk about something else, okay?"

"Well, but it's true," she insisted. "That was one of their techniques: torture the children in order to make the parents talk. And I wasn't even six when it happened; I was five. My mother and I were living in Occupied France then because we hadn't been able to get back to England. And I imagine it must've been difficult, having to sort of hide out all the time, but I still have wonderfully clear memories of the Normandy countryside, and the nice family of farmers we knew. And one day these dreadful men came clumping into the house demanding information about my father. Mummy was very brave, actually: she wouldn't tell them anything until she saw the knife piercing my face – then she broke and told them whatever they needed to know. If she hadn't I might have been killed, or I might have been mutilated for life."

"Yeah," Michael said. "Well, that's a terrible story, all right, and the worst part is I don't believe it. Now, listen, dear. You know I'm crazy about you; you know I'd do anything in the world for you, but I'm not taking any more of this bullshit, do you understand? Christ's sake, I don't think you even know what's true and what isn't."

"Well, I certainly don't see how an attitude like that deserves any comment at all," she said quietly. She got out of bed and walked away, and from the tense shape of her back he thought she might be ashamed, but then she turned and gave him a calm, appraising look. "You're very brutal, aren't you," she said. "At first I thought you were a sensitive man, but you're really very brutal and unkind."

"Yeah, yeah, yeah," he said, trying for a tone of great weariness.

That was about as bad as things got during the fall, and even then he knew they would pick up. If he allowed her to sulk for a while, and to take a shower and change her clothes, he knew she would find some easy, face-saving way to become a sweet companion again; and by that time he'd be willing to have her back on any terms.

He never tired of showing her off to other men – even to strangers, even in restaurants of her choosing that he couldn't really afford – and he happily brought her along to a bar uptown to meet Tom Nelson once, when Tom was in the city for the day. He knew Tom's face would go slack and weak with envy at the sight of her, and it did. That particular afternoon came close to being wrecked, though, when Jane leaned attractively across the table and said "What do you do?"

"Oh, I'm a painter."

"Modern?" she inquired.

Tom Nelson blinked several times behind his glasses to

272

suggest it had been a good many years since anybody had asked him a question like that. Then he said "Yeah, I guess so, sure."

"Oh. Well, I suppose any kind of work can be fun if you like it, but personally I loathe modern art. All modern art leaves me absolutely cold."

Tom began carefully molding a soaked cocktail napkin around the base of his drink then, and it was time for Michael to fill the silence with whatever quick, inconsequential talk came into his head.

That was another thing about Jane Pringle: she didn't really know very much. Her stepmother had taught her a lot about clothes, and she'd heard enough talk around the office to develop strong opinions on current Broadway shows – she could always tell you which of them were great and which were trash – but she hadn't bothered with many other kinds of learning since her time as an inattentive, daydreaming adolescent in boarding school. Her ignorance was so wide that Michael wondered if her lying might have begun as a way of trying to disguise it.

She told him she would have to spend Christmas with her father and stepmother because they'd been looking forward to it for months; then she called him from their place and said she'd decided to stay over for the New Year's holiday too.

When she finally did get back to Leroy Street she seemed a little distracted. Even after she'd sat down with Michael she kept glancing around the apartment as if unable to believe she had ever really lived here, and once or twice she looked at his face in the same uncertain way.

"Well, I had a glorious time," she told him. "We went to thirteen different parties."

"Yeah? Well, that's quite a – quite a few parties."

She had a new hairstyle now, too short for his liking, and seemed to have acquired a new set of mannerisms to go with it:

crisp, businesslike, no-nonsense. Someone had given her an amber cigarette holder of the kind designed to trap poisonous tars, and she used it faithfully for the rest of the winter, allowing it to distort her face in a clenching, squinting way that made her look ten years older and not very smart.

In February she said it would be more sensible to have a place of her own, and he agreed with her. He helped her study the "Apartments Available" columns of the *Times* as carefully as if she were his own daughter starting out in the world. They found a suitable place in the West Twenties, overlooking the gardens of the General Theological Seminary, but Jane declined the landlord's offer to have it painted before she moved in: she wanted to paint it herself, she said, "so it'll feel more like my own apartment."

And that meant Michael had to stand with her in paint-and-hardware stores while she hesitated much too long over choosing just the right shade of off-white, just the right kinds of paint rollers and brushes; it meant he had to wear spattered jeans and climb a stepladder and breathe the paint fumes and tire himself out, wondering all the while what the hell he was doing this for.

Once when Jane was high on another stepladder, dressed in a too-scanty pair of shorts and a too-scanty halter, reaching out to touch up the molding of a front window, there came a happy chorus of cheers and whistles from young Episcopalians in the shrubbery across the street. She laughed and waved to them; then she arranged herself into a slightly more provocative position on the ladder, and blew them a kiss.

Later, she told Michael she wanted her bedroom painted black.

"Why?"

"Oh, just because. I've always wanted a black bedroom. Doesn't it seem sort of delightfully sexy?"

When the paint job was finished, black bedroom and all, he decided to leave her alone for a few days; maybe even for a week.

The next time he went to see her she seemed as eager as ever to have him in her bed, but in the aftermath of it she wanted talk in a way he didn't find congenial. She explained to him, in language she could only recently have learned from some book of pop psychology (*How to Love*, by Derek Fahr?) that she thought their "relationship" might be more "valid" now that it was "structured on a more realistic basis."

"Yeah, yeah, okay," he said. "So when d'ya wanna do this again? Tuesday?"

On another evening she said "Two of the Seminary boys dropped in today; they were terribly nice, both very shy. I gave them tea and fig newtons – oh, not the little cheap ones; the good imported English kind – and we had a delightful time. Then one of them had to go to a class or something, but the other one stayed for hours. His name's Toby Watson and he's just my age. After he graduates he's going to work his way around the world. Isn't that exciting?"

"No."

"He's going to go all the way down the Amazon and all the way up the Nile, and he's going to climb one of the Himalayas alone. He said it may take two or three years out of his life, but he said 'I think I'll be a better person for it, and a better priest.' "

"Yeah, well, okay."

The end of it came abruptly, on the phone, when he called one day to ask if he could come over that night.

"Oh, no," she said, sounding frightened, as if "no" might not be enough to stop him from coming over anyway. "No, tonight's out, and so's tomorrow; so is every other night this week, actually."

"How come?"

275

"What d'you mean, 'how come'?"

"You know; I mean why?"

"Because I have a house guest."

" 'A house guest,' " he repeated, hoping to make her see how false it had sounded to him.

"Well, certainly. In a normally active social life, having occasional house guests is a perfectly normal part of social activity."

"So do you want me to quit calling you altogether, then?"

"If you wish. That's entirely up to you."

For hours after he'd hung up the phone, knowing he didn't have a girl anymore, feeling he'd never really had this one at all and wondering if he'd ever really wanted her anyway, Michael walked around whispering "The hell with it; the hell with it."

"Well, shit, it's too bad, though," Bill Brock counseled him, "because she was a *pretty* girl. I could've killed you when I saw you leaving the party with her that night. Still, you don't want to let yourself sink back into isolation, Mike; that's the worst thing you could do. There's plenty of good stuff around, if you put your mind to it."

And for a while it seemed he was putting his mind to nothing else. It was almost as if sex itself, or rather a determined venereal questing, had taken the place of ambition in his life.

There were two girls, one after the other, who each had separate, carefully explained reasons for not wanting to see him again after a single night. Then he spent five or six weeks with a muscular woman who lived on unemployment checks but had enough yellowed newspaper clippings to prove she was a dancer, who often cried and complained that what he felt for her was "something less than love; something a lot less than love," and who ultimately confessed that she'd lied to him about her age: she wasn't really thirty-one; she was forty.

And there were times when he struck out – when he would sit in an agony of conversation at some restaurant table with a girl who'd keep looking around the room, or down at her plate, until the time came for him to take her back to wherever she lived; then she'd say "Well, it's been nice," and all the way home his mouth would taste of failure.

By the end of that spring he was daunted enough to look for easier ways of spending his time. There were agreeable couples to visit; there were other single men to drink with; there were even books to read – he had almost forgotten about reading – and as his daily work improved it often left him too tired for adventurous evenings anyway.

A young writer named Bob Osborne and his girlfriend Mary, both in their twenties and planning to be married any day now, were the couple he found most agreeable to visit. He always felt so good in their company that he was careful not to go to their place too often, or ever to stay too long, for fear of seeming to impose on their youth and generosity; so it was a nice surprise when the girlfriend appeared at his door one afternoon, and he greeted her like a jovial friend of the family: "Well, Mary; good to see you."

"Look," she said, "I can explain everything."

And he was slow even to recognize that remark. He asked her to sit down; he went into the kitchen to get her a drink, and there he remembered that the last time he'd seen this couple he had made them both laugh by pointing out that "Look, I can explain everything" was the most commonly used line of dialogue in the history of American movies – the same little joke that had won the approval of Tom and Pat Nelson in their upstairs apartment in Larchmont, years ago. Sometimes it seemed that he'd said six or eight funny things in his life, and that what passed for his sense of humor would always depend on a skillful recycling of old material, over and over again.

"You and Bob get married yet?" he asked the girl as he brought the drink to a low table near her chair, and that was when he remembered her name: Mary Fontana.

"Well, not quite," she said, "but it's set for the twenty-third – that's eight days from now, I think. Oh, thanks, that's lovely."

Then he sat across from her, smiling in courtesy as she talked, allowing himself to admire her long bare legs and her fresh summer dress. Everything about her looked nice.

Bob had decided to hole up alone at their country place this week, she told him, because he wanted to make the final changes in his book and have it done before the wedding, so she'd stayed in town to take care of a few last-minute things – shopping, closing out her old apartment, meeting Bob's mother for tea at the Plaza; stuff like that.

"Well, good," he said. "I'm glad you stopped by, Mary."

But he didn't begin to get the overwhelming point of her visit until he had almost obliged her to spell it out for him.

". . . So I talked it over with my analyst today," she said in a steadily weakening voice, bending to put her glass on the coffee table, "and I don't think he approved, exactly, but he didn't raise any – didn't raise any objections, either. So anyway . . ." She sat straight again, swept back a heavy lock of her dark hair, and looked gravely into his eyes. "Anyway, here I am. As you see."

"Well, Mary, I guess I don't quite under – Wow." And he swallowed. "Oh, Jesus. Oh, Christ Almighty."

They both stood up at the same time but he had to get awkwardly around the coffee table before he could take her in his arms; then she melted against him with a moist little moan he would never forget. She was tall and supple and smelled of lilac perfume with a faint tang of lemons, and her mouth was marvelous. He couldn't believe this was happening, but it did make its own kind of sense: the nicest girls in the world might be frightened of marriage when the time came, might impulsively turn away from it, if only for a few days, with some other available man who'd caught their interest – and only a God damn fool could fail to be honored by a thing like that.

Soon her fresh summer dress was on the floor and so were the little drifts of her weightless underwear, and she slid into his bed while he fought free of his own clothes.

"Oh, Mary," he said. "Oh, Mary Fontana."

Then he was all over her, making a feast of her flesh with his hands and his mouth, making her gasp and whimper, but it wasn't long before a wave of fear broke over him: What if he couldn't get it up for this girl?

And he couldn't. The important thing at first was to keep her from knowing it, and that took him into ever-more elaborate preliminaries, stalling and stalling, until all her liveliness ebbed away.

". . . Michael? Are you all right?"

"Jesus, I don't know; I can't seem to – can't seem to get started, is all."

"Well, that's not really very surprising," she said, "considering the way I sort of – burst in on you with all this. Let's just wait awhile, okay? Then we can try again."

But at midnight and later they were still trying. Nothing worked. They were a couple of laborers engaged in a subtle, self-defeating job that could only make them weak with frustration and fatigue. And during the long intervals, sitting up with cigarettes in the darkness, they both found solace in auto-biography.

Oh, it hadn't been easy to be an Italian girl at Vassar. It hadn't even been very nice to be an Italian girl at Coward-McCann, because some of the people there seemed to assume she'd be sort of cheap and on the make. It often seemed that nothing in her life had been very nice, for that matter, until she met Bob. Or was that the wrong thing to say? Did it bother him when she talked about Bob?

No, no, of course not; that would be silly. They both knew what was going on here.

And they both knew too, all too well, that nothing was really going on here at all.

Well, he couldn't really say what had gone wrong with his marriage, even now – and maybe nobody ever could, about any marriage – though he guessed it probably did have something to do with his wife's money. And the story of his wife's money would take a little explaining; it might be difficult to understand even then; but did Mary want to hear it?

Mary did, and after hearing it she said it was wonderful that he'd taken such a firm stand and stuck to it all those years. She didn't think she'd ever known a man as "principled" as that.

Well, but hell; who knew? Maybe if he'd floated along on Lucy's fortune they might both have been an awful lot happier, and Laura too; maybe he could even have gotten more work published.

But then he would've had to be somebody else, Mary pointed out. He couldn't have been who he was without that essential integrity. Besides, if he weren't who he was, she wouldn't be here.

And Michael thought that was nice – she was a girl who knew how to pay a compliment – so he took the cigarette from her fingers and stubbed it out in the ashtray along with his own. Then he kissed her slowly a few times, murmuring her name and saying she was lovely, and began to fondle and stroke her again. He kept her sitting beside him on the bed until his hands had persuaded her that everything would be all right this time; then he let her turn and bring up her legs and lie on her back. But it was no better than the times before.

The following day, jittery from too little sleep, he tried to appease his shame by taking Mary Fontana for a long slouching walk through the Village. She clung to his arm and gave it pleasant little squeezes now and then, but he did most of the talking, saying charming things in a flat, jaded voice that had come to sound a little like Humphrey Bogart's. If he couldn't be a man for her, at least he could be a character.

When they went to the White Horse, though, he stopped trying to entertain her. All he could do there was discover once again what a pretty girl she was, with her long neck and dark eyes and sweet mouth; it was almost as if the beer and the afternoon light were conspiring to make her more desirable than his wretched state of mind could stand.

But there was still time – they had the better part of a week left – and he knew it would be disastrous to abandon hope too soon.

Back at his place she made a shy, irresistible suggestion – "Want to take a shower together?" – and in the shower she was magnificent. He could have stared all afternoon at the nodding and swaying of her small, proud tits as she soaped and rinsed herself, and he was fascinated with the way her lovely thighs didn't quite come together at the top: the generous little space between them there was wide enough for two or three fingers and dense with the hanging curls of her big pubic bush, as though nature had meant her to be more emphatically a woman than most other girls.

Oh, Jesus, if he was ever going to have her it would be now. And he was more and more sure it would happen as they went about the business of toweling each other dry.

"Now," he kept murmuring. "Oh, now, baby . . ."

"Yes," she told him. "Yes . . ."

They were scarcely able to walk in their need to embrace, but they made the distance to the bed and lay ready for the consummation that would settle their lives.

Nope. No luck. No luck that time, either. And almost the worst part of these things now was that he'd run out of apologies: he didn't know what to say to her.

But once again they went on trying far into the night.

". . . Baby, do you think you could sort of tickle me? With your fingers?"

"Here, you mean? Like this?"

"No, I meant up here. Both sides. Both hands. There, that's it. Not quite so hard. Oh, yeah, yeah, that's good. That's good. . . ."

"Does it feel – are you getting – am I doing this right?"

"Well, never mind now, dear; it's gone. I lost it again. . . ."

At last she said "Oh, I think it's my fault. It must be my fault."

"No, come on, Mary, that's dumb; don't say that."

"I think it's true, though. I think you sort of basically despise me for being here instead of with Bob, and maybe I sort of despise myself."

"That's crazy," he told her. "I think it's tremendous that you're here. I love your being here. You'd never dream of despising yourself if I could – you know – if I could make it with you; and I will."

And they discussed those two points of view at some length, getting nowhere, until Mary said she would have to sleep because there were a lot of things to do tomorrow.

She spent the morning uptown, shopping for clothes and other wedding necessities; when she got back she changed into a new dress and went out again to see about her old apartment.

He was left alone so much that day that he had plenty of time to think in unprofitable, circling ways about impotence. Did other men go through it? If so, why was it so seldom discussed except in jokes? Did girls laugh and tattle about it among themselves, and did they think of it privately with revulsion and disdain? Was it something that a word or a glance or a drink could fix, at the right moment, or were you supposed to spend years in psychoanalysis trying to get to the root of it?

It was after she'd come back that afternoon, while they sat having a drink together, that Michael felt himself giving in to a reckless new idea: if some imponderably dumb failure of sex had caused all this trouble, an infusion of love might help.

And so he began to tell Mary Fontana that he loved her, that he'd been helplessly in love since the first night he'd met her at Bob's place, that he'd thought of her all the time and had scarcely been able to bear the idea of her marriage because he wanted her so badly for his own. "So do you see, Mary?" he concluded. "Will you try to understand? I love you, that's all. Love you."

And she was clearly embarrassed, blushing attractively as she looked down into her drink, but he could tell she was pleased, too. If nothing else, there might now be no further question of despising herself. She could easily shy away from making any declaration of love in return – that would take a lot more than she'd bargained for, after all, when she'd showed up at his door the other day – and even so, there could be a new romantic tenderness in their every maneuver from now on.

But the best part was that Michael had salvaged something important for himself. Even if revulsion and disdain were appropriate feelings to have about a man who couldn't get it up, they couldn't very readily be applied to a man in love.

"Oh, listen, Mary," he said, "I didn't mean to embarrass you; I just think it's better for both of us if you know the truth. I'd

283

have been lying if I hadn't told you." And he thought he could detect a quiet new authority in his voice: the desperation was gone. Love had made a difference.

They had another drink as if in celebration, with currents of love running as strong in the air as the whiskey in their veins; then soon they were naked in bed and eagerly determined to make everything new. As always before he began by stroking her thoroughly, as if to find out how she was made; then he brought her nipples out, one in his fingers and the other in his mouth, and fondled them until her hips began to move in the familiar rhythm of their own accord. For a while he tried to make her come with his hand, working two fingers in the warmth and moisture at the core of her and saying he loved her over and over again; then he went through the ritual rearrangement of both their bodies in order to have her with his mouth. But he'd known all along, since their first afternoon, that Mary didn't care for preliminary climaxes unless she could tell they would promise the big one later, the real one at the end. If you lingered too long over trying to bring her off with your hand or mouth she could always sense your trouble; then she'd unwittingly lose interest and her hips would stop. And if you timed things well enough to make your move before that happened – if you mounted her in the hope of a miracle, as Michael did today – it was like trying to push a length of rope: nobody can push a rope. Love may have helped, but it hadn't helped enough.

On the day she had arranged to have tea at the Plaza with Bob's mother she said she couldn't go through with it. She had never met any of Bob's family but they were all rich and Anglo-Saxon and that whole side of the thing had been preying on her mind for months and months. Oh, God, how could she possibly face the woman now?

"Well, baby," he counseled as he fastened her into the

expensive, elegant dress she had bought for the occasion, "I don't know why you can't just go up there and charm the hell out of her. She'll love you. Besides, it isn't as if you had anything to – you know – anything to reproach yourself with."

And Mary turned to him with a small, surprisingly cynical smile and said she guessed he was right.

When she got back from her meeting, a little exhilarated because it had gone pretty well after all – better than she'd expected – she arranged herself demurely in a chair to accept the drink Michael fixed for her. Then she glanced around the room and up into his face and down again: she seemed almost to be asking who he was and how she'd come to know him, and what she was doing in this funny apartment in the first place. He was reminded of the way Jane Pringle had looked around on coming back from her thirteen parties, and he knew it was time to start saying he loved her again.

"See?" he said. "I told you there was nothing to worry about. I knew she'd be crazy about you; anybody can tell you're an exceptional girl. You kind of make your own rules, but that's what all exceptional people do. Know something? I haven't heard you say a single cliché the whole time you've been here. Oh, I guess when you talk about your analyst you've come close to it once or twice, but that's because analysts *teach* people to speak in clichés. That's what they're in business for. I imagine you may have started going to that asshole because you felt a little out of the ordinary, but I'm not worried: he can't do you any harm because you *are* out of the ordinary, in ways he'll never be able to touch. You remind me a little of a girl I've admired for years and never even gotten close to. Girl named Diana; she's married now to some guy in Philadelphia. She told me once she liked a poem of mine called 'Coming Clean,' and I remember thinking Okay, that's it. If Diana Maitland likes 'Coming Clean'

I don't care if anybody else in the whole fucking world likes it or not. I've always been partial to out-of-the-ordinary girls, you see. Girls who know who they are and make up their own minds for their own reasons. . . ."

Listening to the rise and fall of his voice as he watched her face, he wondered how many cool, reserved girls he had tried to win over with this kind of flattering talk, going all the way back to certain girls around the air base in England, and he wondered if they'd all thought it was bullshit. Besides, there probably wasn't anything out of the ordinary about Mary Fontana: she was just a girl who'd wanted to get laid with a stranger before she got married. But he couldn't stop talking: he seemed to be afraid that if he stopped she might get up and leave, or that she might evaporate right there in her chair.

"Michael?" she said as soon as he gave her a chance to speak. "Let's take off our clothes and just be together in bed for a while, okay? I don't care if all we do is lie there."

And she apparently didn't care if all they did was lie there for however few days and nights were left until their time ran out. Michael didn't know what to make of that, but he had to admit it was a relief.

During the several hours that remained to be whiled away in the White Horse they were like an old married couple, or like a boy and girl who hadn't been out together before and didn't feel like starting anything sexy yet, exchanging agreeable remarks for no other purpose than to keep silence from closing in. Once, as he made his way up to the bar for another round and hoped she was watching his back, he found he was enjoying himself – feeling pretty good – and that knowledge was deeply frightening: If you could make a romance out of impotence, you must be crazy.

Then it was their last night. Tomorrow afternoon Mary

Fontana would take a train to Redding, Connecticut, and the following day, after her parents and sisters and friends had arrived on another train, she would be married in a "charming" Episcopalian chapel.

For a while all they did was lie there, between fresh sheets – he had changed the sheets three times this week because it would have been terrible to have them stale and sour through all this failure – and they talked a little but couldn't think of much to say.

When he began to stroke her with his hands he wondered if his hands would ever know any girl as well as they'd come to know this one. Then came the nipples, the moving hips, the flow of moisture, and the hazardous question of timing.

But the remarkable thing tonight was that he did manage to work himself inside her: it wasn't very solid but he was in there, and he knew she could feel him.

"Oh," she said. "Oh. Oh, I'm your woman."

He would remember thinking it was awfully nice of her to say a thing like that, but then he'd always known she was a nice girl. The trouble was that he could tell she was faking it; she'd said it only because of all the times he'd told her he loved her. She felt sorry for him; she wanted to give him something to keep on this last night – and in the very few seconds it took him to understand all that he shriveled and fell out of her. Afterwards, there was nothing more between them than there had ever been.

She had to pick up a few more things at Lord and Taylor's, she explained the next day, but that wouldn't take long, and her train didn't leave until five – and so they arranged to meet at the Biltmore at four, to have a couple of drinks and say goodbye.

"Well, but wait," he said. "Let's make it three-thirty, so we'll have more time."

"Okay."

When she'd left he began to make meticulous plans for how things would go at the Biltmore. There would be no sad, defeated, self-pitying looks across that cocktail table: he would be jaunty and witty for her, wearing his best clothes; it might even turn out to be as brave and bright a goodbye as a girl ever had on the day before her wedding.

But when the phone rang at three o'clock he knew it would be Mary, calling it off, and it was.

"Listen, I don't think the Biltmore's a very good idea after all," she said. "I think I'd rather just go to Grand Central by myself and – you know – get on the train."

"Oh. Well, okay." He wanted to say, Don't forget me, or, I'll never forget you, or, I love you, but none of those things would have sounded right, so all he said was "Okay, Mary."

And for a long time after they'd hung up he sat with his head in his hands, scratching every part of his scalp with all ten fingernails.

Mary would almost certainly tell Bob Osborne where she'd spent this week – she was too nice a girl not to do that, and soon – but she would almost certainly tell him, too, that nothing had "happened"; and the more Bob pressed for further information and details, the more and more she would tell. In the end, there would be nothing left of Michael Davenport at all.

He was useless to himself for many days. He was sick; he lost weight; he couldn't even begin to work. He knew this must be better than dying, but there were hours when he wasn't entirely sure of it.

Still, not even chagrin can last forever: the thing to do was lie low and wait for some unexpected renewal. And one morning later in the summer there was a brief, terse phone call from his agent that seemed faintly promising: an adaptation of one of his

288

old one-act plays would soon be produced on Canadian television, at a "minor" studio in Montreal.

The money he would earn from it was barely enough to cover a trip to Montreal and back, but he decided at once that there could be no better way to spend it. Whatever kind of botch they might make of his play, the cast of it would have to include one or two pretty girls.

At first he considered asking Bill Brock to go along with him, but Brock might make too strident a traveling companion; then he got a better idea: he called up Tom Nelson.

". . . I mean we'd have to use your car, of course," he said after he'd explained the thing, "but I'd buy the gas and we could take turns with the driving."

And Tom was quick to comply. Any excuse for a trip, he said, was good enough for him.

They set out together on a clear, pleasingly warm day, and Tom looked trim and peppy when he took the wheel. He wore a khaki Army shirt with shoulder tabs, the kind only officers were supposed to have, and he was full of wry little jokes.

But they hadn't even reached Albany before Michael began to wonder if Bill Brock might have been a better choice after all – or, better still, if it wouldn't have been smarter to have made the trip alone, on the train or the bus.

"Still got that English girl?" Tom inquired.

"Well, no, we kind of went our separate ways after a while. Had her for about five months, though."

"Good. And how about since then? Been getting much?"

"Oh, I've kept pretty busy."

"Good. And I'm beginning to get the picture on this Montreal business, too. You figure there'll be some nice girl in the show, and she'll come up to you with big eyes and say 'You mean you're the *author*?'"

"That's it," Michael said. "You got it. Kind of like the little museum girls who come up and say 'You mean you're Thomas *Nelson*?'"

And Nelson glanced away from the road with a smile that contained too much mockery to be engaging. "So are you prepared?" he asked. "You bring your rubbers?"

There was a package of them riding in Michael's pocket, but he was damned if he'd confirm or deny it.

"Don't worry, little soldier," he said. "There'll be enough for both of us."

They got lost several times in Montreal before finding the television studio, but they weren't late. A nervous young director said he hoped Michael would like the production; he gave him a mimeographed copy of the script, and Michael read enough of it to know the play had been badly tampered with: the dialogue was bloated to soap-opera proportions, the pacing was lost beyond hope, and the ending would probably be wreckage.

"Excuse me; are you Mr. Davenport?" And a young girl was looking hopefully into his eyes. She said her name was Susan Compton and she'd be playing the lead tonight; she said she was awfully glad to meet him; she said she knew the television version was "awful" because she'd read the original when it came in and found it "beautiful"; she said she was afraid she'd have to go now but hoped they could get together later because she'd "love" to talk to him. And as Michael watched her move gracefully away into a cluster of other actors, he knew he couldn't have found a better reason for coming all the way up here.

Then he and Tom Nelson were seated in a glass booth high in the back of the studio, near the sound engineer, watching the play on a "monitor" screen that hung at the level of their eyes. Except for repeated nudges and frowns there was no way for Michael to explain to Nelson that this wasn't his own play at all, but after a while he decided it didn't matter. A girl would be waiting when the messy thing was over – a girl whose every turn and move were nice to watch in the medium shots, and whose face, in the close-ups, was very pretty indeed.

The ending was almost as much of a sellout as he'd feared, but as soon as the studio lights came up he found his way down to the set and made straight for Susan Compton and told her she'd been wonderful; then he asked if he could buy her a drink.

"Well, I'd love to," she said, "but the thing is we're all going out together. It's sort of a cast party, you see, though of course you and your friend must come along with us."

Soon they were in some big, bright Montreal restaurant where the waiters had neatly shoved a number of tables together for the party. Susan Compton sat at one end, in the place of honor, with the director on one side of her and the leading man on the other; then came the other actors and a few technicians, two by two, with Tom Nelson and Michael hunched at the far end as unexpected guests.

For a while Michael considered saying, Look, Tom: I think I might get somewhere with this Compton girl, so maybe you'd better take a hotel room and go on home alone tomorrow, okay? But the longer he watched her up there, talking and laughing and making little gestures in the air with her brandy snifter as if it were the very symbol of her triumph tonight, the longer he hesitated. When the party was over she might easily give him a quick, brandy-scented kiss, out on the sidewalk, and disappear into Montreal with some actor's arm around her waist, while Tom Nelson stood watching – and if that happened, Nelson's teasing would be merciless all the way back to New York.

No, getting rid of Nelson could wait: the first thing to do was get the girl. As soon as he had the chance he would go up and ask if he could take her home. If she said yes, the problem of Nelson would resolve itself: a few quick, amiable words would take care of it – or maybe only a significant wink, if Nelson was ready to be agreeable. Then the author of the original play would be free to find a taxicab for the girl and himself, and the rest of the night would be rich with promise.

And his plan almost worked: he had to shoulder his way through any number of smiling television people as they rose and turned away from the table at last, but he got the girl – or at least he got within speaking distance.

"Susan? Can I take you home?"

"Well, that'd be lovely; thanks."

"Car's right outside," said Tom Nelson.

"Oh, wonderful," she said; "you have a car."

So there were three of them in the damned car, finding their way to some suburban fringe of the city, and Michael rode with a sense of defeat.

Susan Compton explained that she lived with her family – she hoped to have a place of her own soon, but the apartment shortage was terrible in Montreal – and when they arrived at her parents' house all the windows were dark.

She led them in whispers down to the basement and flicked on the lights of a surprisingly spacious oak-paneled room, the kind of "game room" that upper-middle-class families always seemed to take pride in.

"Can I get you a drink?" she asked, and there was indeed what looked like a well-stocked bar at one end of this ample place. There were two or three deep, handsomely upholstered sofas, too, and Michael began to see that the night might still have possibilities if only Tom Nelson would get out of here. But

Nelson had a drink and then another one, strolling around the room to inspect the paneling as if for tiny imperfections, or perhaps for places where his watercolors might be hung to their best advantage.

"I can't tell you how I wish we could've done the play the way you wrote it," Susan Compton was saying. "All those changes were so cheap, and so unnecessary."

She was settled in one of the sofas and Michael sat facing her on a leather hassock, feeling a pleasurable tension in his very posture.

"Well, I guess that's what you have to expect in television," he said. "Still, I thought your performance was beautiful. You were just the way I imagined the girl to be."

"Do you mean that? Well, I think that's the nicest compliment I could have hoped for."

"It's often seemed to me," he said, "that acting and other kinds of performing must be the crudest of all the arts – cruel in the sense that you never get a second chance. You can't go back and revise your work. Everything has to be spontaneous and finished at the same time."

She said there was a lot of truth in that, and that he'd put it very well; and there was no mistaking the light that had come into her eyes: she thought he was "interesting."

Then she said "Still, I think creative work is what I'll always admire most – making something out of nothing; putting something into the world that wasn't there before. Have you written many other plays, Michael?"

"Oh, some; mostly I write poetry, though. That seems to be what I do best, or at least what I'm most interested in."

"Well, my God," she said, "I can't imagine a more difficult form than a poem. It's all purity: it depends entirely on itself. Have you – published much?"

"Two books, so far. And I wouldn't want to recommend the second one; I think the first is okay."

"Is it still in the bookstores?"

"Oh, not anymore. You could probably find it in the public library, though."

"Wonderful. And I'll look for the other one, too."

Then it was clearly time to turn the talk back to her, so he said "No, but really, Susan, I'm awfully glad I came up here for the show tonight. You really – you really gave me something I won't forget."

"Well, I can't tell you—" And she lowered her eyes. "I can't tell you how humble that makes me feel."

And still Tom Nelson wouldn't leave them alone. When he seemed to have tired of patrolling the walls he came back to sit down with them, and to ask Susan if she'd lived in Montreal all her life.

Yes; she had.

"You have a big family?"

"Well, three brothers and two sisters; I'm the oldest."

"What kind of work's your father do?"

And it went on that way until Susan Compton began to look less like a professional actress than a sleepy girl longing for the silence of her bedroom, where a dozen old stuffed animals might be lined up and waiting to remind her of childhood.

In the end she told them she would have to be back at the studio at ten in the morning to do a children's show, so she guessed she'd better get some sleep. And she said they were welcome to spend the night here; there were blankets and stuff in the cabinet; she hoped they'd be comfortable.

Then she was gone, and the worst of it was that Michael found he couldn't even say Christ's *sake*, Nelson, why didn't you take off? If he said that it would only spoil their long drive back to New York; besides, nobody spoke to Thomas Nelson that way. Thomas Nelson had grown so accustomed to admiration and deference that he moved through the world with the serene absentmindedness of a man on whom anger would always be lost. He was too "cool" for reproach.

And Michael had to acknowledge too, as he turned and pulled a blanket over his shoulders, that it might have been hopeless anyway to think of having the girl in this basement room. Her whole family lay upstairs beyond a door that didn't even lock; she might have frozen and recoiled when he made a move for her, whether she thought he was interesting or not. Well, the hell with it.

In the morning, while they folded their blankets and put them away, Tom Nelson said "Let's get started soon as we can, okay? Because I really oughta get back to work."

"Okay."

Upstairs, in the front hallway of the house, they could hear the sounds of the family at breakfast behind a closed door.

"Know what'll happen if you knock on that door?" Nelson said. "Some nice middle-aged lady'll open it and put her head out" – he expertly mimicked the craning smile of a nice middle-aged lady – "and say, 'Coffee?' and we'll be stuck in there for hours. Come on."

It wasn't until they were on the road again, with the drab Quebec landscape drifting past the car windows, that Michael was seized with a spasm of regret. Why *hadn't* he knocked on that door? Why hadn't he gone in and accepted a place at the family breakfast table, with Susan smiling tall and grown-up among the younger children? He could have gone along with her to the studio for her ten o'clock show; then afterwards he could have taken her to lunch, with martinis, and they might have held hands all afternoon. For Christ's sake, there wasn't even any reason why he couldn't have stayed for a week in Montreal.

And all this led quickly into a new, worse, uglier line of thought: Maybe it was cowardice. Maybe he'd been secretly frightened of Susan Compton all along, and secretly glad of the chance to escape. Maybe that ravaging week with Mary Fontana had left him so sick that he'd be frightened of any desirable girl, ever. Dreaming of seduction and terrified of impotence, he would be the kind of self-deceiving, self-defeating man who always balks and runs away.

That was when Tom Nelson began laughing to himself in the driver's seat, as though something uncommonly funny had just occurred to him.

"Know what that girl probably thinks?" he asked.

Michael could guess at once what the answer would be, and he knew he wouldn't care if he never saw Tom Nelson again.

Then Nelson delivered his punch line: "She probably thinks we're a couple of fags."

Things began to fall apart in August. He would get four hours' sleep one night, three hours the next, and none at all the night after that; then sleep would hit him like a heavy blow in the daytime, and he'd wake in his twisted clothes with no idea of what time it was, or what day.

He could tell he was drinking too much because empty bottles were gathering on the kitchen floor. And he had to force himself to chew and swallow small amounts of food, at longer and longer intervals, because the smell and taste of any kind of food had come to repel him.

Was everything he'd written in the past six months trying to tell him how lousy it was? If so, that was something no professional would need to be told. He put all the manuscripts in a brown paper bag one night, took it out to the street and pressed it deep into a municipal trash container, and that left him so exhilarated that he walked twenty blocks before he realized he wasn't wearing a shirt.

On another night he stopped drinking with a theatrical finality: he smashed his last bottle of whiskey in the sink and stared down at the mess of broken glass like a victor; then he was dizzy with fear that he might now go into what drunks called Withdrawal, so he lay trembling and waiting for hallucinations or convulsions or whatever the hell else Withdrawal might bring.

But on what must have been the next day he was out and walking again, fast, dressed in the whole of his *Chain Store Age* costume: a dark winter suit and a silk necktie. People and things might have a funny, jiggling look on the street and he couldn't always be sure they were there at all, but walking was important because staying home was worse.

For many days now his thoughts had been racing in the useless, desperate, circling way of incipient madness; whenever he could make them stop, even for a minute, he felt he was saving himself.

And he made them stop once at a newsstand on lower Broadway, somewhere near City Hall, long enough to grab up a copy of *The New York Times* in order to find out what day it was. It was Thursday; that meant he would have to be ready for a weekend with Laura tomorrow.

"Mister?" the newsdealer inquired through a mouthful of rotten teeth. "Want me to loan you a dime to buy the fucking paper?"

When he found he was sitting at home again, in different clothes, he couldn't tell if it was Thursday anymore. His watch read nine o'clock but he didn't know if that meant morning or night, and the gloomy pinkish color of his windows might have meant either one. He dialed the old Tonapac number anyway – he *had* to dial it – and while talking with his daughter he heard a shy hesitation and then a rising, uncomprehending fear in her voice.

Then Lucy called him back: "Michael? Can you tell me what the trouble is? . . ."

It wasn't very long after that before Bill Brock was at the door, smiling in a way that looked both canny and self-conscious – "Mike? You okay?" – and that turned out to be the end of the pre-Bellevue period.

Chapter Two

When they let him out of Bellevue he found he was afraid of everything, all the time. The sound of a siren in the street, even in the distance, was enough to chill his blood, and so was the sight of a cop – any cop, anywhere. He shied away from young male Negroes, too, if they were big enough, because they looked as if they might be Bellevue orderlies.

If he'd owned a car then, he would have been afraid to drive it, or even to start the engine and put it into gear – any unspeakable thing could happen once you'd started a car and put it into gear. Walking was frightening enough, when it came to crossing wide streets; he didn't even like to walk around corners because you couldn't know what might be on the other side.

And it seemed to him now that this cowering timidity, concealed or not, had been at the core of his nature all his life. Hadn't he always been secretly afraid of other boys in the schoolyard? Hadn't he hated football and tried to play it only because he was expected to? Even boxing had frightened him badly at first, until he was taught how to move his feet and his weight and his hands. As for his service as an aerial gunner, the one part of his life that seemed to have impressed so many people for so many years, he had known all along that "courage" or "guts" weren't the appropriate words. You were trapped in the sky with nine other men; you did what you could, and what sustained you was the old Army virtue of keeping a tight asshole. You knew it was late enough in the war for the odds to be in your favor – no mission was really very likely to last forever – and it was always a pleasure, back in England, to hear the other guys say they'd been scared shitless too.

Now, trembling at the medicine cabinet, he swallowed his psychiatric pills at their appointed hours every day, never missing a dose; and once a week he crept faithfully back to Bellevue to see the Guatemalan psychiatrist in charge of his outpatient treatment.

"Consider your brain as being like an electrical circuit," the man told him. "Far more complex, of course, but similar in this respect: if you overload a single element" – and he held up one forefinger to emphasize the point – "you blow the whole system. The circuit is dead; the lights are out. Now. In your case the danger is real, the source of it is clear, and there can be only one answer: Don't drink."

So Michael Davenport stayed away from alcohol for a year.

"For a solid year," he would later insist to anyone who seemed to doubt it, or to others who didn't seem to find it all that great an achievement. "Twelve months without even so much as a glass of beer – can you imagine that? – and all because some clown of a doctor scared me shitless by saying it'd short-circuit my brains. Well, I'm still scared shitless half the time, like everybody else in the world, but I'm not a God damn coward anymore and that's the difference."

He had discovered he could get laid again, too, and he was so grateful to the girl who proved it that he might have wept and thanked her with all his heart the minute it was over, though he managed to check that impulse.

She was one of the secretaries at *Chain Store Age,* and she told him she had never cheated on her boyfriend before. She would have felt funny about coming down to Leroy Street this afternoon, she said, if she hadn't recently found out that her boyfriend had cheated on her. Still, she felt she was mature enough to understand and accept her boyfriend's infidelity: he was just starting out in a new dental practice in Jackson Heights and had been under a great deal of emotional stress.

"Yeah," Michael said, feeling like a million dollars. "Well, I guess a thing like emotional stress can really – really get you into trouble, Brenda."

In the summer of 1964, after his third book came out, he was invited to lecture and to read some of his work at a two-week writers' conference in New Hampshire. The thing took place on a picturesque little campus high in the mountains and miles from any town: enough rambling old residence buildings to house three hundred paying participants, an ample kitchen and dining room, and a light-filled lecture hall where the talk never stopped and writing was the only topic ever discussed.

The director of the program was Charles Tobin, a man of fifty or more whose novels Michael had always liked and who turned out to be an engagingly jovial host. "Come on over and join us at the Cottage as soon as you're settled, Mike," he said. "See over there across the road?"

One small frame house with a porch around it, set well apart at the far end of the campus, was used as the faculty gathering place – a kind of club where only privileged outsiders were made welcome. A flood of drink was poured and served there in the hour or two before lunch every day, and an ocean of it in the hours before dinner; then there would often be song and drunkenness far into the night. Charles Tobin's hearty endorsement of all this seemed based on his view that writers worked harder than most other people – harder perhaps than most other people could imagine – and so deserved a break for a couple of weeks every summer. Besides, writers understood self-discipline; he knew they could all be trusted.

But by the end of the first week Michael Davenport had begun to sense that he might be going under – or rather that he might be going up and over and out. And it wasn't just the drink, though that certainly didn't help; it was the lecture hall.

He had read his poems aloud to small groups in the past, but never before had anybody asked him to stand at a lectern and speak from the heart to a hushed, attentive audience of three hundred people. They wanted to know about the stern and delicate craft he had practiced for twenty years, and he told them. His lectures were either extemporaneous or drawn from a few scribbled notes, but each of them seemed to achieve its own firm design and structure. He was a hit.

"That was a damn good job, Mike," Charles Tobin said time and again as they left the lecture hall together, but Michael didn't need to be told because the long, intoxicating applause would still be going on in the hall behind them.

People clustered around him with copies of his books to be autographed; they sought him out for breathless private talks about problems in their own work; and there was a girl for him, too.

She was a slender, dead-serious girl named Irene, one of the young apprentice writers who waited on tables in the dining room in exchange for "scholarships" to the conference; she would knock shyly on his door every night, then whirl inside and fall into his arms as if this were the very kind of romance she had wanted all her life. She praised him in as many ways as he could remember having heard from any girl, even in the early times with Jane Pringle; then, very late one night in his bed, she said "You *know* so much" – and that took him all the way back to Cambridge in 1947.

"No, listen, don't say that, Irene," he told her, "because in the first place it's not true. These lectures of mine are coming out of the air, coming out of the sky; I don't know where the hell they're coming from, but they're making me sound an awful lot smarter than I am, do you understand me? And in the second place, that's the same thing my wife said to me once before we were married and it took her a whole lot of years to find out how wrong she was, so let's not have any more shit along that line, okay?"

"I think you're very tired, Michael," Irene said.

"Oh, baby, you said a mouthful. I'm tired as hell, and that's only the beginning of it. Listen. Listen, Irene. Don't get scared, but I think I may be going crazy."

"You may be what?"

"Going crazy. Listen, though: it's no big deal, if you'll let me explain a couple of things. I went crazy once before and came out the other side of it, so I know it's not the end of the world. And I think I've caught it earlier this time. I may even have caught it in *time,* if you see what I mean. I'm still mostly in control. If I'm terrifically careful with myself, with the booze and the lectures and all the rest of it, maybe I can still get through this thing. There're only three or four more days left here anyway, aren't there?"

"There are six days left," she said.

"Well, okay, six. But the thing is, Irene, I'm really going to need your help."

There was a significant pause before she said "In what way?" And both the pause and the timorous, guarded tone of the question let him know at once that he'd taken too much for granted with this girl. Except that they'd writhed and humped together here for a week they were almost strangers. She might have romanticized him sane, but that was no reason to suppose she would ever know what to do with him crazy. If "help" was needed, she would first have to be very sure she understood what kind of help he had in mind.

"Oh, hell, I don't know, baby," he said. "I shouldn't have put it like that. All I mean is I'd like you to stick around. I'd like you to sort of be my girl, or pretend to be my girl, until this whole thing is over. Then later we'll have a better time; I promise."

But that wasn't right, either. When the thing was over she'd be going back to graduate school at Johns Hopkins, too far from New York for frequent visits even if frequent visits were what she might wish to have. And he should never have said "pretend to be my girl" because no girl in the world would want to consider a plan like that.

"Why don't you just try and get some sleep now," she told him.

"Okay," he said. "Only first come a little closer so I can — there. There. Oh, Christ, you're a pretty girl. Oh, don't go away. Don't go away, Irene. . . ."

He was walking unsteadily toward the lecture hall the next morning when Charles Tobin fell into step with him and took him by the arm and said "This won't be necessary, Mike."

"How do you mean?"

"I just mean you don't have to face that crowd again today; somebody else can fill in for you." Tobin stopped walking, obliging Michael to stop too, and they stood looking at each other in the dazzling sunshine. "As a matter of fact," Tobin said, "I've already arranged for somebody else to fill in."

"Oh. So I've been fired."

"Oh, come on, Mike; nobody gets 'fired' from a place like this. I'm concerned about you, that's all, and I—"

"Where do you get 'concerned'? You think I'm going crazy?"

"I think you've pushed yourself too hard up here, and I think you're exhausted. I probably should've spotted it sooner, but then after what happened in the Cottage last night I—"

"What happened in the Cottage last night?"

Tobin appeared to be scrutinizing Michael's face. "You don't remember?"

"No."

"Oh. Well, listen, let's go back to your room to talk, okay? There're a few too many – onlookers out here."

And that was true, though Michael hadn't noticed it: any number of people, from college kids to ladies with powder-blue hair, had stopped in their tracks on the bright grass, or on the road, in order to witness this confrontation.

Michael had begun to tremble badly when they got to his room; it was a relief to sit on the bed. Then Charles Tobin sat facing him, hunched in the only chair, and told him what had happened last night.

". . . And you kept pouring drinks for yourself out of Fletcher Clark's bottle. I don't think you knew what you were doing, but the trouble was you went on doing it even after he'd asked you to stop. Then when he did get mad you called him a cocksucker and took a swing at him, and it took about four of us to pull you apart, and the big table got broken. You don't remember any of that?"

"No, I – oh, Jesus. Oh, my God."

"Well, it's over now, Mike; there's no point in torturing yourself. Afterwards Bill Brodigan and I brought you back here, and you were very calm by then. You said you didn't want us coming into the room because it would upset Irene, and that seemed reasonable, so we stayed at the end of the hall and watched you go inside, and that was it."

305

"Where is she now? Where's Irene?"

"Well, it's almost lunchtime, so I expect she's busy in the dining room. Don't worry about Irene. Irene'll be fine. I think the best thing would be to get undressed and under the covers, don't you? I'll stop back to see you in a while."

And Michael would never know how little or long a while it was before Charles Tobin came into the room again, followed this time by a smaller, younger man in a cheap summer suit.

"Mike, this is Dr. Brenner," he said. "Dr. Brenner's going to give you an injection and then you'll have a good rest."

There was a needle in one buttock, keener and swifter and less humiliating than any of the Bellevue needles; then he was fully if sloppily dressed again and walking down the hall between Tobin and the doctor, shrugging off their hands to prove he could walk alone, and they went out across a brilliant stretch of grass to where a cream-colored four-door sedan stood waiting in the road. A sturdy young man all in white got out of the back seat and held the door open, and they helped Michael into the car as carefully as if he were very old and frail. Nothing could have gone more smoothly. But he was rapidly losing consciousness as the car moved away through the vivid green and shade of the campus, and he either saw or dreamed a great gathering of oddly assorted people in summer clothes along the roadside, all their faces startled and embarrassed as they watched their favorite lecturer being taken into custody.

He spent a week in the psychiatric ward of a general hospital in Concord, New Hampshire; but the place was so clean and bright and quiet, and the personnel so unfailingly courteous, that it didn't seem like a psychiatric ward at all.

He even had a room of his own – it took him a few days to realize that its door was always kept slightly ajar onto a murmurous corridor that was locked from the outside; but still, a room of his own – so there was never any need to meet and mingle with the other disturbed patients; and surprisingly succulent meals were brought to his bedside, always right on time.

"These medications you're getting now should do the job for you, Mr. Davenport," said a spruce young psychiatrist, "if you go on taking them at home. But I wouldn't underestimate what happened to you up here at the whaddyacallit. The writers' conference. You appear to have had a second psychotic episode, and it may suggest a continuing pattern of further episodes in the future, so if I were you I'd watch my step. I'd certainly go easy on the alcohol, for one thing, and I'd try to avoid any emotionally stressful situations in the course of my – you know – of my life. Your life."

And when he was alone again he lay slowly trying to sort things out in his mind. Could he still divide the years into pre- and post-Bellevue periods, or not? Would this new thing require the establishment of a new historical era in its own right? Or would it, like the Korean War, serve mainly to show that history couldn't be expected to make much sense?

Irene came to see him one afternoon. She sat on the bedside chair with her nice legs crossed at the knee and talked about her plans for the coming year at Johns Hopkins. She said more than once that it would be "fun" to "get together" with him in New York, and he said "Well, sure, Irene, we'll be in touch," but they said those things in the automatically graceful manner of promises never meant to be kept.

At the end of the visiting hour she rose and bent to kiss his mouth, and he could sense that she'd come here today not only to say goodbye but to have a brief sample, for curiosity's sake, of how it would feel to pretend to be his girl.

One of the orderlies brought him a pad of paper and a pen,

and he spent hours drafting a letter to Charles Tobin. It wouldn't have to be a very long letter; the important thing was to find and sustain the right tone. It would have to convey humility and apology and gratitude without ever sinking into remorse, and it would be best if he could conclude it on the note of wry, self-effacing bravery that was characteristic of Tobin's own style.

He was still working on the letter the day they released him from the hospital, and he continued to sound out certain phrases of it, just under his breath, on the plane back to New York.

Everything in the Leroy Street place looked drab to the point of wretchedness when he first walked into it, carrying a suitcase full of dirty laundry, and it was smaller than he'd remembered. He got the Tobin letter finished and into the mail; then it was time to get back to work.

Work might not be all there was in the world, but it had come to be the only thing Michael Davenport could trust. If he eased up on it now, if he ever let his mind slide away from it, there might be a third episode – and the third one, here in New York, might easily take him back to Bellevue again.

One of the ways he could tell he was getting older, during the next few years, was that Laura looked different every time he met the train from Tonapac.

Until she was thirteen or so he had always been able to spot her at once in the crowd coming out through the gate at Track Ten because she was the girl he had known all her life: skinny and quick, with her best clothes worn a little awry and her white socks beginning to sink out of control into the heels of her shoes. Her face would always be bright with expectation as she ran the last of the distance into his arms – "Daddy!" – and he'd hold her close and tell her how good it was to see her again.

But along about the time her troublesome socks were

replaced by nylon hose, other changes began. She grew slower and heavier and less openly glad to see him; her smiles became an effort at civility, and sometimes she seemed to be thinking Isn't this dumb? Why am I supposed to visit my father when all we ever do is get on each other's nerves?

When she gained forty pounds in what seemed no time at all, at fifteen, Michael almost wished he wasn't expected to meet these trains anymore. Where was the pleasure in having a big high-shouldered lump of a girl come plodding at you with a sullen and evasive look?

"Hi, baby," he would say.

"Hi."

"That's a nice dress."

"Oh. Thanks. Mom bought it at Caldor's."

"Want to have lunch before we go downtown, or afterwards? We'll do whichever you like."

"I don't care."

But she lost nearly all that weight by the time she turned seventeen; that seemed to make her happier, and seemed to make her brighter, too. He couldn't get used to the sight of her carrying a lighted cigarette when she walked out of the train gate, but it was good to have her talking again – and it was nice that not all of the things she said were commonplace.

One night when he was alone there was a phone call from Lucy – the first in years – and after a few shy preliminary courtesies she got down to business: she was worried about Laura.

". . . Well, I know adolescence is a difficult time," she said, "and I can certainly see that hers might be more difficult than most. Oh, and I've read as much as anybody else about how crazy everything's supposed to be for kids these days, with all this 'hippie' stuff breaking out, so that's not the point, either. It isn't

Laura's interests or activities I mind, you see, it's something worse: it's her lying. She's turned into a liar.

"Let me give you just one example. I had some people here for the weekend and their car was in my garage, and Laura sneaked it out and drove it away one night. I don't know where she went or what she did before she put it back in the garage, but that's secondary. The main thing is she lied about it. We found a fairly heavy scrape in one fender, you see, and when I asked Laura if she knew anything about it she made me ashamed for even asking. She said, 'Oh, Mom. You really think I'd take somebody else's car?' But then when we opened the driver's door we found Laura's change purse there on the front seat.

"So do you see what I'm getting at, Michael? I don't *like* the clouded, stupid look that comes into her face when she gets caught at something like that. It's the look of a submissive criminal, and it's frightening."

"Yeah," he said. "Yeah, well, I see what you mean."

"Oh, and then there's so much else I don't understand about her anymore." Here Lucy paused for breath, or perhaps in surprise at herself for talking so easily to a man from whom she'd been estranged for years. "You may not be aware of this, Michael, unless she's let it slip, but the times you see her in New York are by no means the only times she's there: She gets into the city quite a lot, and there isn't any way I can control it. She did let it slip to *me* once, during one of the brainless talks we have about 'values,' that she knows a beautiful boy named Larry on Bleecker Street – oh, and needless to say, her ways of explaining what makes him so beautiful were enough to curl your hair; he has 'a beautiful soul,' and so on. So I said 'Well, dear, why don't you ask Larry out here some weekend? You think he might enjoy a few days in the country?' And that surprised her, of course, but the funny part was she agreed to it. I could almost see her making up her mind: having Larry of Bleecker Street to show off, right here, in person, might turn out to be the social triumph of the year among the kids at Tonapac High.

"Then one day I looked out the window and there he was, standing around with her in the front yard: this kid with a ponytail down his back, wearing a dirty leather vest with no shirt under it. And I mean except that there weren't any lights in his eyes he didn't look sinister or anything; he just looked like a boy who needed a bath. So I went out in the yard and said 'Hello; you must be Larry.' And he took off running – up the road and out across the fields, heading for this rotten old abandoned barn about two hundred yards away.

"I said 'What's the matter with him?'

"And Laura said 'He's shy.'

"I said 'How long has he been here?'

"And she said 'Oh, about three days now. He's staying in the barn. There's a lot of old straw in there and we fixed up a nice little place.'

"I said 'How does he eat?'

"And she said 'Oh, I've been bringing him stuff; that's okay.'

"Well, I guess I'm making all this sound sort of funny," Lucy said, "and I guess it was; but I'm getting away from the point. I think the question of her interests and activities will tend to resolve itself – and she might as well get all this bohemian nonsense out of her system now as later – but the lying is something else."

And Michael said he agreed with that.

"She's too old to be 'punished,'" Lucy went on, "and how would you punish a child anyway when the offense is lying? One lie simply hooks into another until a whole fabric of lies comes into being, and then the child is living in a world devoid of substance."

"Yeah," he said. "Well, I think you're right to be concerned. I am, too."

"So here's the thing. This is why I called. The only therapist I know around here is Dr. Fine, and I've come to have decidedly mixed feelings about him; I suppose what I mean is I wouldn't want to trust him with something like this. So I wondered if you might be – acquainted with someone you could recommend in New York. That's really why I called, you see."

"No, I'm not," he told her. "And I don't believe in that stuff anyway, Lucy; never have. I think the whole 'therapy' industry is a racket." And he might have gone on at some length in that vein, saying things like "Sigmund fucking Freud," but decided he'd better stop. It had been only reasonable for her to assume he'd be "acquainted" with some shrink, after two breakdowns; besides, if they had an argument now it would spoil this spontaneous and pleasant phone call. "So I guess I can't help out there," he said. "But look: she'll be in college soon and she won't be bored half to death all the time the way she is now. There'll be things to challenge her mind and they'll keep her busy. I think we'll find that makes a difference."

"Well, but college is still a year away," Lucy said. "I was hoping we might get – you know – get something started now. Well, okay, then," she said in a way that meant she was concluding the talk. She would probably arrange for Laura to visit Dr. Fine, despite her mixed feelings. "Oh, and speaking of college, Michael," she said in an afterthought, "I've talked with the girl who's the new whaddyacallit here, the new guidance counselor at the high school, and she says Laura can have her pick of quite a few good colleges. And she said she'll be calling you in on this, too; that's the policy."

"The 'policy'?"

"Well, you know: where there are divorced parents, the

father is always consulted too. She's nice – extremely young for a job like that, I'd think, but very capable."

The guidance counselor did call him a few days later, wanting to know what afternoon he could come in for a two o'clock appointment. Her name was Sarah Garvey.

"Well, tomorrow's not so good," he said. "How about the day after that, Miss Garvey?"

"Okay," she said. "Fine."

He'd had to make it the day after tomorrow because it would take that long to get his only suit cleaned and pressed. Ever since the divorce he had cut back heavily in the assignments he took from *Chain Store Age* each month, to provide himself with as much time for his own work as possible. Lately, though, finding he was down to one suit and that all his other, mismatched clothes were ready to fall apart, he'd begun to wish he had a university job, like most other poets. He was tired as hell of living in the Village, too: it might be all right to be a ragged kid in the Village but not a ragged middle-aged man, and Michael was forty-three years old.

Still, when he was freshly shaved and everything he wore was freshly cleaned, he always knew he looked all right. It even struck him sometimes, when he caught his reflection in passing plate-glass windows, that he looked better now than he had ten or twenty years ago.

He felt okay riding out on the Tonapac train, and the good mood persisted even as he made his way through boisterous high-school corridors, though he'd always hated the thought of his daughter enrolled in a dumb, blue-collar school like this. Then he was at the door of Sarah Garvey's office, and he knocked on it.

★

313

Mothers of Tonapac High School students might sit talking with Sarah Garvey in a businesslike way, asking courteous questions and getting courteous replies, careful not to overstay their appointed time – but the fathers must all have been stricken in this tiny room, helplessly imagining how Sarah Garvey would look naked and how she would feel in their hands, and how she would smell and taste, and how her voice would sound in the delirium of getting laid.

The walls of her office were made of perforated white peg-boards with nothing pegged to them, and the plainness of that background made it easy to believe you were looking at the loveliest girl in the world. She was slim and supple, with dark shoulder-length hair and limpid brown eyes and a wide, full-lipped mouth. When she was seated behind her desk you couldn't tell what she was like from the rib cage down, but she didn't keep you waiting very long. Twice during the interview she got up and walked to a tall filing cabinet, and then you saw the whole of her: perfect legs and ankles beneath a straight skirt; a trim little ass with just enough curves to make you ache for it. Your first impulse might be to lock the door and have her here, on the floor, but it wouldn't take much self-control to follow a more sensible plan: get her out of here, take her somewhere else, and have her there. Soon.

Could Sarah Garvey guess what was going on in your mind? If so, she gave no sign of it. All this time she'd been talking of Vassar and Wellesley and Barnard colleges, and she may have mentioned Mt. Holyoke, too; now she'd begun to talk at length, and with some enthusiasm, about Warrington College in Vermont.

"The arty little place, you mean?" he said. "Well, but aren't all the girls there expected to be precocious at some – you know – at some art form or other?"

"I suppose it may have acquired a reputation like that," she said, "but it's a very open, stimulating environment and I think Laura would do well there. She's an extremely bright and sensitive person, as you know."

"Well, sure she is, but she can't *do* anything. Can't paint or write or act; can't play a musical instrument or sing or dance. She hasn't been raised that way. There were never any leotards in our house, if you see what I mean."

And that earned him a small, qualified smile from Sarah Garvey's beautiful eyes and lips.

"What I'm getting at, Miss Garvey," he said, "is that I think she might be intimidated by all those talented girls. And being intimidated is the last thing I want for her, in college or anywhere else."

"Well, that's very understandable," she said. "Still, you might want to look into Warrington anyway; I have the catalogue here. And the other factor, you see, is that her mother seems to feel it would be the best place for her."

"Oh. Well, I guess that means her mother and I'll have to talk it over."

Their business seemed to be concluded – Sarah Garvey was stacking papers and folders and putting them away in a desk drawer – and Michael wondered if he would be expected to leave before he'd even had a chance to get her out of here. But then she glanced up at him in a way that seemed too shy for such a pretty girl.

"It's been really nice meeting you, Mr. Davenport," she said. "I've admired your books."

"Oh? Well, but how did you ever happen to—"

"Laura lent them to me. She's very proud of you."

"She is?"

Too many surprises had hit him at once, and when he sorted

them out he found that Laura's being proud of him was the best. He could never have guessed a thing like that.

Steel lockers were being slammed all up and down the corridors now – school was out, and that made it easy for him to ask her out for a drink. She looked briefly shy again, but said she'd love to.

As she led him out into the faculty parking lot he guessed it wouldn't matter even if Laura did happen to be in the crowd of kids who watched them go: she might think they were only adjourning to some more comfortable place for a further discussion of her college plans.

"How does someone get to be a guidance counselor?" he asked Sarah Garvey when they were on the road.

"Oh, it doesn't amount to much," she said. "You take a few sociology courses in college; then there's some graduate work, and then you look for a job in a place like this."

"You look too young to've been to graduate school."

"Well, I'm almost twenty-three; that's a little younger than average, but not much."

So there were twenty years between them – and Michael felt so good that twenty years seemed a tidy and even an attractive span of time.

She was driving through a part of the Tonapac countryside that he didn't recognize, which was just as well – he wouldn't have wanted to pass the old "Donarann" mailbox, or anything like that. Glancing down, he found she had taken off her shoes to work the floor pedals with her slender stockinged feet, and he thought that was one of the prettiest things he had ever seen.

The bar and restaurant she took him to was a place he didn't recognize, either – a lot of new business must have come into town since his time – and when he said it was nice she gave him a quick look to see if he was kidding. "Well, it's not much," she said as they settled beside each other in a half-circular leatherette booth, "but I come here a lot because it's convenient; my house is sort of right around the corner."

"Do you live alone?" he inquired. "Or . . ."

And in the moment it took her to reply he was afraid she'd say "No, I live with a man" – that had lately become stylish among even the youngest and prettiest of girls, and they always seemed to say it as though they were boasting.

"No, I share an apartment with two other girls, but it's not working out; I'd much rather find a place of my own." Then she lifted the heavily beaded glass of an extra-dry martini, straight up, and said "Well: Cheers."

Cheers indeed. It had begun to seem that this might turn into Michael Davenport's most cheerful, cheering afternoon in years.

It was hard to believe that any girl so young could have such composure. And there couldn't be much of a life for her here in the shabbier part of Putnam County – working at a job that must be only sporadically interesting, having roommates she didn't like, taking meals in this ordinary restaurant. The only way to make it all add up was to assume she must escape into New York every weekend, and into the arms of some man who could let her know who she was.

"You get into the city much?" he asked her.

"Hardly ever," she said. "I can't really afford it and I never have a very good time there anyway."

And so he was able to breathe again.

Because he was closer to her here than in the office, and less shy than in the car, he could see clearly now what he'd only been able to guess at before: the texture of her skin was what had made him want to pull off her clothes the moment he'd seen her. It was like the surface of a flawless apricot or nectarine; it glowed; it needed to be taken and eaten. A small edge of white lace could be glimpsed just inside the V-neck of her dress, moving with each breath and quivering when she laughed, and that frivolous, unconscious touch of flirtation made him heavy with lust.

With the second drink they fell easily into using each other's first names, and she said "I guess I'd better tell you something, Michael; or maybe you've figured it out already. There wasn't any reason for you to come out here today. Everything we discussed in the office could easily have been done on the phone. I wanted to meet you, that's all."

And he kissed her mouth for that, wanting to make it as urgent as a boy's kiss but careful not to let it be the kind of kiss that could get a man thrown out of a family restaurant.

"It must be wonderful," she said a little later, "to put a poem together that won't fall apart – can't fall apart. I've tried and tried that – oh, not much anymore; mostly in college – and they've always fallen apart before I could even get them finished."

"Most of mine fall apart, too," he told her. "That's why I've published so few of them."

"Oh, but when yours stand," she said, "they really stand. They're built to last. They're like towers. When I got to those final few lines of 'Coming Clean' I was all gooseflesh – all over – and I cried, too. I can't think of a single other contemporary poem that's ever made me cry."

He might have wished she'd picked another poem – "Coming Clean" was everybody's favorite – but what the hell. This was nice.

When a waitress laid dinner menus on their table they both knew that having dinner was out of the question.

"Can we go to your place?" he asked against the side of her fragrant hair.

"No," she said. "There's never any privacy there at this time of day. They'll be everywhere, blow-drying their hair or making their chocolate-chip cookies or whatever it is they do. But there's a—" and he would always remember that she drew her head away in order to look into his eyes when she said this – "there's a motel not far from here."

Because his imagination had been undressing Sarah Garvey all afternoon there was no real surprise when her clothes came off in the big, locked, dead-silent motel room: he knew how lovely she would be. And from the moment he had her luminous skin in his hands he knew he could abandon the last dim thoughts of Mary Fontana that had haunted him for years with other girls. There would be no failure here tonight.

It was as if neither he nor Sarah Garvey could be complete unless they were joined. Until then they might as well have been dying for each other: there wasn't enough air for either of them to breathe; there wasn't any way for their racing blood to settle. Only in coupling were they fully alive and strong, taking their time, bringing each other along and up and over the unendurable crest of what they had made; and when they fell apart at last it was only to wait, not even having to speak, until they could be joined again.

By the time daylight shone blue in the Venetian blinds, it was understood that they would spend as many nights and weekends together as they could manage. That was the only plan they needed for now; falling asleep, they knew there would be plenty of time for figuring out the rest of their lives.

Chapter Three

Bill Brock had left *Chain Store Age* to take a public-relations job, which he often described as a piece of cake. And he'd given up trying to write novels: he considered himself a playwright now.

"Oh, listen, though," he said in the White Horse one night, holding up one hand to ward off Michael's envy. "Listen, Mike: I know you wrote plays for years without ever quite getting them off the ground, but I've always felt that was because you're essentially a poet. Well, now you're an established poet and everybody knows it. I couldn't write a poem to save my ass, but you can. You do. You've found your line, and I've found mine.

"One thing, I know I've always been good at dialogue. Even in the shittiest rejection letters I'd get for my stories and novels, there'd always be a line like 'Mr. Brock handles dialogue very well.' So I figured, what the hell; fuck it. If my strength lies in dialogue, I'll write for the stage."

He had recently completed a three-act play called *Negroes* – "Well, sure, it's kind of a stark little title, but that very quality of starkness is what I was after" – and he felt that his gift for dialogue had served him well in exploring the artistic possibilities of American Negro speech.

"For example," he said, "all through this play the characters keep saying 'muh-fuh'; 'muh-fuh' – and I've spelled it just that way. Well, the word is 'motherfucker,' obviously, but sometimes if you write what your ear tells you to, you find you're really getting inside your material. Anyway, I think this play's solid, Mike, and I think the times are right for it."

And his first step toward getting it produced had been to mail it, with a brief and friendly covering letter, to Ralph Morin at the Philadelphia Group Theater.

"Jesus," Michael said, "Why him?"

"Well, why *not* him?" And Bill was instantly ready for an argument. "Why *not* him? That's the more intelligent question, don't you think, Mike? I mean, shit, we're all grownups; all the stuff between Diana and me was over years ago; why should there be any bad feeling? And besides" – he took a deep drink of beer – "besides," he said again, wiping foam from his mouth, "this guy's a comer. You can read about him in the fucking Sunday *Times*. He's built that little Philadelphia project into something that's got practically a national reputation. When he gets a good commercial play – and I mean a *good* commercial play – he'll kiss Philadelphia goodbye, bring it up here and be one of the top directors on Broadway."

"Okay."

"Well, so anyway, he wrote me back this really nice, really gracious letter. He said 'I've told Mrs. Henderson that I love your play, and she'll be reading it over the weekend.' "

"Mrs. who?"

"Well, see, she's the money behind the whole operation down there; she underwrites everything they do, so they can't make a move without her approval. And I guess she must've liked the hell out of *Negroes* too, because the next thing was that Ralph called me to find out how soon I could get down to his office and talk it over. Well, shit, I dropped everything: I was there the next day."

"Did you see Diana?"

"Oh, yeah. Yeah, I sure did, and it was all very pleasant, but that came later. Let me give you the first part first, okay?" And he leaned back comfortably in his wooden chair. "Well, for one thing, I found I really liked the guy," he said. "You can't help liking him. I mean, you can tell he's very sensitive and all that, but he doesn't try to impress you with it: he comes on in a very calm, straightforward, no-bullshit way.

"So he said 'Let me level with you, Bill.' He said 'All the characters in your play are Negroes, and of course that's fine; that's what you set out to do.' He said 'You've captured their oppression and their rage and their terrible sense of helplessness, and it's a powerful piece of work.' He said 'The difficulty for us, though, is that we have another script here on a racial theme, also by a new playwright, only this other one is an interracial love story.' "

Bill came heavily forward then, both elbows on the damp table, shaking his head with a rueful little smile. Michael could remember trying to explain to Lucy, long ago, that one of Bill Brock's more endearing traits was his way of shrugging off or laughing off his failures. "I'm afraid I don't see that at all," she'd said. "Why doesn't he succeed at something, and then be endearing about that?"

"Well, by the time he got that far," Bill was saying, "I knew I was losing the ball game. Then he told me about the other play. It's called *Blues in the Night* – the title struck me as a little corny, but what the hell; you never know. There's this very young, aristocratic Southern white girl who falls in love with a Negro boy, you see, and her first impulse is to run away with him to some distant place, some foreign country, but the boy won't budge: he wants to stay home and brazen it out. Then the girl's father gets wind of it, so the trouble starts, and you begin to get this relentless building to total tragedy at the end. Well, shit, I've abbreviated the thing a lot more than he did, Mike, but you can see how material like that could be dynamite on the stage.

"But then he started telling me about the problems they've had trying to find the right girl for the role. He said 'She's got to be young as hell, but she can't just be a good actress – she's got to be brilliant.' And you can see what he means by that, too: put some girl in there who's less than great and the whole play might be open to charges of being – you know – of being in questionable taste, and so on. Then he said 'So even supposing the perfect girl does turn up – what can we do then? We can't promise her a Broadway opening, and we sure as hell can't expect her to work for peanuts in Philadelphia, right?'

"So you see what he was telling me, Mike? He was saying that if this other play falls through in the casting, he and Mrs. Henderson might want to go for my play instead – that's why he'd asked me in for a talk in the first place. And I thought it was very decent of him to lay his cards on the table that way. Very decent."

"I don't get it, though," Michael said. "How come he couldn't have told you that on the phone, or in a letter?"

"Wanted to meet me, I guess," Bill said; "and that's fair enough; I wanted to meet him, too. So I was just getting ready to leave when he said 'I hope you don't have to rush off, Bill; I told Diana you'd be here today, and she said she'd try to drop by.'

"Then – whammo. It happened right on cue. The door flew open and in she came, dragging these three little boys. Diana Maitland. Jesus. First time I'd seen her since nineteen fifty-four."

And Bill got up from the table to reenact the scene. "She came in like this," he said, and he pantomimed falling against a wall, staggering, recovering, and lurching forward.

"And I must say," he said when he was settled in his chair again with the same little smile he used for shrugging off his failures, "I must say, that really brought back a few memories. Because that was the one thing I never liked about her, you see. That awkwardness. I can remember thinking, Well, sure she's pretty, and sure she's nice, and sure I love her – or at least I think I do – but why can't she be graceful, like other girls?"

For a second or two Michael wanted to reach across the table and pour his full stein of beer over Bill Brock's head. He wanted to see the shock and the blind bewilderment in Brock's face as his hair and his shirt were soaked; then he would stand up, put a few dollars on the table, and say You're an asshole, Brock. You've always been an asshole. And he would be rid of him forever.

Instead, sitting still and controlling himself, he said "She always looked graceful to me."

"Yeah, well, you never had to live with her, buddy. You never had to – ah, never mind; the hell with it. Fuck it. Forget it. *Any*way," Bill said, easing back into the Philadelphia part of the story with evident relief, "I gave her a little kiss on the cheek and we sat around making small talk for a few minutes, all very pleasant; then I suggested we go out for a drink, but Diana said the boys were too tired or something, so we all went down and said goodbye out in front of the office building, and that was it. No, but I mean really, I came away with an essentially good feeling. I'm glad I sent the play to Morin, and I'm glad I met him. I feel I've made a good contact and a good friend."

Yeah, Michael said silently, yeah, and you'd eat shit with a rusty spoon, too, wouldn't you, Brock?

He was halfway home from the White Horse, walking fast and tense with anger, before it struck him that he no longer needed to hate Bill Brock for having once had Diana Maitland, nor would he ever again have to long for Diana Maitland over impossible spaces of distance and time. The only reason he'd come out to drink with Brock at all tonight was that it was the first time he'd been alone in six weeks: Sarah Garvey had spent all the other nights with him; she'd be back again tomorrow; and Sarah Garvey was as fine, as fresh and as nourishing a girl as Diana could ever have been.

Back in the apartment he found his unfinished resume rolled in the typewriter, where he'd left it when Brock called, and he stayed up late to get it done. He would give it to Sarah tomorrow; she would get it photocopied at the office of the Tonapac High School, and then he'd mail it out to the English departments of as many American colleges and universities as he could find in the public library.

After years of swearing that an English teacher was the last thing he would ever want to be, he was ready for it now. And he didn't care what part of the United States it might take him to because Sarah said she didn't care either; she could probably find work in a high school anywhere, if that turned out to be necessary; if not, she wouldn't bother. The only important thing, for both of them, was to start a new life.

"Hey, Sarah?" he asked her a few nights later, when they were having dinner at a restaurant he liked called the Blue Mill. "Have I ever told you about this guy Tom Nelson, up in Kingsley? The painter?"

"I think so, yes. Is he the one who works as a carpenter?"

"No, that's the other one; they're worlds apart. Nelson's an entirely different story." And it seemed to take him a long time, then, to explain what an entirely different story Nelson was.

"It sounds as though you envy him quite a lot," she said when he was finished.

325

"Well, yeah, I guess I do; guess I always have. We haven't been on very good terms for years because we took a trip to Montreal once that turned out badly and I got pissed off at him; the only times I've seen him since then were at one or two of his gallery openings, and I only went to those because it's a way of meeting girls. But anyway, he called me up today, out of the blue – very shy, very nice – and asked me to a party out there Friday night. I got the impression he wants to be friends again. And the thing is I'd really like to go, Sarah, but I don't want to go unless you come along."

"Well, that's not one of the more – ornate invitations I've received lately," she said, "but sure. Why not?"

Only a few cars were parked in the Nelsons' driveway when they got there. Several men among the early arrivals were strolling nervously in the living room – and that room, with its intimidating thousands of shelved books, was enough to make anybody nervous until the drink began to flow. The women seemed mostly to be in the kitchen helping Pat, or more likely pretending to help, since Pat could always manage everything by herself, and Michael proudly steered Sarah out there to introduce her.

"Good to meet you, Sarah," Pat said, and she did look pleased that Michael had such a nice young girl; but there was a touch of amusement in her eyes too, as if he were in his fifties rather than his forties, and he didn't like that part of it.

When he asked her where Tom was, she made a face of exasperation. "Oh, out in the backyard playing with his toys – he's been out there all day. Why don't you go get him, Michael, and tell him his mother says it's time to come home."

The backyard was long and wide, like everything else on the Nelsons' place, and the first thing he saw at the far end of it was a girl standing with her arms folded across her chest and her hair blowing slightly in the wind; it took him a few more seconds, walking, to recognize her as Peggy Maitland. Then he saw Tom Nelson squatting near her feet and facing away from her, hunkered down over a ridge of dirt as intently as a boy at a game of marbles. And only then did he make out a third figure ten or fifteen yards away, a man reclining on his side and propped on one elbow, dressed all in denim: it was Paul.

Across the carefully sculpted terrain of their battlefield, most of the combat troops were dead. All permissible field artillery fire was over – the two plastic dart pistols lay unloaded and cast aside in the grass – and now was the time for peace and commemoration.

Tom Nelson greeted Michael heartily enough, saying it was great to see him, but he was almost jubilant in his need to explain that this had been one of the finest battles he'd ever fought.

"This guy doesn't just fool around," he said admiringly of Paul. "He really knows how to protect his flanks." Then he said "Wait right here, Paul, and don't touch anything. I'll go get the camera; then we can lay down some smoke and take some pictures." And he hurried away toward his house.

"I'll be damned, Paul," Michael said when Maitland had gotten up to shake hands. "I'd never've expected to find you here."

"Well, things change," Maitland said. "Tom and I've become good friends in the last couple of years. We have the same gallery now, you see; that's how we met."

"Yeah? I didn't know you had a gallery, Paul; that's terrific. Congratulations."

"Oh, well, they don't sell *much* of my work, and they haven't given me a show yet; still, it's better than no gallery at all."

"Well, sure it is," Michael said. "That's really good news."

RICHARD YATES

Paul Maitland worked his spine a little this way and that, wincing, taking the kinks of warfare out of his muscles, and his fingers adjusted the blue bandana around his neck. "No, but I've been really surprised at how much I like Tom," he said. "Surprised at how much I've come to like his work, too. I used to think of him as sort of a lightweight, you know? An illustrator and all that? But the more you look at his pictures the more they sort of grow on you. You know what he does, at his best? He manages to make difficult things look easy."

"Yeah," Michael said. "Yeah, I've often thought that too."

And then Tom Nelson came loping back over the yard with his camera, causing Peggy Maitland to clap her hands in delight like a little girl.

An hour or two later, when the party had come alive – there must have been fifty people in the house – Michael asked Sarah if she was having a good time.

"Well, sure," she said, "but you know. Everyone here is so much older than me that I sort of don't know what to do or what to say or anything."

"Ah, just be yourself," he told her. "Just stand there being the prettiest girl anybody's ever seen, and all the rest of it'll be easy. I promise."

There was an art historian currently engaged in a monograph on Thomas Nelson; there was an aging, distinguished poet whose next book would be published in a limited edition, at two hundred dollars a copy, and would contain a Thomas Nelson illustration on every other page. There was a celebrated Broadway actress, too, who said she had been drawn to Nelson's house "as a moth to a flame" because she'd been so "moved" by an exhibition of his pictures at the Whitney Museum. And there was a novelist, recently acclaimed for having made no artistic mistakes in any of his nine books, who had never met Tom

328

Nelson before tonight but now had begun to follow him through the rooms, clapping him on the back of his paratrooper's jacket and saying "You said it, soldier. You said it."

After Sarah had gone into the kitchen to "hide" with a few other young people, and at about the time Michael was beginning to feel all the drink he'd taken in, Paul Maitland drifted over and asked him what he was up to these days.

"Looking for a teaching job," he said.

"Well, I've made the same move," Paul said. "We'll be going out to Illinois in the fall – did Tom tell you this? – the University of Illinois at Champaign-Urbana, or whatever it's called. Funny." And Paul fondled his mustache. "I've always vowed I'd never go into teaching, and I expect you have too; still, it does come to seem the only appropriate thing to do, at our age."

"Right. Sure does."

"And I imagine you'll be pleased to be rid of *Chain Saw Age*."

"Store."

"How's that?"

"It's called *Chain Store Age*," Michael said. "It's a publication for all kinds of retail stores that operate in – you know – in chains. Get it?" Then, slowly shaking his head in dismay, he said "I'll be God damned. All these years, as long as Brock and I've been telling you what we did, you thought we were talking fucking chain saws."

"Well, I've got it straight now," Paul said, "but yes; I did have the impression you were both concerned with – publicizing chain saws, and that kind of thing."

"Yeah, well, in your case I suppose it was a reasonable mistake. Because you never do listen very carefully, do you, Paul? You never have paid a hell of a lot of attention to anybody in the world but yourself, have you?"

329

Paul stepped back a pace or two, blinking and smiling as if trying to discern whether Michael was serious.

And Michael was serious, all right. "Let me tell you something, Maitland," he said. "Way back when Lucy and I first met you and your sister we thought you were both exceptional. We thought you were superior beings. We'd gladly have bent our lives out of shape if that could've helped us be more like you, or brought us any closer to you – oh, shit, do you see what I'm saying? We thought you were fucking enchanted."

"Look, old man," Paul said, "I seem to've offended you in some way and I certainly never meant to; whatever it was I'm terribly sorry, okay?"

"Sure," Michael said. "Forget it. No offense meant, none taken." But he was weak with shame for the nakedness of his outburst: the line "We thought you were fucking enchanted" still hung in the room to be savored by other party guests; the only mercy was that Sarah was well out of earshot in the kitchen. "Wanna shake on it, then?" he asked.

"Well, of course," Paul said, and they were both drunk enough to make an excessively solemn business out of shaking hands.

Then Michael said "Good. Now. Let's play a game. You can go first." He opened the coat of his only suit and pointed to the middle of his shirt. "Hit me as hard as you can," he said. "Right here."

Paul looked bewildered only for a moment before he seemed to understand. This might have been a game once played at Amherst; in any case, the years of manual labor had kept him strong. His punch was fast and solid enough to send his man dancing backwards and fighting to keep from buckling over.

"Nice," Michael said as soon as he could speak, and he stepped back into range. "That was a nice one. Now it's my turn."

And he took his time over it. He closely inspected Paul Maitland's face: the intelligent eyes, the humorous mouth, the fearless iconoclast's mustache. Then he set his feet, gathered his strength and put everything he had into his right hand.

The remarkable thing was that Paul didn't drop at once. He backed off wincing, with glazed eyes; he even managed to say "Not bad" in a small voice; then he turned away as if to seek a new conversational companion, and he took three or four wobbling steps before he fell sprawling over an antique wooden chair and lay unconscious on the floor, on his back.

Among those close enough in the crowd to have seen the action there was a woman who screamed and another who shrank away and covered her face with both hands, and there was a man who took Michael firmly by the arm, saying "You better get out of here, buddy."

But Michael sized up the man in a glance and said "Fuck off, sweetheart; I'm not going anywhere. This is a game."

Peggy Maitland went fluttering down to cradle her husband's head in her arms, and Michael was afraid she would now look up with the same terrible reproach he'd seen in young Mrs. Damon's face, long ago, but she didn't.

Between the two of them, Michael and Peggy brought Paul around and up to one trembling knee and then to a standing position, and they helped and guided him so carefully through the crowd that some observers might not even have known he was hurt.

Paul managed not to vomit until they were out in the driveway, where nothing could be spoiled; then he did, and when the spasms were over he seemed to gain a little strength.

It wasn't hard to find the Maitlands' car among all the others ranked in the moonlight: theirs was the only high, dull, stubby one, the only one made before 1950. When Michael opened the passenger's door and helped Paul inside there was a heavy scent of gasoline and mildewed upholstery. The Maitlands would have a gleaming new middle-class car soon enough, when Paul became a professor in Illinois; in the meantime, this was the car of a nonunion carpenter who had tried for many years to paint pictures at home.

"Hey, Paul?" Michael said. "Listen, I didn't mean to hurt you; do you understand?"

"Oh, of course. Goes without saying."

"Hey, Peggy? I'm really sorry about this."

"Little late for that now," she said. "But okay. I mean I know it's a game, Michael. I just think it's a dumb, dumb game, that's all."

And Michael turned back to confront the Nelsons' big, brilliant house. The only thing to do now was walk around on the grass to the kitchen door, get Sarah out of there, and take off.

Very few colleges replied to Michael's application, and the only job offer that seemed worth considering was from a place called Billings State University, in Kansas.

"Well, Kansas does sound a little bleak," Sarah said. "Unnecessarily bleak, I mean. What do you think?"

But neither of them could tell. He had grown up in New Jersey and she in Pennsylvania, and they were almost total strangers to the rest of the United States. He waited a little while to see if something better would turn up; then he accepted the Kansas job for fear it might be given to somebody else if he didn't.

And the only thing left to decide now was how best to spend the many weeks of Sarah's summer vacation. They chose Montauk, Long Island, because it had an ample sweep of ocean beach but was far enough away from the more fashionable towns, "the Hamptons," to be cheaper. Their summer cottage was so small and narrow that a single person might have found it unendurable, but it was a shelter with walls, and with windows for light and air; that was all they needed because all they did there, every afternoon and again every night, was get laid.

As a boy he had believed that men in their forties, like his father, began to lose this kind of energy, but that only proved what false things a boy could believe. Another of his boyhood assumptions was that men in their forties usually settled for women of their own age, like his mother, while girls would always prefer to copulate with boys – but the hell with that one too. Young Sarah Garvey, fresh from the windswept beach and tasting of salt, had only to whisper his name to let him know she didn't want a boy at all; she wanted him.

Once when they were walking together along the firm part of the sand, close to the breaking water, she impulsively clasped his arm with both hands and said "Oh, I think we were made for each other, don't you?"

And looking back it would always seem that their plans for marriage had begun at that moment.

By the end of the summer, only the details remained to be taken care of: they would spend a few days with Sarah's family in Pennsylvania and arrange a simple wedding there; then, together, they would go out and face whatever "Kansas" might mean.

Chapter Four

The place they rented in Billings, Kansas, after they were married, was the first modern, efficient house Michael had ever known – and Sarah said it was the first of its kind in her life, too. It was built all in one story, a "ranch house," and didn't look like much from the road: you had to go inside to find how generously long and wide and high it was, with a bright hallway connecting its several spacious rooms. Each room held a window air-conditioner against the late-August heat, and there were thermostats to control the brand-new furnace that promised steady protection in the winter. Everything worked.

He would walk these solid floors despising the memory of the funny little house in Tonapac, chagrined that he could ever have imposed such daily discomfort on Lucy and Laura for what now seemed no reason at all. Still, only fools consumed themselves with regret; and whenever he looked ahead, thinking of Sarah, it surprised him all over again to know that the world was ready to give him a second chance.

Sarah had been right on one important point, though: there *was* something unnecessarily bleak about Kansas. The earth was too flat, the sky was too big, and if you had to be outdoors on a clear day there was no way to escape the punishing sun until it finally, splendidly, went down. Cattle stockyards and a slaughterhouse lay a mile or two beyond the university, and when the afternoon breeze came from that direction it carried a faint, nostril-puckering stench.

The house provided an excellent place to hide from all that for the first week or two – Michael even managed to complete a short poem called "Kansas" that seemed good enough to keep, though he would later throw it away – but then it was time for school.

And except for that brief series of lectures in New Hampshire, where the very exhilaration of lecturing had apparently been enough to drive him crazy, he felt unequipped for this kind of work. *Chain Store Age* might have been a repugnant way to make a living all those years, but nothing about it had ever frightened him; now he was clammy with fear each time he walked into a classroom. He couldn't read the faces of these young strangers, couldn't tell whether they were bored or daydreaming or paying attention, and the allotted time for each period was always much too long.

But he survived the lecture classes and the "poetry workshop" classes without incurring cause for shame, and survived the easier hours of conference with individual students as well; then, at home, he would hunch with a pencil over their lame, flimsy poems or their earnest and point-missing "papers" on poetry, and so he was able to believe he was earning his salary.

"Well, but why do you spend so much time at it?" Sarah asked him once. "I thought the whole point of a job like this was that it would give you some freedom for your own work."

"Well, it will," he told her. "Once I get the hang of this I'll be doing it with my left hand. You'll see."

★

335

Only one drugstore in the college town carried the Sunday *New York Times,* and Michael bought it every week in order to frown for an hour over the Book Review section, learning of how younger poets he despised were building excellent reputations while older ones, a few of whom he liked, were rapidly losing ground.

Sometimes, after that small torture, he would pick through the theater pages too; that was how he found out that *Blues in the Night* had become the first smash hit of the Broadway season.

. . . Rarely if ever before on the American stage has a doomed interracial love affair been treated with the dignity, the delicacy, and the overwhelming gut-level power of this landmark work by Roy Kidd, under the brilliant direction of Ralph Morin.

It isn't an easy play to watch – or rather it might not have been, if it weren't for the extraordinary performances of Emily Walker as an aristocratic white Southern girl, barely out of her teens, and of Kingsley Jackson as her stubbornly defiant black lover. Both of these remarkable young people went out onto the Shubert stage as newcomers last Tuesday night, and both came back as stars. In at least one reviewer's opinion, this show deserves to run forever.

Michael skipped the paragraph or two about the playwright because he didn't want to know how young the son of a bitch was, and didn't want to see him called a "dramatist"; then, further down in the column, he read this:

. . . Still, perhaps the highest accolades for this electrifying evening belong to Ralph Morin. As director of Philadelphia's Group Theater for some years, he earned a reputation for skill and sensitivity in any number of productions. But Philadelphia isn't New York, and even a play as strong as *Blues in the Night* might have languished in obscurity if Mr. Morin hadn't done everything right: assembled a near-perfect cast, drilled them with consummate artistry until every sound and silence was just to his liking, and then brought the show to town.

Interviewed in his Manhattan hotel suite yesterday, wearing a robe and pajamas though the hour was well past noon, Mr. Morin said he was "still in shock" over the play's extravagant success.

"I don't quite believe any of this," he said with a disarmingly boyish smile, "but I hope it keeps on happening."

At forty-two, with the kind of theatrical good looks that let you know he was once an aspiring actor himself, Mr. Morin can accurately be called a director who has paid his dues.

His wife Diana came up from their Philadelphia home for opening night but had to return the following day to look after their three small sons. "So the next thing now," he said, "as soon as I can get my act together, is to find some decent place here for all of us to live."

And it would seem that neither Diana nor the boys need have a moment's concern about that: Ralph Morin is very, very good at getting his act together.

"What're you reading?" Sarah inquired.

"Ah, some bullshit, is all. Some Sunday puff-piece about a guy I met once; he's married to a girl I used to know. He's directing a hit play on Broadway now."

"You mean what's-his-name? *Blues in the Night* and all that? Where'd you know him from?"

"Well, it's a long story, dear. You'd only get bored if I tried to tell it."

But he told it anyway, going easy on the part about his long infatuation with Diana, telling of Paul in a way that required no mention of the traded punches; then he tried to round it off with a disparaging account of Bill Brock's visit to Philadelphia, but he could tell her attention was wavering because Bill Brock was someone she'd neither read about nor ever met.

"Oh," she said when he was finished. "Yes, well, I can see how it all would sort of – connect for you now. It does sound like kind of a trashy play, though, doesn't it? Oh, very ambitious and 'relevant' and everything, but trashy anyway. If it were a movie they'd call it an exploitation flick."

"Right," he said, and he was glad she'd said it first.

One afternoon he drove home from school and found two bright new bicycles standing near the garage – a surprise from Sarah – and he went quickly into the house to thank her.

"Well, I thought it might be good to get a little exercise," she said.

"It'll be great," he told her. "I think it's a great idea."

And he meant it. They could ride away down the road over this endless prairie every afternoon; he could work the poisons of the job out of his system by pedaling hard with the wind in his face, gulping fresh air. And by the time they got back to the house, to take hot showers and change into clean, soft clothes, his tingling blood and quiet nerves would feel so good that he might not need more than a drink or two before dinner.

But there wasn't any pleasure in their first day on the bicycles. She flew away from him like a bird – he couldn't imagine where all the power came from in that delicate body and those slender legs – while he struggled to keep his wheels straight on the asphalt. He might still be able to deliver a knockout punch in Tom Nelson's living room, but his legs had gone rotten; that was the first of his bad discoveries this afternoon, and the second was that his lungs were rotten, too.

He knew the only way to overtake her was to stand up on the pedals, hunch over the handlebars, and pump his heart out; so he did that, with burning knees and a loose-lipped gasping for breath, and although he was nearly blind with sweat he could tell when he'd drawn up alongside her bike and finally passed it.

"How're you doing?" she called.

Then he was obliged to let her get ahead of him again, because any athletic coach in the world would have told him he needed a rest. He let the bike come to a stop, crouched to one side of it, and forcibly emptied one and then the other of his nostrils onto the road; if he hadn't done that he would have had to retch and puke in order to breathe.

When he was breathing again he looked into the shimmering distance and saw that Sarah was much too far away to permit his ever catching up; then he watched her make a wide turn to the other side of the road and begin the long ride home. When she approached and came sailing past him she smiled and waved, seeming to say it would be all right with her if he wanted to start his own journey home from here, so he turned the bike around and trailed her at an ever-lengthening distance. The main trouble now was that he kept veering out to the very edge of the asphalt, where it flaked off into irregular crusts and chunks that shuddered his tires and his spine; whenever that happened, with tall yellow weeds beginning to whip at his spokes, he would have to wrestle the handlebars to bring himself up onto the solid part of the road again before he could make any headway.

He saw Sarah rise and stand on her pedals to pump swiftly up the little hill of their concrete driveway, then coast into the shadows of their garage, and he vowed to save enough strength so that he too could accomplish that final bit of the ride with authority and ease; but from the moment he hit the base of the driveway he knew it was out of the question. He had to get off the damned bike and walk it up to the garage, hanging his head, holding his jaws shut tight to stop himself from greeting his wife with something like Well, I guess you think you're pretty fucking young, don't'cha?

Later, after soaking in the shower and putting on a clean shirt and pants, he sat hunched over his whiskey in the living room and told her it wasn't going to work. "I can't do this, baby," he explained. "I just can't do this shit, that's all. Just can't."

"Well, look, it was only the first time," she began, and it chilled him to find that both her tone and her words were like Mary Fontana's, or perhaps like those of any other nice girl trying to comfort an impotent man. "I know it'll come back to you soon," she was saying. "It's only a knack, after all. The main thing is not to fight it, or strain for it; just try to relax. Oh, and next time I won't be such a show-off; I won't go tearing off way ahead of you like that. I'll wait and ride along with you until you're more comfortable, okay?"

Okay. And just as an impotent man might well be touched by such kindness in a nice, nice girl – knowing all the while that she didn't know the half of it, fearing that the wretched business could never be set right – he agreed that they would go on "trying" with the bicycles every day.

There were faculty parties several times a month in Billings, and the Davenports went to most of them until Michael began to complain that they were all alike.

The walls in most faculty homes displayed giant black-and-white photographs of old movie stars – W. C. Fields, Shirley Temple, Clark Gable – because this kind of decoration was said to be "camp"; in some houses too an entire wall would be given over to the spectacle of an American flag hung upside down, as proof of bitter and wholehearted opposition to the war in Vietnam. Once, finding his way to the bathroom in such a house, Michael came upon a mock recruiting poster:

Join the Army
Visit Exotic Places
And Kill People

"And I mean what kind of horseshit is that?" he asked Sarah as they drove home that night. "Since when has it made any sense to blame the war on the soldiers?"

"Well, it's not a very good poster," she said, "but I don't think that's what it was meant to suggest. I think the idea is more that everything about the war is wrong."

"Then why isn't that what it said? Christ's sake, all the kids in the Army today are there because they were drafted, or because they couldn't find work anywhere else. Soldiers are the *victims* of wars; everybody knows that." Then, after a few miles of silence, he said "I don't think I'd mind these parties so much if the people weren't all so busy being 'political.' You get the feeling that if it weren't for the Anti-War Movement they wouldn't have anything in their lives at all. Or maybe all I'm trying to say is that I wouldn't mind them so much if I could ever count on getting a halfway decent drink. Jesus; wine. Wine on top of wine. And all of it warm as piss."

So they found ways to avoid most of the parties, until one day when the English department chairman stopped Michael in the corridor, gave him a friendly tug of the sleeve, and made a half-joking suggestion that it might soon be time for the Davenports to have a party of their own.

"Oh," Sarah said that night. "I didn't realize these things were sort of – obligatory."

"Well, I don't think they are, necessarily," he told her. "But we have been acting a little aloof, dear, and that's probably not a very good idea in a town as small as this."

She seemed to be thinking it over. "Okay," she said at last. "But if we're going to do it, let's do it right. We'll have real whiskey, with a whole lot of ice, and we'll put real bread and meat on the table instead of all this crackers-and-dip nonsense."

On the afternoon before the party there was a phone call from a young man with a shy, hesitant voice. "Mike? I don't know if you'll remember me – Terry Ryan." And the voice did sound familiar, but the name might not have helped if he hadn't followed it quickly with "I used to be a waiter at the Blue Mill restaurant, in New York."

"Hell, of course I remember you, Terry," Michael said. "I'll be damned; how are you? Where you calling from?"

"Well, the thing is I'm in Billings for a couple of days, and I—"

"Billings, *Kansas*?"

And Terry Ryan gave a brief, self-effacing laugh that brought him instantly alive in Michael's memory. "Sure," he said. "Why not? It's sort of my Alma Mater, after all – or at least it would have been, if I'd ever been able to pass the foreign-language requirement. All that was before I went to New York, you see."

"So what're you up to now, Terry? What're you doing?"

"Well, that's the funny part. I got drafted; then I guess the Army managed to get me trained, more or less, and now I've gotta be in San Francisco tomorrow afternoon."

"Oh, Jesus; are they sending you to Vietnam?"

"That's what I hear, yeah."

"What branch are you in?"

"Oh, the infantry, is all. Nothing fancy."

"Well, Jesus, Terry, that's – that's really bad news. That's lousy."

"But I took this little detour, you see, to see some friends of mine here in Billings; then when I heard you were teaching here I thought I'd give you a call. Thought you might come out for a beer or something."

"Good," Michael said, "but I've got a better idea. We're having a party at my house tonight, and we'd be delighted if you can come on over. Bring a girl."

"Well, I can't promise the girl," he said, "but the rest of it sounds fine. What time?"

And even before they'd finished talking, Michael had begun to feel privileged and kind.

Terry Ryan had been younger, smaller, and skinnier than any of the other Blue Mill waiters, and he'd clearly been the brightest of them, too. His quick, nervous face always let you know when he had something funny to say; then he'd say it, usually while putting dinner plates on your table, and he'd get away fast every time, heading back for the kitchen or the bar, before there could be any hint of an intrusion on your privacy. And on some nights, after his working shift was over, he and Michael would drink together at the bar until closing time. Terry's ambition was to be a comic actor – he alluded modestly to having been told he had the talent for it – but his greatest fear was of ending up as what he called a theater bum.

"You're a little young to be worried about ending up as anything, aren't you, Terry?"

"Well, I see what you mean. Still, everybody's gonna end up some way, sometime, right?"

Right.

"Sarah?" Michael said, ambling over to where she stood at work with the vacuum cleaner. "Listen. We'll be having a special guest tonight."

The department chairman and his wife, John and Grace Howard, were among the first to arrive. They were both in their fifties, and often said to be a lovely couple. He was tall and straight, with a closely trimmed mustache; she had retained the dimpled, "cute" good looks of a much younger woman, though her hair was white, and she usually wore full skirts cut short enough to emphasize her attractive legs. At another recent party they had waltzed together on a cleared floor for twenty minutes, Grace lying back in John's arms to gaze up at him in girlish rapture, and most of the people watching them agreed it was the prettiest thing they'd ever seen.

"You're to be congratulated, Michael," John Howard said. "It's about time somebody served an honest drink in this town."

And that opinion was echoed by a number of other guests – people who always showed up at these parties whether they liked one another or not because there was hardly anything else to do in Billings, Kansas. Most of them were teachers but there were graduate students, too, with their wives or girls – some smiling as uncertainly as children at a gathering of grownups, others leaning against the walls and observing everything with thinly veiled expressions of disdain.

When Terry Ryan came in he looked even smaller than Michael had remembered – he must have been barely tall enough to qualify for the Army – and he'd chosen not to wear his uniform: he wore jeans and a gray pullover sweater that was too big for him.

"Come on, Terry," Michael said, "we'll get you a drink and

then we'll find you a place to sit down. All the introductions can wait. Far as I'm concerned you're the guest of honor tonight. Hey, listen, though: you remember Sarah?"

"I don't think so."

"No, I guess I didn't start taking her to the Mill until after you'd quit working there. Anyway we're married now, and she wants to meet you. See the one over there by the window? With the dark hair?"

"Nice," Terry said. "Very nice. You've got good taste, Mike."

"Well, what the hell: why marry some plain girl when you can get a pretty girl instead?" From the tone of his own voice Michael could tell he had begun to drink too much, too fast, but he was sober enough to know he could still repair the damage by staying away from whiskey for the next hour.

"Wait right here," he told Terry, who was perched on a tall wooden stool brought from the kitchen and nursing a bourbon and water. "I'll go get her."

"Baby?" he said to his wife. "Would you like to come and meet the soldier?"

"I'd love to."

And from the moment he left them together he knew they would get along. He went to the kitchen and drank water. Then he busied himself at the sink, washing out glasses to kill as much as possible of the time before he could go to the liquor table again. When two or three students drifted into the kitchen he conversed with them in a quiet, humorous, good-host kind of way that seemed to prove he was getting better, though his watch said there was still almost half an hour to wait. He strolled back into the living room to give other people the benefit of his presence, and he almost collided with John Howard, who looked tired and ill.

"Sorry," Howard said. "Damn good party, but I'm afraid I'm not used to the hard stuff – or maybe I'm too old for it. I think we'd better be on our way."

But Grace wasn't ready to leave. "*Go*, then, John," she said from the sofa where she sat among her friends. "Take the car and *go*, if you want to. I can always get a ride." And it occurred to Michael that this was undoubtedly true: all her life, Grace Howard must have been the kind of girl who could always get a ride.

When the whole of his hour was mercifully over, he felt righteous as he fixed himself a good one at the liquor table. And that oddly bracing sense of righteousness persisted after he'd turned back to mingle with his guests; it seemed to enhance the joviality of his drawing the more sullen students away from the walls, winning their smiles and even their pleasing laughter. It *was* a damn good party, and it was getting better all the time. Looking around the room he could see men he thought of every day as fools, or bores, or worse, but now he felt a comradely affection for all of them, and for their nicely dressed women. This was the old fucked-up English department; he was an old fucked-up English department man – and if they had suddenly begun to raise their voices in the opening verse of "Auld Lang Syne" it would have brought tears to his eyes as he sang along.

Soon he had lost count of how many times he'd replenished his glass at the liquor table, but that no longer mattered because the evening was well past the strain of its early stages. And his greatest pleasure was in watching Sarah move gracefully from group to group, the perfect young hostess. Nobody could have guessed at how reluctantly she had organized this thing.

Then he turned and saw Terry Ryan on the tall wooden stool with no one to talk to. It was possible that Sarah had taken him around to meet other guests and that he'd come back after running out of polite things to say; but it was possible, too, that he'd sat here all this time, allowing his last night of freedom in the United States to evaporate before his eyes.

"Can I get you something, Terry?"

"No thanks, Mike; I'm fine."

"You met any of these people?"

"Oh, sure; met quite a few."

"Well," Michael said, "I think we can do better than that." And he stepped around to stand beside him, firmly clasping one thin shoulder beneath the fabric of his sweater.

"This young man," he announced in a voice loud enough to leave no doubt of his intention to address the party as a whole – and most other talkers in the room fell silent – "this young man may look like a student, and that's what he was at one time, but not anymore. He's an infantry soldier on his way to Vietnam, where I imagine his personal problems will soon be a great deal worse than any of our own. So suppose we all forget about college for a minute, please, and let's have a hand for Terry Ryan."

There was some clapping, though nowhere near as much as he'd expected, and even before it was over Terry said "Kind of wish you hadn't done that, Mike."

"Why?"

"I don't know; just because."

Then from across the room Michael saw Sarah looking at him in disappointment or disapproval. He felt as if he'd just traded punches with someone in the Nelsons' house, or just been told he had called Fletcher Clark a cocksucker at the writers' conference.

"Well, Jesus, Terry, I didn't mean to embarrass you," he said. "I thought they ought to know who you are, that's all."

347

"Oh, I know; it's okay; forget it."

But it was a thing that wouldn't be forgotten.

Grace Howard was on her feet and making her way through the smoke, bearing down on Terry Ryan with one stiff index finger aimed at his chest.

"May I ask you something?" she inquired. "Why do you want to kill people?"

And he smiled bashfully. "Oh, come on, lady," he said. "I never killed anybody in my life."

"Well, but you'll have your chance now, won't you? With your automatic rifle and your hand grenades?"

"Hold it, Grace," Michael said, "you're way out of line here: This boy was drafted."

"And maybe they'll give you a little radio, too," she went on, "so you can call in the artillery and the bombs and the napalm on women and children. Well, listen—"

"Oh, *stop* this," Sarah called, hurrying to Terry's side as if to protect him.

"—Listen," Grace Howard said. "You're not fooling anybody for a minute. *I* know why you want to kill people. You want to kill people because you're so *small*."

Some of Grace's friends managed to take charge of her then: they turned her around and walked her back across the room and out the front door, which closed with a little slam.

"Terry, I'm sorry as hell about that," Michael told him. "I knew she was drunk, but I didn't know she was crazy."

"Look, the hell with it, okay?" he said. "Fuck it. The more we talk about it, the worse it's going to get."

"Exactly," Sarah said quietly.

Later, when everyone else had gone at last, Sarah made up the bed in the spare room so that Terry could spend the night here. But there wasn't much left of the night: they had to get up early

348

to drive Terry to his friends' place. There he changed into his Army uniform, which Sarah said was "very becoming," and picked up his duffel bag, and they drove him twenty miles to the airport. There was some mild and pleasant talk in the car – all three of them had reached the stage of easy good humor that sometimes follows a night of too little sleep – but none of them mentioned Grace Howard.

When it was time to say goodbye at the gate to Terry's flight, Michael shook hands with him in a little excess of old soldier's heartiness: "Well, stay loose, Terry. And keep a tight asshole."

Then Sarah opened her arms for him. She was taller than he was, but that didn't make it an awkward embrace. She held him, however briefly, in the way a man ought to be held before going to a war that nobody would ever understand.

They rode in silence for much of the drive home, until Michael said "Well, hell, the whole damn thing was my fault; I know that. I never should've made that dumb little speech." Then he said "But the point is, baby, when I was in the Army you wanted people to pay attention the night before you went overseas. It was nice to have civilians make a fuss over you – and they did, if you were lucky."

"Well, I know," Sarah said, "but that was another time. That was before I was born. Before Terry was born, too."

And when he glanced away from the road again he found she was quietly crying.

She went to sleep as soon as they were back in the house; that gave him a chance to drink two cold beers in the kitchen and try to get his brains together.

Then the telephone rang. "Michael? John Howard here. Listen: who was that kid you had in your house last night?"

349

"Friend of mine from New York, is all; he was just passing through. Why?"

"Well, I understand he was very rude and offensive to Grace after I left."

"Oh?" And Michael instantly knew there would be no point in trying to clear up this messy business. Terry Ryan was a thousand miles away in the sky now, rid of Billings, Kansas, forever; nobody's brave words could defend him any longer. "Well, I'm sorry there was any unpleasantness, John," he said with what he hoped was an edge of scorn, and he hung up the receiver before Howard could say anything more.

If Howard called back at once to persist in his false grievance there would be nothing to do but tell him the truth about what Grace had done. And the phone didn't ring a second time.

He wished Sarah were awake, so she could assure him he'd done the right thing. Still, it was probably better to have her asleep; that way there might be no need to talk it over, ever again.

One evening at the end of the school year, in June, Lucy Davenport called Michael to tell him their daughter was gone.

"Whaddya mean 'gone'?"

"Well, she's supposedly heading for California," Lucy said, "but I don't think there's any clear destination. She wants to be a vagabond, you see. She wants to bum around with all the other dirty, smelly little vagabonds on the road – any road, anywhere. She wants to be wholly irresponsible and wholly self-indulgent, and she wants to wreck her mind with all the hallucinatory drugs she can get her hands on."

Laura's freshman year at Warrington College had apparently taught her nothing but bad habits, her mother reported – "I think there must be a very extensive traffic in narcotics on that damned little campus." When she'd come home from there yesterday she seemed "all funny," and she'd brought along three friends, presumably as weekend guests: another Warrington girl, also acting "funny," and two boys that Lucy found difficult to describe.

"I mean they're *townies*, Michael. They're proletarian kids; children of textile-mill workers kind of thing. All they can do is grunt and mumble and try to imitate Marlon Brando — except that I don't suppose Marlon Brando's ever grown his hair down to his belly-button and his buttocks. Am I making any of this clear?"

"Yeah," Michael said. "Yeah, I think I'm getting the picture."

"And they were here less than twenty-four hours before Laura announced they were going to California. I couldn't reason with her, couldn't talk to her at all, and the next thing I knew she was gone. They were all gone."

"Well, Jesus," he said. "I don't know what to say."

"Neither do I. I don't understand any of it. I only called because I thought — you know — I thought you ought to know."

"Yeah. Well, I'm glad you did call, Lucy."

Sarah told him there probably wasn't anything to worry about. "Laura's nineteen," she said. "That's practically grown up. She can go off on an adventure like this without risking any damage to herself. The drug-taking does sound a little scary, but I think her mother may be exaggerating that part of it, don't you? Besides, every kid in America is fooling around with some kind of drugs, and most of them aren't any worse than alcohol or nicotine. The main thing to remember, Michael, is that if she does get into any kind of trouble she'll call you. She knows where you are."

"Well, she does, that's true," he said. "But here's the thing, you see: This is the first time since she was born that I haven't known where *she* is."

Chapter Five

One advantage in being twenty years older than your wife was that you could afford to take a fond, tolerant attitude when she developed interests that had nothing to do with your own.

Michael might have been startled and even frightened, years ago, when Lucy brought home *How to Love*, by Derek Fahr; but the coffee table of this Kansas house soon came to hold book after book by a dismaying variety of more recent authors – Kate Millett, Germaine Greer, Eldridge Cleaver – and they seldom caused him a moment's discomfort.

He wasn't even ruffled when Sarah joined a dead-serious organization called Women's International League for Peace and Freedom, though he had to acknowledge that once or twice, watching the car take her away to those meetings, he was reminded of Lucy disappearing into the privacy of her appointments with Dr. Fine.

Well, what the hell; girls would always be a mystery. The important thing was that this particular girl still chose to spend most of her time at home – and, in the hours when she wasn't absorbing propaganda, she could be a lively and engaging talker.

By now she had told him a great many interlocking episodes out of her brief, full life – college; high school and grammar school; parents and family and home – until he'd begun to feel he knew her almost as well as he would ever know himself. And he was always charmed by the honesty and humor and the pithy selection of detail in those reminiscent stories; they might ramble and digress, but they never strained to portray her in a flattering way, or in a pitiable way, either, and they never even came close to boring her listener.

What a girl she was! There were evenings, watching her talk in the lamplight on their secondhand sofa, when Michael could only marvel at his luck in finding her and at the glowing safety of his having her here. He knew she wouldn't tell so many intimate, self-revealing things unless she loved him completely – unless she was counting on him to keep these small and terrible secrets to himself until death.

One night in bed, speaking in a very soft voice, she suggested they have a baby.

"Right away, you mean?" he asked, knowing at once that the question betrayed his fear, and he winced in the darkness. He was too old for this; oh, Jesus, too old.

"Well, I meant within a year or two," she said. "How does year after next strike you?"

And the more he thought about it, the more sense it seemed to make. Didn't every healthy girl want a baby? Why would any healthy girl get married, after all, if not in the hope of having one? And this was the other point: it might be a good thing to raise a new child of his own – to have a chance to atone for all the aching mistakes he'd made over the years with Laura.

"Well, okay," he said after a while. "But I'll sure as hell be an old father. Know what I just figured out? By the time this kid is twenty-one, I'll be seventy."

"Oh?" she said, as if that hadn't occurred to her. "Well, then, I guess I'll have to be young enough for both of us, won't I?"

★

When the operator asked if he would accept a collect call from Laura in San Francisco he said "Sure I will," but when Laura's voice came on the line – "Daddy?" – it was so faint he thought they must have a bad connection.

"Hello? Laura?" he said, raising his own voice as if that would help.

"Daddy?" And this time he could hear her plainly.

"Are you okay, baby?"

"Well, I don't know. I'm still in – you know – still here in San Francisco and everything, but I'm not feeling very well, is all. Things keep closing in. I mean I was fine in the Outer Limits, but then ever since we – ever since I got back I've been all – I don't know."

"Is that some club out there? The Outer Limits?"

"No, it's more a state of mind."

"Oh."

"And I've only got about a dollar and thirty cents, you see, so there really isn't much I can do to fix myself up – depending on what I mean by fix myself up, of course. Depending on what you think I mean by fix myself up."

"Well, listen, dear. I think I'd better come out there right away, don't you?"

"Well, I guess that's what I was sort of hoping you'd – yes."

"Okay. If I leave right now I can be there in three and a half or maybe four hours. But first you'll have to give me the street address where you are." And he wagged his hand urgently at Sarah for a pencil.

"Two ninety-seven," Laura was reciting "– no, wait; two ninety-three South Something-or-other Street—"

"Come on," he said. "Come on, baby: South what? Try to remember." And when she was able to spell out the street name

355

at last, with what he could only hope were the right numerals, he said "Okay. Now the phone number."

"Oh, there aren't any phones in the building, Dad. I'm calling from a pay phone on the street, somewhere else."

"Oh, Jesus. Well, listen: I want you to go straight back to your place and wait for me there, however long it takes. Promise me. No more going out tonight for any reason, okay?"

"Okay."

Sarah drove him to the airport, taking a few close chances in the passing of other cars. There was a San Francisco flight ready for boarding when he rushed up to the ticket counter, and he made it, hurrying breathless through what may have been the same gate where they'd said goodbye to Terry Ryan. And just as it had undoubtedly been for Terry Ryan, the flight to San Francisco was the easy part.

"You sure you got this right?" the cab driver kept asking, even after stopping to confer and frown with two other cab drivers over the obscurity of Laura's address. Then, once he found he was taking his fare in the right direction, he said "Well, I don't know; you go into some of these old run-down neighborhoods, it's like going into another world. I wouldn't give you shit for this area along in here. This area isn't even fit for the blacks – and mind you, I've got nothing against the blacks."

Everybody in America had begun to say "black" instead of "Negro"; it might be only a question of time before everybody began saying "woman" instead of "girl."

There were no tenants' names on any of the doorbells, and Michael decided after pressing three or four of them that all the bells were probably out of order – several of them had fallen loose from the wall and were dangling by their own dead wires. Then he discovered that both locks on the big front door had been smashed: he could get inside just by turning the knob and lunging heavily with one shoulder.

"Is anybody here?" he demanded, walking into the ground-floor hallway, and four or five heads appeared out of partly opened doors – all of them young, more of them boys than girls, and all the boys wearing their hair in styles so wild that nobody would have believed the sight of them a few years ago.

"All right, listen, you guys," Michael said, not caring whether it sounded like an impersonation of James Cagney or not. "I'm Laura Davenport's father and I want to know where she is."

The young faces either withdrew or stared at him blankly – was it the blankness of fear or only of drugs? – but then a resonant male voice spoke up from the shadows at the far end of the hall: "Top floor, all the way to the right."

There could have been four, five, or six floors in that building; Michael didn't count them. He would achieve one flight of littered, piss-and garbage-smelling stairs, stand gasping until his strength came back, then go to work on the next flight. The only way he knew he'd made the top at last was that there were suddenly no more stairs.

All the way to the end of the right-hand corridor was a dirty white door. He paused for breath again, if not for prayer, and then he knocked on it.

"Dad?" Laura called. "You can come on in; it's open."

There she was, lying on a single bed in a room so small that there wasn't even space for a chair, and the first thing that struck him was that she was beautiful. She had lost too much weight – her long legs were too thin in greasy jeans and her upper body looked as frail as a bird's under a greasy workman's shirt – but her pale and famished face, with its great blue eyes and delicate, thin-lipped mouth, made her look like the heartbreaking debutante her mother might always have wanted her to be.

357

"Wow," he said, sitting on the edge of the bed near her knees. "Wow, baby, am I ever glad to see you."

"Well, me too," she said. "Could I have one of your cigarettes, Dad?"

"Sure, here. But listen: I get the impression you haven't been eating a hell of a lot. Right?"

"Well, I guess it's been a little over two weeks now since I—"

"Okay. So the first thing we'll do is feed you a good dinner somewhere; then we'll find a hotel for the night, and tomorrow I'll take you back to Kansas. How does that sound?"

"Oh, it sounds – okay, I guess, except that I don't know your wife or anything."

"Sure you do."

"Well, but I mean I don't know her as your wife, is all."

"Oh, Laura, that's dumb. You'll get along fine. Now. Is there anything here you want to keep? And do you have a bag to pack it in?"

In policing the narrow floor he found two black, elastic-strap bow ties of the kind worn by restaurant waiters, the kind Terry Ryan used to wear on duty at the Blue Mill, and when he pulled her smudged nylon "backpack" away from the wall a third one fell out from behind it. Had three young waiters been up here and had her and left their accidental souvenirs? No; more likely it had been one waiter, three times – or five or ten times, or more.

("Hey Eddie, where you been?"

"Been making it with the tall skinny one I told you about: top floor, all the way to the right. She comes on like Gangbusters, man."

"Well, okay, but shit, Eddie, I wouldn't mess around in that house if I was you; all those kids are crazy."

"Yeah? You mean crazy like me, or crazy like you? Listen: I get my pussy where I find it, man.")

"Are you ready, dear?" Michael asked.

"I guess so."

But they couldn't get a cab on this street; they had to walk many blocks before they found one that would stop for them.

"Is there someplace where we can get dinner at this time of night?" Michael asked the driver.

"Well, at *this* time of night," the man told him, "the only place I can take you is Chinatown."

And it would always strike him as a ludicrous touch that Chinese food was the best he could provide for his starving child. Egg Foo Young, Pork Fried Rice, Shrimp with Lobster Sauce – stuff that most Americans eat only once in a while, for a change, when they're not very hungry anyway – this was what Laura took for nourishment in steadily rhythmic forkfuls, and she didn't speak or even look up until the last empty dish had been cleared away.

"Can I have another cigarette, Dad?"

"Sure. You feeling any better?"

"I guess so."

Another cabdriver recommended a hotel, and there, as they stood waiting in line at the front desk, Michael was afraid the room clerk might easily misinterpret everything: a nervous-looking professor type with a sweet, doped-up hippie girl.

"I need accommodations for my daughter and myself," he began carefully, looking the man straight in the eyes, and he realized in the same breath that this was exactly the kind of thing a quivering old lecher might be expected to say. "For one night only," he added, making it worse. "I think the best arrangement would be two connecting rooms."

"Nope," the clerk said with finality, and Michael steeled

himself to be asked – or told – to leave the place at once. But it turned out, as his lungs began to work again, that there was nothing to fear. "Nope; can't give you any connecting rooms tonight," the clerk said. "Best I can do for you tonight is a double room with twin beds. Would that be suitable, sir?"

And it may have been the "sir," as much as the rest of it, that lightened Michael's step as they walked across the carpeted lobby and into an elevator. More than two thirds of his life was gone, but he hadn't yet learned to take it for granted when another man called him "sir."

Laura slept so soundly that she didn't move or turn all night, but her father lay awake in the other twin bed. Toward morning, as he'd sometimes done on other sleepless nights, he began to whisper his way through the long final poem from his first book, the one called "Coming Clean" that Diana Maitland and Sarah Garvey had liked. His whispering was so faint that nobody could have heard it more than a few inches away from his pillow, but it was an accurate and precise recitation – getting the most out of each syllable and silence, rising and falling in just the right places, never making a mistake because he would always know that poem by heart.

Damn. Oh, Jesus God, it was the best thing he had ever written. And it wasn't lost yet, though the book was long out of print and increasingly hard to find in public libraries. Oh, it wasn't lost yet; somebody could still pick it up and get it published again in a classy-looking anthology that might become a standard text in all the universities.

Then he began to recite it again, taking his time, from the beginning.

"Dad?" Laura called from her bed. "You awake?"

"Yup." And he was afraid she would say she'd heard him whispering, so he anxiously prepared a quick explanation for her: Guess I must've been having a nightmare or something.

"I'm a little hungry, is all," she said. "You think we could go down and have breakfast pretty soon?"

"Sure. You go on in and use the bathroom first if you want, dear, and I'll get dressed."

He was relieved that she seemed not to have heard the whispering; but then it occurred to him, as he zipped up his pants, that she might have heard it and thought it "weird" or "bizarre" but decided not to mention it. Hippies were said to respect the privacy of one another's trips. Do your own thing.

That afternoon, as their plane lay floating impossibly high over the earth, Laura turned away from her window and said "Dad? There's a thing I guess I'd better tell you. I think I may be pregnant."

"Oh?" And Michael smiled to prove he wasn't stunned by the news.

"Well, I mean it could be just that I've missed a couple of my periods because I haven't been – you know – haven't been feeling well and everything, but I'm not sure. And I don't know who it – you know – who the boy was. My memory's sort of blurred on a lot of the stuff that's happened this summer."

"Oh," he said. "Well, dear, I don't think you need to worry about that anymore. We'll take you to the university hospital and have them do a test; then if it's true we'll get it taken care of right away. Okay?" And he felt warmed by his own kindness. He told her he knew a doctor at the hospital who could make unofficial referrals to a certain clinic in Missouri where "D. and C.'s" were quickly arranged and performed; he promised her she would be all right.

But once the need for reassurance was past, after Laura had turned back to the window again, Michael sat riding the sky with a look of desolation. His daughter might be pregnant at nineteen, and would never know the father of her child.

When Sarah met them at the airport she gave Laura a hug and a little kiss to show she wasn't a guidance counselor anymore, and the three of them drove home in a mood of uncertain camaraderie.

Laura said the landscape here looked "funny, if you're used to a city." Then she said "We didn't come through Kansas at all on our way out; we went across Nebraska instead."

And now that she'd said "we" and "our," Michael could barely suppress a question that had nagged him ever since he'd found her alone in that wretched house last night: what the hell had happened to her friends? With all their bleating about "love," weren't hippies supposed to stick together and look after their own? How could those kids have abandoned a girl in a harsh and alien place?

He didn't say anything, but he knew he would urgently need to talk to Sarah tonight, once they were alone.

Like an infant, Laura was ready for sleep again as soon as she'd been fed. Sarah took her down the hall to the spare room, and Michael brought a freshly made drink to the mantelpiece because that seemed a good place to stand while he tried to sort things out.

When Sarah came back into the living room she sat on the sofa, facing him, and listened with no apparent surprise to the news of what Laura had told him on the plane.

"Well, we can take her over to the hospital tomorrow for a rabbit test," she said. "It may be nothing, and until we find out I don't see any point in worrying about it."

"I know, I know," he said quickly. "That's what I told her. And I told her I could arrange for an abortion, too. Still, it hit me pretty hard – and the worst of it is her not having any idea who the boy was. Isn't that the God damndest thing?"

Sarah lit a cigarette. She smoked only four or five cigarettes a week, during peaceful interludes, and he had long come to interpret it as a sign that she was trying to understand him.

"Oh, well," she said, "I imagine that's in keeping with the general hippie way of life, don't you? And I imagine the girls have found it useful as a sort of shock-your-father tactic, too."

He went out to get another drink, and he barely made it back to the mantelpiece before he was crying. He turned quickly away and tried to hide it from her – no young wife should ever see an aging husband in tears – but it was too late.

"Michael? Are you crying?"

"Well, I didn't get any sleep last night," he said, covering his face with his fingers, "but the main thing is I'm proud of myself for the first time in – first time in years. Oh, Jesus, baby, she was all alone out there and she was lost – she was lost – and maybe I've never done anything right in my whole life, but son of a bitch I went out there and found her and got her and brought her home and now I'm fucking proud of myself, that's all." But he suspected even then that it wasn't quite all, and that the rest of it couldn't be told.

When he'd pulled himself together, apologizing, artificially laughing to prove he hadn't really cried, allowing Sarah to lead him to their bedroom, he knew he had been reduced to tears by the final lines of "Coming Clean" – lines that had thrummed in the pressurized cabin of the plane today and now continued to roll and ring in his head – and by the knowledge that he'd written that poem when Laura was five years old.

The rabbit test was negative – Laura might never be pregnant now until after she'd married some young man who would take as keen an interest in rabbit tests as she did – and so the worst of the pressure was off.

But the next thing, which Michael might have tried to avoid if it hadn't been Sarah's idea, was to take Laura in to see one of the university-hospital psychiatrists.

For an hour, fighting his nerves, he sat alone in a waiting area full of orange plastic chairs; then the doctor brought Laura back from his consulting room so she could wait here while he conferred with her father. And Michael was grateful at least that they hadn't gotten some young smart-ass; this one was courteous and dignified and fifty or more, and he looked very settled, very much the family man in his conservative suit and highly polished brown shoes. His name was McHale.

"Well, Mr. Davenport," he said as soon as they were seated, with the door closed on their privacy, "I think we can consider this a clear psychotic break."

"Now, wait a minute," Michael said. "Where do you get 'psychotic'? She's been taking a lot of drugs, that's all. Don't you think 'psychotic' is kind of an ugly word to throw around?"

"I think it's the most accurate word we have. Some of these drugs do induce psychosis, you see. There's a severe disorientation; there are 'highs' and 'lows' and hallucinations, so ultimately the pattern is that of a conventional psychotic episode."

"Well, okay, but look, Doctor. She's stopped taking all that stuff now. She's living very quietly with her stepmother and me. Can't we just give her a chance to get well on her own?"

"In some cases I might agree with that, yes; but your daughter is very troubled and confused. I'm not suggesting she be hospitalized, at least not for the present, but I'll want to see her here twice a week. Three times might be preferable, but we can begin with two."

"Jesus," Michael said. "She must've acted an awful lot crazier in here with you than she does at home." But he could tell he was losing the argument: he had always lost arguments with these slippery bastards before, and probably always would. "I mean she doesn't act quite *right* at home yet," he said, "but it's mostly just that she's kind of lazy and sluggish all the time."

"And not very talkative?"

"No; not at all."

"Well, then," the doctor said with a sly look that contained the distressing suggestion of a wink, "I don't suppose you've had occasion to hear about the 'Outer Limits,' and that kind of thing."

One morning a crisply typed letter arrived from Warrington College, forwarded in Lucy's handwriting; its message was that Laura would be permitted to return there for her sophomore year "on a probationary basis."

"Well, big fucking deal," Michael said. "Listen, baby, I don't ever want you going anywhere on a probationary basis. Fuck Warrington College, right? Let 'em take their leotards and stuff 'em up their ass."

And not until then did he remember that Sarah, now quietly eating her breakfast, was the calm and thoughtful young counselor who had recommended Warrington College in the first place.

"Well, okay, I'm sorry, dear," he said. The words "dear" and "baby" and "sweetheart" had flown around this house in such profusion lately that he would sometimes lose track of which girl he was talking to, but this time he knew he meant Sarah. "And listen, it was a nice try. But I never did think Warrington was right for her: she could probably get a better education here at *Billings* than in that little flower factory. Besides, if she goes to Billings she can go on seeing Dr. Whaddyacallit for as long as that takes; then if she wants to transfer to some classier school she can do that later."

RICHARD YATES

And Sarah agreed, after thinking it over, that this sounded like a reasonable plan.

"It's funny, you know?" Laura said from across the breakfast table, and her eyes and voice had taken on a dreamy quality. "I really don't remember much of anything about Warrington now – it's all kind of a blur. I remember afternoons when a bunch of us would go walking out across the fields to the highway, and we'd wait there for a certain car to come along. Then the car would pull up and stop, and the guy would roll down his window so we could give him our money, and then he'd hand over these little brown paper bags. Tabs of acid, different kinds of amphetamines, coke and hash and even plain old marijuana; then we'd walk back to school – oh, and sometimes there'd be beautiful sunsets over those fields – and we'd all feel rich and wonderful because we knew we'd be able to make it through another week."

"Yeah," Michael said. "Well, that's very nostalgic and very bucolic and all that, sweetheart, but I want to tell you something. You're not a hippie anymore, do you understand me? You've had all the irresponsibility and all the self-indulgence you're ever going to get. You're a psychiatric patient now, and your stepmother and I are doing the best we can to help you put your brains back together. So listen: if you've finished eating, why don't you go in and take one of your four-hour naps or something useful like that?"

"Don't you think that was a little excessive?" Sarah asked him after the girl had gone.

And he could only stare down grimly at the yolk of a cold fried egg. It wasn't yet nine o'clock in the morning, and already he had lost his temper twice.

That day the registrar's office at Billings State University told him it was now too late for Laura to enroll for the fall semester;

the best that could be done was to have her fill out application forms for admission in February. And so all three of them, in a house that had come to seem much too small, would be stuck with one another for five months.

"Well, I imagine we'll survive," Sarah said. "And I don't think she's ready for college work yet anyway, do you? I don't think she has the concentration."

Soon there was a letter from Lucy. It was very short and neatly centered on the page, and the care taken over its form and content suggested she had written it several times before finding the right tone.

Dear Michael:

I am extremely grateful for the way you stepped in and took responsibility for Laura this summer. You were there when she needed you, and you seem to have done everything wisely and well.

My regards to Sarah, and my thanks for her help too.

All best, as always,

L.

P.S. – I'll be moving to the Boston area soon; Cambridge, I think. Will let you know the details.

"Well, of course I only met her that one time," Sarah said, "but she did impress me as being a very – decent woman."

"Oh, very decent, sure," he said. "All three of us in my little family are very decent people; it's just that two of us are crazy."

"Oh, Michael. Are you going to start this nonsense about being 'crazy'?"

"How is it nonsense? Would you prefer the kind of words the shrinks use? 'Psychotic'? 'Manic-depressive'? 'Paranoid schizophrenic'? Listen. Try to understand this. Way back when I was a kid, before anybody in Morristown had ever heard of Sigmund Freud, we recognized three basic categories: there was sorta crazy; there was crazy; and there was crazier'n hell. *Those* are the terms I trust. And I've often thought I wouldn't at all mind being *sorta* crazy, because that can make a man terribly attractive to girls, but I'd be a liar if I tried to squeeze myself into that category for you. I'm crazy, and there are documents to prove it. Laura's crazy too, at least for the time being, and unless she and I play our cards right we're both gonna be crazier'n hell. Simple as that."

"Do you know what you do sometimes?" Sarah asked him. "You let your own rhetoric run away with you until you don't even know what you're saying. It's like when you try to tell me about Adlai Stevenson and end up making him sound like the crucified Jesus. I certainly hope you have better control than that in your teaching, or you may have a lot of very bewildered students on your hands."

After a little while – however long it took him to decide not to be angry with her – he said "I think we'd better let the teaching and the students be my business, don't you?"

Then he went away to hide in his workroom, fairly confident that he'd delivered his last sentence with the right kind of quiet dignity.

She *had* overstepped the line a little that time, impugning his "control" as a teacher. For once, in these small but increasingly frequent quarrels, she had been ever so slightly in the wrong, and she would probably acknowledge it. Oh, she wouldn't apologize right away; more likely she would wait until all the difficulties of the day and the evening were gone, until they could lie down together at last, dappled in the pale light and shadow of the rising Kansas moon; then, in his arms, she might say she was sorry. Or maybe, by that time, it would no longer be necessary.

"Hey, Laura?" he asked his daughter one day. "How come you never make your bed in the morning?"

"I don't know. What's the point of making it when I'll just be getting back into it?"

"Well, I guess that's reasonable, in a way," he said. "So what's the point of combing your hair when it'll just get tangled up again? What's the point of taking a shower when you'll just get dirty again? And maybe we could all agree not to flush the toilet more than once a month – does that sound like a good idea?"

He moved in close then and wagged one forefinger at her cringing, wincing face. "Look, baby. It seems to me you've got a choice here. Either you're going to live like a civilized girl or you're going to live like a rat. You think it over and decide, okay? And I'd like to have your decision sometime during the next thirty seconds."

There would probably have been more scenes like that, worse and worse, if it hadn't been for Sarah's steadying influence. It was Sarah, as he tried to tell her many times, who made these months endurable. She was scarcely five years older than her step-daughter, but she was always quietly in charge. She would go about the daily housework never seeming to notice whether Laura helped her with the cleaning and cooking or not; she would drive Laura into town to keep her appointments with Dr. McHale; several times, while waiting for the psychiatric hour to be over, she shopped around and bought a few tasteful, stylish clothes for her.

At school, in his classrooms or his office, Michael began to allow himself a comfortable sense that things would be all right when he got home, and they usually were. On their best days, during the time of peace and measured alcohol in the late afternoon, the three of them could sometimes sit conversing as pleasantly as if Laura were a child of the people next door – an "interesting" girl, too young to offer much in the way of originality, but deferential and well-mannered as she sipped at her can of Coca-Cola. Still, none of them were fooled: they all knew it would take a great deal more than this before she was well.

Once he came home and found her in the big easy chair, wearing a fresh new dress and absorbed in the Modern Library edition of *The Scarlet Letter*.

"Good," he told her. "I'm glad you're reading again, dear. That's a great book, too."

"I know," she said, and as he passed the chair he looked down to see what page she was on: 98. He went into his workroom then and hunched over many student papers and student poems – the whole trick of teaching was to get this part of it out of the way in a day or two, if you could – and it must have been two hours later when he walked back past Laura's chair and saw she was still on page 98.

Well, shit, what *was* the matter with this kid? Hadn't that asshole psychiatrist done anything at all for her? What the hell could she be thinking about behind those big, blue, heart-breaking eyes?

Sarah was there in the kitchen, opening a tray of ice cubes to fix a drink for him because it was five o'clock, and all he could say was "Oh, Jesus, you're wonderful."

He had to wait until they were in bed that night, with two closed doors and a stretch of hallway to muffle the soft-spoken words, before he told her about Laura and the book.

"Oh," she said. "And you're sure it was the same page?"

"Of course I'm sure. Why would I tell you as creepy a thing

370

as that about my own child if I wasn't sure?"

After a thoughtful pause she said "Well, I suppose I see what you mean by 'creepy,' though it might be better if we could find a more useful word. Still, it's very – distressing, isn't it. Because I thought she was getting so much better, didn't you?"

Early in the winter, when they'd decided it was time for Laura to take up some constructive activity, a new commercial typewriting school was opened for business in town. Sarah's own typing was "rusty," she said, and Laura had never really learned to type at all; it would be helpful for both of them to sign up for the course together.

So they went off to their typing class nearly every day, on a schedule carefully arranged to leave time for Laura's psychiatric sessions, and Michael hesitantly assumed it would be a good thing. Typing was a mindless kind of work that could sometimes take your thoughts away from your troubles – unless, of course, you were trying to type up your own poems. And he remembered days and nights long ago, in New York and Larchmont and Tonapac, when he would flinch and curse the machine for all the dumb fucking mistakes it made in his lines, when he would rip out the paper and roll in new paper and make still other and worse mistakes, until it was time for Lucy to take over. She had always been able to type the poems for him quickly and perfectly at one sitting, like the most desirable kind of secretary.

One afternoon a few weeks after the typing course began, Laura came blundering into the house to confront him while Sarah was putting the car away in the garage.

"Look, Dad, it's a thing I just can't do, okay?" she said, and her face and neck were red with the need for tears. "You know how some people can never learn a foreign language or a musical instrument and stuff like that? Well, I can't type, that's all. I've

371

been using two fingers for so long I don't even understand the fucking keyboard, and they all make me feel so dumb in that class. They make me feel so dumb I want to puke." At the word "puke" her welling eyes spilled over, and she wiped them with her hand as she went quickly down the hall to her room. It was the first time in years that he'd seen her cry.

Sarah had come in from the garage in time to witness the last of Laura's outburst, and now she tried to explain to him: "It wasn't a very good day. The teacher kept getting impatient with her, and a few of the other kids laughed."

"Well, shit," he said. "I don't want anybody laughing at her in the shape she's in. I don't want anybody laughing at her ever, for that matter. I've always thought ridicule is about the most hateful thing in the world."

Sarah gave him a brief, testy look. "Then why do you ridicule her all the time?"

And he might have said "That's different," if he hadn't caught himself. Instead he said "Well, okay, you're right. I do, and it's a thing I'll have to watch. Even so, I must say it was kind of a relief to see her cry. After all this zombie behavior, I mean."

"Well, now you've lost me completely," Sarah said. "Ridicule is the most hateful thing in the world, but crying is good for you? Crying is 'therapy' or something? Isn't that the kind of thinking we're all expected to outgrow by the time we're about sixteen years old?"

She walked firmly away into the kitchen then, though it was much too early for dinner preparations, and he knew better than to follow her. He stood slumped at one of the storm windows, looking out over flat fields mottled white and gray from yesterday's light snowfall, and his heart contracted with foreboding. If Sarah ever did decide to leave him ("Well, now you've lost me completely") he believed he knew how it would feel.

Things seemed to improve at the typing school. The two girls would often come home laughing together, and at the end of the course they displayed for him, with mock pride and ill-concealed pleasure, their two corny little certificates of graduation.

"Well, but I mean how did she manage to graduate?" Michael asked as soon as Laura was out of earshot.

"Oh, she caught on to the knack of it eventually," Sarah said. "It's only a knack, after all; that's what I tried to tell her from the beginning, and what the teacher told her too. And I think she'll be much better prepared for college now, don't you?"

There were other preparations. Sarah had found the shopping facilities "skimpy" here in the college town, so she began taking Laura into the nearest neighboring city, where the airport was and where any girl could find whole streets of fashionable shops and stores; that was how Laura acquired a plentiful, good-looking new wardrobe for winter and spring. She would surely be among the best-dressed girls in all of Billings State, and nobody would ever guess how she'd looked as a vagabond.

It was just after he saw their car return from one of those shopping trips, on an unseasonably warm afternoon at the end of January, that Laura opened the front door, thrust her bright, pretty head inside and called "Dad? Okay if I borrow your bike?"

"Sure, baby," he called back. "Take it away."

And he went to the front windows to watch them go. Laura might have done everything she could to wreck her health in the past few years, but she was as strong as Sarah when they pedaled swiftly up the road together and into the distance, with their hair streaming. He couldn't have said which was the more light or fleet or graceful of those lovely, fast-disappearing girls.

On the day they took Laura to her four-girl suite in a sophomore residence hall, with all her clothes, there were hugs and kisses but no prolonged goodbyes. They would be living only a few miles apart; they'd be seeing one another from time to time, and so there was nothing to say now but good luck – oh, good luck, dear – and so long.

The house was suddenly ample again. It had resumed the look and feel of the house they'd been so pleased to find on first coming to Kansas: the best house either of them had ever known, the surprisingly well-designed, modern house where everything worked.

"Well, baby," he said, "I could never have gotten through these months without you, and neither could she."

They were standing in the living room like visitors who haven't yet been asked to sit down, and he reached out to clasp both of her hands so that she'd look up at him. What he wanted now was to take her down the hall to their bedroom, where they could have each other all afternoon and long past nightfall, never caring what sounds their gasps and cries might make in a house that was once again, and finally, their own.

"I think you're glorious," he told her.

"Well," she said, "you're not so bad yourself."

She was allowing him to steer her easily out of the living room into the hall, and he took that as a heartening testament of faith. However cool and crisp this girl might sometimes seem, she was still the girl who had first suggested, in the restaurant down the road from her prim little guidance-counselor's office, that there was a motel not far away. Oh, Lord God; oh, thank

Christ Almighty, Sarah would always be a girl who wanted to get laid.

And he had her. He had her all to himself on that Kansas prairie for a year and a half and more before the time came to fulfill the promise he'd made.

"How does year after next strike you?" she had asked him the year before last – time gets away from everybody – and so there was nothing to feel but pleasure and pride at Christmastime, in 1971, when she told him she was pregnant.

Chapter Six

During the months of Sarah's pregnancy they took a number of automobile trips around the Middle West – discovering the fucking country, as Michael explained it – and once, when they found themselves in central Illinois, he decided to look up Paul Maitland.

It would be chancy but worth the risk. Michael had been nagged for a long time by the dismaying memory of that night at the Nelsons', and now a jovial afternoon in Paul Maitland's company might easily set things right.

Sweating in a roadside phone booth, dropping dimes into the coinbox while enormous trailer trucks came roaring up and moaned away beyond the glass, he got through at last to Paul Maitland's voice.

"Mike! Good to hear from you."

"Are you sure?"

"Am I what?"

"I said are you sure it's – you know – good to hear from me, is all. I thought I might be on your shit list."

"Ah, don't be silly, man. We were both smashed, we traded punches, and yours was the better punch."

"Well, shit, buddy, yours was all right too," Michael said, and he was breathing more easily now. "I could feel that punch of yours for about a week."

Paul asked him where he was calling from; then there came long and explicit directions for how to get to the Maitlands' place. Leaving the phone booth, Michael was so pleased that he held up one hand to make a triumphant circle of thumb and forefinger in the sunshine, and Sarah smiled at him behind the windshield of the parked car.

". . . Well, we're a long way from Delancey Street, old timer," Michael was saying an hour later as they sat around the Maitlands' living room. "Long way from the White Horse, too." He didn't like the bogus heartiness in his own voice but couldn't seem to suppress it – couldn't even manage, in fact, to stop being the only talker in the room.

Paul acknowledged his nostalgia with pleasant little mumbles and a melancholy smile or two; Peggy remained silent – but then, Peggy had been known to remain silent for hours – and Sarah hadn't yet been able to contribute anything beyond small courtesies.

The Maitlands had two blond little girls now, both born during the years since Michael had left Putnam County: they came shyly in from another room to be introduced, then got away again as soon as politeness would permit. And their mother rose and followed them to wherever they'd gone, staying long enough to suggest she preferred their company to that of the visitors.

In the silence Michael noticed for the first time that Paul was wearing a white shirt and well-pressed khaki pants instead of the old denim outfit; then he sat back and looked around to inspect what little could be seen of the house. He knew there would no longer be a toolbox at the front door with muddy work shoes ranked beside it; even so, he could never have pictured Paul Maitland enclosed in as tidy and prim, as middle-class a living room as this, and he wondered if Diana would think he was "dying" here.

"So how do you like teaching, Paul?" he asked, because it seemed once again that somebody ought to say something.

"Well, it's difficult if you've never done it before, but it can be satisfying, too, in some ways. I imagine you've found the same thing."

"Yeah," Michael said. "Yeah, it's about the same for me. You getting enough time for your own work?"

"Oh, not as much as I'd like," Paul said. "I've found I have to do an awful lot of reading just to keep ahead of my lectures. I came out here knowing almost nothing about African art, for example, and that's what a great many of the kids want to learn."

Only now, with a puckering of the palate and throat, did Michael fully comprehend what was the matter with this visit: There hadn't yet been any offer of a drink, or even of a beer. What's the deal? he wanted to say. You off the sauce, Paul? But he kept his aching mouth shut. He knew what being off the sauce meant, and he guessed he'd better not inquire into Paul's case. That kind of thing was a man's own business.

Then Peggy came back into the room wheeling a little cart that carried a coffee service and a plate of big raisin cookies on its top tray, with four cups and saucers and spoons tinkling on the tray beneath.

"Those look wonderful," Sarah said of the cookies. "Did you make them yourself?"

And Peggy modestly divulged that she did all her own baking, even her own bread.

"Really?" Sarah said. "Well, that's very – enterprising."

Michael declined a cookie – it looked like a meal in itself – and waited until most of his unwanted coffee was down before he opened a new topic with his host:

"I see where your brother-in-law's made quite a name for himself."

"Oh, that, yes," Paul said. "Well, it's remarkable how a play can sometimes catch fire commercially that way. It's made enormous changes in their lives – mostly changes for the better, of course, because they've got more money coming in than they'll ever need, but possibly a few for the worse, as well."

And to expand on what he meant by changes for the worse, he told of a few days that he and Peggy had spent with the Morins in New York last year. Diana had looked "lost" in the luxurious high-rise apartment that was now her home – he couldn't remember ever having seen her look that way before, even as a child – and the boys had seemed bewildered, too. Ralph Morin had been almost constantly on the phone, talking business, or else on the run: there were urgent meetings every day about the show, or about other, future shows.

"It was all a little – uncomfortable," Paul concluded. "Still, I imagine it'll settle out in time."

Michael replaced his empty cup in its faintly chattering saucer.

"You ever hear from Tom Nelson, Paul?"

"Oh, we've exchanged a few letters. He writes terrifically funny letters, as I'm sure you know."

"Well, no, as a matter of fact, I've never had a letter from Tom. He used to send me little cartoons once in a while, with captions, but no letters." And even that was an exaggeration: there had been only one cartoon, a caricature of Michael frowning sternly in an academic cap and gown, with the caption: ARCHITECT OF YOUNG MINDS.

"I'll always regret not getting to know Tom years back," Paul said, "when you first suggested it. I was foolish about that."

"No, I could understand how you felt," Michael assured him. "Anybody who makes it big in a commercial way at twenty-six or -seven is bound to be a little intimidating to strangers. If I hadn't met him by accident I probably never would've – you know – never would've sought him out, or anything. Might have been better off all around, too."

"Well, but the word 'commercial' isn't really appropriate for Tom," Paul objected. "It may apply to a flukey kind of luck like Morin's, but that's an entirely different thing. Tom's a professional. He found his line early and he's stayed with it. You have to admire that."

"Well, I guess you have to respect it; I'm not sure it's something you necessarily have to admire." And Michael didn't like the way this talk was going. Not very many years ago he had tried to defend Tom Nelson against Paul Maitland, only to find his lines of defense falling apart under Paul's attack; now the roles were exactly reversed, and he had an uneasy sense that he was about to collapse again. It didn't seem fair – there ought to be more consistency in the world than this – and the worst part was that nothing could be said to be at stake anymore for either adversary: they had both been reduced to eking out a living in farm-state colleges, probably for life, while Tom Nelson went serenely about the business of success.

"His standards are as high as those of any painter I know," Paul was saying, warming to the argument, "and he's never sold a picture he doesn't believe in. I don't see how anyone can ask more of an artist than that."

"Well, okay, you may be right about the professional part of it," Michael conceded, with the deliberation of a strategist abandoning one position in order to strengthen another. "But the man himself is something else. Nelson can be a prick when he puts his mind to it. Or if not a prick, at least a real pain in the ass."

And almost before he knew what his talking mouth was up to, he had launched into the story of the trip to Montreal. It took longer to tell than he'd thought it would – that was bad enough – and there seemed to be no way of telling it that didn't portray himself as something of a fool.

Sarah's calm, brown-eyed gaze was leveled at him above her neatly held coffee cup while he talked. She had wept in silence after his drunken bungling at Terry Ryan's expense; she had been openly disappointed in him time and again since then ("Well, now you've lost me completely"); by now there had come to be a certain resignation in her way of waiting for him to discredit himself.

". . . No, but the point is Nelson *knew* I could've had that girl that night," he heard himself saying, trying to explain and redeem the story after it had been told. "He was half sick with envy – you could see it all over his face – but he knew too that all he had to do was hang around and be a nuisance, which wouldn't cost him anything because none of his other friends were there to see it happening, and then he could make sure I'd be out of luck. So that's the way the little son of a bitch decided to play it, and you could see the decision in his face too: Sly. Smart-assed. Pleased with himself. Oh, and as for his remark on the way home, about the girl thinking we were fags, the funny part there is that Nelson's spent his whole *life* afraid of being mistaken for a fag. He's obsessed with it. I remember days on end when he couldn't talk about anything else, and I always figured it might help explain his wanting to dress up like a soldier all the time."

But neither the story nor its explanation had gone over very well with this particular audience: all three of their faces looked unconvinced and unsatisfied.

"I don't get it, though, Michael," Sarah said. "If you really wanted the girl, why didn't you stay in Montreal a few more days?"

"Good question," he told her. "I've been asking myself the

same question ever since. I guess the only answer is that I was so snowed by Tom Nelson then I'd go along with whatever the hell he felt like doing."

"That's a curious expression, 'snowed,'" Paul said thoughtfully. "I certainly came to admire Tom, once I knew him, but I don't think I've ever been 'snowed' by him."

"Yeah, well, there's the difference between you and me," Michael said. "That's probably why you get letters from him, and all I get is fucking cartoons."

Mercifully, then, they managed to change the subject; their talk turned to summer vacations.

The Maitlands hadn't been able to afford an extended trip this year, Paul said, but next summer they planned to spend the whole of their time on Cape Cod.

"That sounds lovely," Sarah said.

"Well, but I think I like the Cape even better in the off-season," Peggy pointed out. "We used to know some wonderful people there during the winters. Carnival people. They were gypsies."

And Michael knew she would now tell the same little anecdote about the sword-swallower that she'd told in Putnam County at least ten years ago, when it had driven the young, stagestruck Ralph Morin into peals of artificial laughter as he pronounced it the very heart and spirit of the entertainer. Sure enough, when she came to the punch line she delivered it word for word:

". . . So I said 'Doesn't that hurt?' And he said 'Think I'd tell *you*?'"

Sarah rewarded her with an agreeable laugh and Michael was able to chuckle too; Paul Maitland only fondled his mustache as if to mask his having heard the thing far too many times in the past.

Half an hour later, out in the driveway, the Maitlands stood smiling and waving goodbye as attractively as if they were posing for a snapshot – a comfortable Illinois art teacher and his wife, good people who couldn't afford very many extended trips but at least would never be "snowed" by anyone, sensible people a long way from Delancey Street and willing to settle, with African art and home-baked bread, for a great deal less than the stuff of their dreams.

"Well, Paul's very nice, of course," Sarah said when they'd settled down for the long drive back to Kansas, "but I didn't sense anything out of the ordinary about him. I can't imagine how you could've romanticized him all these years."

"Whaddya mean? I don't think I've ever done that."

"Oh, sure you have. Come on, Michael. Just before you knocked him out that night you were telling him you'd always thought he was 'enchanted.'"

"Jesus," he said. "I thought you were in the kitchen all that time."

"Well, I'd been in the kitchen, but I'd come out. Then after you hit him I went back in, because I knew you'd be coming around to look for me there."

"I'll be damned. And how come you never mentioned it until now?"

"Oh, because I knew you'd explain it to me, I suppose," she said, "and because I didn't want to hear the explanation."

A son, James Garvey Davenport, was born to them in June of 1972. He was healthy and well-formed, and Sarah made what one doctor called a reasonably quick recovery, but the birth itself was extremely difficult.

According to the way Michael heard it, the baby began to emerge from her upside down, and some fool of an obstetrician kept trying to turn it over with forceps. Then a number of other men were summoned to the delivery room to frown and mutter over the case; in the end they had to wheel Sarah unconscious into an elevator and down to another floor, where an emergency cesarean section was finally performed – almost, it seemed, in the nick of time.

"Kansas!" Michael said at her bedside, while she lay weakly sipping from a paper cup of ginger ale through a paper straw. "This kind of blundering incompetence couldn't happen anywhere else but fucking Kansas."

"Oh, that's silly," she told him. "Anyway, I think he's awfully nice."

And he thought she meant one of the doctors, some fatherly Kansas asshole who might have murmured a few pleasant words to her as she came out of the anesthetic. "Who?" he demanded. "Who's awfully nice?"

"The baby," she said. "Don't you think he's an awfully nice-looking boy?"

All he had seen, through the plate glass, was a wrinkled, wobbling head that didn't look much bigger than a walnut, with its mouth stretched open in a cry that couldn't be distinguished from the cries of all the other newly born on every side.

"Well, he did look a little blue at first," an elderly nurse confided to him outside the nursery window, wearing her sterile mask beneath her chin to show she was off duty. "He *was* blue when we got him, but then we put him in the incubator and he pinked right up."

That night, trying to chew and swallow an overcooked hamburger in a restaurant that wasn't even licensed to serve beer, he allowed his mind to speculate on children of the kind who had been born "blue babies." Did their eyes look funny? Did they learn only to smile and drool and stammer incoherently, rather than to speak? Did they walk with a softly lurching gait in well-supervised groups, carefully instructed to hold hands with one another when they came to street crossings? Was basket weaving about the most you could expect of them in the way of educational attainment?

Well, but then surely the lady wouldn't have been so cheerful in reporting that this particular blue baby had "pinked right up" – she probably wouldn't have told him about the blue part of it at all if she hadn't meant the pinking-up to be reassuring news.

Even so, as he paid his check and got out of that lousy restaurant and made his way home, he was willing to acknowledge that he wished it had been a girl. Oh, having a son was said to be a splendid thing – there were even men who openly expressed disappointment at the birth of daughters, and who saved all their primal exultation for sons – but Michael didn't feel up to any of that Old Testament bullshit tonight.

Girls were – well, nicer than boys; everybody knew that. All you had to do with a girl was throw her in the air and hug her and kiss her and tell her how pretty she was. Even after she grew too big to ride on your shoulders you could take her to the zoo and buy her a box of Crackerjack and a balloon (you always had to tie the string of it around her wrist so it couldn't float away), or you could take her to a matinee of *The Music Man* and see her sad little face transformed into pure rapture at all the unexpected wonders on the stage. Then came the achingly tender years: once when Laura was thirteen, and possibly at her mother's suggestion, she had called him up from Tonapac to say "Daddy? Guess what! I'm menstruating!"

And sure, of course there could be trouble later: A girl might develop a piercing, near-deadly talent for shock-your-father tactics; she might languish around the house for months, having to be bullied into making her bed, never quite able – for God only knew what reasons – to get past page 98 of whatever the hell she was pretending to read. Still, even in the worst of times like that, there would always be signs that she was going to be all right. A girl could come out of almost any kind of slump because girls were amazingly resilient. They were graceful; they were swift and smart.

But oh, Jesus, a boy could be a real pain in the ass. If you feigned sparring with a boy in his little drop-seat pajamas at bedtime he might expect to be known as "Slugger," and might pucker up and cry if you ever forgot to call him by that name. At nine or ten he would pester you to take him out in the backyard and teach him how to throw, whether you were altogether sure you knew how to throw or not; then there would be vigorous outdoor father-and-son activities, organized by the fire department or the VFW, where you might find you didn't know what to say to any of the other fathers or their shitty little sons.

At sixteen or so, if he was turning into a humorless, intellectual kind of kid, he might want you to sit down with him for serious talks about honor and integrity and moral courage until your head swam with those abstractions; or, worse, he might become a surly, slouching, spitting youth who would rarely speak at all except in monosyllables, and who would care about nothing in the world but cars.

Either way, by the time he was of college age he would almost certainly come to stand in the doorway of a room where you were trying to get some work done, and he'd say "Dad? Do you know how much alcohol you've taken into your bloodstream today? Do you know how many packs of cigarettes you've smoked? Well, listen: I think you're trying to kill yourself. And I want to tell you something: if you're going to kill yourself I wish you'd hurry up and get it over with. Because frankly, you see, it's not you I'm concerned about. It's Mom."

Oh, shit; and there were still other possibilities too dreadful to contemplate. What if, in response to things that struck him as funny, your son took to saying "I love it" or "Oh, how delicious"? What if he wanted to walk around the kitchen with one hand on his hip, telling his mother about the marvelous time he'd had with his friends last night at a really nice new place in town called the Art Deco?

It was nearly three o'clock in the morning when Michael Davenport went to bed at last, too drunk even to realize it would be the first time he had slept alone in this house. All he knew for certain, as he pulled the bedclothes sloppily around and over him, was that none of it was fair: he shouldn't be expected to endure any of this because he was too fucking old. He was forty-nine.

For many months the house seemed almost to tremble with fragility and tenderness and long silences. Though still frail and tired at first, Sarah was an ideal young mother. She took a girlish pride in breastfeeding; she carried her son very slowly up and down the hall to the tune of a charming little music box that one of the faculty families had sent as a gift; she would always place a forefinger at her lips and say "Sh-sh" to her husband after laying the baby down in the crib and softly closing the door behind her.

And Michael found he could go along with the reverence – he liked it, if only because it showed Sarah in a fine and admirable new light that any man would be a fool not to cherish – but his only previous knowledge of this kind of thing was well over twenty years in the past. He could have sworn that the infant Laura had never smelled this bad or soiled this many diapers, that she hadn't cried this long and loud, or puked this often, or inflicted such a general, around-the-clock strain on his nerves.

All right, you little bastard, he would say just under his breath during the times when it was his turn to walk the baby in the sweet tinkling melody of the music box, while Sarah slept. All right, you stubborn little son of a bitch, but you'd better be worth it. You'd damn sure better turn out to be worth all this shit, or I'll never forgive you. Is that clear?

Surprisingly, and perhaps because he had to steal the time for it, Michael wrote well during his son's first year. New poems began to come easily, and so did ideas for how best to salvage and restore a number of old, failed ones. By the time Jimmy Davenport was able to stand and take hesitant sidling steps, using the edges of the coffee table for support, there was enough finished manuscript on his father's desk to comprise a new book.

And Michael was prepared to admit there might not be much brilliance in this fourth collection, but he felt there was nothing in it to be ashamed of, either: the things he'd learned about professionalism over the years could be sensed on every page.

"Well, I think it's – quite good, Michael," Sarah said one evening when she'd had time to read the whole manuscript at last. "All the poems are interesting, and they've been nicely worked out. They're very – sound. I couldn't find any weak places."

She was seated under a good lamp on the living-room sofa, looking as young and pretty as he'd ever seen her look before, frowning slightly now and fingering back through the pages as if in search of weak places that might have escaped her notice on the first reading.

"You have any particular favorites?"

"I don't think so, no; I think I liked them all about equally well."

And he had to acknowledge, as he went to the kitchen to refill their whiskey glasses, that he'd hoped for higher praise. This was the book he'd been writing as long as he'd known her; it would have her name on its dedication page. It might have seemed only fair of her to come through with some show of excitement, even if she'd had to fake it; still, he knew it would be a mistake to let her know he was disappointed.

"Well, look, dear," he said, bringing two fresh drinks back into the room. "I've come to think of this as kind of a transitional book – kind of a plateau performance, if you see what I mean. I think I still know how to do the big stuff, how to take the big risks and bring them off, but those things will have to wait now until the next book. The fifth book. And I'm already working on one idea for that one that feels about as ambitious and encouraging as anything I've done since – you know, since 'Coming Clean.' All I'm going to need is time."

"Well, that sounds – that sounds good," Sarah said.

"Meanwhile I think this collection is worth publishing, and I'm very, very pleased if you think so, too."

"Yes," she said. "Well, I do."

"Tell you one thing I've decided, though," he told her, slowly pacing the carpet. "I've decided not to send it off right away. I think I'd rather hold it back for a while, because the new work I'll be doing might help me find ways to make it better. I mean, it seems like a finished book now, but a few of the poems might still break open and need to be fixed."

And he hoped she would object to that plan – he wanted her to say No, Michael, it *is* a finished book; I'd send it off just as it stands, if I were you – but she didn't.

"Well," she said, "I suppose you have to trust your own judgment about something like that." Then, setting the manuscript aside on the sofa, she said she didn't really want the drink he'd brought because she was terribly sleepy.

When the warm weather came around again they took to having picnic lunches in their backyard, on a blanket spread over the grass. That was nice. Michael liked to recline on one elbow with a cold beer in his other hand while his lovely wife arranged the sandwiches and the deviled eggs on paper plates; he liked to watch his son toddle through sunlight and shade as earnestly as if he were discovering the world.

Well, you're getting the general idea, little buddy, he wanted to say. Part of it's bright and part of it's dark, and those big things over there are trees, and there's nothing here that can ever hurt you. All you have to remember is not to go out beyond the edges of it, because everything is slippery rocks and mud and brambles out there, and you might see a snake and it might scare the shit out of you.

"Do you suppose kids of this age are scared of snakes?" he asked Sarah.

"No, I wouldn't think so; I don't think they're scared of anything until older people tell them what to be scared of." Then after a moment she said "Why snakes?"

"Oh, because I can't remember a time when I wasn't scared of snakes, I guess. Also because snakes have something to do with a kind of big, complicated idea I've been trying to work out."

And he thoughtfully plucked and inspected a blade of grass. Talking over his ideas with Sarah had been profitable in the past – the clarity of her questions and comments could sometimes cut through muddled parts of his thinking – but he wasn't sure if this particular idea would lend itself to discussion. It might be too big and too complicated; besides, he knew he might be sorry if he gave it away: it was the material for his most ambitious and encouraging poem since "Coming Clean."

Still, Sarah was here and ready to listen; the sky was a deeply satisfying shade of blue and the beer was excellent, and so he didn't hesitate very long.

"The thing is, I want to write about Bellevue," he said, "and I want to have it connect with a lot of other events in my life both before and after the time I spent there. Some of the connections will be easy to make; others are going to be subtler and more difficult, but I think I'll be able to work them all into the pattern."

Then he began to tell her about daily life in a psychiatric ward – crowds of barefoot, half-clad men made to walk to the wall and turn, walk to the opposite wall and turn again – but he kept it brief because he knew he'd described it to her before.

"And whenever you make a disturbance, you see, the orderlies grab you and give you a forced injection of some knockout sedative and throw you into a padded cell and lock it, and they leave you alone in there for hours."

He had told her this part too, but it seemed important now to go over it and make it as vivid as possible.

"You have to imagine one of those cells, if you can. There's no air in there; you're entirely enclosed in canvas mats, and they're very bouncy, and you don't even have much sense of gravity: you can't tell up from down.

"So I'd come very slowly back to consciousness with my face pressed into a floor mat – oh, and they're dirty as shit, those mats, because they haven't been changed for years – and that's when I'd think snakes were crawling all over me. Or other times I'd think a string of anti-aircraft shells had just exploded up close and I'd been killed but didn't know yet."

Sarah was chewing the last of a sandwich, looking attentive but turned partly away to watch the baby.

"And then after I got *out* of Bellevue," he said, "I was afraid all the time. Afraid to walk around street corners. There weren't any more snakes, but the fear of anti-aircraft fire was persistent as hell. I used to think if I went more than a few blocks up Seventh Avenue I'd walk into the flak, right into the exploding shells, and that would be the end. Either I'd be dead, or cops would come and take me back to Bellevue – and I couldn't have said which would be worse.

"Well, of course all this is only part of it; there's a great deal more. But the central idea, you see, is the inseparability of fear and madness. Being afraid drives you crazy; going crazy makes you afraid. Oh, and there has to be a third element in there, if I want to get the most out of the other two."

He paused to let Sarah ask what the third element was; then, when she didn't ask, he told her anyway.

"The third element is impotence. Not being able to get laid. And I've had a little – personal experience along that line, too."

"You have?" she said. "When?"

"Oh, a long time ago. Years ago."

"Well, that's supposed to be fairly common among men, isn't it?"

"I guess it may be about as common as fear," he said, "or as common as madness. I'll be dealing with three fairly common conditions, you see, showing how all three work together, suggesting that maybe they all amount to the same thing."

He knew then that he wanted very much to tell her about Mary Fontana; that was probably why he'd brought up the third element in the first place. It had always been easy and pleasurable to tell Sarah about other girls – he had made a tidy little comedy for her out of the Jane Pringle story, and he'd done well with lesser stories too – but Mary Fontana had remained his secret, all this time. And there wasn't any reason why that miserable week on Leroy Street couldn't be openly discussed here, now, in the Kansas sunshine: Sarah might even provide the necessary words to make it settle down and recede in his memory at last.

But Sarah was busy at the moment. She had gathered the paper plates and put them into a paper bag; she had gotten up and shaken all the crumbs from the blanket; now she was neatly folding the blanket in half and into quarters, for carrying.

"Well, I'm afraid I wasn't listening very carefully to any of that, Michael," she said, "because it all sounded morbid to me. You've been talking about 'madness' and 'going crazy' as long as I've known you, and of course it was understandable at first because we both wanted so much to tell each other everything about ourselves; but that was years ago, and you've never stopped. You didn't even let up on it when Laura was with us, and that was certainly a time when it might've been a mercy if you had. So you see I've come to think this whole line of talk is just a self-indulgence of yours. In a curious way it's both self-pitying and self-aggrandizing, and I don't see how you can ever make it attractive, even in a poem."

Then she started back for the house, and there was nothing for him to do but hold his warm, empty beer can and watch her go. On her way across the grass she stopped, reached down, picked up her son and settled him on her hip, and the two of them looked completely self-sufficient.

According to several national magazines, the idea of being a single mother had become a new American romance. Single mothers were brave and proud and resourceful; they had "needs" and "goals" that might set them apart in a strictly conventional society, but today, with changing times, they could find refreshingly open communities. Marin County, California, for example, had now become well known as a lively and inviting sanctuary for recently divorced young women, many of them mothers – and for swinging, stomping, surprisingly nice young men.

While he sat alone on one of the orange chairs in the waiting area outside Dr. McHale's consulting room, Michael found that the palms of his hands were damp. He blotted and dried them on his pants, but the moisture came quickly back.

"Mr. Davenport?"

And as he got up to go in, Michael was able to confirm that his first impression hadn't been wrong: McHale was still courteous and dignified, still very settled and very much the family man.

"Well, this isn't about my daughter, Doctor," he said when they were seated behind the closed door. "My daughter's fine now, or at least I think she is. Hope she is. This is something else. It's about myself."

"Oh?"

"And before we begin I want to tell you that I've never believed in your profession. I think Sigmund Freud was a fool and a bore, and I think what you people call 'therapy' is usually a pernicious racket. I'm only here because I have to talk to somebody, and because it has to be somebody who can be trusted to keep his mouth shut."

"Well, then." The doctor's face conveyed a calm and expert willingness to listen. "What's the problem?"

And Michael felt as if he were stepping off into a void. "The problem," he said, "is that I think my wife is going to leave me, and I think it's going to drive me crazy."

Chapter Seven

Getting out of Kansas and going home – that had become the dominant idea in Michael's mind, and in his talk, by the time he was fifty-two. And his visions of "home" had nothing to do with New York; he was always clear and emphatic about that. He wanted to go back to Boston and Cambridge, where everything had come alive for him after the war, and he felt he couldn't wait much longer for the break that would make it possible.

Sarah often said she thought Boston would be "interesting," and he took heart from that, though she sometimes said it in what sounded like an absentminded way.

"And I mean it doesn't necessarily have to be Harvard," he explained to her, several times. "I've got applications in at other places all over those towns; something certainly ought to come through.

"Oh, and it's not as if I were asking for more than I deserve, do you see? I've earned this move. I've done well here, I'm ready for a better job, and I'm old enough to know where I belong."

Paul Maitland might allow his life and talent to seep away in Middle Western mediocrity, but that, like the willful blandness implicit in his staying off the sauce, was something only Paul Maitland could account for. Other lives and talents would always need a bracing environment – and one of the ways Michael could tell he needed a bracing environment was that for a very long time now, ever since Sarah had dampened his interest in the Bellevue poem, he hadn't written anything.

Still, in his heart, he knew the real reason for all this urgency: whether it made sense or not, he felt that if he could get Sarah to Boston he might have a better chance of keeping her.

Every day he held his breath when he approached the big tin mailbox at the base of the driveway; then one morning he found a letter there that seemed to make all the difference.

It was from the chairman of the English department at Boston University, and it was a clear and definite offer of employment. The final sentence of it, though, was what sent Michael loping up to the house and into the kitchen, where Sarah stood washing the breakfast dishes – this was the sentence that weakened his knees and strengthened his back as he thrust the trembling letter a little too close to her startled face:

Apart from the business at hand, let me say that I have always considered "Coming Clean" to be among the finest poems written in this country since the Second World War.

"Well," she said. "That's really very – really very nice, isn't it?"

It was nice, all right. He had to read it three more times, walking around the living room, before he could believe it.

Then Sarah came to stand in the doorway, drying her hands on a dish towel.

"So I guess it's all settled then, about Boston," she said. "Right?"

Right; all settled.

But this was the girl whose very skin had once been made "all gooseflesh, all over," and who'd been made to cry, too, by the concluding lines of that poem; now she looked as calm and plain as any other housewife considering the practical aspects of moving to a new place, and he didn't know what to make of the transformation.

"Well, good," Dr. McHale said. "Sometimes a change of scene can be very helpful. You may find it gives you a new perspective on your – domestic situation."

"Yeah," Michael said. "A new perspective; that's what I'm hoping for. Maybe a sense of new beginnings, too."

"Exactly."

But Michael had long grown impatient with these weekly sessions. They were always embarrassing and always fruitless. You always knew the doctor didn't really give a shit about you; how, then, could you be expected to give a shit about him?

What did this particular Kansas family man do when he went home at night? Did he sink into the sofa facing the television set – flanked, perhaps, by whichever one or two of his adolescent children had nothing better to do than come and sit with him? Would his wife provide popcorn? Would he eat it greedily by the heaping handful? And when he became wholly absorbed in the show he was watching, would his mouth slacken and hang slightly open in the mottled blue light of the picture tube? And would there be a rivulet of melted butter down his chin?

"Well, in any case, Doctor, I'm grateful for your time and your help. I don't think I'll be needing any more of these appointments now, before I leave."

"Good, then," Dr. McHale said. "And good luck."

At the airport, on the day of his flight, Sarah was in a hazy, dreamy mood. He had seen her like this before, on mornings after she'd had a few drinks; it was an agreeable kind of hangover that would always vanish with an afternoon's sleep, but it didn't seem quite appropriate for a time of saying goodbye.

She strolled far away from him across the enormous floor, with their son treading beside her and clutching her forefinger. She looked as interested in everything as if she'd never seen an airport before, and when she came back to where he stood with his ticket she said "It's funny, you know? Distance doesn't matter anymore. It's almost as if geography didn't exist. All you do is doze and float in a pressurized cabin for a while – and it doesn't even matter how long, because time isn't important, either – and before you know it you're in Los Angeles, or London, or Tokyo. Then if you don't happen to like wherever it is you find yourself, you can doze and float again until you find yourself somewhere else."

"Yeah," he said. "Well, look, I think they're boarding over there. So take care, dear, okay? I'll call you as soon as I can."

"Okay."

"Well, I think you're going to find this is kind of a transitional book, Arnold," Michael told his publisher at lunch in a New York restaurant. "Kind of a plateau performance, if you see what I mean."

And Arnold Kaplan nodded over the brimming of his second martini in a way that suggested patience and understanding. His company had published all of Michael's earlier books and lost money on them every time. But then, it wasn't exactly the profit motive that impelled you to publish a poet; if anything, it was your knowledge that some other commercial house might be ready to pick him up and absorb his losses if you let him go. Well, it was a funny line of business; everybody knew that.

Michael was explaining now that he thought he could still do the big stuff, still take the big risks and bring them off, but

Arnold Kaplan had begun to let the words flow past his hearing.

Years ago, when they were college classmates, Arnold Kaplan had been "literary" too. Arnold Kaplan had worked as hard as anyone else at finding a way to put his voice on the page and giving it something to say. Even today, on the floor of his basement in Stamford, Connecticut, there were three cardboard boxes full of old manuscripts: a collection of poems, a novel, and seven short stories.

And it wasn't bad stuff. It was perfectly decent stuff. It was stuff that almost anybody might want to read and enjoy. How had it come about, then, that no words by Arnold Kaplan had ever been set into type for printing? What was the deal?

He was called a senior vice-president at the office now; he made more money than he could ever have imagined as a boy; but the price of it was that he had to spend too many hours like this – getting half smashed on his expense account and pretending to listen to a boring, rapidly aging striver like Davenport.

". . . Oh, I wouldn't want to give you the idea this is sub-standard work, Arnold," Michael was saying. "I like all of it. If I didn't like it I wouldn't be submitting it. I think it's very – sound. My wife likes it, too, and she's a tough critic."

"Good. And how *is* Lucy?"

"No," Michael said, frowning. "Lucy and I've been divorced for years. I thought you knew that, Arnold."

"Well, maybe it was a thing I knew and just forgot; that can happen sometimes. So you have another wife now."

"Yeah. Yeah; she's – very nice."

Neither of them ate much – you weren't expected to eat much at lunches like this – and by the time their messy plates were cleared away they had both fallen silent except for dutiful exchanges of small talk.

399

"So how you getting up to Boston, Mike? The plane or the train?"

"Well, I think I'll rent a car and drive up," Michael said, "because I want to make a stop along the way, to see some old friends."

The car he rented was big and yellow and took to the road so easily it seemed almost to be in control of itself, and in that unearthly way he found he was very soon in Putnam County.

"No, there's nobody home but the two of us," Pat Nelson had told him on the phone, "and we'd love to see you."

"Pretty nice boat, Dad," Tom Nelson said in the driveway, when Michael had brought the yellow car to a stop and climbed out of it. "Classy set of wheels." And only after having that small joke did he come forward to shake hands.

He looked older, squinting and a little wizened, but this was a look he seemed to have been cultivating for years. Once long ago, before he was thirty, some admirer had taken a photograph of him outdoors, under a stormy sky, that had strangely caught that middle-aged quality in his youthful face, and Tom had kept an enlargement of the picture on his studio wall. "What's this?" Michael had asked him. "What's the deal on displaying pictures of yourself?" And Tom could only say he liked it; he liked having it there.

As they went into the house together Michael saw that Tom had acquired still another costume: an authentic old Army Air Force "flight jacket" that could only have been made and issued in the early nineteen-forties. He must have touched on every branch of the service by now.

When Pat came smiling across the big living room with both arms held out – "Oh, Michael" – he thought she looked remarkably good, better even than she'd looked as a girl. Given enough luck, enough money, and a good bone structure in the first place, some women seemed never to age.

With the pouring of first drinks they settled into a pleasant grouping of sofa and chairs, and the talk began to flow. All four of the Nelsons' sons were "fine," though all grown and gone from home now. The oldest boy was a source of particular pride to his father because he'd become a professional jazz drummer – "Never had any trouble getting *his* union card" – and two of the others were also doing exemplary things; but when Michael asked about Ted, the boy who was Laura's age, both parents lowered their eyes and seemed to be searching for words.

"Well," Pat said, "Ted's had a few problems trying to – you know – trying to find himself. But he's much more stable now."

"Yeah, well, Laura went through a difficult time, too," Michael told them. "She didn't like Warrington, and then she kind of drifted for a while; but it didn't take her long to get straightened out, and she's done very well in Billings."

Tom looked up with a kindly, puzzled expression. "Very well in what? In 'Billings'?" He said that as though he thought "Billings," like Accounts Payable or Data Processing or Personnel, might be a department of some clean and well-managed business office where the safe harbor of commercial employment had been found at last for a drifting girl.

"Billings State University, in Kansas," Michael told him. "It's an institution of higher learning, okay? You might say it's sort of like Harvard or Yale only with prairies, and with a funny smell that comes off the stockyards every day. It's where I make my fucking living."

"Oh, *I* see. And Laura went to school out there, right?"

"Right," Michael said, and now he was ashamed. The last thing he wanted to do, in this house, was to play the failed and exiled former neighbor.

401

"We never get to see Lucy anymore," Pat said. "Never even hear from her. Do you know how she is? And do you know what it is she's doing there in Cambridge?"

"Well, I don't suppose she's necessarily 'doing' anything," he said. "She's never had to earn money, you know. Never will."

"Oh, well, of course I knew that," Pat said impatiently, as if it had been boorish of him to point it out. "But she certainly did keep busy around here. For years. I've never seen such drive and energy – or such stamina. Anyway, if you see her when you're up there, or talk to her, will you be sure to give her our love?"

And Michael promised he would. Then Pat went off to the kitchen "to see about supper," so he followed Tom into the studio for a conversational stroll.

"Well, Lucy tried just about everything," Tom said, and he hunched up the shoulders of his flight jacket to put his hands in his pants pockets as he walked, the way a real flyer might do in discussing a mission that hadn't gone very well. "Everything in the *art* line, I mean, except music and dancing, and I guess you have to start those when you're a whole lot younger. Tried acting; tried writing; tried painting. Really threw herself into each thing, too; worked hard as hell – only, the painting part of it turned out to be a little embarrassing for me."

"Embarrassing how?"

"Well, because she asked me to criticize her pictures and there wasn't anything I could say. I sort of improvised a little praise, but she didn't fall for that. I could tell how disappointed she was and it made me feel lousy, but there wasn't any way I could help.

"So then I started thinking back: Well, if she's not a painter, maybe she wasn't a writer, either, or an actress, either – and look, I know this may sound harsh, Mike, but there's an awful lot of women running around *trying* things. Oh, you'll find men doing it, too, but the men seem to have a few more options in their

402

lives, or else they're not all that dead-serious to begin with. It's the women who can break your heart. And I mean they're mostly good, bright, admirable girls – you can't dismiss them as 'silly' or anything – and they keep on trying and trying until their brains get scrambled, or until they're so tired they're ready to drop. Sometimes you want to put your arms around a woman like that and say 'Hey, listen, dear; take it easy, okay? What's the big deal? Nobody ever said you had to do this.' Ah, well, hell; that's not exactly what I meant to say, but it's close."

"Oh, I think you put it very nicely," Michael said.

All three of them seemed as eager to be finished with their light supper as if this were a party night: they wanted to get back into the living room, where there'd be brandy and coffee and another hour or two of talk – and all Pat Nelson wanted to talk about, apparently, was Lucy.

"Well, but the one thing I could never understand about her," Pat said when she'd taken her place on the sofa again, "was her belief in psychiatry – her trust in it, her reliance on it. She seemed almost to make a religion out of it, so you'd feel that any disparaging or joking thing you might want to say would be a sacrilege. And I mean there were times when I could hardly keep from taking her and shaking her and saying 'But you're too *bright* for this, Lucy. You're too smart and funny a person to be taken *in* by all this humorless Freudian rigamarole.'"

"Yeah," Michael said.

"Oh, and wait. Wait." Pat turned to her husband. "Who was the sort of schlocky, pop-psych man," she inquired, "who made millions of dollars back in the fifties?"

"The *How to Love* guy, you mean," Tom said helpfully, but it was left to Michael to supply the author's name:

"Derek Fahr."

"Right. Derek Fahr." And Pat squirmed deeper into the sofa

cushions. She seemed to be taking an almost voluptuous pleasure in whatever it was she had to tell about Lucy now, and Michael watched her with apprehension. But he had begun to feel a nice, brandy-flavored detachment, too – an immunity to these two old friends who might never have been friends at all – and so he was ready.

"Well," she began, "Lucy came over here all breathless one afternoon – she looked *radiant* – and told us she'd just spent half an hour on the telephone with Derek Fahr. She said it had taken her days and days to get his phone number, and she said when she made the call she was so shy that all she could do at first was apologize to him, but he came on saying very pleasant, reassuring things in a nice voice. How did she describe his voice, Tom?"

" 'Mellow,' I think."

"Exactly. This very 'mellow' voice. And then he asked her what the problem was.

"Well, you know Lucy," Pat said with a twinkling smile of old fondness. "She didn't go into *that* part of it with us; she skipped that part. She'd always been a very reserved, private person. But she said she couldn't get over the way he kept having these 'incredibly rare, intuitive insights' into everything she told him – and that's just how she put it.

"Well, I may be making all this sound a little unkind," Pat admitted, "and you have to realize she'd probably had a couple of drinks before she came over that day; still, what sticks in my mind is the way she summed it up for us. She said: 'Derek Fahr taught me more about myself in half an hour than my own therapist has been able to do in eleven years.' "

Michael couldn't tell whether he was expected to smile or frown or shake his head in sadness, but he didn't want to make any of those responses, so all he did was come slightly forward in his chair and hide his mouth in his drink.

It was probably time to get back on the road. It wasn't even easy to remember, now, why he'd made this stop in the first place. He guessed it was because he'd wanted to let Tom Nelson know he was still alive. And if the talk had gone a little differently tonight, he might have seized on almost any conversational opening to tell Tom Nelson what the man at Boston University had said about the poem.

". . . Are you sure you don't want to stay over?" Pat was saying. "There's plenty of room, and we'd love having you; then you could get a fresh start in the morning. Or you could stay through the afternoon, if you'd like; that way you could meet these wonderful new friends of ours from up the road. They're sort of – celebrities, so it's never easy to say their name without seeming to 'drop' it. The Ralph Morins; you know? *Blues in the Night*?"

"Oh. Well, as a matter of fact I know them. Only met him once, but I've known her a long time."

"Really? Well then you *must* stay. Aren't they nice? And isn't she marvelous? Isn't she an extraordinary creature?"

"She sure is."

"It may sound silly to say," Pat said, "but I think she has the most beautiful face I've ever seen. And her whole manner: her poise, her carriage, her way of seeming to electrify everyone in the room the moment she walks in."

"Yeah," Michael said. "Oh, yeah, I agree. Funny thing: the first time I met her I knew I was sunk. I knew that in some dopey, half-assed way I'd be in love with her for life."

"Oh, and so young," she said. "So fresh and unspoiled."

"Well," he said in a tolerant, qualifying way, "not all that young. Not really young at all anymore, Pat; none of us are."

And she looked so baffled that he was baffled, too. Then she said "Oh. Oh, no. You must mean the much-hated *first* wife. I meant Emily Walker, you see. The actress."

It took two or three seconds for Michael to sort out the information. Then he said "Where do you get 'much-hated'?"

"Well, Ralph can barely refer to her without shuddering – that's *one* way you can tell – and he's described her once or twice as 'drab.' He told us the marriage had really been dead for years before he – you know – before he put a stop to it; and now she's holding him up for some huge amount of money every month. She certainly doesn't *sound* like much of a prize."

"Well, okay; but has he ever happened to mention that she's Paul Maitland's sister?"

The Nelsons gave each other stunned, blank looks and turned quickly back to Michael; then Tom asked, rhetorically, if this wasn't the damndest thing.

"Well, we were both terribly fond of the Maitlands," Pat explained, "but you see we only *knew* them for a year or two before they moved away, so it's hard to remember now if Paul ever even talked about his sister."

"No, he talked about her, dear," Tom said. "Talked quite a lot about her. He asked us over there to meet her once, when she and her kids were visiting, but we couldn't make it that day. Only, the funny part is I always got the impression she was married to some plodding, small-time Philadelphia guy." Then, after a moment's reflection, he said "Son of a bitch."

"Well," Michael said, "sometimes it takes a while to get acquainted."

They seemed to hover over his departure – getting his raincoat from the closet, turning on the porch lights for him, walking out into the driveway with him for the ritual handshake and the small, ritual kiss. It was as though both the Nelsons wanted to apologize but didn't know what there was to apologize for. He could tell from their faces that they probably wouldn't feel like themselves until he was gone.

It must have been an hour later, on the Boston turnpike, that the big yellow car swerved alarmingly in its lane. Fighting the wheel to bring it straight again, he heard his own voice speaking aloud in the emptiness, and in rage:

"Oh, and another thing. One more thing, Nelson. I think you'd better take off that flight jacket now, you hear me? Because if you don't take off that flight jacket I'm gonna tear it off your fucking back, and then I'm gonna punch you right in the mouth."

Chapter Eight

The only uncomfortable thing about Michael's room at the Sheraton Commander Hotel, in Cambridge, was that it held a big full-length mirror. Frowning, smiling, slumped or standing straight, there was no way to escape the sight of a fifty-three-year-old man. When he came naked out of the shower it always took him by surprise – Hello, old man – and then there would be an urgent need to cover himself with clothes. What could be said for legs too weak to ride a bicycle? Where was the beauty in a ruined middleweight? When he talked on the phone, he found he couldn't resist turning around now and then to take a look at the old man talking on the phone.

He called Sarah every day, whether there was anything new to tell her or not, and he looked forward to those calls as anxiously as if her voice might save his life.

On the fourth or fifth afternoon he began to dial the Kansas number before remembering he wasn't supposed to call until after the longdistance rates went down at five o'clock: he'd made that mistake yesterday, and Sarah had mildly scolded him for the waste of money. So he sat waiting at the little cream-colored telephone table with nothing better to do than peek around his shoulder at the hunched, waiting old man.

After a while, and almost as if for no other purpose than to kill time, he took the city telephone book from its little shelf, thumbed the pages, and looked down the list of Davenports until he came to Lucy.

She sounded pleasantly surprised to hear he was in town – "Oh, I thought you'd be in Kansas" – but she hesitated for a second or two when he asked if she would have dinner with him tonight. Then she said "Well, yes; why not? That might be nice. How about seven o'clock?"

And when they'd hung up he was glad he'd obeyed the impulse to call her. It *might* be nice. If they could manage to be courteous and careful with each other, he might find ways of talking that would settle things he'd wanted to know about her for years.

Then his watch told him it would be all right to call Kansas now, and in a minute he was talking to Sarah again.

". . . Still nothing to report on the apartment situation, I'm afraid," he told her.

"Well, I hardly expected there would be," she said. "You've only been there a few days."

"I must've seen a dozen real-estate agents, but none of them have anything much to offer. And aside from that, you see, a lot of my time so far's been taken up with college business; getting the job settled."

"Sure. Well, that's all right. There's no hurry."

"Oh, and I met the boss today. You know? The guy that wrote the nice letter? Funny thing: I expected him to be an older man – I always think people who praise my stuff are going to be older than me – but he's only about thirty-five. Very nice, though; very welcoming."

"Well," she said. "Good."

"So I guess most of my readers'll be younger than me from now on; probably have been for years. If I have any readers left at all, that is."

"Well," she said, "of course you do," and the tiredness in her voice let him know that he'd required that kind of reassurance from her too often in the past.

"Anyway, I'll be able to spend the rest of this week looking for a place, and all of next week; then if nothing's turned up in the city I'll start trying the suburbs."

"Okay. But really, there isn't any pressure about this. Why don't you just let it take however – you know – however long it takes. I'm perfectly comfortable here."

"I know you are," he said, and the phone was beginning to feel moist and slick in his hand. "I know you are. But I'm not. In fact I'm a little desperate, Sarah. I want to get you up here before I—"

"Before you what?"

"Before I lose you. Or maybe I've lost you already."

And he couldn't believe how long the silence went on. Then she said "That's a funny way of putting it, don't you think? Does a person 'lose' another person? Is that really what happens?"

"You're damn right it's what happens. You bet your sweet ass it's what happens."

"Well, but wouldn't that imply a state of ownership to begin with? And how would that make any sense? I think I'd prefer to believe that everybody's essentially alone," she said, "and so our first responsibility is always to ourselves. We have to make our own lives as best we can."

"Yeah, well, now, look: I don't know what the hell you've been reading, Sarah, but I'm not going to take any more of this feminist horseshit, is that clear? If you want to talk jargon you'd better find some boy of your own age. I'm too old for it. I've been around too long and I know too much. I know too much. Now. There's one more point I'd like to make in this delightful little talk. Will you listen?"

"Certainly."

But he had to wait for his heart and his lungs to slow down before he could speak again.

"It wasn't really very long ago," he began, in an almost theatrically quiet voice, "that you told me you thought we were made for each other."

"Yes, I remember saying that," she said. "And the moment I'd said it I knew you'd be reminding me of it, sooner or later."

This time the silence was deep enough to drown in.

"Shit," he said. "Oh, shit."

"Well, in any case, this question of Boston will probably have to wait awhile," she told him, "because I think I'll take Jimmy to Pennsylvania and spend a few weeks with my parents."

"Oh, shit. How many weeks?"

"I don't know; two weeks, maybe three. I need some time by myself, Michael; that's the whole point."

"Yeah," he said. "Well, okay, and how's this for a scenario? Spend three weeks in Pennsylvania, then get on another plane and doze and float your way out to Marin County, California."

"*What* county?"

"Oh, come on. You know. Everybody knows. It's the sexiest place in America. It's where all the young single mothers go to meet men. You'll have a wonderful time there. You'll be able to open your legs for a different man every Saturday night. You'll be able to—"

"I'm not listening to this," Sarah said, "and I don't want to talk anymore. I'd rather not hang up the phone on you, Michael, but I will, unless you hang up first."

"Okay; I'm sorry. I'm sorry."

Wow. Wow. This was almost too much.

Alone and silent again at the cream-colored table, he knew that everything he'd said was wrong. Would he always shoot his

411

mouth off? Hadn't the world taught him anything at all in fifty-three fucking years?

There was a clean pad of Sheraton notepaper on the table, with a white Sheraton pen beside it, and those fundamental tools of his trade were the only heartening things in sight.

Sometimes, if you wrote out your thoughts, it could help you put them in order. And so, bending over the job like a calm and steady professional, he wrote this:

> Don't torture me, Sarah. You're either going to come here and live with me or you're not, and you're going to have to make up your mind.

That looked right; it seemed to achieve the right tone; it might even be the kind of lucky first draft that would never need revision.

Lucy Davenport's address turned out to be one of the very old wooden houses considered the gems of the Cambridge real-estate business; that seemed entirely appropriate for a woman with something between three and four million dollars. But when she opened the door he thought at first that she didn't look at all well: she was thin and gray, and there was something the matter with her mouth.

Very soon, though, when they were seated across from each other in a better light, he could see she was probably in excellent health. The small, strange contortions of her mouth must have been caused by a spasm of shyness in the doorway, of not knowing which of several kinds of smile to wear in greeting him (formal? reserved? friendly? affectionate?) and so, at the last flustered moment, of trying them all on at once. But her mouth was as controlled as the rest of her, now; and the rest of her –

thin limbs, well-dressed gray hair and the kind of woman's face called "handsome" – could be explained in an instant by her being forty-nine years old.

"You're looking very well, Lucy," he said, and she told him he looked very well, too. Was this the way long-divorced couples would always try to ward off silence when they began their hesitant little talks?

"I'm afraid I can't offer you a drink, Michael," she said. "I haven't kept hard liquor in the house for years; but there's some white wine. Would that be all right?"

"Sure. Fine."

And while she was gone in the kitchen he looked around her place. It was as high and spacious as an heiress's home ought to be, with a generous number of windows, but it was almost bare: a table, a sofa, and the fewest possible other places to sit. Then he noticed that none of her curtains matched. They were all hemmed to the same length and tied back with sashes made of their own fabric, but no two were alike. A red-and-white-striped curtain at one side of a window was paired off with a blue polka-dot curtain at the other; then in the next window a curtain of bright flowered chintz hung in contrast to one of rough, oatmeal-colored cloth – that was the way it went around the room. If he'd ever visited this house as a stranger, and especially as a boy, he would have thought some crazy lady must live here.

"What's the deal on the – on the curtains?" he asked when she brought the glasses of wine into the room.

"Oh, that," she said. "Well, I'm sort of tired of it now, but when I first moved in it seemed like an interesting idea: having everything clash on purpose. It wasn't meant to suggest I'm an eccentric, you see, or that I'm a bohemian, either. It was meant more as a parody of both those possibilities."

"A 'parody'? I don't get it."

413

"Well, I don't think there's necessarily anything to 'get,'" she said in some impatience, as if reproving the kind of dull-witted listener who assumes that every story must have a point. "Still, I suppose it was a little on the overly self-conscious side. I'll probably put up regular curtains eventually."

She wanted to hear about Laura, so he told her of a good time they'd had a year ago when Laura had brought three other girls over to the house.

". . . And then toward the end of it they were all sitting around on the floor, giggling over inside jokes about boys and secrets, and I swear there wasn't a single 'cool' or 'hip' or any other kind of smart-assed girl in the bunch of them. They were just girls, being silly together because they felt like it, acting younger than their age because they'd all had enough of trying to act older."

"Well," Lucy said. "That does sound – encouraging. I don't quite see the point of graduate school, though. And why in Kansas? And why in a funny field like sociology?"

"Well, I think it's mainly because she's interested in a boy who's in that department," he explained. "That's what girls tend to do, you see; they tend to go along with boys."

"Yes; I suppose they do."

Then she went to get a raincoat, hooked two fingers into the neck of it, and slung it jauntily over one shoulder, and he was reminded of a sweet Radcliffe girl who used to carry her raincoat around town the same way.

They walked several blocks to a dimly lighted restaurant called Ferdinand's, the kind of place where you can tell at once that nothing on the menu will be worth half its price, and the way the headwaiter said "Good evening, Lucy" made clear that she was a regular customer.

"None of this faggoty stuff was here in the old days," Michael said over his first drink.

414

"What faggoty stuff?" She looked as though she might be ready for an argument.

"Oh, well," he said quickly, "I didn't mean this place, necessarily, but there's a slick, fake, 'campy' atmosphere all over Cambridge now. I keep seeing little cafés with names like the 'Déjà Vu' and the 'Autre Chose.' It's as if everybody in town had decided to fall in love with bad ideas. And you can even see it beginning to happen in Boston itself."

"Well, styles change," she said. "There's nothing anyone can do about that. We can't have it be nineteen forty-seven forever."

"No; no, we sure can't." And now he wished he hadn't said anything. They weren't getting off to a very good start. He kept his eyes down and didn't look up at her face until she spoke first.

"How's your health been, Michael?"

"Mental health, you mean? Or the other kind?"

"Both kinds; all kinds."

"Well, I don't think my lungs are in very good shape," he said, "but that's nothing new. And I don't even think about going crazy anymore because it's fear that drives you crazy; then in the end it's going crazy that leaves you with nothing but fear."

It was the same thought he'd tried to express to Sarah, on the day of the bad picnic lunch, but this time he seemed to have put it more clearly. Maybe the difference was that Lucy's curtains had made him suspect she might be a little crazy herself; or maybe – and this was probably closer to the truth – it was just that some things would always be easier to discuss with someone of your own age.

"There was a while there, back in Kansas," he told her, "when I thought I might get a poem out of all that – make some big-assed statement about fear and madness – but I scrapped it. Dumped it. The whole idea began to seem morbid." Only after saying "morbid" did he remember it was Sarah's word. "And the funny part," he said then, "the funny part is I may never even have gone crazy in the first place. Isn't that possible? Maybe Bill Brock was more than a little out of line that night; maybe his signing that commitment paper says more about him than it ever will about me. I don't want to insist on that, but it's worth considering. And here's another one: Isn't it possible that psychiatrists give themselves a whole lot more credit than they ever deserve?"

Lucy looked thoughtful, but he wasn't sure if he would get an answer until she said "Well, I think I see what you mean. I spent a very long time with that therapist in Kingsley, and afterwards it all did seem to have been pointless. Utterly pointless."

"Good," he said. "I mean, *you* know; it's good that you see what I mean, is all." Then he raised and held out his drink across the table. "So listen" – and he winked to let her know she could take it as a joke if she wanted to. "Listen: Fuck psychiatry, okay?"

She hesitated only a moment before picking up her own glass and clinking the rim of it against his. "Okay," she said without smiling. "Fuck psychiatry."

This was better. It could almost be said that they were getting along.

When the waiter had set heavy plates before them, Michael thought it might be safe to open a new topic.

"What brought you back here, Lucy? Is it okay to ask you that?"

"Why wouldn't it be okay?"

"Well, I just meant I don't want to inquire into your personal life, that's all."

"Oh. Well, I suppose I moved back because it seemed sort of like coming home."

"Yeah; I've had that sense of 'home' about it, too. But I mean

416

everything's so different in your case. You could easily go anywhere and do—"

"Oh, sure: 'go anywhere and do anything.' I can't tell you how often those words used to occur to me. But the question is greatly simplified now, you see, because there's hardly any money left. I've given almost all of it away."

This was something that would take a little while to sink in. Lucy without money? In all the years he'd known her, he could never have imagined such a revelation: Lucy without money. And he didn't even want to think of what his own life might have been if Lucy had been without money from the start. Better? Worse? How would anybody ever know?

"Well, Jesus, that's – Jesus, that's really something," he said. "Would it be okay to ask who you've given it to?"

"I've given it to Amnesty International." And she pronounced that name with a shyness and pride that let him know it meant the world to her. "Are you familiar with the work they do?"

"Well, just barely; just from reading the papers. But I know it's an – admirable organization. I mean those people aren't just fooling around."

"No," she said. "No, they certainly aren't. And I've become very active with them now, too."

"How do you mean 'active'?"

"Oh, I serve on some of their committees and help organize some of their meetings and panel discussions, and I write a lot of their press releases; things like that. They may send me to Europe in a month or two; at least that's what I'm hoping for."

"Good. That's very – that's very good."

"I like this work, you see," Lucy said, "because it's real. It's real. Nobody can deny it; nobody can shrug it off, or make fun of it, or ever take it away. There *are* political prisoners. There *is* injustice and oppression all over the world. When you do this kind of work you're in touch with reality every day, and that simply wasn't true in any of the – any of the other things I've tried."

"Yeah," he said. "Well, I heard you'd tried a few things."

The quick, slight lifting and hardening of her face made clear at once that he shouldn't have said that.

"Oh," she said. "You heard. How did you hear?"

"Well, from the Nelsons, is all. And I think they really miss you, Lucy; they wanted me to be sure to give you their love."

"Ah, yes," she said. "Well, they're both very good at teasing, aren't they, those Nelsons. Teasing in the sense of ridicule, I mean, as well as in the sense of eternally coy flirtation. It took me years to figure that out."

"Well, now, wait. Where do you get 'ridicule'? I don't think anybody's ever 'ridiculed' you. You're too tough a girl for that."

"Oh?" And she narrowed her eyes. "Would you like to bet? Well, listen: maybe you were spared from knowing this – and I think I must always have been at considerable pains to *spare* you from knowing it – but sometimes when I look back over my life I can't find anyone there but a ridiculed, picked-on, wretchedly unpopular little boarding-school girl whose only friend in the world was her *art* teacher. And I may never even have told you about the art teacher, because she was one of my secrets for years until I tried to put her in a story once, long after you'd gone.

"Miss Goddard. A funny, lanky, lonely girl not very much older than me; very intense; very shy – oh, and possibly a flaming dyke, too, though that side of it never occurred to me at the time. But she told me my drawings were beautiful, and she meant it, and it was almost more than I could bear.

"I was the only girl in school allowed into Miss Goddard's apartment to have sherry and English biscuits in the afternoons, and I felt sanctified. I felt awed and sanctified at the same time; can you imagine? Can you imagine a more wonderful combination of feelings than that, for someone like me?

"All I wanted then was to be eligible in some way – to qualify – as a participant in what Miss Goddard always called 'the world of art.' Isn't that a sad, fanciful expression, when you think about it? 'The world of art'? And for that matter, isn't 'art' itself a maddeningly shifty little word? In any case, I think I'd like to propose another toast, if I may." And Lucy brought her wine glass up to the level of their eyes.

"Fuck art," she said. "I mean really, Michael. Fuck art, okay? Isn't it funny how we've gone chasing after it all our lives? Dying to be close to anyone who seemed to understand it, as if that could possibly help; never stopping to wonder if it might be hopelessly beyond us all the way – or even if it might not exist? Because there's an interesting proposition for you: what if it doesn't exist?"

He thought it over, or rather made a grave little show of pretending to think it over, holding his own drink firmly on the table.

"Well, no, I'm sorry, dear," he began, knowing at once that the "dear" should have been edited out of the sentence, "I can't go along with you on that one. If I ever thought it didn't exist I think I'd – I don't know. Blow my brains out, or something."

"No, you wouldn't," she told him, putting her glass down again. "You might even relax for the first time in your life. You might quit smoking."

"Yeah, well, okay, but listen. Do you happen to remember the long poem in my first book, years ago?"

" 'Coming Clean.' "

"Right. Well, that's what got me hired here at whaddyacallit. At Boston University. The guy even wrote me a letter and told

419

me so. He said – he said he thinks it's among the finest poems written in this country since the Second World War."

"Well," she said. "Well, that's certainly very – I'm very proud for you, Michael." She looked quickly down, perhaps in embarrassment at having said as intimate-sounding a thing as "proud for you," and he was embarrassed, too.

Soon, then, they were walking quietly back through the Cambridge whose style he no longer understood and wouldn't even want to find out about now, if he could manage to settle on the Boston side of the river. But it was good to be walking with such a nice, brave, forthright woman – a woman who knew how to speak her mind when she felt like it, and who understood the restorative value of silence.

When they reached her house he waited until she'd found the key to her door; then he said "Well, Lucy, this has been really nice."

"I know," she said. "I enjoyed it, too."

He took hold of her shoulder, very lightly, and gave her a kiss on the cheek. "Stay well, now," he said.

"I will," she promised him, and there was just enough light in the street to suggest that her eyes were glistening. "And you too, Michael, okay? You too."

As he walked away and hoped she was watching his back – did other men ever want women to watch their backs? – it struck him that Sarah had scarcely come into his mind for three hours.

Well, his mind would be filled with her again soon enough. The words he'd written on that Sheraton note pad would still be there on the table – "Don't torture me, Sarah" – and might by now have been picked up and scrutinized by some Sheraton chambermaid, working the late shift, who had let herself into the room to turn down his bed.

And what a lousy line! Maudlin, hysterical, asking for grief,

420

"Don't torture me, Sarah" was about as bad a line as "Oh, don't leave me" or "Why do you want to break my heart?" Did people really say things like that, or was it a kind of talk heard only in the movies?

Sarah was too nice a girl ever to be charged with "torturing" a man; he had always known that. Still, she had never been the kind of girl who would collaborate in allowing her future to fall apart, and that was something he'd always known about her, too.

Soon, now, fifteen hundred miles from here, she would be putting the Kansas house in order for the night: the child asleep, the television blind and silent, the dishes washed and put away. She might be wearing her knee-length cotton robe – blue, with a pattern of strawberries – the one he'd always liked because it showed her legs off well, and because it had always meant she was his wife. He knew how it smelled. She would almost certainly be thinking over what they'd said to each other on the phone this afternoon, and the little vertical crease between her eyebrows would be deep with perplexity.

The Sheraton was still some distance away – the glowing red sign on top of its roof could barely be discerned from here – but Michael didn't mind walking; nobody had ever died of it. And he'd begun to find there were small satisfactions in having lived more than half a century: your very way of walking along the street could suggest how peaceful and responsible you had grown; there would be no more plunging ahead in pursuit of ephemeral things. Given good-enough clothes and shoes, you could always look dignified whether you were or not, and almost everybody could be counted on to call you "sir." The bar at the hotel would be open for business; that was nice because it meant Michael Davenport could sit in its murmurous shadows, alone with his skepticism, and have a drink before going upstairs.

She might come and live with him; she might not; and then

421

there was another dreadful possibility: she might come and stay with him only a little while, in a spirit of tentative compliance, waiting for her better judgment to set her free.

". . . Everybody's essentially alone," she'd told him, and he was beginning to see a lot of truth in that. Besides: now that he was older, and now that he was home, it might not even matter how the story turned out in the end.